HAPPY VALLEY COLLEGE

Dick Carlsen

authorHOUSE®

AuthorHouse™
1663 Liberty Drive, Suite 200
Bloomington, IN 47403
www.authorhouse.com
Phone: 1-800-839-8640

First published by AuthorHouse 7/19/2007

ISBN: 978-1-4343-1268-6 (sc)

Library of Congress Control Number: 2007903215

Printed in the United States of America
Bloomington, Indiana

This book is printed on acid-free paper.

To my dear, sweet, lovely bride,
and to the memory of
Sergeant Paul B. Woolford, U.S. Army,
killed in action 10 NOV 1969, Vinh Binh Province,
South Vietnam.

ACKNOWLEDGEMENTS

Valuable insight, perspective and timeframes on the Vietnam War were gained from a review of the following texts:

1. *Vietnam A History*, Stanley Karnow, The Viking Press, New York, and Penguin Books Canada Limited

2. *Vietnam The Decisive Battles*, John Pimlott, Macmillan Publishing Company, New York

3. *Vietnam At War The History: 1946 to 1975*, Phillip B. Davidson, Presidio, Novato, California, 1988

4. *Pay Any Price, Lyndon Johnson and the Wars for Vietnam*, Lloyd C. Gardner, Ivan R. Dee, Chicago, 1995

Ron Kurth, a college buddy and retired U. S. Navy Captain and pilot, provided information on Naval aircraft used during the Vietnam War.

My Sister, Pam, provided helpful feedback and editing.

I would still be flailing away at the computer had it not been for the timely and excellent Word Perfect assistance from Mindy Sawyer and Steve White.

Photo Credits

I am grateful to Jeffrey Teeter for permission to use his Trinity Hall photo for the book cover as first shown in the California State University, Chico, Alumni Magazine.

The front cover black and white inset photo is credited to Robert Hunt Picture Library.

Honour is purchas'd by the deeds we do:
  Honour is not won
Until some honourable deed be done

Christopher Marlowe
Hero and Leander, Ses I, I.276

PROLOGUE

There was silence. No one spoke. And there were tears.

Silence was the unspoken command. It was understood by all present. We all took slow, halting steps. No rush. Everyone was dealing with this event in his or her own way.

It was a gray day in May, which that day was appropriate.

The portable, "moving" Vietnam War Wall had been set up on Naval Air Station Patuxent River, Maryland in conjunction with the annual air show. It was early on a Saturday morning, before all the other air show festivities started up, and of course all the visitors to the base in rural southern Maryland that day were anticipating an exciting performance by the Navy's Blue Angels.

I found the directory and looked up the name of my drill sergeant from Army Basic Training, Fort Ord, California, 1969. I felt numb as I looked at his name. He was blessed with so much vitality and energy, and looked so "strack" in his DI uniform.

Other people were doing the same thing as me. And it was so quiet, out of reverence for those who perished during the Vietnam War, and more so because of the private way each person was confronting this reminder of a crazy time in U. S. history. Our hearts and our shoulders were heavy with the weight of those memories.

I walked slowly to the appropriate Wall section, deep in thought, instantly overcome with a plethora of emotions, feelings and memories that flowed like whitewater charging downstream, that included the hell-raising years in college, college life in the 60's in general, the many unanticipated affects of the Vietnam War on my personal life, and decisions I had made along the way. Some good. Some bad. Part of growing up.

I found his name on the Wall and put my hand to it. And I stared at it, and kept staring at it, like it was not real, like somehow if I thought and prayed hard enough he could be brought back to life. My God, but how unrealistic, and yet the Wall had me in its grip and would not let go. It brought excruciating and heart wrenching pain. I had no idea now what was going on around me. I was totally oblivious to it. I was in a "zone" that blocked all else from cognition, and I could not break myself away from that spot. It was like a magnet and I was "attached" to that Wall. I felt a lot of things. Respect for him. Sadness at his loss of life, knowing he wanted to be in that war. I was certain that his decision and desire to serve in Vietnam was an end in itself and not unlike the early Greek ideals surrounding Agonism. Drill Sergeant Becker's motive was purely to serve his country and to find satisfaction in that experience. I felt guilt for my early indifference toward the war and maybe even for enjoying so much the best four years of my life at Happy Valley College in northern California during the mid-60's where I reveled in playing sports, drinking beer at fraternity and sorority keggers and with my "independent" buddies and fellow "jocks", cruising around on my motorcycles, and so much more. So many wonderful friends and memories. But most important, the portable Wall provided me the opportunity for closure and to finally say, "Thank you, Drill Sergeant, for what you represented in my life. Thanks for what you did, for giving your life for a cause I know you believed in, and for the affect you had on my life."

I was finally able to pull myself away from that spot where I stood, mesmerized by the sanctity of what the Wall represented. His name was planted forever in my mind. Before I left, I also looked up a couple of names of junior high school and high school classmates I did not know very well but that had also lost their lives in Vietnam, as well as the name of a grade school neighbor.

As I left the Wall that morning my final thought was one of satisfaction with a major decision I had made in my young life many years ago that derived from Drill Sergeant Becker and the Vietnam War.

I awoke the next day to a beautiful, brisk morning. The kind that beckons you to a window to gaze out at a crisp, clear blue sky and dew on the leaves. It was going to be a beautiful, exhilarating day in southern Maryland. The clean air and the gentle breezes off nearby Chesapeake Bay offered the promise of a new season. Another winter of near isolation was history. As I stretched and squinted into the bright sun I thought of how long it had been since I was back home to see family and college friends. The sweet, albeit sometimes treacherous, smell of nostalgia was incessantly lapping at the shores of vast lands of good memories. Call it daydreaming. Call it a Peter Pan Syndrome. Call it whatever you want.

The only sound in the air was that of jet aircraft being prepared for the air show activities that day. On a normal day the sweet jet noise was from aircraft being prepared for the Navy test pilots for their work. On a good day I could get a whiff of JP4 jet fuel.

I didn't wear a uniform, and my job wasn't directly related to the combat mission of the Navy. I was a Field Representative for the Navy's recreation and club program, which meant I traveled to bases worldwide reviewing their quality of life programs. Throw in some inspections of slot machine operations overseas, too. Sweet job. I was on the road about 90% of the year, spending two weeks in Jacksonville, the next two weeks in Orlando, then maybe on to Key West, to New Orleans, to Japan and Taiwan for a few months, and so on. You get the idea. I saw my home base for only a few weeks a year. Otherwise, my mission was to travel, which was what I wanted to do. I learned early in my life that travel was in my blood.

My most recent business trips included more travel than many Americans enjoy in a lifetime. I had just completed an assignment in New England. From there, I had flown out to Kentucky for a few days to attend the Kentucky Derby with my

3

Brew Crew friends from graduate school at Indiana University, where I had enjoyed a wonderful experience, though somewhat less carefree and more academically demanding than Happy Valley College. At Indiana I played rugby and took in the whole Big Ten sports experience. After the derby I traveled to our Navy base at Argentia, Newfoundland, followed by a weekend layover in New York City enroute to Iceland. While on assignment at the base in Keflavik, Iceland, I took a weekend charter flight to Dublin, Ireland, also passing through Glasgow, Scotland. I remember well how intrigued the local Dublin bar-goers had been with the fact I worked for the United States government as we drank and shared stories in a bar near the River Liffey.

Yeah, things were well in my life. No nine to five rut for me. I had a job with a lot of travel and I was generally solo and on my own.

Nate, the office driver that ran the Field Reps to airports, picked me up at 9:30 AM for our drive to Washington's National Airport. We were well up route 235 when he asked, "Where you goin' this time, Mr. Pedersen?"

Nate was good people. He worked in the audio-visual department, but spent a lot of time on the road between Pax River and the Washington, D.C. airports shuttling us world travelers around. Black, kind of tall, but walked with a little bit of a slouch.

"I'm going to San Francisco and San Diego, Nate," I finally replied after being deep in thought. "I'm stopping off in San Francisco to see family and college friends before going on to San Diego for a special assignment down there."

"How often do you get out that way?" he asked.

"Not often enough. I really miss my old college buddies. Lots of good memories," I told him. Great ones, I thought to myself. Be nice to relive them again. Okay. I know what you're thinking already. Get out of the past. But, hey, it's okay to reflect and smile and ponder on past friends and on good times. They were carefree times, too. For the moment, we'll forget that they gradually slipped away because of some other stuff, namely the Vietnam War, going on during the mid to late 60's when I was in college.

I had started the day with a good run, which helped put some of the emotionally exhausting aspects of the previous day behind me. There's nothing like going for a morning run and it's just you, the darkness, silence, and nature, listening to your breathing, the birds, and your footfalls, alone with your thoughts. I call it the great equalizer. I generally didn't feel all that talkative, but the beautiful weather, the relaxing drive through the southern Maryland countryside, and the prospect of a weekend back home brought me out of my introspective shell.

This was to be a different weekend for me. Home with family a few flight hours away, and a few beers with college friends.

My senses rebounded as we sped across the Woodrow Wilson Bridge toward the Virginia side of the Potomac River and I took advantage of being a passenger to stare at the magnificent scenery of the nation's Capital. It was breathtaking, with the monuments, the Capital, a city alive and pulsating with wealth, new and old, and power. Gave me goose bumps every time I took in that view. It wasn't home, but it was nice to feel a part of it and to be on my way to National Airport to board a plane for a business trip.

A short drive up George Washington Parkway after passing through the middle of historic Alexandria and we were at the airport.

"What airline you travelling out on today, Mr. Pedersen?" Nate politely asked.

"American, Nate," I said quietly as I came out of some more deep thought. "And thanks, by the way, for the drive up." I needed to collect my thoughts as I prepared to enter the airport and make necessary arrangements for my flight.

Nate pulled up in front of the American Airlines terminal, edging in ahead of a taxi. The taxi driver's quick blast on his horn didn't faze us. Another short-tempered taxi driver. So what?

I jumped out, grabbed my luggage and wished Nate well.

"Have a good weekend, Nate, and I'll see you when I return. And by the way, I like your ballcap."

"Thanks, Mr. Pedersen. And you have a good flight and a nice visit with your family," he offered with his big smile.

The plane departed from the gate on schedule, and minutes later after a short taxi we were airborne. I wasn't hungry, so I decided to pass on the in-flight meal. They usually gave me gas anyway, and waiting for the clean up or a clear aisle to the restroom only made matters worse. Instead, I placed my seat in a reclining position, closed my eyes, put my head back, and welcomed the tranquility as I eased my mind into a recollection of the happiest period of my life.

I smiled and wondered to myself how I survived and was not tripped up by the college administration, and how, more importantly, I made it out of college alive, particularly when I think of all the times I had a few beers with the guys and cruised around on my Honda 250 Scrambler looking for some action. I could not help but think, too, of the pain, anxiety, frustration and challenges presented by the Vietnam War, the draft, and military service obligation. Behavior notwithstanding, the transition from my early carefree years at Happy Valley College to the reality of the draft and Vietnam War my junior and senior years was an unexpected journey that would never be forgotten. Along the way, there had been many friends and a book-full of growing-up experiences. The biggest and most traumatic decision was how to handle various options concerning my military obligation and the Vietnam War, particularly because I had fallen in love with a young lady with whom I wanted to spend every waking hour. She was my equivalent to the Sirens of Greek mythology.

The quiet "whrrr" of the plane's engines and the deep state of my reflections put me in an intensely sublime state as the plane sped me home high above the puffy clouds.

1964

CHAPTER ONE

My twin brother Dan had been up at Happy Valley College working his butt off in 100-degree heat for double-day freshman football practices. He had left home two weeks prior to my departure to work out with the team and during phone calls home had extolled the beauty of the campus, the quaintness of the town, and had spoken of many new friends. Most of the guys on the team were from the San Francisco Bay Area, which made for an exciting prospect of meeting people from near our hometown of Danville that I certainly would not have met otherwise.

The drive to Happy Valley with Mom and Dad seemed to take forever. Dad had worked in the area so he knew the roads well. Travelling due north from Danville, we bypassed Davis, skirted the eastern side of Woodland, passed through the one street town of Knights Landing, then drove through Yuba City and a couple other smaller towns before arriving in Happy Valley. Most of the towns along the way existed as support for the region's farmers in this richly endowed agricultural belt. Other than passage through the "agi towns," the entire length of the highway from Davis north was bordered on both sides by farmland – rice, wheat, you name it, for it grew there. And dairies. Another trademark of the region was the bugs the front of the car collected on a drive through the area. A couple years later I was to make that same trip on a motorcycle. That was not fun.

It was a typical hot day in the valley as Dad sped north so I was wearing bermuda shorts and a tee-shirt and still perspiring like hell. The weather in the Sacramento Valley could hang in the 100 degree range for days during the daytime. You got used to it, but then you had no choice, particularly since our home in Danville didn't have air-conditioning and temperatures could oftentimes equal those in the valley. Anyway, hot is when you have to keep a bowl of water in the car and washcloth wet to dab over your skin while driving through the intense heat of the California and Arizona deserts. Again, no air-conditioning. Talk about commitment! If our family could have envisioned the discomfort due to extreme heat on that particular vacation trip in 1958 I'm sure we would have opted for the great Northwest vice Navajo Indian mountain dwellings, the Petrified Forest, and the Grand Canyon.

While the heat was tolerable as we drove to Happy Valley, the emotional state of Mom, Dad and me was slightly strained. It was a quiet emotion. We knew what was happening and we accepted it. Dan and I were making a transition, starting a new chapter in our lives going off to college, while Mom and Dad were relinquishing a chapter in their lives.

Conversation was minimal. At various times along the way I probably came out with such inane and rhetorical statements as, "Boy, it's a hot day," or "the Sacramento River is dry," and "I wonder how Dan's doing." Simple crap like that.

I just wanted to get the trip over. That 3-hour drive seemed like an eternity, as I was torn by conflicting emotions. I was anxious for my college experience to begin on the one hand, but nervous as hell about being on my own and subjected to a tougher academic setting. High school was history, and the summer after graduation was neatly tucked away with memories of a "summer flame". Work at a local gas station, trips on days off to the Santa Cruz beaches for rollicking, body surfing and "cruising", and high school friends and acquaintances were fading away like a freighter steaming over the horizon as departure for college loomed near.

I kept my emotional state concealed, as that was my nature. I too often internalized my thoughts and emotions, feeling more inclined to work things out on my own.

Later on, I would have a greater appreciation for the emotion Mom and Dad were battling. Their melancholy behavior during the trip and the anticipation of leaving Dan and me in Happy Valley was not unlike the sailor standing on the rail amidships heading out to sea. The sailor is torn between the excitement of new challenges and experiences in far away places he is going to, and the realization that he is leaving a part of him behind from the recent port call. And while Mom and Dad felt that reluctance to accept our departure, there was also a sense of pride and hope for us.

It's entirely possible that as we made our way north Mom and Dad were re-living the camping trip that Dan, me, and three of our high school pals took after graduation. Everyone, including parents, envisioned a relaxing, trouble-free fishing trip up the Feather River Canyon in northern California. That is how it started out, and how it was described to parents, but not how it finished up. We took a right turn and headed to Lake Tahoe to check out the girls and drink some beer. We got a little too frisky, took in a Jim Burgett dance at the lake, and ended up causing some significant damage to our rented RV camper.

With confessions to parents when we returned home and explanations of how the RV damage occurred, as well as how the hell we ended up at Lake Tahoe, we paid the damages on the camper with fond memories of an innocent graduation trip. Mom and Dad may have been reflecting on that particular week thinking of the possibility of more ridiculous behavior by their sons.

Mom and Dad had been very restrictive parents with regard to the age we could start dating, who we dated, what guys we could hang out with, and were hell on parties. I'm not suggesting that was all bad. It taught us boundaries, but those boundaries were largely moot the day they left me off in Happy Valley.

The arrival of Mom, Dad and me in Happy Valley was both exciting and relieving. Relieving in the sense that arrival meant emotional good-byes were imminent. It was time for release from the dependency and security provided by the home environment, and a time for a very different form of growth. The next four years would be what Dan and I made of them. They would hopefully be something to cherish and to look back on with fondness and positive feelings, with a multitude of social contacts. I began to realize all this my first day on campus.

With Mom and Dad headed back toward Danville, Dan was eager to introduce me to some of the guys he had met on his freshman football team. "C'mon Dave, I want you to meet Jack. He went to Acalanes and also has a twin brother." Acalanes was in nearby Lafayette, and was in our high-school athletic conference, and had a reputation for having a student body that came from homes a cut above the average economic strata. An Acalanes student wore Gant shirts, pressed slacks, and penny loafers. In cooler months I'm sure they had a sweater tied around their neck. "Ivy League", you know.

Dan and I headed back into the dorm and up to room 404 to see if Jack was in. The door opened to a person that fit the Acalanes image. Jack wasn't wearing slacks, but his bermuda shorts were creased, and he was wearing a visibly clean and pressed madras shirt.

"Dave, meet Jack," Dan stated. I extended my hand and we shook hands. His friendly smile told me we were going to get along well. He had a relaxed, unpretentious manner about him, contrary to the "stuffy Acalanes image."

"I understand you went to Acalanes, Jack. I was on your campus last Fall as part of an exchange assembly. You might remember the act I was in. Six guys, calling themselves the 'Black Cons', sang a few songs and even got an encore from your student body."

"I remember that," said Jack, "yours was the best part of the assembly."

Jack was good people from the start. We would find out that his handsome looks caught the attention of more than a few campus girls. He only had to shave every other day, which gave him a boyish appearance. At 5'10", Jack was a bit taller than Dan and me, and he had a good build from his wrestling days in high school. With his Ivy League haircut (we all wore our hair relatively short; in fact my Mother threatened to cut off my allowance if I didn't keep my hair short while away at college), blue eyes, and an excellent taste in clothes, Jack was not someone that would have any problem getting dates at Happy Valley.

The three of us walked from our dorm over to the Student Union, commonly called "the CAC", for Campus Activity Center. Most of the students had not arrived on campus yet, so it was quiet and still as we strolled through the middle of the campus. From our dorm, we went past the women's dorm, Lissen Hall, and across a six-foot wide footbridge (about 70 feet long) over Sutter Creek (a pretty, gurgling stream that ran through campus and that we were able to inner-tube on in the Springtime when the water level was up). To our left as we crossed over the bridge, we could see a small park with a few picnic tables and benches that we would come to find was used for various official social functions at Happy Valley. Personally, I would learn it was a great place to take a date for some privacy day or night, but particularly late at night when I had nowhere to romance. We marveled at the picturesque beauty and tranquility of our new surroundings. Once over the bridge, we veered left, walking between the dining hall on our left and the campus bookstore on the right, both fairly diminutive, one-story stucco buildings, we then turned right onto what was the main campus walkway. Past the front of the bookstore on our right and the west end of the Administration Building on our left, we passed the Industrial Arts Building, another one-story structure, before entering the "quad", with its grassy area bordered by sidewalks and large kelly green wooden benches. The quad was the central and focal point of the campus, where students congregated to study, socialize, or otherwise hang out between classes and after classes.

As we approached the CAC, Dan spotted a few other teammates that must have had the same idea about going out for a stroll and to looking for friends and something to do in the evening hours free from football practice and team meetings. Obviously, the "double days" of football practice in the scorching valley heat were behind them.

"Hi, Tim," yelled Dan to get the group's attention before they inadvertently turned away and left the CAC.

"Hi, Dan." There were three of them, all from the Concord area. It was interesting how Dan, Jack and I were together and represented an athletic conference in one part of the east Bay Area, and the three of them came from the same athletic conference in another part of the East Bay.

Dan took the lead on introducing me. "Dave, I want you to meet Tim Templeton and Brad Stevens, who went to Mt. Diablo, and Paul Eiselman from Ygnacio Valley. They're all on the football team. Dave's my twin brother," he added, "and just got up here today."

"Hi," I said, shaking hands with them. Brad had a handshake like a vice grip. Strong SOB. He was about 5'11" and 190 pounds, with a stocky build. Short, curly hair sat atop a large, squarish face with an upper lip that protruded a bit.

I asked Brad, "Do you know John Farrell?"

"Sure do," he answered. "How do you know that crazy guy?"

"I met him on a date last summer. He came out to Danville to pick me up so we could double date with his girlfriend and a girl living in San Francisco that I had met up at the lake at Twain Harte earlier in the summer. Nice guy, and we had a good time." Nothing like mutual acquaintances to start off a friendship.

We talked for a little while, mostly about the football team and some of the other players, then said good-bye and returned to our respective dorms. In reflecting back on that meeting of the six of us at the CAC, Dan and I were always close and stayed very close as brothers over the years, Jack was a roommate three of the four years of college, and Brad was one of our group through our years at Happy Valley, remaining a close friend after college. The creation and evolution of friendships is always an interesting reflection. How, when, and what experiences helped form the bond that will always exist and endure the ultimate geographical separations? There is hardly an emotion in a man that can equal the satisfaction, security, and strength of a good friendship.

As Dan, Jack and I walked back through the campus to the dorm, they told me about various guys on the freshman team as well as some of the "crazies", like Rob Fine, playing varsity football. They also told me about Trout Hole.

"Wait 'till you see Trout Hole," Dan excitedly told me. I could tell his excitement was based on a clear vision of a recent experience there, and an anxious yearning to return to that spot. "You won't believe this place. I've seen nothing like it before."

"Picture-book stuff?" I interjected with a grin. "Idyllic?"

"Yeah," Dan said agreeably, adding, "It's out in Sutter Park, and you have to travel on a gravel road for a mile or so to get to it. Then you have to climb down a trail on the side of a 40' rock cliff. But it's worth the trip. There's a natural, deep swimming hole about forty feet long and about the same across, bordered by large rocks and a small sandy beach for sunbathing, and with an overhanging tree that has a rope attached for swinging out into the water. The water's cold, and there's seldom more than a handful of people there. Probably because it's so much trouble to get to. But the place is dynamite, and felt great after a tough practice in the heat."

My appetite was sufficiently whetted. I couldn't wait to see this place myself. "When do you suppose we can get out to Trout Hole?" I asked, which was almost a rhetorical question in that none of us had our own cars at Happy Valley. For someone whose parents were going to be financially stretched to help out with college expenses, possessing a car at college was not one of those matters dwelled on at all. We were not poor, but Mom and Dad did not have the kind of money to buy cars for their kids. We understood that, and it was never an issue.

"Well, a couple of the guys on the team have cars, particularly the locals from Happy Valley and Durham, so maybe we can talk them into loading up the cars for a trip out there in the next weekend or two," Dan replied with optimism and hope.

"Sounds great," I said. "I can't wait to get out there and see this place."

Sutter Park comprised the majority of the city park system in this northern Sacramento Valley town with a population of about 17,000 people. The park was named after General John Sutter, the founder of Happy Valley whose beautiful Victorian mansion sat off The Boulevard and adjacent to the college property, and was used for a 1930's movie: "Robin Hood". The Boulevard was a four-lane road from the center of town north, divided by a median strip dominated by large oak trees with grass immaculately cut and trimmed year round, and lined by clean, stately homes large and small. It also had a number of fast food outlets, a Mr. Smorgy Boys "all you can eat" smorgasbord (that during our stay at Happy Valley we would come to love and hate after overindulging), and the nicer travel motels in town.

Sutter Park was on the east side of town, and for a small town the park was immense. It was one of the largest municipally owned parks in the United States. Sutter Creek meandered through the park, and the developers had taken advantage of the natural vegetation to create rather private picnic areas and swimming holes at numerous spots along the road that winded parallel to the creek. The park was noted for its natural beauty, with its large oaks and sycamores laced with wild grape vines. At what was called "One Mile" and "Five Mile", small dams had been constructed to produce mammoth natural swimming holes that could accommodate hundreds of swimmers at any time. There were grassy areas on both sides of One Mile for picnicking, napping, sunning, or just laying on a blanket with a girlfriend or date. The golf course was located at the far eastern end of the park past Five Mile. That's where the paved road ended, becoming the gravel road that ran further out into the park toward Trout Hole, passing Deer Hole, another favored swimming hole with large boulders for sunning.

That evening back at the dorm we sat in Jack's room. He didn't know yet who his roommate would be. I felt fortunate in that respect, in that Dan and I would be sharing a room that first year. I suppose it took a little bit of the edge off the anxiety surrounding the first year in college, particularly as it related to the uncertainty of a roommate and his lifestyle and behavior. In fact, there had not been much for me to do when I arrived at the dorm, as Dan already had the room arranged.

Our dorm was called Sierra Hall, and was a straight, four-story brick building sitting east and west, with one-story lounge areas off the center, north and south. Just inside the front entrance and to the right was the door that led into the first floor, east wing. A large foyer separated the two lounge areas. To the right of the foyer was the front desk, where the Resident Assistants pulled their duty and where the Dorm Mother, "Ma", stationed herself to meet residents, parents and guests. Her quarters were connected to the desk area, on the east wing. A double set of doors opened up to the stairwell, with plain concrete steps to the second, third and fourth floors. A small lounge area and a payphone booth were located on each floor between the wings. The rooms serving as our living quarters were furnished frugally and with Spartan intent. This wasn't the Ritz. This was your basic, no frills, college dormitory. Two single beds, two metal combination desk and drawers that ran along the entire window wall, so that study areas were to the far right and left, with space in the middle to place typewriters or, if lucky, a phonograph. Okay, a record player. Closets were on each side of the door wall. Jack had brought up a record player, which we affectionately called "the mono", as in monophonic vice stereophonic. Really.

Across a short paved walkway, bordered on each side by two large lawn areas, was Lissen Hall, the women's dorm. Just past Lissen Hall were the creek and the footbridge connecting the dorm area with the main campus. The women's dorm was of the same design as Sierra, so that the south side of Sierra faced the north side of Lissen, about 150 feet away and easily within shouting range.

Most of the buildings at Happy Valley College were constructed of brick, with the Administration Building and its' domed rotunda, the Auditorium, and CAC being the original buildings constructed of brick. From a focal point on First Street, which for the most part was the southern boundary of the campus, the Auditorium sat to the right of the Administration Building and the CAC to the immediate left. A large lawn separated the buildings from the street, and numerous trees in that area provided a shady retreat for relaxation or study in the warm, sunny afternoons. The Library was to the left of the CAC, and the Business Building across the quad and rose garden from the CAC to the north. To the east of the Auditorium was the Biology/Physical Sciences Building, and across the creek, to the north, the Sociology/Psychology Building. The Gymnasium and athletic complex was located in the northwest part of the campus, with our dorms to the east of the gym across a large parking area. The buildings just described made up the perimeter of the campus and were the predominant structures. Like I said, it was a small campus. A few butler-type buildings had been placed near the parking lot and next to the creek to create additional classroom space. Sad to say, the buildings constructed in recent years were of varying designs and incorporated differing building materials. Notwithstanding some architectural voids created by the college planners, Happy Valley was still a gorgeous campus with its integration of structure with nature.

The topic of academic majors came up as we sat in Jack's room that first night. He asked, "What is your major going to be, Dave?"

"Business and accounting," I answered. "I changed my major from Biology after talking to a friend of my parents who is in the insurance business in Portland. The potential in business seems much more appealing."

"That's great," Jack exclaimed. "Mine is business also. What about you, Dan?"

"Architecture," he said.

Little did Dan know as our first day together on campus came to an end that a few days later he would have a different major.

And little did we know, too, that over the course of the next four years we would establish a close bonding unknown to us in our more frivolous high-school days. Our friendship had a depth and quality surpassing any such relationship in high school. We would laugh together, drink together, raise some hell together, and share our deepest thoughts and sorrows. We were inseparable, until girls came into the picture, anyway. We would suffer embarrassments and disappointment and make mistakes, but revel in the athletic victories and accomplishments we would experience, each of us stroking the other, encouraging and lifting up, and loving one another like brothers. Dan and I already had an edge there.

We grew together, but stumbled occasionally. We found a way to laugh at the falls, finding strength from each other. Our four years together were not unlike those experienced by our contemporaries at other colleges in California, or in Ohio or Florida for that matter, but it was made different by our own

aggregate blend of personalities and backgrounds. We experienced an incredibly wide range of emotions, including happiness, sorrow, tragedy, and fear, but we were "foot loose and fancy free", without a care in the world. Exams, and practice and competition in our chosen athletic endeavors, were definite exceptions to our carefree existence.

The warm valley air still hung unmercifully outside portending another 100 degree scorcher as the three of us exited the dorm together the following morning and I prepared to spend my first full day on campus.

CHAPTER TWO

I was alone most of that first day. Dan, Jack and the other new friends had a football meeting in the morning and practice that afternoon. In between sessions they found a cool place to relax and re-energize themselves. That meant sitting around the dorm rooms or in the lounge downstairs with its vinyl upholstery that felt cool to the bare skin as they sat around in shorts and t-shirts.

I wandered around my new surroundings, getting a feel for the layout of the campus and marveling at its beauty. I also walked downtown. Main Street, with its mix of office buildings, retail stores and a small city park, was just off campus, so I strolled up and down a few of its blocks. The land bank office, western wear shop and countless pick-up trucks reminded me this was just a big "agi" town. Taco Bell and McDonalds had not yet arrived. To my surprise, the Woolworth's had a soda counter, unlike its counterpart back home in nearby suburban Walnut Creek.

I nodded a greeting or said hello to some of the people walking by me. I know what they were probably thinking on that early September day: "Well, it's been a quiet summer. Those college kids are arriving back in town so it's time to batten down the 'ol hatches."

Eager to talk to someone, I stopped at the college bookstore as I crossed the campus on my way back to the dorm. It was apparent they were still in the process of getting the store ready for the onslaught of students buying books and supplies a week hence. Unopened cartons lay in the aisles stacked atop one another, and there was a quiet flurry of activity getting shelves stocked. It was easy to gain the attention of a saleslady, which I did to ask a few questions about articles of clothing and some other insignificant items. I noticed with great interest a couple of jackets with Happy Valley logos, and told myself to make it a point to buy them when I had the necessary funds.

As I crossed the footbridge over Sutter Creek I lingered a moment to look at the park area on the north side of the creek with its large oak trees, freshly cut green grass, a picnic table or two, and the alluring gurgle of the creek. A soft breeze moved through the trees. It was very quiet on that footbridge so all I heard was the rustle of leaves, birds chirping, and the sound of water rolling over rocks and pebbles below. I was mesmerized by the cacophony. I was alone. I was very much taken by the natural beauty of my new surroundings.

That evening was far from lonely. Dan and Jack had a football team banquet to attend, so I went off by myself.

"What are you doing tonight, Dave?" Dan asked as we sat in our dorm room in the late afternoon.

"Terry told me about a party over at 4th and Cherry and that it would be open," I replied with a mixture of excitement and apprehension. Terry was a friend from our high-school graduating class. After all, I thought to myself, I wouldn't know anybody there and didn't even know where the hell 4th and Cherry was located.

"That's where the Beta Pheta Chi's have their parties," Dan informed me. "You might see Ronny Braniff there since he's a Beta Pheta," he added. Ronny graduated two years ahead of us at San Ramon High School, and while we were all in sports I really cannot say that I knew Ronny very well. I was a lowly sophomore during a senior year for him when he excelled in football, basketball, and baseball. Not your average bubble-gummer strolling the high-school halls. He was a star.

I got some directions from our dorm resident assistant and found the place quite easily. What a frigging night. I no sooner got both feet in the door and was in the process of asking someone what it cost to buy into the keg when I hear a loud, "Pedersen!" It was Ronny Braniff. He greeted me like I was a long lost pal or had just returned from a fortnight or more on Crusoe's island. The rest, as they say, is history.

My first college kegger is one I shall never forget.

"Ronny," I answered somewhat timidly, "how you doing?"

"Great," he bellowed (he had a head start on the beer), "good to have you and your brother up here."

"Thanks," I offered, beginning to shed some shyness.

"How much is the kegger?" I yelled above the blaring stereo playing Beach Boys music coming from the far corner of the room.

"A buck," Ronny answered. "Come here. I want you to meet a few people that are fraternity brothers of mine."

"Sure," I said, "but let me fill my cup first." I had worked up a bit of a thirst from walking around all day, but more than that I was eager to be a full participant at this first college party I attended.

Ronny introduced me to a fraternity brother named Vince Costello and to Vince's freshman brother Eddie. Vince was a cheerleader and from what I could gather that night by observation was very popular on campus.

It wasn't so much the party and its merry participants that made the night memorable, but what happened after the party. I found my way home, navigated to my room all right, and quietly undressed so as not to awaken Dan.

This being the first time I had really gotten sloshed, I had no idea what to expect. I laid down in bed, closed my eyes, and holy s ...! what's happening? Simultaneously, I was achieving that nauseous feeling one attains when spinning the Disneyland "Mad Hatters Teacup Party" vehicle uncontrollably round and round, and felt as though I was the center spoke on a child's merry-go-round spinning wildly without stopping. Hey, this wasn't part of the deal or the price of admission!

Somehow, Dan awoke and realized his brother was ripped big time.

"You okay?" he mumbled.

"Really, no," I said swimmingly.

"You drank too much?" he asked.

""How'd you guess?" I could get away with being a smart-ass at the moment.

"How do you feel?"

"Like death warmed over. I think I'm going to get sick. I can't believe how sh … I feel. Damn."

"I hope it's not going to happen in this room, cowboy."

I'm damn near dying and he's got the nerve to get rasty on me! "I'll see what I can do about it. Let's hope I don't unload my lunch in the general region of your bed."

I was able to get one foot on the floor, followed slowly and agonizingly by the second foot. I didn't want to rush things, but my stomach was beginning to tell me that the college dining hall's best breakfast, lunch and dinner would be served up on our newly waxed floor if I didn't make it to the bathroom FAST! The fifty feet down the hall seemed like fifty yards, but I made it in time. Thirty minutes later I dragged my weakened body back up the hall, fell into bed, and awakened the next morning feeling like I was playing my own version of the "Death March."

As I pulled myself out of bed, Dan was quick to comment. "Geez, Dave, you look like death taking a s…!"

"Gee, thanks, bro, that's just the kind of encouragement I need to hear."

"Well, you deserve it, getting drunk like that."

"No lectures, please. I am fully capable of making my own decisions, using some poor judgement, and paying the consequences where due."

Needless to say, I held off a few days before touching another beer, which was tough to do because the pre-semester parties were cranking up everywhere around campus.

Registration for classes took place a couple days later. It was hardly what one would call an art form in the 60's. It was trench warfare. Not blood and guts, but pronounced mental trauma, although there were occasions when you wanted to kill the asshole that weaseled into line ahead of you and got the last card for that certain class you just had to have to fit into your frequently changing class schedule. This was particularly the case if that class was your third or fourth choice!

For Dan and me registration was a piece of cake that first year because students in the alpha category "P" were among the first to enter the "arena" on day one of registration that semester. Jack, in alpha category "L", was distraught over his time slot late on the second day. With all three of us being business majors, since Dan made a last minute change from architecture, we had hoped to get some if not all of our business classes together. Dan and I did fine. While in line that morning outside the gym waiting to enter for registration Dan and I met Jim Preston, a freshman whose home was Los Angeles. Jim became a good friend of ours even though he went the fraternity route early on. A few years later Jim was in the right place at the right time and saved me from a calamity. More on that later.

At about 4:30 P.M. on day two of registration a drained, downcast Jack dragged his tired fanny into the dorm room shared by Dan and me. He flung himself down on one of the beds, with his elbows bracing him up on the bed and his back against the wall, and slowly shook his head in disbelief.

"That bad, huh?" Dan queried cautiously.

"I can't believe it," he started, adding in a weak, despondent tone of voice, "I spent three hours in there, hustling my ass from line to line to get a class card. I either waited in line for 10 to 15 minutes to get a class or saw all too frequently a sign telling me a class I wanted was filled and not available. What a royal mess. And to make matters worse, I was forced to sign up for accounting, which is generally a second year course requirement."

"Damn," I sympathetically replied truly from the bottom of my freshman fear and anxiety heart. That is a hell of a way to start the school year. "What a ball buster," I concluded.

"This first year will be tough enough on me without adding a course like accounting. I sure hope I make it through okay. I'm just going to have to work my butt off in that class," Jack said.

"You'll make it, Jack," Dan replied on an optimistic note.

A couple of weeks into the school year I had my first date at Happy Valley. No big deal really, except for one thing that occurred. I had been told by Bob, a member of the freshman football team who came from Walnut Creek, which was a few miles from Danville, that a girl he had gone to high school with wanted to go out with Dan or me. Since Dan was seeing someone else, she decided I would be all right. Really. She was cute, too. Bob introduced me to Sue Ellen and the two of us made plans to rendezvous at her dorm one night. Jack got his roommate's VW bug and we drove out to Ramsey Hall to meet Sue Ellen and Jack's blind date to go for a little drive. Jack's date was a cute but rather plain looking blond named Jean. We headed out to Sutter Park, trying to impress the girls with our knowledge of the city's geography, where we stopped the car in one of the many turnoffs along the creek, and made small talk both collectively and date to date. Unbeknownst to Jack and Jean, Sue Ellen and I were catching some hugs in the rear seat when the conversations waned. This quite startled an uncooperative Jean when a moment before turning her head and seeing Sue Ellen and me embraced said, "Sue Ellen, you know, we hardly know these guys." Sue Ellen and I were quickly getting to know each other intimately. Well, with hugs and kisses, anyway! I felt bad for Jack, who as the chauffeur in a VW bug with front bucket seats had an unmemorable and frustrating night and the raw end of the deal. Not that Jean was ready to rock 'n roll, though.

The evening offered an embarrassing moment for me. As the four of us were leaving the dorm for the car a girl named Carol, whom I had been seeing occasionally, strolled into the lobby from her upstairs room. Our eyes locked on one another. Carol and I did not see any more of each other after that episode, needless to say. I got over that pretty quick, though, just as I didn't have any second thoughts when I told Sue Ellen after a few dates that I was not interested in taking her out anymore. It was quite simple. College was still a new dimension in my life and I didn't want to compromise it by getting involved in a serious relationship.

There was a steady bombardment of new experiences, new friends, different study habits dictated by varying routines and requirements of my professors, and a new element in my life called football practice.

Watching Dan and the guys practice football and attending their first game of the season became increasingly agonizing to me. I wanted the physical activity, but more than any other thing I wanted to be a member of a group, to be a part of the team and share in the camaraderie. I had not played football since my freshman year in high school, but my eagerness to participate overshadowed that deficiency. It didn't hurt, too, that Happy Valley was not a football scholarship school, so in reality everyone was a "walk-on". Don't get me wrong, there were some damn good athletes out there, including Dan. But for reasons of size and the immutable fact that they were a distinct level below big-time football players in overall size, speed and ability, these athletes were at Happy Valley on a non-scholarship basis and because they wanted to go to a school where they knew they could play.

For these reasons I mustered up the courage to see Fred, the head coach of the freshman team.

With my heart pounding and with some trepidation, I knocked on Fred's office door in the gym.

"Come in," I heard a gravelly voice say.

Entering, I found him in his usual and customary outfit of shorts and tee-shirt. Fred was slim in build, being a runner, was middle-aged, with crew-cut blond hair that was beginning to show some gray. He had heavily wrinkled skin on his face that no doubt came from the many hours he had spent outdoors in various coaching and teaching activities under an unrelenting valley sun. I think he taught a golf class, too. The wrinkles made him appear to have a scowl, but that belied his instant attention, interest and friendliness. After all, he wasn't the head coach of the mediocre varsity football team, so how stressed could he be?

"Coach Johnson," I started, "I'm Dave Pedersen. My brother Dan is on the team, and I'm going nuts watching him and the other players practice. I didn't play much in high school, but I'm in pretty good shape and I want to play football. Can I join the team?"

"You really want to play?" he asked, giving me a look through squinting eyes that appeared harder and more piercing due to all those natural wrinkles. "We've already had a few weeks of practice," he went on, "and it will be tough trying to gain a position and learn our system. I can't guarantee you'll even play."

"I understand, sir, but please just give me a chance. I want to be a part of your team."

"Okay. Go to Ray this afternoon and he will issue your equipment. Practice starts at 3:30, and here's a play book you can start looking at."

"Thank you, sir. I'll be there." I left his office excited, but a little nervous. What was I getting myself into?

Wow, I did it. I wasn't too "jacked"! I'm part of the team, I joyously thought to myself as I walked the short distance over to the dorm. I was anxious to tell Dan and Jack the good news. Prior to going to Fred I had discussed the idea of going out for the team with the two of them in our dorm room one night after dinner and during a study break. We had a lot of study breaks, by the way. They had been supportive and encouraged me, which helped tremendously in the mental gymnastics of my decision process.

Life at Happy Valley had a certain routine for us. We were occupied with attending classes, studying, going to football practice Monday through Friday, and having a game on Saturday afternoon. Saturday night we usually had a few beers somewhere and went to the varsity game and a dance afterwards. When the varsity had away games things were notably quieter for us, although we still ended up having a few beers and finding a party somewhere.

During those days sans "wheels", since none of us were privileged to have a car at school, we relied on friends on the team that had cars. The guys from the local area commuting to classes generally had one. One such person was Rob Maguire, a slim, blond haired, good-looking guy that had great success dating senior girls at his former high school in Durham. When not spending time with the girls on Saturday nights, Rob drove out to campus and picked us up in his new, blue Ford Mustang that had four on the floor. We'd drink a few beers and cruise around looking for a party.

Otherwise, we walked. Fortunately, there were a lot of apartments within an easy walk of the dorm, and some of those apartments had upper-classmen that bought the kegs and held the open parties. We also found ourselves walking the long distance to Baker and Ramsey Halls way the hell out 3rd Street past the railroad tracks. The men were in Baker, and the women in Ramsey. Baker and Ramsey were both new dorms and were occupied for the first time. Their design was a new concept, with four occupants to a room and sharing a common bathroom. While four people to a room might be too much, it sure beat our situation in Sierra where a whole wing used a common bathroom.

It was commonplace to walk to Ramsey to sit for a few hours in the lounge with a girlfriend under the watchful eye of the dorm mother. No hanky-panky, uh-uh. Nope. Mrs. Spencer, the dorm mother, was known to interfere when things appeared to go beyond holding hands. Later she would get hers, however.

Yes, all was normal until a couple of events, both of which set a tone for the ensuing four years and signaled the potential for a lot of big time screwing around.

Dan and I were walking back from a mid-afternoon class and talking about football and our classes we had together. In our wildest imagination we could not have foreseen what awaited us back at Sierra Hall, room 303. I inserted the key to our room, looking forward to the opportunity to lay down on the bed and relax for a while before going to football practice, but was both shocked and reviled at what I saw. Nothing in the room was in its original place as we had left it that morning. Everything was literally turned upside down. A foot from the swing radius of the door was a bed that had been propped on top of a desk, which had been placed atop the other desk. The other bed was merely on end leaning against a wall, as we found out after crawling through and under a desk opening to enter into the room. Trash cans were placed on the bed that was atop the desks, and lamps and the radio were on the floor. As an extra touch, the assholes had sprinkled clothes soap all over everything.

"Sonovabitch! Those damn assholes," was all Dan could say.

"What the hell? I don't believe this." I mean, what else could I say? Chalk up that day. We were ready to kill or maim. Furious and irrational, we would have let loose on the first person that came upon us at that moment hinting at any claim of personal or contributory responsibility for our "tossed" room. Our room was a shambles, a disaster zone.

Shortly after we started putting furniture back in place, Jack came along with a few other guys to see our room and, because as it turned out they were responsible, gauge our reactions. They were not prepared for our barrage of emotions. They quickly showed great remorse and apologized, and then helped us undo the damage. Later, we would joke about it, but at the moment we were pretty upset at what happened to our room. After things were back in place and emotions cooled, Jack explained that he had borrowed a master key from the floor resident assistant, or RA as we called them, and had even explained to the RA what they needed the key for! I couldn't believe a RA would condone this. Jack also told us the names of the other contributing violators. One of them was a wimp down the hall. That night he got "pennied" out of his room and the dorm maintenance staff had to be called to gain entry to his room by outside ladder and entering through the window. During our stay in Sierra we "pennied" a number of people both in and out of rooms simply by heavily taping a few pennies either over the inside button or forcing a number of coins in the exterior door jamb on the side of the door knob. Either way, the door would not open. We would normally lock a person in his room for a few hours before removing the coins.

The second event I alluded to involved our membership by invitation to the Raiders, a jock organization on campus classified as GDI's --- or God Damn Independents. Of course, with only five fraternities on our small campus it was easy to be an independent by proxy. But being a Raider, a GDI, was special.

An invitation to join had been extended to certain members of the freshman football team by nomination of some of the varsity players.

"What do you think, Dave?" Jack asked me as we sat in our dorm room one night. The three of us, Dan, Jack and I were together constantly. We ate together and studied together, except when Jack had some particularly tough accounting work and needed uninterrupted study time. We took study breaks together, walking over to Lissen Hall when the mobile food wagon stopped there each school night to sell snacks to the dorm residents, and went almost everywhere together when not asleep or in class. We became quite close and trusted one another with things we would not discuss with anyone else. We bonded as friends. It was during one of our study breaks, when we would sit on a bed, our backs against the wall, relaxing, with legs extended off the edge of the bed, that we talked about the invitation to join the Raiders. None of us had heard much about the Raiders. We knew that it was an informal organization of athletes, and that the better athletes on campus that were not in a fraternity were members.

"Sounds good to me," I said. "It doesn't cost much, that's for sure. There's no dues, and the only thing we would need to buy now is our sweatshirts."

"I think we should go ahead and join," Dan added. "There's some good men in Raiders, and 'Rancher' said they would really like to see us in."

"I agree. And someone said they have a lot of parties," I said.

"I think we ought to do it," Jack stated firmly.

"Then it's decided. We join." Dan concluded.

With that, it was simply a matter of going to the meeting one evening later that week to be formally accepted into Raiders and to buy our sweatshirts. The excitement we felt the night of the meeting as we walked across campus to the Business building, where the meeting was to be held, was almost like an adrenaline rush. After the meeting and the hand shaking with fellow Raiders we headed back to our dorm with sweatshirts proudly in hand. We wore them to classes the next day, with the "frat pin", an inch long bolt with nut, attached to the shirt.

We were beginning to feel quite independent and in control in our new surroundings. The anxiety and mystery of college had worn off. We were all in a groove with classes, studies, and extra-curricular activities, and being a member of Raiders created an overall feeling of self-confidence that put us on a perceived level of importance higher than the average student at Happy Valley. With Raiders, we were a part of a group that both enjoyed a good reputation because of its parties, and was disliked by certain members of the student body, particularly the fraternities, because we were just flat out rowdy.

Raiders was an informal group even though quasi-formal recognition by the school came in the form of a faculty advisor, Professor Mervin, an older, tenured, balding and heavy-set member of the faculty who even permitted himself to be included in our group photo. The limited recognition was not enough, however, to get our photo into the school yearbook. The school had to draw the line somewhere. We didn't have any bylaws, secret handshakes or a "house" like the fraternities. We did, however, have Raider Henry's.

Raider Henry's was an apartment complex that consisted of ten bungalow-type units off Colley Avenue, a few blocks west of the campus and past some small agriculture warehouses and over the railroad tracks. The complex was old, and the units small but large enough to accommodate four people comfortably in two small bedrooms. When I first saw the complex it reminded me of migrant farmer quarters I had seen in the San Joaquin Valley. The kitchens in each unit were sparce and the lone bathroom was tiny and along the back wall of the unit. The Bluebird Club, a local redneck bar, was across the street from Henry's, and Luige's Pizza was a half block south near the bridge over Sutter Creek. Five units on each side of a narrow driveway faced one another. A few small trees grew in front of the units. The parties were never inside, but were held on the driveway in the complex. There was no room for parked cars in the complex during parties, so parking was off the side of the road on Colley Avenue. We usually walked to Henry's from the dorm. Using the roads from the dorm required us to walk through campus, down First Street a few blocks to Colley Avenue and up a couple blocks to Henry's. That was too long and out of the way, so we cut across the college athletic fields, squirmed under a cyclone fence, and walked across the Southern Pacific railroad tracks that put us on the back of Henry's property.

Some Raider upperclassmen lived at Henry's, most notably "TJ", the black center on our basketball team, Nick Pressley, a hot-shooting guard on the same team, and "JJ" Howell, another guard on the team and the most versatile and well-rounded pure athlete at Happy Valley. When these guys decided to have a party, word spread fast among the Raiders and anticipation levels grew as we looked forward to a wild and entertaining evening.

There was no telling what would happen, but you could be certain that "Buzzard" would hang a "BA" on the roof of one of the apartments. Buzzard lived in Sierra Hall and was a speedy receiver from Ventura County that played on our freshman football team. He was the jokester and was never at a loss for something outrageously funny and original to say or do. Whenever he was around our insides were already laughing and in the cocked position just waiting for something new and hilarious to come forth from his lips or body language. He was the author of such things as "give me a blow-me and cheese sandwich", giving some of our friends in Lissen Hall names like Sally-mander and Beth Boa-constrictor, and referring to urinating as "choke my duck" and "drain my lizard". To say Buzzard took a lighthearted and loose view of things is an understatement. He certainly wasn't bothered with the exposure of his bare ass on the roof at Henry's. With his black hair cut close to the scalp, and elongated nose, high forehead, long neck, thin face and close-set eyes, he really did look like a buzzard.

But the overwhelming image of Henry's was the shoulder-to-shoulder people crowded on that little driveway and the wait to put a cup back under the keg spigot to get a refill. The driveway was a mass of blue Raiders sweatshirts. People that were not members of Raiders or invited guests knew better to stay away ... unless you were a girl, and you assumed the risk of attending.

If some conversation could be heard, one would undoubtedly hear, "I wonder where Buzzard is?" or "I wonder when Buzzard's going to do his thing?" And then it was just a matter of time before we would all hear a loud, chorus of, "Buzzard!" That meant he was on a roof, and a few moments later was seen by all in the evening shadows created by a full moon or a dim bungalow porch light.

And that's about the time 'ol Henry came out. Henry lived in an end unit close to the railroad tracks and was the owner and landlord. He was a short, nervous, crotchety, gastric old man in his 70's and walked with a bit of a hunch. He never walked outside without his old, tattered wide-brim hat on top of his head of thin, gray hair. We never really knew when he would pop up, so were generally caught by surprise when he started talking to the first group he encountered and threatened with, "I call police." The unlucky group would merely shrug their collective shoulders and walk away. Sometimes he called the police, and other times he didn't. Normally, TJ, JJ or Nick would get word of his threats and talk to him gently.

"What's up Henry?" Nick asked.

"Too much noise," Henry answered.

"We'll turn it down some, Henry."

"Okay. What's that young man doing on top of the roof?" Henry asked.

"Oh. He's just checking out some loose roof tiles."

"Oh." Henry replied. "Tell him to get down."

Nick turned toward the roof and yelled, "Buzzard, get down off the roof!"

With that, Nick gently turned Henry around and started walking with him in the direction of his bungalow. He assured Henry things wouldn't get out of hand (as if they weren't already!) and that he really didn't want to call the police and ruin the nice time everyone was having at Henry's place. You could tell Henry was thinking the situation over as he shuffled along, head bent low. He mumbled something unintelligible and walked into his unit.

Ten minutes later the police arrived, telling us to keep things down, and drove off. If they had to return the party was over, as happened on more than one occasion.

To our good fortune, the police in Happy Valley were reasonable, easy to get along with, and tolerant of the college students. We didn't hassle them, and they gave us a lot of rope before bringing down the hammer. You really had to give them a hard time to find yourself taken to police headquarters. Dan crossed over that line once, but was rescued by a friend opening the back door of the squad car when the police were preoccupied so he could run the hell away.

The police didn't have to worry about most of us at Happy Valley. We didn't go around calling them "Pigs", and we respected them for the job they had to do. We were just fun-loving people that liked our beer, our parties, our shenanigans, and that tried to stay out of harms way regarding the police. Most of us had not been in any trouble with the police back home and were not going to start now. We didn't want to disappoint our parents, either. They had high expectations of our being in college and were doing all they could to support us. But anyway, dealing with police was no fun.

Let's face it. We were not gifted students academically like those fortunate enough to matriculate at Cal, UCLA, or Stanford. Studies didn't come easy to us, so we had to work hard. When not studying or attending football practice, which occupied the majority of our time, we relaxed and let off some steam. We opened up the release valves "full throttle" on the weekends, as Buzzard would say. Hey, we were just a bunch of average guys trying to get a college education, but having a good time along the way. The issues of the day were not of great importance to us. Sure, we knew about the election of LBJ and the escalating American involvement in South Vietnam. We were aware that the increased involvement translated into more American personnel of one sort or another sent over to Southeast Asia, and that somewhere, someone had come up with the number of 500,000 American troops needed for the war. But we were only 18 years old and not even able to vote. Who really cared about issues, except when they were on a Poli Sci or History exam? Most of the American people supported LBJ's actions at that time anyway. Our high schools spoon fed us everything we needed to know for college prep and did so without discussing issues of the day. In fact, I had a Biology teacher that was berserk over the space program, so given the opportunity he talked about the space program and its successes.

Our routine at Happy Valley didn't permit us much TV other than some televised ballgames on the weekends. After dinner we congregated outside the dorm to unwind for a little while before opening the books for the evening. Reading the dorm's copy of the local news tabloid was impossible anyway because it was scattered to every corner of the lounge before noon. I guess we were somewhat insulated from what was going on in the world around us, but then aside from the trend of increasing black riots in our nation's inner cities things were relatively calm in 1964. The 50's and 60's were times of relative prosperity and tranquility in the eyes of the freshman class at Happy Valley. One day I was in suburban Danville with its unmistakable contribution to the good life. The next day I was over 100 miles away at a small state college in a distinctly rural agricultural community in northern California that was light years removed from the struggles of our federal government in Washington, D.C. Let alone the struggles and festering hatred emanating from our inner cities. When I was home in the Bay Area there were just certain streets and neighborhoods you stayed away from while traversing Oakland and San Francisco. We were told by our parents to roll up our car windows and lock the doors if we should somehow find ourselves driving on those "dangerous" streets. Well, I did neither. I had some trust in my fellow man, and did not care about the color of skin.

Happy Valley was our vacuum, where we were not only insulated but were safe and secure. It was really more like a Shangri-La for us, for it met our needs in every way and provided immeasurable good feelings and happiness in a beautiful setting.

So who cared about issues? Crack the books, work hard at athletic endeavors, find a date or a set of wheels for the next weekend, find a party, and by all means don't get anybody pregnant! As if that was a possibility – having sex was an anomaly for most of us anyway, as most "nice girls" in the 60's kept their legs closed, if you know what I mean. Pretty simple life, and particularly something you wanted to preserve and hold on to. Life at Happy Valley was a hell of a lot of fun, especially with guys like Buzzard around.

CHAPTER THREE

"Good evening, Mrs. Thatcher," Dan, Jack and I chimed together.

"Good evening, boys," Mrs. Thatcher replied in that soft, sweet, southern voice of hers. She marked our dining hall cards for the appropriate day and we continued on to pick up a tray and dinnerware before entering the food line.

"All right!" exclaimed Jack, "it's tacos for dinner. I can really eat a bunch tonight. Let's see who can eat the most."

"You're on," I replied. It was Saturday night and we all had a healthy appetite. Normally, we dragged in our sore and wounded bodies smelling of "heat balm" after football practice. Because of the intense heat and the lost fluids during practice all we could think of was something to drink. Chugging a few glasses of soda or kool-aid before eating does marvelous things for the appetite, however. We would nibble our way through an otherwise good dinner and then wonder why we were so ravenously hungry at 9:00 PM as we cussed out the mobile sandwich van for being late.

As we started down the food line we heard a familiar voice say, "Hello, Mrs. Thatcher." It was Brent Nelson. The four of us usually ate together every evening.

"Hello, Brent," Mrs. Thatcher answered. She called him by his first name. How nice. She obviously didn't consider "gentleman Brent" as one of the dining hall troublemakers. We looked at "Nellie" and wrinkled our faces as we mouthed the words, "hello, Brent." Nellie chuckled quietly to himself.

"Hey, Nellie", I yelled. Mrs. Thatcher's head snapped so fast you could almost hear the bones grind. Her eyes lowered, she squinted and stared at me, and didn't move a muscle, which was her way of saying she didn't much appreciate my lack of decorum in her dining facility.

"Hey, guys, how's it going? Thanks for waiting up for me back at the gym," Nellie said in a tone respectful of Mrs. Thatcher, but critical of our leaving him behind to get to dinner. Nellie took long showers.

"Great, Brent. You were taking too much time in the shower as usual. Tacos tonight," Jack responded with a tinge of enthusiasm.

"Contest?" Brent asked.

"Do bears do it in the woods?" Dan replied. This caused another scowl from Mrs. Thatcher, but what the hell. She'll get over it.

Brent Nelson was an end on the football team and came from San Rafael, on the Marin County side of the Bay. He had a gentle look about him and a friendly face. And he always conducted himself like a gentleman, particularly to ladies like Mrs. Thatcher. Given a little time with us, he would change. Like all of us, he had an Ivy League haircut. Brent roomed three doors down from Dan and me in room 310 and had the misfortune to have an odd, but likeable, bookish non-athletic roommate named Irwin. Why bookish Irwin was at Happy Valley I will never know.

Brent was not a large physical specimen. He had a medium build with about 180 pounds soaking wet on a 5'10" frame, and was slightly bowlegged. While he had a studious look about him, and was ever the smiling, friendly, sincere person, a football uniform transformed him into an aggressive, hungry player that never quit. It was the hungry quality that made him a defensive starter on our freshman team.

At our table around the corner from the main dining area the conversation turned to our planned activities for the evening and to women. Our freshman team had a bye that weekend, but the varsity had a home game against Southern Oregon.

"What time you guys want to head over to the game tonight?" someone asked.

"About 7:45 sounds good to me. There's no sense in getting there too early," I said. "I'm sure someone on the team will be saving some seats for us."

"Sounds fine. I'll be ready by then, so just bang on my door when you want to walk over to the stadium," Brent said.

"Okay," said Jack. "Brent, you be sure and be ready when we bang on your door, now. I know you're going to put an extra dab of Brut on for the girls at the dance," he teased good-naturedly.

"Yeah, right, Jack," Brent replied, blushing some.

Dan and Jack went to the food line and returned with plates loaded with tacos. "I hope Lynn Mandaris is at the dance tonight," I stated. Lynn was in the Early American Literature class that Dan and I had three mornings a week at 8:00 AM. She was from the peninsula part of the San Francisco Bay Area, and with her dark eyes, black hair and olive complexion, not to mention a petite figure and a friendly personality, was definitely someone with which I wanted to enjoy a few dances.

"Maybe Connie will be at the dance", Dan mused. Connie was a striking blond with a nice figure, and caught the attention of a lot of guys. She was a local girl and had been introduced to Dan by Rob, our football teammate from Durham, while on campus one day a few weeks prior. Dan was rendezvousing with her on campus occasionally and calling her a couple nights a week. Serious stuff. He sure wasn't seeing her much in the evenings, for she lived way the hell out Colley Avenue, almost to the Sacramento River Road, in a converted motel called Elon Hall that the college leased and used as a dormitory. In fact, there were a few other good looking girls that lived at Elon, including Phoebe Miller and Margie Henderson. Phoebe was blond, buxom, and bubbly with conversation, and Margie was cute, had a healthy body, and nice, shapely legs. She was a bit standoffish, and not as friendly as Phoebe.

"Connie lives out at Elon, doesn't she?" Jack asked.

"Yes she does, unfortunately," Dan replied.

"Boy, they've got more than their fair share of nice looking ladies out there," Jack continued almost dreamily.

"You've got that right, Jack," I said. "Nellie, what about you? Anyone in particular you have your eyes on?" I asked. We all knew Brent wasn't seeing anyone in Happy Valley. He was a little on the shy side, but more important had a girlfriend back home in San Rafael. Melissa was her name, and we had no idea what she looked like, for she had never been up to Happy Valley. There were some feelings there between the two, but we could read between the lines and see that the relationship was fading. Happy Valley during one's freshman year was no place to hold on to a long distance relationship. Jack was experiencing the same thing with a girlfriend back in Lafayette. We were changing too much and too fast and were not the same people from our high school days. I, too, had already forgotten about a girlfriend from the past summer. The survival rate of those type relationships was zilch. Zero. Forget it. The combination of distance and the excitement of college life at Happy Valley was a killer of long distance relationships.

"Maybe we'll have a good turnout at the dance," I said with optimism. While there were certainly other girls I would dance with, Lynn was particularly attractive to me and I couldn't get her off my mind. I really hoped she would be at the dance. She was a cute girl and there would be many other guys asking her to dance. Dan's problem was a little different. Connie had caught the attention of some of the upperclassmen, particularly guys on the varsity football team, and may have had a date that night and not even make it to the dance. I'm sure that thought made him miserable. It was also tough competing against upperclassmen because they oftentimes had a set of wheels.

We got off the subject of girls and got into a playful mood at our dinner table. There was four tables in the alcove where we sat, and none of the other tables were occupied. It was always that way when we sat back there. People knew better.

Poor Mrs. Thatcher. Lillian was her name, though we didn't dare call her by her first name. She was without a doubt in the wrong place at the wrong time. Her southern charm was sweet and nice, and she had no problems with other classes and other individuals, but the freshman class living in Sierra Hall was different, which she would find day by day and week by week. There wasn't just the four of us. There was a rowdy group from Orland – Rich, Tim and the Wilson twins, Mike and Matt – and Buzzard and Ron from Ventura County. All were on the freshman football team but Rich, who played soccer, and Ron, who was a sophomore and on the varsity football squad.

Lillian was thin, about 5'3" tall, about 65 years old, and always had her gray hair in a bun. She walked with a surprisingly straight posture for her age. We wondered at times if she was a holdover from the Mayflower, for her fashion of dress, if you want to call it that, was early puritan. With a collar on her dresses that was buttoned to above the Adams apple, we never saw her neck.

Sunday nights were special in the dining hall. Students were required to wear their Sunday best, which meant a coat and tie for the guys. Gag! Lillian was always in "seventh heaven" on Sunday night as she wore her finest dress and paid compliments to all for their appearance as they went by her table. We didn't like the coat and tie bit, and decided to rebel by altering our fashion.

Jack definitely had the right idea as he walked into our room that first rebellious Sunday night to anxiously display his idea of dressing contrary to the code. He had done a great mix and match job, just as we had talked about.

"You look great, Jack," I screamed in delight as I burst into laughter. "You did good." And he had done good. He was wearing our standard black low-cut Converse tennis shoes, blue denim slacks, a multi-colored rainbow of a madras shirt, a brown tie with zig-zag vertical and horizontal lines (where in the hell he got it is anyone's guess), and to top things off, a Harris tweed sport coat. Jack's attire that night was a mass of busy lines and contrasting colors. Dan and I, with great eagerness, dressed the same. We put on sunglasses and walked out of the dorm to confront Lillian.

We had never walked so rapidly to the dining hall as we did that night, for we were anxious to get Lillian's reaction. Of course, there was a minor concern that she would be wise to our little charade and "call the jamb off on us" by directing us to change into more suitable attire before we could return for her special Sunday night dinner. Our fears were soon allayed.

"Good evening, Mrs. Thatcher," we said with great effort and control, for our guts were ready to burst into raucous laughter. We had to restrain ourselves or she would certainly catch on to our prank.

"Good evening, boys. You look very nice tonight," she said softly, but with a slight noticeable hint of vexation and uncertainty in her voice. If anything, she probably wondered to herself who had taught these three young men how to dress!

We almost blew it as we moved past her desk to the food line, but aborted a possible outburst by restraining ourselves until we got to our table in the alcove. I'm sure she heard our laughter, but had no idea what precipitated it. And the other students noticed but could do nothing but feel envy for our non-conformity.

Midway through the football season Coach Johnson instituted Sunday practices. We took advantage of this, explaining to Lillian that we did not have adequate time to go back to the dorm to dress up for dinner and could you please make an exception for us? She obliged, so we were able henceforth to enter the dining hall legitimately wearing typical jeans and tee-shirt. At the end of football season we were spared from reverting to Sunday dress-up. The policy had been eliminated by the administration and we were all permitted to wear informal attire for Sunday nights, much to the chagrin of Lillian.

The next to last week of our short football season arrived. We were to have a home game that coming Saturday night against Cal-Davis. Being on the team had made my first semester at Happy Valley that much more special. I had met and become friends with a great bunch of guys from all over the state of California, including San Jose, Fillmore, San Rafael, Woodland, Orland, Sacramento, Herlong, Happy Valley, and even Sonora in the Mother Lode country. The Orland guys were crazy, and Chip from Sonora would fight at the drop of a hat. He was typical of a number of guys from small northern California towns who were accustomed to using their fists in inter-town clashes.

As the football season progressed, Dan, Jack and I developed a growing friendship with Benny Martinez, a back-up quarterback and defensive back. He was quick on his feet, and had a good arm, but at 5'8" lacked the height to give him a shot at displacing Neal, a hometown guy, at quarterback, who was a little over 6' tall and had a rocket for an arm. Benny was from up in the mountains northeast of Happy Valley, up Highway 70, in the small logging town of Herlong. An excellent athlete, Benny had lettered in three sports at the high school in town. As is the case in the state of Indiana, the town of Herlong, as well as other nearby communities, was fanatical about basketball, which is what Benny had excelled at. He had told us that the winters in that part of the state were harsh, with snow drifts over six feet high on the main street of town commonplace. We rarely saw even a dusting of snow in the Bay Area.

By coming to Happy Valley, Benny, like a few others from Herlong in his graduating class, had escaped the expected and routine transition of going to work for one of the logging mills in town. That distinction didn't change anything, however, when the guys in college went home at the holidays and for the summer. The locals were a tight bunch and did their share of beer drinking and hell-raising when they all got together after a grueling day in the forest working for the logging company. They also got in their share of fights in the summer months, particularly when they strayed into nearby Chester to check out all the girls who had come up to beautiful Lake Almanor from their cozy homes in the San Francisco Bay Area. For some reason, the Chester boys got a little too possessive over their local girls.

Unlike Dan, Jack and I, Benny was living in a boarding house of sorts off Rio Plumas his freshman year. His roommate was Dan Talmadge, a junior on the swimming and water polo teams. Benny was constantly telling us stories of his roommate's successful heroics in sneaking his girlfriend in and out of their room. The best part of the stories, however, was when Benny would tell us of Talmadge's sexual exploits while Benny was presumed to be asleep in the room.

On Saturday night, Dan, Jack and I walked over to the gym to suit up for our game. On the way over we discussed our plans for the evening after the game.

"Dan, what are your plans for tonight?" Jack asked.

"I'm not sure, really. Connie is going to wait for me after the game, and I think we'll go to Larry Sanford's place. His roommates are having a little party and invited us over since Larry will be out of town for the varsity game. Connie's got her parents car so we're set for the evening. What about you, Jack?"

"I'll be with my family tonight. They're on their way up for the game, so we'll probably go out for a late dinner afterwards. How about you, Dave?"

"I don't know. Sue Ellen is going to be at the game and meet me after, but beyond that I really haven't thought about what to do. Maybe I can find a party somewhere that is within walking distance."

Neither Jack nor I got into the game that night against Cal-Davis, for they were in the lead the entire game and ended up beating us in a close score. What we needed was for us to get a lopsided, or at least comfortable, lead on an opposing team so Coach Johnson would put in the subs. Not that night. In a losing effort, though, Dan had a good game, scoring a touchdown and catching a few passes out of the backfield.

I was extremely disappointed and walked slowly off the field with Jack. The two of us felt quite dejected.

"Damn, Jack, it sure would have been nice to get some playing time tonight," I said somewhat bitterly.

"Yeah, I agree. It's tough standing on the sideline the entire game, waiting for the coach to call your number, when you've worked your butt off all week in practice." Ah, the frustration of the bench warmer.

Coming out of the locker room I said goodbye to Jack, then spotting Sue Ellen walked to her slowly. She could tell I was in a pensive mood.

"Hi," she said in a quiet way, putting her arm in mine. That thoughtful, sensitive gesture began to heal my wounds to the ego and told me all was not lost for the night. "I can imagine how you feel," she added with a sincerity that was real.

"Thanks, Sue Ellen. I just wanted to get in that game in the worst way tonight."

Before I could say anything else, she said, "Why don't we just take a walk over to the park and talk?"

"Sure. Sounds fine to me."

We walked to the park, my arm around her shoulder, and her arm around my waist, making small talk as we crossed the dorm parking lot and headed for the entrance of the small, peaceful park alongside gurgling Sutter Creek. There were no lights in the park, so it was easy to enjoy some privacy save for a small number of other couples that occasionally wandered in with the same goal of privacy.

We lay down on the cool grass, and with her head resting on my arm I began to relax and improve my disposition. We talked a bit, and I occasionally put my hand tenderly to her cheek and gently put her lips to mine. We laid close to each other, whispering sweet things, kissing, for a couple of hours before I realized it was late and time to get her over to Lissen Hall where she was to meet a girlfriend for a ride back to Ramsey Hall.

At Lissen, I said, "Thanks for coming to the game tonight. I know we didn't do anything terribly exciting like go to a party, but I enjoyed our togetherness in the park."

"I enjoyed it, too," she warmly replied. "When will I see you next?" she asked.

"I'll call you tomorrow, but I don't plan on going out your way. I'll see you on campus next week." Sure, I had a nice evening. Having someone to cuddle with after the game and its distress was pleasurable and much needed, but I was not looking for any romantic entanglements.

"Okay," she answered, adding, "I'll see you then. Goodnight." She went into the dorm to meet her friend and I walked the short distance over to Sierra to see if Jack was back. I knew damn well Dan wouldn't be back by this time.

The three of us had breakfast together Sunday morning. Jack had had a nice evening with his family, who were heading back down to the Bay Area early that day, and Dan had the same type of evening as me, although he at least had a party to attend. None of us were enjoying enlightened sex lives. We were all dating "nice" girls who were looking for a steady relationship. Bull…. on that. Some companionship was fine, but who needed a girlfriend?

The following Saturday was our last game, and it was to be at Sacramento State, a road trip.

Dan and I were sitting in the quad on the Wednesday before the game when Jack approached.

"Hey, guess what?" he yelled excitedly still twenty feet away from us, "Dave and I made the travel squad to Sac State!"

"All right!" I screamed out, not caring who might have heard me. I jumped up on top of the bench, yelled once, "I made the travel squad!" I then quickly jumped back down to the ground and sat on the bench before anyone could figure out what the hell was going on. Making the travel squad definitely improved the odds of playing in the last game of the season.

"That's good, Dave," Dan offered. He wasn't able to share the enthusiasm felt by Jack and me. After all, he was a starter and getting an ample amount of playing time. With some luck, he and the other starters would share some of that playing time with the subs this Saturday.

At dinner that night all Jack and I could talk about was our upcoming trip to Sacramento.

Saturday morning finally arrived and the excitement level increased in anticipation of boarding the team bus for our trip south. As we walked over to the gym after breakfast to gather our equipment, Jack and I speculated about our prospects for getting in the game and hoped our families would be able to see us play. I felt like a little kid as I walked proudly out the back door of the gym to board the bus sitting on the narrow strip of asphalt separating the gym from the stadium fence.

Late in the fourth quarter of the game Sac State had a two-touchdown lead when I heard my name called.

"Dave Pedersen!" Coach Johnson yelled. As I pulled up quickly to his side he said, "After the next play go in for Bennett. I want you to stunt in between their guard and tackle. Get as low as you can."

"Yes, Sir," I replied, somewhat in a daze. The rush of adrenaline hit immediately. The moment the next play ended I charged onto the field. "Bennett," I yelled as I got near the huddle, and took his place. I was jacked! This wasn't USC and Notre Dame, but for me it was big time!

"Hey, Dave, good to see you here," one of the guys said, smiling.

The defensive play was called and I got in position. My heart was pounding and my legs felt like jelly. I had been waiting for this for so long and now it was here. S..., I was really in over my head, but was determined to play aggressively. What the hell! Plus, I was probably playing against their subs, so we would all be running around looking for someone to hit.

At the snap of the ball I sliced in but nothing was there as the ball and runner went in the other direction. They had obviously done their scouting work and had decided to run the ball in the opposite direction of me! Right! The next play I held back to cover the middle but the pass play was further downfield and incomplete.

I was in for three series of downs and got my hands on the ball carrier a couple of times. My uniform was getting stained from the grass and for once I looked like I got some legitimate action. After my third series I was replaced by another sub that needed some playing time.

Boy, it felt great. After the final gun sounded we walked off the field.

"Hi, Dad," I beamed with pride and satisfaction.

"Way to go, Son," he said. "I'm proud of you. You played hard out there." Mom walked up too, gave Dan and I a hug and added her congratulations. Now it was picture time. "Okay you two. Get next to each other for a photo," Dad said. "That's it. Good." A couple photos were taken and Dan, obviously more physically and emotionally drained from the game than me, excused himself and headed for the locker room. I lingered a bit longer, taking in the moment and savoring thoughts of my play and a dirty uniform.

This was just another contest to many of the guys, but a real honest to God achievement for me. I had gone from a meeting with Coach Johnson to a final game in which I had made the travel squad and seen action in the game. Now I was really part of the group and had more to talk about than our practices, wind sprints, and running the bleachers.

CHAPTER FOUR

The end of the football season meant a more active social life for us, which also translated into more beer consumed.

The following Saturday after our last varsity football game we decided to have a few drinks before going to the dance in the South gym. It would be no problem getting one of the older Raiders to buy the booze. The problem would be where to drink it. We decided to ask a fellow Sierra Hall resident, "Plug", for help. "Plug" was just that, a short, squatty guy that looked like a fireplug. The nickname was his invention.

"Plug," a couple of us said in near unison as we caught him outside the dorm after dinner one night early in the week, "are you using your car this weekend?" His car, an old beat up station wagon with near bald tires, faded and chipped paint, and a bent radio antenna, would work out great since Merv, an oriental friend of ours that was on the freshman basketball team, wanted to join us.

"No," he answered haltingly, for he wasn't exactly anxious to loan his car out. "Why?"

"Well, we've arranged to get some booze but we need a place to drink it before going to the dance," I replied.

"How about it?" Jack queried.

"I don't know, you guys. I'd like to help out, but what happens if the campus police catch you drinking in my car?" It was obvious Plug wasn't eager to cooperate.

"Hey, we'll be careful. We can duck down and hide. We won't get caught. Come on, Plug, what do you say? We'll just need it for a couple of hours, and we don't want to drive it anywhere," Dan stated.

"Well, okay," he resignedly said. "Come by my room Saturday before dinner and I'll give you the keys."

"Great! We appreciate that, Plug, and we'll be very careful and on the lookout for campus police," I said.

Things were going well on Saturday. We got our booze with no problem – Country Club malt liquor for the three of us, and vodka and orange juice for Merv. It was a rainy night, so we dashed out to the parking lot, found the car, and hopped in. The back seat was down, creating a large flat area behind the front seat. Merv and I sat in the back and Dan and Jack occupied the front seat.

"This is great," Jack said as we started popping open our Country Clubs.

"Sure glad Plug gave in and let use the car. I didn't feel like having to find someplace else to drink. And this way, we're a stones throw from the gym for the dance. Problem is, this Country Club stuff tastes like s…," I said. That was a major problem.

"Here, Dave, you can have some of my vodka and OJ," Merv thankfully offered.

"Thanks, Merv. You're all right. I don't care what the others say about you. I sure don't want to be the only one without a buzz when we go to the south gym for the dance."

A moment later someone saw a light in the parking lot. "What's that over there? Looks like a flashlight beam. Just our luck it it's coming from a campus policeman."

We watched with interest, then increasing concern and fear as the light appeared to meander through the parking lot from side to side, first one direction seemingly away from us, then working its way back toward us. It did not appear to be someone casually or randomly wandering through the parking lot, but a more repetitive pattern like a policeman checking each row of cars and looking inside cars. Fearing the worst, I said, "Damn, it's a cop. We're deadmeat, amigos."

"We'll be okay," Jack answered in a reassuring tone. "Get ready to duck down if it comes this way. He shouldn't be able to see us if we're below the window line. Just in case, let's stash the booze now."

As if the cop wouldn't be able to smell the brewery upon opening the door to an airtight car made so because of the rain outside!

The light kept getting closer. "Duck!" Dan yelled quietly. We all got down as low as we could. If that was a cop and we got caught with booze on school property our collective asses were grass and the Dean was the lawnmower! I'm sure it would mean expulsion. Who knows? Hell, we were just freshmen. All we needed was to get expelled and show up on our parent's doorsteps trying to explain how we got in trouble with the school administration. Or better yet, having to make the proverbial phone call home to announce the news. The dialogue would no doubt go something like this: "Hi Mom and Dad, this is one of your favorite Sons. I have some good news and some bad news. First, the good news. You no longer have any college expenses for us. No, we didn't get a scholarship. The bad news is that we have been expelled from school." Imagine the torment and discomfort of the parents. Okay… anger. What do they say when the friends and neighbors ask, "How are the boys doing in college?" The reply? "Well, the boys were unreasonably mischievous and have been given the boot by the college."

You get the idea.

We all were scared s…less. Things were getting more hairy and tense by the moment as we saw the light beam shooting around in different directions, occasionally beaming from a distance through our car as it got closer.

All of a sudden the source of the light was next to the car and the light was shining brilliantly inside. We were ready to pee in our collective pants. Under our breaths we were praying and cussing. The door on Jack's side opened up. At the same moment that Jack stared into the light he saw that the chubby little hand holding the flashlight belonged to none other than Plug!

We were relieved, but not enough so to refrain from verbally reaming out the sonovabitch. "You damn c…-sucker, Plug," Jack yelled hysterically. "You scared the living piss out of us!"

"That was my intention," he responded calmly. "I just wanted to play a little RF on you. I really had you worried, didn't I?"

"Damn right you did. I thought we were dead," Merv replied on our behalf.

"Damn," was all I could mumble as I reflected on seeing my college days pass before my eyes. We really felt like strangling the fat little bastard, but were so relieved it was him and that it was only a practical joke that we let matters lay. Plus, it was his car we were using!

"I'll see you guys. Have fun at the dance," Plug said before leaving to walk back to the dorm, probably to down a box of cookies. His pudgy face was all smile from ear to ear.

"You know," I said, "that little jerk and his prank just took the starch out of me. What do you say we take a few more sips and head over to the dance?" Everyone was in agreement, so we stashed the booze in the car and headed to the dance. The dance was okay, but not the same without a few drinks to just loosen up a little.

During registration week I had signed up for a physical education class in gymnastics, having always wanted to try the sport. The instructor was the varsity gymnastics coach, Mr. Jensen, and toward the end of the semester he told me that I had good potential. I went out for the varsity team during the second semester and because of my late entry into the sport decided to concentrate on the sidehorse. I was fortunate to have an understanding teammate that spent a good deal of time working with me. I improved rapidly and through tryouts landed a spot on the team and the opportunity to compete in the meets. In my first meet I captured a third place against an uncharacteristically weak University of Oregon team, and the coach commented to a news reporter that I was improving and showing good strength.

What was particularly captivating about all this was that for the first time in my life since junior high school sports I excelled in a sport. I was on "cloud nine", and my friends at Happy Valley were encouraging, yet envious, while they watched me compete on a varsity team as a freshman.

At dinner one night Jack asked me, "Dave, how does it look for a varsity letter for you this year?"

"Jack, I'm cautiously optimistic. I've been competing in all the meets and have placed in most of them, so I would think my chances look pretty good. I really don't know, however, what the coach's criteria are for an award. I don't want to worry about that right now. But I just can't believe it's all happening. Never in my wildest dreams could I envision being on a varsity team up here, let alone having a shot at getting a varsity letter."

"That's fantastic. I sure hope you make it," Jack replied. "And I'm keeping my hopes up for a good season when I go out soon for the wrestling team."

"I can't believe it either, bro. You've picked it up so fast and are doing pretty good," Dan interjected.

"Thanks," I replied, adding in a tone that I didn't want to appear overly optimistic, "I just hope it all works out okay. Getting that second place last week in the invitational meet and the second at Nevada the week before should help me considerably."

I had a good initial season, and the highlight of the season was competing in the state college championships held at Sacramento State. One of the memories from that meet was that, none other than Bob Diamond, who as a child starred in "My Friend Flicka", was a fellow competitor. He was a super gymnast, especially in still rings and parallel bars. The real highlight of the season, however, was when coach Jensen recognized the Block HV award winners by drafting individual memos to recipients so they could take same to the college bookstore to order a Block HV jacket. The jacket was red wool with cream color leather sleeves and a white HV on the left front.

While I was fairly certain I had won a letter, one of only two freshmen on the squad to do so, to say I was extremely elated and proud when the coach put the memo in my hand would be understatement. My palms were sweaty and my heart was thumping 100 beats per minute. It was truly a dream come true. I almost got choked up in the coach's office, for that award meant so much to me and represented my first ever varsity letter in anything.

"Coach, I really appreciate this," I said in all sincerity.

"Don't thank me," he replied flashing a warm smile, "you earned it. Try to practice during the summer and lift weights. But I'm telling you for the last time, don't do so many curls!" Coach reproached me often when he visited the weight room and saw me doing curl exercises with barbells and dumbbells. Since I did sidehorse he wanted me to concentrate more on tricep muscle exercises.

"Yes, Sir," I said in a somewhat detached tone. I was real anxious to leave his office so I could go to the bookstore.

At the bookstore I found a jacket my size, tried it on, found that it fit fine, paid the clerk, and then, although it was about 90 degrees outside that afternoon, wore the jacket outside. I walked through the quad to get a couple comments of congratulations, and then made a beeline for Sierra Hall so Jack and Dan could see my new possession.

"Wow," Jack said enthusiastically, "that's beautiful. Congratulations Dave. You did it, big guy. All right! Freshman with a Block HV jacket. How about that?"

"Way to go, bro," Dan said. "You done good."

I thanked them and then, with great reluctance, took the jacket off to be carefully hung up.

As the spring semester progressed into March the weather started to warm up and we started to think of trips to swimming holes after classes and on the weekends. Some of those trips took us to Trout Hole. Others took us to Deer Hole, which was also in Sutter Park. Deer Hole had a couple nice places to swim, and was better for sunning than Trout Hole. It was more out in the open, didn't have any trees nearby to block the sun, and had huge granite boulders lining both sides of the water that were flat and could accommodate at least half a dozen sunbathers apiece. It was a great place to take a date and to stake out a rock for some privacy and sweet talk between plunges into the icy cold water that felt fantastic after lying in the hot valley sun.

But seldom did we go up to Sutter Park, for Rob had shown us a place that was equally as idyllic as Trout Hole. It was a long-ass way from campus, but the destination was worth the drive. Called Nelson's Bar, it soon became a Raider destination. Thank God Rob had a car, for we would have enjoyed few trips out there otherwise. Rob was a mathematics major, and quite frankly had a more demanding academic load than us, but he lived at home so it was usually easy to talk him into a few hours at the swimming hole before he headed home at the end of the day. A couple times a week he would stop by the dorm to visit after lunch, and that's when we would propose a drive to Nelson's Bar. Really had to twist his arm!

On one particular scorching Thursday the inevitable suggestion was made. "Rob," I said, "how about all of us spending the afternoon sitting by the cool waters of Nelson's Bar?"

"Sounds fine to me. I've got an easy day tomorrow," he replied on an eager and encouraging note. It didn't take us long to get ready. Throw on swimsuits, grab a towel and the wallet, slip on some sandals, and away we went. We all piled into Rob's Mustang that he had parked on one of the side streets near our dorm, and he fired up his machine. Just outside of town I made the other inevitable suggestion.

"Hey, let's stop at the Oxen Hill store on the way and get a six-pack."

"Sounds like a good idea, Dave," Jack said. "I've got a lot of homework in accounting, but what the hell. I can catch up this weekend."

"That's the spirit, Jack," I said. "Never do today what you can put off until tomorrow." Jack and the others chuckled, but I knew Jack was a little concerned about his schoolwork situation. We just didn't like passing up an opportunity to go to Nelson's Bar.

Getting there meant driving about 13 miles south of town on route 89, and turning left on the Oxen Hill Road. The road led up into the foothills and we were soon swallowed up by the hills and valleys heading east to Oxen Hill. The two lane road was generally bordered by mile after mile of farm land stretching out for miles in either direction over gently rolling hills covered by short brown grass and scattered bunches of oak trees. About five miles back off the highway we came to Oxen Hill store. Even at 18 years old we had no trouble buying beer at this small hole-in-the-wall mom and pop country store. Once back in the car with our beer we embarked on the final leg of the drive, which took us up and down some small valleys and around a couple of horseshoe turns bordered by solid rock. About three miles from the store we came to the trestle bridge over Disabla Creek. Just before crossing the bridge we pulled off the road onto a dirt shoulder that could handle maybe six cars at best. Getting to Nelson's Bar late on a weekend day meant parking along the side of the road and a longer walk to the swimming hole. The location was also popular with Paradise High School students and other locals, but they normally stayed on the east side of the water or went to other spots up and down the creek.

After negotiating a short, winding walk down a gradual sandy decline in between large rock boulders, we walked out onto a nice, hidden sandy beach area that was a little larger than a tennis court in size. The creek and a natural swimming hole that was about sixty feet across was to our right. A granite rock sat in the middle of the water and was large enough for about four or five people to sit on at one time. Water flowed through the swimming hole at a slow rate, but the current was enough to keep the water clean and clear. The beach area was bordered on both sides by large outcroppings of granite rock that protruded from the hill in back of the beach down to the water's edge, thus enclosing the beach on three sides. Across the water on the other side was a smaller sandy beach bordered on the north side by a flat-faced rock about thirty feet high. In later trips to Nelson's Bar we would jump off that rock face into the cool blue-green water and hear the shrieks from the girls on our way down to the water.

Nelson's Bar was our place to get away from it all on a sunny day at Happy Valley. We could be carefree and forget our studies as we sat against a rock on the beach or on the rock in the middle of the swimming hole and drank our beer. We were still a couple of years away from the tension that would visit us due to the Vietnam War with its' vivid news telecasts, hungry draft boards, and scattered accounts of ill fortune that befell friends and acquaintances from back home serving in the "rice paddies". In retrospect, it was as if we were being given a message, "Enjoy the purity of play and lightheartedness. Live for the moment, for soon world events will force you to make decisions not foreseen nor wanted and cheat you of some of your youth." Those events would also rob some of our friends of their lives.

"Hey, guys, I think it's time to split," Rob suggested as we lay peacefully on the hot sand. He was right. The sun was getting ready to dip behind the rocks, and we had polished off a couple six-packs of beer.

"I guess you're right, 'ol buddy," I answered with lament and a touch of sorrow, "but this all feels so damn good." I was in no hurry to get back to the dorm and books.

We grabbed the trash and our belongings and loaded into Rob's car for the trip back. At Oxen Hill store we stopped to grab a snack to eat on the way home. A couple of us simultaneously saw the cattle in a pasture next to the store.

"Hey, let's go chase some cows," Jack suggested. It was the effect of the beers. The four of us jumped the fence and started chasing anything near us. Jack was whistling like a banshee. This went on until we saw the bull. Goodbye, cows.

Jack, Dan and I walked over to the dining hall with large appetites after Rob dropped us off at the dorm. Lillian knew when we had consumed a few too many beers, for our behavior was more raucous than normal. We would sit back in the alcove and make a disgusting amount of noise. Occasionally, she would walk back to where we were sitting and say, "Shhuusshh, boys, please."

"Yes, Ma'am," we would politely answer, but when we were in one of those extremely loose and playful moods it was difficult to turn it off.

CHAPTER FIVE

In early March the campus started buzzing with the preliminary activities of Western Week, a campus-wide extravaganza that touched everyone in varying degrees depending on which organization they belonged to and how involved they were with that organization. Sierra Hall had called some meetings in February to generate interest in the activities but we Raiders did not attend and therefore did not participate in the activities as part of an organized group.

While Dan, Jack and I were walking back to the dorm one sunny afternoon in mid- March, Jack asked, "Who are you guys going to vote for as 'Little Daisy'?"

"I don't know, Jack," I replied, "but Julie Stein from Gamma Epsilon is really good looking so maybe I'll vote for her." We didn't know the upper class girls so our votes that first year were cast strictly on looks. The men on campus voted for a Little Daisy, or queen, and the women voted for a Marshall, or king.

"I think Mary Bellarmine of Zeta Chi will have a good chance," Dan interjected.

"Yeah," Jack added, "I think it will be between those two."

"You know, even though we're not involved with the dorm I understand that everyone wears cowboy boots and cowboy hats during the time leading up to Western Week and especially during the festivities. We should go out to a western wear store and buy some boots and hats," I said. It was important that we at least look the part.

"Sounds good," Dan replied. "What do you say we do that this Saturday after my baseball game?"

"Great," I said, adding, "You know, I hear that a lot of the guys grow beards as well. I've seen some of the guys in Sierra Hall and around campus with their scraggly initial growths. But I don't think I want to mess with that."

"I agree," said Jack. "Of course, I don't really have much choice. I probably couldn't grow much of a beard if I tried."

We all laughed. "Jack," I said, "I agree. I don't think you'd better try that. That sparse peach fuzz wouldn't look very pretty!"

We were all excited about the prospects of Western Week, even though as freshmen we had limited knowledge of what it involved. It was already obvious, however, that this was a campus-wide affair and that all the major organizations took it seriously, particularly the fraternities and sororities. The school newspaper ran some stories about the event and there were campaign posters everywhere one turned extolling Marshall and Little Daisy candidates. The various organizations wanted your vote, for, as we would find out, much prestige was associated with being victorious in the elections and other aspects of Western Week.

The culmination of Western Week included a parade down Main Street and Broadway in town, and was always the first Saturday in April. Two Fridays prior was when things really heated up with parties and keggers. The Raiders had some parties of their own, but the fraternities, in their effort to generate votes and interest in their respective candidates filled the eight day period before the final voting with kegger after kegger and pulled out all the stops. Anything the Raiders sponsored was small and paled in comparison to the open parties held on the grounds of the frat houses. The attraction of the frat parties was that they were catering to the female voters for their respective Marshall candidates, so the women were invited to those keggers and showed up by the hundreds. Since Happy Valley already was known to have a higher ratio of women to men, which frankly didn't benefit us much our freshman year, the frat keggers were collectively the place to be.

On that first Friday of the festivities the three of us met at the dorm as prearranged at 3:30 PM. We donned our Raider sweatshirts and walked over to the gym to lift weights. After our workout we walked out the rear door of the gym, headed across the women's athletic fields, and through the fence to Henry's. By the time we arrived the kegger was already in full swing and there were Raider sweatshirts everywhere. There were even a few brave girls to be seen.

"Buzzard!" We yelled as we crossed the railroad tracks and entered Henry's property. Buzzard and a few of the Orland boys were already there and looked to be in a mischievous mood.

"Hey, guys," he yelled back as we made our way to the keg, "get over here and get to work on this keg."

"Sounds like a super idea, Buzzard. We just worked up a thirst working out in the gym," Jack stated.

"Working out? Who are you guys trying to impress?" Buzzard asked teasingly.

"Gotta stay in shape," Dan commented.

We gave our dollar bills to "JJ", one of the resident Raiders, grabbed a cup, and slid them under the tap nozzle for some ice cold brew.

"Boy, this tastes great," I said. There's nothing like the taste and enjoyment of the first cup of beer at a kegger on a warm day.

"Gentlemen," Jack offered, "I propose a toast to our first Western Week."

"All right!" Dan said agreeably.

"Yessir. This is it, boys," I added.

We all tapped our cups together, took a long drink, then walked over to where Buzzard was holding court to the background of Beach Boys music blaring from "JJ's" cottage unit.

"Hey," Buzzard said as we approached, "it's the Me-Off twins, Joe and Jack." Everyone laughed, not so much at the joke, since we all said it so many times ourselves, but at the funny twinkle in

Buzzard's eyes and the special gift he had to make anything sound funny, original and like you had just heard it for the first time.

The night was typical Henry's. Buzzard did a ball-walk about 10:30 that night from on top of "JJ's" bungalow, and about 11:30 a strange, stand-offish group of girls from Ramsey Hall got a Raider Henry's welcome when twenty guys, on the order of "drop trou"! dropped their drawers and mooned the unsuspecting girls.

The words, "how gross", and "I don't believe it", were overheard from the group of girls, who also quickly looked away in embarrassment. Never saw them back at one of our parties.

And about midnight Henry came out and followed up with his threat to call the police. It was Western Week and they had obviously received marching orders to crack down a little on the students to keep things from getting out of hand. We could see from a distance the police were checking IDs, so the three of us walked out the back of Henry's and made our way to the dorm. A good night and no problems other than the police visit.

Being rather blitzed when we got back to the dorm we were in no hurry to call it a night. We decided to heckle a few people across the way at Lissen Hall. Sitting on the bench inside some tall hedges bordering the entrance to the women's dorm we talked and joked loudly and made "kissing" sounds when we noticed a couple kissing goodnight before the girl slipped into the dorm. The couples gave us a look of disgust, said goodnight to one another, and the guy walked away. At lock-out time we walked back to Sierra Hall, hit the vending machines for some much needed munchies, and walked upstairs to our rooms where we talked about the evening before calling it a night.

On Saturday, Rob came by and we went out to Nelson's Bar. There were already some other Raiders out there when we arrived, and a few of them had brought dates.

"Hey, you guys, how you doing?" asked Jim Farragut as we made our way onto the beach with beer and hotdog fixings in hand. Jim was a junior from Yuba City on the football team, and was known for his aggressive, "crazy" style of play. He went by the nickname of "Rancher," and was known to be a scuba diver, which was rather an odd pursuit for land-locked Happy Valley.

"How about that party last night at Henry's?" he asked with a big smile.

"Hi, Rancher," I answered. "That party was a great start to Western Week. You suppose we'll see some of those girls again we mooned?"

"Nope," he answered, adding, "If they don't like our way of having a good time that's their tough luck. Come on over and join us."

"A few minutes later Rancher and a couple other guys walked over to the bridge and proceeded to jump off into the water forty feet below.

"What do you think, Jack?" I asked half-heartedly.

"I'm not sure. I've never jumped into water from that height. I'm not that anxious to try it."

"I know what you mean," I said. We sat there on the beach for a while thinking it over. It sounded like an exciting thing to do, but our bodies were glued to our towels and we could not take the first step toward the trestle bridge. The thought quite frankly petrified us, and we hadn't even seen what the jump would look like from standing on the trestle.

"Go on, you guys. Go for it. Go off the bridge," someone encouraged.

"That's all right, we'll pass this time," we seemed to say simultaneously. A few more guys came back to the beach after having gone off the bridge and were quite animated about their experience.

"Jack," I said in a rather serious tone influenced by the fear and uncertainty of it all, "Let's at least go over to the bridge and give it a look."

"Okay," he replied. We walked over to the bridge, leaned over the rail and looked down to the water.

"Oh, s…," I said. That did it. My mind was made up. "No way, Jose," I continued. "Jack, that's a long ass way down there."

"I know," was all he could say, with fear riveting both of us to the pavement of the road.

With some further encouraging by others we finally got up the nerve to try it. We climbed up on the 9" wide rail that was another four feet above the road surface. Our eyes were now about fifty feet above the water. Looking down from my perch I thought I was on the cliffs of Acapulco. No lie.

"Damn, Dave, this railing is higher than I thought." We stood on the rail for a good 15 minutes, our hands locked around the bars like clamps, and our palms getting sweatier by the minute. It was pure hell. People were jumping off on both sides of us into the jade green depths below, but we couldn't budge. We got down off the rail to make room for others, conveniently, and then got back up a few minutes later with a stronger conviction to jump. We finally talked ourselves into jumping.

We counted together, "one, two, three, jump!" Off we went and oh, my God, what a new feeling as my stomach crowded up to my throat and my whole body tingled from the pull of gravity that sped us to the water. "Sshhii …!" I yelled.

We hit the cold water and came up sputtering expletives as we talked to one another about the feeling of the jump.

"Wow, that was incredible," Jack yelled as he came to the surface. "Let's do it again!"

"Okay," I answered. The second jump took us a couple minutes to rationalize, but after that we were veterans and only jumped a few more times before the novelty wore off.

After a day of beer drinking, the roasted hotdogs tasted great and about dusk we headed back to campus.

Monday night was the real kick-off to Western Week. "Presents", as it was called, was held in the gymnasium and consisted of skits put on by each organization that had a Marshall or Little Daisy candidate. The event played to a full house and the skits were creative and quite entertaining. The skits either consisted of some light drama or singing, with the candidate the center of attention.

Immediately after Presents each fraternity had an outdoor party at their respective house, so from the gym many of the students thronged to the area just off campus where the majority of frat houses were located. The two closest houses were Beta Pheta Chi and Delta Phi Sigma. The latter was a local fraternity whose house left something to be desired. The house really didn't matter, though, for the large grass yard on the property was where the hundreds of party seeking students drank the fraternity's beer that poured from kegs located in back of the house. Delta Phi's Marshall candidate mingled among the crowd and an organized group of Delta Phi's sang some of their campaign songs.

I was in a daze over it all. None of us had ever experienced anything like it. The noise level created by the talk and laughter was deafening and was obviously temporarily tolerated by the local folks living in nearby houses bordering the Delta Phi house.

"Can you believe this?" I yelled to Dan and Jack as we stood near a corner of the yard and surveyed hundreds of students drinking beer and having a good time.

"No, I really can't," Jack answered. "And to think this is a school night. We all have classes tomorrow! Do you realize this is the first time we've had a few beers on a night before classes?"

"I hadn't thought about that," Dan replied with an excitement in his voice. "I'm glad I don't have a 7:30 class tomorrow morning." We would learn over the course of the next few years that a lot of early-morning classes were cut. It wasn't unusual for some professors to cancel a class or two as well during Western Week.

"Hey, let's go over to the Beta Pheta house, Ronny's fraternity, and see who's over there," Dan suggested.

"Let's go," I said. We walked up to the next corner, full beer cups in hand from a trip to the keg before leaving the Delta Phi house. We could hear the music and noise from the Beta Pheta house before we got even within one block of the place. Upon arriving, we saw a scene reminiscent of where we had just been. Hundreds of people were milling around the front yard of the fraternity house, sitting on the steps, on the front porch, on cars parked in front of the house, standing shoulder to shoulder in the yard, and filing in and out of the house singularly and in groups. Music was blaring from speakers that had been placed on the front porch, throwing out tunes from the Beach Boys, Animals, Rolling Stones, The Kinks, and other popular groups.

We ran into a few people we knew, and after draining our beer cups ventured inside to find the keg and get a refill. After a couple beers there and listening to the ever-present campaign songs, we decided it was time to return to the dorm.

None of us were in very good shape the next morning as we met to go over to the dining hall for breakfast.

"I don't know about you guys," Jack half mumbled as he looked at us through blood-shot eyes and wrinkled forehead that further portrayed his acute hangover, "but this much drinking is going to take some getting used to. What do you say we back off tonight and just spend some time in the quad watching the projects go up?"

"I think that's a swell idea," I said, anxious to get to the dining hall to assuage my huge appetite that morning.

Besides the Marshall and Little Daisy honors that the various organizations sought, a judging committee also awarded points for best costumes worn by an organization, best publicity campaign, and best quad project. Every organization had an opportunity to enter all events and a grand prize award went to the organization that totaled the most overall points in all categories. Competition was particularly keen for the projects, so an amazing amount of time, resources, effort and creativity went into the construction of the quad projects. The emphasis was to build a structure that looked authentic and that was as close as possible to being a replica of a structure that may have existed during the 1800's out west. For example, a fraternity that adopted a lumberman theme would dress their Marshall candidate in authentic-looking lumberman's attire and would create a costume that all members of the fraternity would wear during the entire time of Western Week wherever they went, to classes, socials, parties, and so on. They would replicate a sawmill for their project, including moving parts. A sorority might adopt the theme of a small town school and build a schoolhouse. All the projects, having been under some form of construction off campus during the prior two months, were brought to the campus quad in modular fashion Tuesday after 5:00 PM and were erected Tuesday night. Sometimes the erection of a project took all night and a tired, but excited, group of workers would leave the quad just before sun-up.

The final visual effect was that the central campus quad had been transformed into a small western town, or what looked like a Hollywood movie set, replete with a couple of main thoroughfares. Add to that effect many groups of people in their respective look-alike costumes singing campaign songs and taking interested students on short tours of their quad projects and you have the crux of Western Week. At any given time hundreds of students were milling about this mini-western "town" that sprang up Tuesday night and would remain up until the groups disassembled everything Sunday.

This is where Dan, Jack and I spent a quiet and dry Tuesday night, wandering among the structures going up and somewhat mesmerized by the authenticity and splendid workmanship that was so evident. We didn't know many of the people in the Greek organizations, so all we could do was look. In future years, as we got to know more people on campus, we were at times ready helpers and at other times politely asked to leave because our help would have been minimal having just come from a party somewhere.

At lunch Wednesday Jack was the first to mention the ghastly experience that awaited me and a few other guys that night at the Western Week carnival to be held in the football stadium parking lot. The carnival booths were constructed the previous Saturday by active Block HV lettermen society members, with each organization paying a nominal fee for erection of a booth, and then setting up their own carnival-type event. One such event, for example, was the agricultural club's "bronco bull" consisting of a large 55-gallon drum connected to ropes in all four directions that were pulled in varying sequences by men holding the ropes. The rider had a single rope to hold on to and a semblance of a saddle.

"So, are you ready for your initiation into Block HV tonight, Dave?" Jack asked with a big s… eating grin on his face.

"Not really," I answered. "I mean, just how prepared can you get for something like that? You know damn well what I'll be going through. I'm told there is only one way to go through it, and that's s… faced so you don't feel a thing. Larry and I will be going over to the Sanchez's apartment to prepare for it." Larry and I were the two freshmen to letter on the gymnastics team earlier in the year. He was about 5' 3", had muscles on top of muscles, was one of our top still ring and parallel bar performers, and could do an iron cross. I worked at it, but could not quite pull it off. The Sanchez's were Rick and Ron, twins from Vallejo who were "big men on campus", to be trite. Rick was the quarterback and punter on the varsity football team, and Ron was a bruising fullback. They were juniors so lived off campus on Iris Street. It would be my first time to their apartment, which was located across First Street from the campus library.

"I hear it gets pretty messy," Dan added. He and Jack were obviously attempting to psyche me out.

"That's what I hear, too," I replied. "I just cannot imagine what it's like to have eggs thrown at you for 30 minutes. Obviously, that great unknown is why we have been advised to arrive at the carnival feeling no pain." I knew that somewhere along the way the whole affair would have its moments of fun and gaiety, but I also visualized how sloppy things would get.

As it turned out, Larry and I had the time of our lives. I met him at the Sanchez's at 6:00 PM. He and I were scheduled for 9:00 PM to 9:30 PM at the booth, so that gave us plenty of time to drink and walk up the road to the carnival site. We had decided to drink hard cider. To hell with drinking something filling like beer. Our goal was to get ripped as quickly as we could. The Sanchez's had bought the juice for us and it was cold and ready when we arrived. It was a beautiful night, so we sat out front on the steps, sipped our cider, talked about the past gymnastics season, and commiserated over what indecencies lay ahead that night for us.

"Dave, I think it's time to walk up the street." He was feeling neither pain nor fear. His eyes sparkled and he had a grin that said, "Look out, everybody, here we come. Give us your best shot!"

We grabbed a full glass of hard cider before leaving the apartment and, arm over the others shoulder, singing, found our way up Magnolia Avenue to the stadium. Tossing our empty cups away before entering the carnival area, we located the Block HV booth and responded with drunken eagerness when some of the active members running the booth announced our arrival and encouraged us into the pit.

The pit was an area about ten feet deep behind a single sheet of chicken wire. After a delay of a few minutes to change the "targets", someone yelled, "let 'em rip!" and the s... and eggs began to fly. Thank God we were blitzed. We sang and yelled at the customers throwing eggs, and generally encouraged them through various caustic remarks. Fortunately, we had been advised to put some type of oil on our exposed skin, which would inhibit the drying of egg matter on our faces on that warm Spring evening. We were feeling no pain, as our yelling, laughter and general behavior could attest. After 30 minutes we were drenched with egg from head to foot. If you thought Moses splitting the Red Sea was a sight and wonder, you should have seen us create a large pathway as we departed the carnival grounds and people gave us a wide path.

Since Sierra Hall was close by we stumbled over there, took a shower with clothes on, and then headed back over to the carnival after putting on a clean change of clothes. The egg-soaked clothes were trashed, and we still had a hell of a buzz on when we arrived back at the Block HV booth and were officially initiated members. Dan and Jack would have their turn during their sophomore year, after lettering in football and wrestling, respectively, but that night was mine, and it was sweet.

Thursday night was the annual stage play held in the Auditorium. While the play itself was insignificant, the organizations attended in big numbers because immediately after the final curtain the results of the Marshall and Little Daisy voting from that day were announced. The top three finishers in each category would be in the final voting the following day, Friday. The scene during and after the announcements was pandemonium!

In a way, you couldn't feel sorry for those groups that didn't make the cut for Friday. The silver lining to that cloud was that people in the "losing" organizations could "let their hair down" and get more into the party mood with everyone else. After all, the campaigning and requirement for doing things together as a group was hard work and created a lot of strain. It was difficult for them to really get into a festive mood. Sort of. The three fraternity finalists had huge open parties to try and generate maximum votes for the next day and in the process went through over fifty kegs of beer at each house.

Friday night began the culmination of Western Week. A rodeo was held out at the fairgrounds, but the contestants were students, not professional riders. And the events were designed to limit the risks. No Brahman bull riding or bucking bronco stuff. Events consisted of a greasy piglet scramble for the girls, a calf roping event for the guys, and so on, and all done on foot. Each organization was allowed a certain number of contestants, so it was strictly a student affair. Points earned counted toward the Western Week Grand Prize, so there was some serious aspect to it.

We three sat up in the stands for the rodeo that first year. As I watched the event, I told myself, and Dan and Jack, that we needed to get ourselves into the rodeo as contestants. All agreed, wholeheartedly. That's where the excitement was on Friday night, on the other side of the grandstands, sitting on the fences that lined the animal pens and being part of the action from ground level.

The rodeo activity itself packed the stands with people, but most everyone was there to hear the announcement of the final voting that day for Marshall and Little Daisy. Jack, Dan, Rob and I had already left the grandstands and were on our way to Rob's car when we heard repeated roars from the crowd. The announcements were obviously taking place.

"I wonder who won?" I asked, actually rather rhetorically since if it was important to know, all we had to do was stick around a few more minutes to get the news.

"Who gives a damn?" Dan replied. "We'll find out later. Let's get to the car and grab a beer before we go over to the dance." The dance was sponsored by the town and was held in an auditorium adjacent to the rodeo arena.

After about an hour of "cruising" around the dance floor and talking to a few girls that Rob knew from high school, we decided to leave and call it a night. Too young a crowd, and how the hell could any of us pick someone up with all of us relying on Rob's Mustang for a ride home?

We awakened Saturday morning to a gorgeous day for the Western Week parade. If anything, it almost threatened to be uncomfortably hot. The parade represented the only Western Week event that the townspeople got involved in, and they lined Main Street to see all the floats with the Marshall and Little Daisy candidates aboard as well as the victorious Marshall and Little

Daisy in the lead car. As with other events, judging was also conducted for the floats and points awarded accordingly.

Because we all felt a bit dehydrated from all the beer and hard cider consumed during the week, there was unanimous approval to drive out to Nelson's Bar after the parade and all-campus lunch held on the front lawn of the college Administration Building.

Any Happy Valley student or alumnus would agree that the remainder of the school year post Western Week was rather anti-climactic. Call it burnout, attribute it to a concerted effort to compensate for lost study time during the period leading up to Western Week and particularly during that week, but we all had some catching up to do. Final exams were also approaching, but we still found time on the weekends to get out to Nelson's Bar for a few hours in the sun and to take a break from studying.

Before we went our separate ways for the summer, we had filled out request papers for dorm rooms for the following year. Dan and Jack were going to room together in room 304, which was directly over the dorm main entrance, and I would be directly across the hall, in room 303, with Chip Bengston, the "crazy one" from Calaveras County.

We were all excited about the prospects of our sophomore year at Happy Valley. We were familiar with the campus, the town, and the organizations on campus. Through our association with the college athletic programs and our membership in Raiders, we had a lot of friends and knew a number of upperclassmen that would buy our beer for us. The important thing was that among our group, Dan, Jack, Rob, Brent, Chip, Brad Stevens, and me, we would all be academic sophomores. None of us failed any classes or had a grade point average that warranted dismissal. Our sex lives didn't qualify for great locker room talk, but then we were all free of any romantic entanglements that might have had a deleterious effect on our growing involvement with the Raiders and all of its social outlets. We all dated during the year, but nothing serious. Hopefully, our love lives would eventually improve.

Little did we know, as we packed cars with our belongings to travel home for the summer, that we would overstep our bounds and that there would be trouble. Our fun and hell raising would create problems for us with the college administration, dorm mother, police, and others. Would we even get through our sophomore year, and succeed to the next year? We would also find out upon returning to school that some of our friends had dropped out, joined the military, and were on their way to Vietnam.

CHAPTER SIX

When I returned to Happy Valley College in early September I entered a dorm room that was already occupied, just as I had done the previous year because of Dan's early arrival for football. This time, Chip was settled in because of his participation in double-day football practices before the start of the school year. Chip had taken the left side of the room so I put away my belongings on the right side. It was a pleasant surprise to see that my new roommate had brought with him a stereo record player and some record albums. I had a handful of albums myself to offer, but they were older records from my high-school days that included a couple of the first Beach Boys albums, such as "Surfin Safari", and a Johnny Mathis record. However, during the recent summer I had added a dynamite Glen Yarborough album to my limited collection.

Dan and Jack were also settled in to their room due to football double-days. I caught up with them over at the gym, and from there we walked to the dining hall for dinner, catching up on summer news.

It was good seeing Jack and Chip again, as well as Brent, or "Nellie", who joined us for our walk from the gym. I also learned that our good friends Paul and Tim from the freshman team did not go out for the team.

"How was your summer, Dave?" Jack asked as we made our way along the creek on a hot, sultry evening.

"Pretty good, actually. As I'm sure Dan has told you, we worked again for Standard Oil at a gas station in Walnut Creek. Gas jockeys. But at least we had a job and made some money for school this year."

"I know what you mean," Jack said.

We entered through the rear door of the dining hall and after going through a very short line for food, since many dorm students had not yet returned, went to our customary table in the back of the place. There, the conversation about the recent summer continued.

"Tell us all about your trip to Twain Harte Lake, Dave, with some of our friends from San Ramon. I told the guys you were going up there so we're anxious to hear about it," Dan stated. I knew he was disheartened in not being able to make the trip, but football came first and he accepted the disappointment.

"We had a great time," I started, "Spent a lot of time on 'the rock' each day, consumed our share of beer each night, and had a party at the cabin our last night there. The party lead to an encounter with the Twain Harte police when Randy was almost caught javelin throwing the flag pins on the golf course. Oh, and I finally met a girl named Rhonda, who we've seen there before, Dan. Neat girl, and a member of the San Francisco world champion synchronized swimming team. I plan to visit her some time. Anyway, we had a good week."

Jack talked about his summer job working at a hotel in Oakland and some of the more seedy people he came in contact with. He definitely did not work at a five-star place. We all described our more memorable summer experiences. Dan mentioned the many trips he and I made to the Santa Cruz beaches in Randy's convertible, and told the guys about one trip in particular involving some girls. We had started up a conversation with the girls, who were returning to the San Jose area, as we sped along the winding Santa Cruz highway with "Hot Time, Summer in the City" blaring from the cassette player. We eventually got them to pull over, at which time we talked and exchanged phone numbers and addresses. Later in the summer Dan and I dated two of the girls.

Our conversation that day back at school didn't deal with world or national events. Frankly, it didn't concern us much. LBJ was our President, but our group had no opinions on his presidency or policies. That's not to say we were ignorant of what was going on around us. LBJ was relatively popular. We heard and read occasionally that the situation in Vietnam was escalating, and that in 1964 Congress gave the President what he wanted so he could wage war when it passed the Tonkin Gulf Resolution. William Bundy rationalized and justified the war by alluding to rights of the Southeast Asian people, that Southeast Asia had made commitments, that failure was not an option, and that we could win the war. There was some twisting of facts related to hostilities in the Tonkin Gulf, but the President pushed on with the war effort. In early 1964, American officials in Saigon said the country's ability to control the insurgency actions was largely contingent on improvements in the South Vietnamese government and armed forces. But President Johnson believed the South Vietnamese would step up and do what was needed. President Truman had sent 35 military advisors to South Vietnam, Ike had sent 500, and President Kennedy had sent 16,000. President Johnson took a hard line on Communism. He felt strongly that there would be severe consequences in other parts of the world if we bailed out of Vietnam. JFK and LBJ increased our involvement in Southeast Asia, which was contra to views they held before they became president. Polls showed that 85% of the American public favored the conduct of the war, but much of the population paid scant attention to what was happening in Vietnam. Early in the war only five American news organizations had correspondents in Saigon, which also indicated a rather weak interest level in the war. In 1965 the draft call increased to 5,000 men a month. But we were untouchable. We were college students, and having a damn good time at it, I might add. The Vietnam stuff didn't affect us. That was a volatile situation that was occurring thousands of miles from Happy Valley and one-half the way around the world, so what the hell?

Earlier in the summer we watched news broadcasts that informed us of the 62 orbits around the earth by James McDivitt and Ed White in Gemini 4. White had even performed a twenty-minute walk in space. Incredible stuff.

On the down side, though, and something that got our attention since some of us lived near big cities, the Watts riots occurred in Los Angeles. The riots caused millions of dollars in destruction, and injuries to hundreds of people, not to mention the fear that such occurrences placed in all of us. So much for that stuff.

Brent's roommate that year at Sierra Hall was Joe Knapp. Knapp was a couple of years older than us and was transferring into Happy Valley as a junior from Contra Costa Junior College in the San Francisco Bay Area. He had a nice car, a Buick Special convertible, but was reluctant to let anyone use it other than in extreme emergencies. Smart guy! Loaning a car to another student was risky business, as both Benny Martinez and I would learn the hard way later at Happy Valley. But Joe did have a fantastic stereo system in the dorm room, which Nellie was allowed to use, and he had brought a large collection of records. In the evenings before studying and on the weekends a number of us would gather in Brent's room and listen to Motown sounds like Smokey Robinson and Little Anthony. Great music.

I went out for gymnastics early in the year, but after watching Dan, Jack, Chip, Brent, Rob and Brad practice and enjoy the camaraderie of the football team, I decided I wanted to give football another try. My gymnastics coach, Coach Jensen, was very understanding, so I joined the football team with the idea of going back to gymnastics after the football season concluded. I enjoyed being a part of the football team, but one could wonder why I endured the demanding practices every day when I was classified a "red-shirt" and couldn't suit up for the games.

My second year at Happy Valley was quite different in one other aspect. During the summer I had obtained the approval of Mom and Dad to buy a Suzuki motorcycle. Not a big one, but just a 50cc bike, which was all I needed to get me around town. The guys used to kid me about the ferocious sound of my bike, trying to vocally imitate it with a "rrdding-ding-ding-ding-ding, rrddinng-ding-ding-ding ding-ding." Real funny, assholes, but who had the wheels, huh? That's right. She was slow on the hills, but on a straightaway I could crank her up to maybe 50 mph. It was great being self-sufficient for transportation. All I had to do was walk outside the front door of the dorm, kick her over, and I was on my way, wherever and whenever I desired. I let Chip, Dan and Jack borrow it occasionally, shying away from frequent loans.

Jack did not make the travel squad for the football game at Southern Oregon, so on Saturday afternoon he had come to me and said, "Dave, let's go down to Magnolia so I can try to buy some beer." The store was located just far enough away to discourage walking to it, but was within a quick and easy motorcycle ride. The store was a very special place to we 19 year olds because some of us were able to buy beer there. And the prices were right on our poor student's budget. You sure couldn't beat three quarts of Fisher Beer for a buck.

"Okay," I said, and we boarded the bike for the short ride up Magnolia Street. "You really think you can pull it off, 'ol buddy?" I asked lightheartedly.

"We'll see," he answered with a hint of self-doubt.

We walked in the store and said "Good afternoon" to the grocery attendant at the register. She was the only person on duty in this "mom and pop" store. The store had all of three short aisles in its 20' by 30' confines.

"Good afternoon," she replied. She appeared to recognize me, which certainly helped. We tried to look relaxed.

We walked over to the chill box with its glass sliding doors and made the appearance that we were deliberating over our selection. We grabbed two quart bottles of Olympia Beer and proceeded to the counter, where Jack placed down the bottles with an attempted air of confidence.

"May I see your identification?" the clerk asked of Jack.

He froze. "I don't have it on me," he politely said.

"I'll go ahead and pay for it, Jack," I said for the benefit of the clerk. I quickly put my money on the counter, grabbed the beers, and gave a pleasant goodbye to the clerk.

"Good day," she replied.

Jack was visibly annoyed by the refusal but soon got over it after we arrived at the park and took a few swallows of the cold beer. His boyish face definitely presented problems when it came to buying beer under age. Because I felt a little bit of pity for him I was less reluctant to let him use the motorcycle on occasion. One such occasion presented itself a couple of weeks after the Magnolia Street catastrophe. He came across the hall one night when I was studying.

"Dave, Nancy has asked me up to her house in Magalia this Saturday for dinner. I'd really like to go up there, and would like to prevent her from having to come down here to pick me up. Do you think I could use the Suzuki?" Nancy was a pretty blond girl with dominant eyes, and Jack had really fallen for her. She and her father had moved into the Magalia area from Wyoming and Nancy was attending Happy Valley. Magalia was about 12 miles from Happy Valley and up in the hills that bordered Little Magalia Creek. The views from the Skyway were spectacular, and Magalia, with its solid stands of pine trees and small, mountain town appearance, seemed to be in a whole different world from where we lived in the valley.

"Sure, Jack," I answered, "but just be careful with it. Good luck getting up the mountain, because I've done it before and it loses a lot of power heading uphill. I don't know why that little bit of altitude has such an effect on the bike. The bike just has a hell of a time on any hills."

"Thanks, Dave. I'll get it up there all right. I'll take care of it and also fill it with gas for you," he said gratefully.

"That's okay, Jack. It will probably use 25 cents worth of gas up and back." If he made it, that is.

The skies clouded up that Saturday and rain threatened, but Jack headed for Magalia on the Suzuki anyway. Nancy was a good-looking girl and I could understand why Jack was determined to take the bike up the mountain. Nothing was going to stop him from getting to her house that night. It's called young male testosterone.

Brad and I had gone out that night for a few beers, and having nothing else to do late in the evening decided to head up the Skyway and attempt to help Jack if we could intercept him. It was raining like hell. I don't know what made us think we might locate him. We just wanted to try to help a buddy. We were about one-half way up the Skyway, not far from the summit, and the windshield wipers could hardly take the water off fast enough.

"That poor bastard if he's out there in this crap," Brad commented. It was only a few moments later that I spotted a single headlight coming at us from up the road.

"There he is!" I yelled. A few seconds later he zoomed by us racing down the hill, a stream of water flying out behind him. He had his head and body bent down low over the handlebars and was obviously drenched to the skin, head to foot. Brad gave a hurried blast on the horn, then made a quick U-turn. Jack knew it was Brad's car and slowed down so we could catch up.

We pulled along side of him and I rolled down the window. "Jack," I yelled over the noise of the downpour, "we can put the bike in the trunk and give you a lift back to the dorm. What do you say?"

He just smiled. He'd had a good night in Magalia. "I'm okay. It's not really that bad. I can make it. The bike's running fine, Dave."

Sure, Jack, I thought to myself. You're not feeling any pain because you must have experienced some unusual delights.

"Okay, Jack, it's up to you," Brad yelled from his side of the car.

Brad and I drove off, but not until we knew Jack had a good lead and we could follow him into town. On the way down Brad got a little carried away with the throttle and on a wide, sweeping turn we did a 180 degree spin-out and ended up in the other lane facing back up the Skyway! We laughed a bit over it, then Brad got his bearings and we continued on, slower, to town.

When we met Jack at Sierra Hall he was not only drenched but had a blue tint to his skin. It was a long time before he asked me for the use of the Suzuki to go up the mountain. He found other means of transportation.

I used the Suzuki during the late Summer months to explore and visit places I could not get to on my own the previous year without my own wheels. On one warm Saturday I drove up to Trout Hole to see that beautiful swimming area and hike around.

I rode up through Sutter Park, through the golf course, and made my way up the gravel road into the low hills. It was rare to find another vehicle there since it was such a long ride from town, so I was a bit surprised to see a car in the parking area when I arrived. I parked the motorcycle under a tree for shade, and worked my way down the near vertical path worn into the side of the hill to the lovely stream below. I did not see anyone, so decided to just walk up stream a bit. I came around a bend that opened up into a small beach area, immediately smelled pot, and nearly stumbled over a couple wearing beads and shirts adorned with peace symbols and obviously taking some hits on marijuana. They saw me and stopped their activity long enough for us to look at one another. I do not know who was more embarrassed, the couple or me. The awkward silence that was only seconds in duration seemed more like an hour, but it was long enough for me to notice that the middle-aged man was a senior official at the college. I remembered seeing a photo of him in a handout distributed at an orientation for freshmen held at the dorm. I'm sure the lady with him was his wife. Have you ever had that happen to you, where you are just speechless and feel like a real idiot? I am sure that to them I looked like I had just fallen off the turnip truck.

Finally, I merely said, "Oh, excuse me. I'm sorry." There wasn't anything to say. I sure wasn't going to get chatty with them. And they never said a word. Again, what could they say? I then just turned around and started walking back from the way I had come. I had to kind of chuckle, thinking of this guy that maybe wished he was at Cal Berkeley, Harvard or Columbia, but he was at little 'ol Happy Valley College. Then again, what was the big deal over smoking some pot out at a swimming hole and pondering life or the gorgeous surroundings? I climbed up the hill, got on the bike and took off for Sierra Hall. In fact, I didn't even mention it to anyone when I returned to the dorm. It was harmless, but certainly not an activity that they would want known around campus.

CHAPTER SEVEN

As the football season and semester progressed our group became tighter. The doors to rooms 303 and 304 normally stayed open during the evening hours so that we could converse back and forth and slip in and out of the two rooms during study breaks. Which was often. Sometimes Nellie would wander out of his room a few doors down the hall and join us, but that was infrequent because he took a more serious view toward his studies. We all studied hard and when we needed to, but 'ol Nellie was a masochist. A big reason for his study habits was an incredibly difficult Art History course he got stuck taking, to hear him tell it.

Down the hall further was Tim Ballantine, whose father had a Chevrolet dealership in the San Joaquin Valley town of Merced. Tim's good fortune was beyond anything we could relate to. His father had given him a new 1965 Corvette for his sophomore year. It was a beautiful, cobalt blue convertible that certainly didn't hurt Tim getting dates. Tim was a good friend of ours and joined us on a number of our outings, like going to Nelson's Bar after classes, but was not a jock and not a member of Raiders.

Thus, in the dining hall sharing a table for dinner it was usually Dan, Jack, Chip, Brent and me. Because Brad was in Baker Hall and Rob lived at home, we only saw those two members of our group on campus, at football practice, and on the weekends. Benny Martinez, after being unable to obtain a dorm room his freshman year, was now in Sierra Hall, and while he lived on the first west wing where many of the Orland guys like "Mouse", Tim Lucie and the Wilson twins lived, he spent increasingly more time with our group. I suspect it was because he had a tough time breaking into the Orland click. Benny didn't go out for football that year, but joined Mouse on the soccer team, as had Buzzard.

Tim may have had his Corvette, but Chip, thank God, had his 1955 Ford pick-up truck. Without that truck, we'd have had little if any transportation. Three of us could fit into the wide cab of the puke yellow machine, but when we all went out some would climb into the cab and the rest into the truck bed. In nice weather, no one complained. If we were going to a kegger I would follow on the Suzuki. I liked keeping my options open, for it was always fun taking girls for a ride on the motorcycle while at the parties. After all, motorcycles were still a somewhat rare commodity around campus.

Poor Ma. She really had a mischievous group in the Fall of 1965. There was no end to the rambunctious activity.

Ma was absolutely shocked one night as she shuffled her large frame down the sidewalk separating the two dorms on her way back from dinner. "Oh, my God," someone claimed to hear her whisper (I think they were mistaken) as she noticed the collection of articles on the roof of the dorm lounge. I had climbed up on the roof and been handed bikes, garbage cans, ashtrays, and other dorm items which I carefully piled in a unique fashion. It was really a work of art, but Ma didn't appreciate it for one second, thank you, and ordered us to take it all down.

One night the following week we were sitting at our table in the dining hall minding our own business, which we always did, and bothering no one, when we became the target of an RF. Four of our dear friends from the women's dorm thought that they would be terribly humored by throwing some ice cream on us before exiting out the rear door near our table. Brenda, Kathy, Mary Jane and Mandy, all cute girls I might add, bit off more than they could chew.

We quickly mobilized into action. "Get the trays in and let's get after them," Jack yelled.

"And get a supply of ice cream," Dan added.

We each had a couple cups of ice cream and were on our way out the door and to the girl's dorm. They must not have expected us to have anything, for they were waiting for us on the sidewalk leading to Lissen Hall and were apparently intent on seeing the results of their attack on us. We unleashed a counter attack on them and they unquestionably took the worst of it. With that, they challenged us to a water fight. No chance there either. We came supplied with water balloons and anything else that could hold water, and after drenching them the girls cried "uncle!" That night we also went back to the creek to retrieve a dead, smelly fish we noticed earlier and threw it inside the front door of the women's dorm. Lovely odor.

During the football season Chip and I spend a lot of time together. Dan and Jack had steady girlfriends, so Chip and I often found ourselves sitting in our room listening to music before going out to look for parties. We damn near wore out the Beatles "Rubber Soul" record album. One of my favorite tunes on it was "Norwegian Wood", but the entire album was dynamite.

That weekend things went a little too far when a group of us that had not made the football team travel squad to Los Angeles found ourselves in a vehicle joyriding down the sidewalk to the entrance of the girls dorm, then moving onto the lawn between the two dorms. Bad move. We ended up in Student Court but I'll spare you the details. The episode caused all of us some reflection on our behavior. What in the heck were we thinking?

CHAPTER EIGHT

The football season gratefully came to an end. For me, it meant no more practicing for nothing. It also meant jumping back into gymnastics, and for Jack the start of wrestling practices.

At dinner on the Wednesday before the last game, which was to be at home, we made post-game plans. "Well, guys, what's it going to be Saturday after the game?" Jack asked.

"I think we ought to see if Vicki will pull a train for us," I offered. Vicki was a gorgeous brunette with a great body and lived in Lissen.

"Nice try, but I don't think that's in the cards," Dan replied.

"Well, then, I think we should have a stagger," I said. "No dates. Tell the girls you love them but that you'll see them the next day. You and I don't have to worry about that part, Chip."

"Thanks for the reminder, prick. My horns are so long I have to stoop to go through a doorway," Chip jestered.

"Seriously, guys," Jack cut in.

"A stagger sounds good to me," Brent said.

"Me, too," Chip added.

"Count me in," Dan said.

"Okay, it's set. Now, where do we go?" I asked.

"I'll talk to Bill Nathan. Maybe we can go to his apartment," Jack suggested. Bill was a friend of ours, but since he and Jack were on the wrestling team it would be best if Jack approached him. Bill had an apartment just past Magnolia Street Grocery, so it was convenient and nearby.

"Good, Jack," I replied. "Let us know as soon as you can. If Bill says no we'll have to try one of the upperclassmen. But that's marginal since most of them will probably be having their own parties."

"What's it going to be, gentlemen, wine or beer?" Chip queried. It really came down to those two choices, for none of our budgets could handle good booze.

"Wine," Dan answered.

"Oh, boy, look out," Nellie said in a warning tone. We all could handle beer pretty well, but wine was going to get us stinko, and fast.

"We'll get it at Magnolia Street earlier in the day and take it over to Bill's if everything is a go," I said, adding, "Don't forget there's a dance that evening. Having a day game is perfect. We can start our party right after the game and have plenty of time before the dance."

It was an unforgettable day. Immediately after the game, when everyone was ready, we all piled into Chip's truck and Rob's Mustang and made our way up Magnolia Street to Bill's apartment. He was ready and waiting for us, and greeted us with the following pronouncement. "Let's have a good time, but just don't break anything."

"Okay, Bill," we answered simultaneously. The group consisted of Dan, Jack, Brent, Chip, Brad, Rob, Benny, and myself. What a group if there ever was one! Bill stayed around for a while, then left to pick up a date. We didn't see him again until the dance. We didn't break anything, but that was a small wonder, for during the course of the evening we actually found a way and a desire to play football in Bill's living room. It was nothing more than imitation goal-line stands, with resulting "pileups". Pity the neighbors below when the floor shook as we piled atop one another and gave out loud, grotesque yells.

The building was a 3-story wood frame structure that had been converted into an apartment house, and was typical of many in the neighborhood close to campus. The nature of the structure accentuated the noise made by us that November evening.

Leaving Bill's, we drove, miraculously accident and incident-free, back down Magnolia Street where we parked the cars in our dorm parking lot and crossed the street to the South Gym for the dance. We were normally successful in sneaking into the dances, either by rubbing the stamp from the hand of one paying customer to that of another person or by simply bolting through the door when no one was looking. That night was no exception, but it meant we had to carefully avoid checkers all night. We were all wearing our Raiders sweatshirts.

A friend told me the following day that we were actually on the bandstand during the breaks and making quite a ruckus, but no one had said anything to us at the time. And Dan had been kicked out an innumerable amount of times, but had managed to sneak back in.

The band was playing a lot of British rock hits – Rolling Stones, Kinks and Animals stuff. I found Lynn Mandaris so was guaranteed a few dances for the night.

"Brent, Brad, let's go outside for some fresh air," I said at one point during the dance.

We went out, and were talking to a girl when a policeman approached us.

"Let's see your ID's" he said brusquely. He wasn't being friendly at all, which surprised us, and obviously had some special reason to confront us because outside we were acting with proper decorum.

As we pulled our ID's from our wallets I asked, "What have we done wrong, officer? We're just standing out here talking quietly with this young lady." His reply was quick and direct.

"You Raiders have been awfully rowdy and uncontrollable in the dance tonight. I've been watching you." He detained us on the spot for quite a long time while he took the ID's to another officer. Finally, the other officer walked up to us, and contrary to what we expected would happen – a trip downtown to police headquarters – he handed us our ID's. In a firm voice he told us what to do.

"Go on home and do not go back into the dance. You guys are feeling your oats, I see, but I'll let you off easy."

"Yes, officer," we politely answered, pocketing our ID's and walking off toward the dorm before he had a chance to change his mind. The matter was not over, however. The next week we all got an invitation to meet with the Dean.

"Boy, we've had it this time," Chip fretted as we walked to the Dean's office in the main Administration Building the following week.

"I know," I said. "I wonder what's going to come of this? I thought the whole episode was history when the policeman gave us our ID's and told us to disappear." I had no idea what to expect, for it was the first time any of us had come face to face with the Dean in a situation like this. Would there be any punishment? Expulsion? A letter to our parents? But that seemed an incomprehensible manner in which to handle the matter. He could direct a formal dissolution or disbanding of Raiders, but informally we would still be a viable, functional, and active group.

Arriving at the Dean's office we met up with Brad and Brent, Dan and Jack. They all had worried looks on their faces as well. The Dean, a young looking man in his early 40's dressed in a dark business suit and looking very much the former academician, walked out of his office and spoke to us.

"Good morning, men," he said in a no-nonsense voice. He wasn't smiling. "Come in, please." When we were all seated he picked up a piece of paper and continued. "I have a copy of a police report filed by the campus police department. Seems the Raiders were quite in evidence at the dance last Saturday and had a good time." A small, wry smile was visible. Maybe things were not as catastrophic after all, I thought with a slim measure of hope.

"Yes, Sir," Brad said softly and with deference and respect to this man that had all the cards in his hand and in his favor, and who could make life quite miserable for us if he so chose. The

Dean paused and looked each of us right in the eyes before going on.

"These reports are customary, gentlemen, and nothing will come of it." You could hear a collective sigh of relief from us. He added, "While I certainly do not like receiving such reports from the police from our social activities here on campus, what I called you in for was to ask if you had any ideas on improving the dances."

We were all dumbfounded and ill prepared for this most fortunate turn of events that without doubt saved our bacon. He's asking us for suggestions? Talk about asking the fox for ideas on fixing the proverbial hen house! Damn, this was almost embarrassing.

A couple ideas were thrown out, but they were not really of substance. I mean, we were not individually or collectively students of substance! Something about the bands and the attitudes of the police. He made some written notes and excused us, thanking us for our time but emphasizing his final comment.

"You're okay this time around, but I'm telling you that the Raiders had better show some restraint or there will be some problems and possible sanctions. I am also asking you to be available to help, as an organization, for some occasional campus emergent requirements."

"Yes, Sir, we'll take it easy, and we'll be glad to help you as a group if we can," Jack said for all of us as we filed out of the Dean's office and down the spiral stairs in the rotunda in an effort to put as much distance between him and us as fast as we could. In fact, we did not utter a word as we exited the building, fearful that the sound would somehow find its way into his office suite. But the Dean's words caused some reflection.

We received some good news the next day. The football coaching staff announced an end-of-season dinner and awards ceremony to be held at the Student Union. Even the "red-shirts" were invited. Chip and I were definitely in a bind, as we were not dating anyone seriously at the time. But we needed to find a date. This was not the type of event to pass up for lack of one. While the four of us were in Dan and Jack's room one night talking I brought up the subject of the dinner and a possible date.

"I've been considering asking Cindy Coleman to the dinner. She's the good looking blond we've been noticing that lives in Lissen."

"Yes, she is pretty," replied Jack. "I think you should ask her. She seems friendly and always has a smile on her face. Might be a lot of fun for a date."

"But I don't even know her," I countered, showing my true colors of shyness when it came to the opposite sex.

"Just go over to Lissen one day and introduce yourself," Dan suggested.

Sure, I thought to myself before replying, "Easy for you to say. Let me just go ahead and fly to the moon while I'm at it. I've never just walked up to a girl before, introduced myself, and asked her out. At least with Rhonda at Twain Harte we had been running into each other at the lake and around town."

"Well, be that as it may, Dave, if you really want to meet her and ask her to the dinner you're going to have to find a way to get her attention. Plus, if it works, you'll definitely have a classy looking date," Jack stated. Jack was good at that. Always a positive, logical view toward things, lifting others up, and it was helpful.

"Okay, that's what I will do. I'll find out when she returns to the dorm each afternoon after classes, wait for her in the lounge, and introduce myself to her. Sounds easier than it will be!"

A couple of days later, after gaining an idea of her schedule, and at the continued urging of the guys, I walked over to Lissen Hall to wait for Cindy. I was nervous as a whore in church. My palms felt a little moist, and I wished she would return soon so I could get the trauma over with. There she is, as I spotted her through the window, walking down the sidewalk, and she was alone, precluding the awkwardness of a friend having to excuse herself, or worse yet, me starting my dialogue with a second person hearing all. That gave me a moment to prepare. I stood up as she walked in the front door and I then casually moved near the route she would take to go upstairs. No, I didn't "jump" out into her path and block it. This was a smooth move.

"Cindy," I called out. "Could I talk to you for a moment?" I said with as much confidence as I could muster.

"Hi," she answered with a big smile that helped me relax instantly. Maybe this will not be as rough after all, I thought to myself as she walked over toward me. Up close for the first time, she looked prettier than ever, with her blond hair slightly curling up at her shoulders, and friendly blue eyes. I also noticed for the first time that Cindy had the cutest freckles, and she was wearing Shalamar, my favorite perfume.

It all went very smooth. I introduced myself and acknowledged that this all appeared a bit awkward, but explained that the football team was having an awards banquet and that I would feel honored if she would accompany me for the evening.

"I'd love to," she beamed. I told her what night it would be and what time I would call on her. The fact I did not own a car made no difference for our date, for the Student Union was a short walk from our dormitories and particularly from her dorm. Everything was relaxed, to her credit, for as I talked to her it became apparent that she was really a lovely, sincere and friendly girl. We talked for a while and felt very comfortable together on the occasion of our first meeting.

We had a super time at the banquet, and after walking her back to the dorm I sat with her for much too long in the lounge considering the Economics test I had to study for. But, oh, hell, who cared about Econ on a night like this? She was fun to be with and we really hit if off. Cindy was from the valley town of Manteca, and we actually had a couple mutual friends that I had met in my high-school days. I was on cloud nine the rest of that night and couldn't even concentrate on my studying despite protestations by Dan and Jack.

Dan and Jack tried to act with understanding when I wanted to talk about Cindy, but had to remind me frequently that they too had the same Econ test the next day. I sat in their room and kept looking out the window to Lissen Hall and thinking of Cindy.

Cindy and I started seeing much of each other, but it was a shaky relationship at best. I was hungry for a meaningful relationship, and was overwhelmed by her physical attractiveness, but I built too much into her genuinely sweet nature and friendliness. We dated a lot, and I spent a great many study breaks in the lounge of Lissen Hall talking to her late into the evening, or at least until the dorm staff kicked the guys out for the night.

It was during this period in which I was seeing Cindy that Benny and I developed a very close friendship. He was dating her roommate Donna, so we would double date almost every weekend. If Cindy and I weren't doubling with them, we were doubling with Dan and his girlfriend Janie to attend a party at Larry Sanford's. Terry shared an apartment with some other upperclassmen on W. Olney.

But more frequently than not, I spent a good part of each week talking to friends that lived in apartments in an effort to find a place where Cindy and I could go on a Saturday night. Distance was not a problem, for I had the Suzuki. Cindy got used to my picking her up with my bike, which I would park at the front door of her dorm, and our heading off via the Magnolia Grocery to a place where we could be alone and have a few beers together. There wasn't much sexual activity. We just weren't there, but I would find out later why she was less responsive. We talked a lot, and cuddled up to one another, sometimes on a couch, and at times on a bed, but it was all "kissy-face", as Jack referred to it, and some sweet talk, but nothing more. Definitely no "moge and maul", another of Jack's terms referring to the "clinch" and going for it. That did not bother me, for I was really taken by her and falling in love with her more each day. Well, I thought it was love. I would learn later that at that young age, it was more infatuation, but I thought it was love. It sure felt great, whatever it was. All I know was that I looked forward to each day and the opportunity to see her and talk to her, and hold her hand as we walked across campus. The emotions, love or infatuation, build each day and have a way of consuming you to the exclusion of other things in life that should be of equal or greater importance. I was overwhelmed by all the things I found so attractive about her.

One night Benny was able to get Buzzard's Honda 50, so we surprised the girls by pulling up together in front of their dorm on motorcycles, loaded up some records that the girls carried under their arms, and took off for Bill Nathan's, for he had generously granted us the use of his apartment for the evening. The four of us got a pretty good buzz on that night, and the girls took some photographs with an instant camera one of them had packed along.

Our evenings would not have been the same without the proper mood music. Benny and I didn't leave anything to chance. As a quality control measure we made sure that at least three certain record albums were in our party arsenal for the night – Righteous Brothers, Johnny Mathis, and Glen Yarborough. No party could be a success without those three records. We would listen to Beach Boys and Beatles music first, as well as some other British exported tunes, and some Motown, but later in the evening the stereo turntable played Johnny and Glen.

At one of our parties at Larry's I noticed that Dan and Jack were preoccupied with their girlfriends as we sat downstairs in the living room. I wanted some privacy with Cindy so quietly said, "Let's go upstairs."

Cindy and I lay down on the bed, made some small talk and caught some hugs as the sound of the romantic music made its way upstairs to the room we were in. I knew the Mathis album by heart, anticipating each successive musical number.

I thought to myself as "The Twelfth of Never" concluded: here comes "When Sunny Gets Blue." It was one of my favorites. When that number started I turned toward Cindy, pulled her gently toward me, and kissed her. It felt so good. With my right hand I stroked her lovely hair and then let my hand run down her back, softly rubbing it as we kissed. After about thirty seconds of this it was time to come up for air so I just held her very close. I punctuated this with little hugs once in a while.

"You don't know how good this makes me feel, Cindy," I whispered tenderly. I was in another world holding her and listening to Johnny. "When I Am With You" started up next. Great music. Things were really quiet downstairs, too. I wanted more and more of this affection and tenderness, not just that night, but on future nights together. But it was not to be.

CHAPTER NINE

In late November of that year we sat stunned as we watched a TV news program announcing that two anti-war protestors burned themselves to death. We knew about increased involvement in Vietnam by American advisors and troops, but the basic question we asked ourselves was, "what war?" And what was the big deal over Vietnam? I read somewhere that the Joint Chiefs of Staff had their own answer to that question, which centered on the possible disastrous affect of the "domino theory", that America's ability to successfully confront Communism was contingent on winning in South Vietnam. But I also read that Clark Clifford, an advisor to President Johnson, was fearful of the war turning into a quagmire and advised against significant military commitment. And Secretary of Defense McNamara allegedly told two stories, telling reporters after a trip to Vietnam in July of 1965 that we were inflicting heavy losses on the Viet Cong, but telling the President quite the opposite. The conflict was turning into a war of attrition. But why the protest, and was this limited involvement in the affairs of Vietnam and a few lives lost worth taking one's life over? As 19-year olds that had viewed and enjoyed "Victory at Sea" and other World War II documentaries on TV during our youth, and had grown up in the 50's with an eagerness to own military gear for play, the Vietnam situation did not fully grab our attention or concern in 1965. We were admittedly ambivalent towards the war.

We were having a grand time at Happy Valley, although we were somewhat of an irritant to the college administration. There was never an end to the RF's pulled off in the dorm. Much of it was harmless, but some of it was unmistakably dangerous.

Some of our co-residents played a little too hard and were a bit overzealous with matches. About once a month someone from the 4th floor would light off some sort of firebomb in a trashcan in the stairwell at the end of our hallway. Fortunately, the extent of damage was no more than a lot of black smoke and charred brick walls near the can. Occasionally, paint was used for the firebomb and the incident left paint spewed on the charred walls.

Water balloons were used frequently in our antics around the dorm. We had tremendous water fights between 2nd East and 3rd East that were talked about for days after, although the occasion of the first fight was definitely questionable and ill timed. For homecoming that year Sierra Hall had voted Brenda Higgins of Lissen Hall to be their queen candidate. Unfortunately, the night Brenda and a number of other girls came over to Sierra to work on the homecoming float in our recreation room was also the night we decided to have a water war. Anything that held water was used – balloons, buckets, extinguishers, coffee cans, surgical hoses, and so on. Before it was over, 1st West also managed to get into the fray. Participants ran up and down between floors and threw water anywhere they could. Along with our wet clothes and bodies, the halls were covered with water, and the hard-working girls downstairs listened and watched in horror as the tempo of the skirmish increased in intensity, participation and water volume. Water cascaded down the stairwell from the 3rd and 2nd floors to the 1st floor, creating a small waterfall. With half the men in Sierra engaged in this monumental struggle to see who could out water the other, the girls simply returned to their dorm until a more propitious time for work on homecoming matters. Someone had discovered a large bag of some white powdery substance in a janitorial closet and had thrown that down the stairwell, which significantly added to the mess.

With all the guys involved in the water fight how the hell my name ended up on a short list of participants that would be submitted to the Dean I will never know. Rumor had it the incident would put me out of the dorm and possibly out of school. We all did some quick politicking with the RA that held the list, promising to clean the mess up with all due haste. As it turned out, the RA didn't give a rat's ass about the situation and was thinking about quitting anyway, so ripped up the list and let us go.

Christmas break did not come soon enough for the administration, for they had certainly had their fill of reports of damage and pranks at Sierra Hall. Many of those pranks were harmless, but like the overzealous resident that let off small firebombs, others in the dorm also got a little carried away. We would occasionally see where a trashcan had been thrown through a window, or a trashcan had been set on fire in a restroom, not to mention toilet paper dispensers ripped from bathroom walls, cushions in the lounge set ablaze, furniture in the lounge set askew, bonfires on the front lawn, and all too frequently the fire alarms set off.

During Christmas break I used a day off from my gas station job to drive up to Manteca so Cindy and I could exchange Christmas gifts. I began to sense a hesitation in her, but was powerless to do anything about it, and did not want to say something that might be considered premature.

As if that wasn't traumatic enough, upon returning from Christmas recess we all found a letter in our mailboxes from the Dean of Housing. There was a hint of desperation and pleading in it. While we were cognizant of the substantial damages around the dorm, the scope, as compared to the other dorms, was staggering. We sat in dismay as we collectively read the letter.

"I can't believe this," I said in utter amazement. "It doesn't seem possible."

"I can't either," Jack said, his mouth hanging open and jaw dropping. Suddenly, the pranks around the dorm were serious business. "The Dean says that the total damages in Sierra Hall for the first part of this semester exceeded five times the amount of damages for all the other housing units on campus combined. Incredible."

"I'm glad you find that so incredible, Jack," Chip stated, "but I'm more concerned about the twenty dollar fine each of us in Sierra Hall is being assessed to pay for some of the damages."

Jack answered sharply. "I agree, Chip, but there's nothing we can do about that now. Maybe we should all be more restrained around here. And it's not like any of us have not contributed in some way to this alarming situation."

"Sure, Jack. Tell that to the guys that really do most of the damage. I don't know about the rest of you guys, but this sure as hell puts a bite in my spending budget this month."

"Okay, okay," I broke in. "No sense getting heated over this. We'll just pay our twenty dollars and be over with it." For most of us, that was easier said than done. Twenty dollars represented a week's wages from the dining hall or CAC, the student union, and was damn near a months spending allowance. I continued, "Maybe this letter will get everyone's attention and things will quiet down some." Chip was still incensed over the charges, and I suppose rightly so.

"I hear you guys, but we didn't cause that damage. In fact, very little except for the water fight damages. Other guys and the mysterious firebomber upstairs caused most of this. I'm going to tell Ma I refuse to pay the fine, and see what happens," Chip added in a rebellious tone.

"Good luck, roomie," I said.

It turned out that Chip ended up paying the fine. He was given a choice, to pay the fine or move out of the dorm. Since he wasn't anxious to look for new quarters off campus, discretion won out.

Things were relatively calm the next few weeks around the dorm. Either the Dean's letter and the fine hit home, or people were too busy studying for final exams. I'm sure it was a combination of both.

Shortly after the Christmas break Benny was there for me one night in my dorm room in a way I will never forget. He told me Donna had told him that Cindy was still pretty tight with a boyfriend from her high school days back in Manteca. This shattered me and I felt helpless in trying to hold back any tears as my throat ached, constricted and screamed for relief. Benny, feeling my hurt and anguish, experienced similar emotions.

Benny told me, "Dave, you can't let it affect you this way. She's got an ex that she thinks she still cares about, but she's confused as hell, too. Everything will turn out for the best. Let her go."

My mind and body felt tortured, and all I could say was, "Thanks, Benny, but I was really in love with her. We've had some great times together." I had never felt so attached to a girl before, ever.

"I know, I know", he replied, "but just don't get your expectations up, because I don't think she can be there for you the way you want."

Part of my problem was that while had not had that many serious relationships with girls, when I did "fall in love" I really fell hard and allowed it to absolutely consume me. I was one of those "hook, line and sinker" kind of guys when it came to love, with no holding back.

"All right," I managed to say. "This is really going to suck, you know?"

Benny shook his head in agreement.

Cindy and I saw each other briefly between Christmas and the semester break the end of January. I could tell she was confused. She didn't make matters any easier when she went to a lot of trouble to make a book for me from phrases cut out of magazines that, put together, told me about the things she liked in me. Neat.

Because I was in training for a gymnastics meet during the semester break, I declined to attend a Block HV party just prior to semester break at Doug Jensen's, an upperclassman that was a splendid all-around athlete. I was in the dorm room just hanging out when Jack stumbled in with a big grin on his face. I had missed a good party evidently.

He left the room for the bathroom, and I didn't see him for a while. Not until Rob walked in, asked about Jack, and we both walked down to the bathroom to look for him. We found Jack sprawled on the floor of a toilet compartment. Rob and I got him up and outside, took him for a long walk across the Happy Valley High School athletic fields that were across the street from the back of the dorm, and put the poor guy to bed.

I'm not sure why, but I did rather poor in my gymnastics meet during the break. Maybe it was boredom I felt sitting alone all day in the dorm until practice, and maybe it was thinking of Cindy and that disaster. I played a lot of solitaire, which Rob had taught me earlier in the week when he came by to visit one night, and I must have played the Beatle's "Rubber Soul" album a hundred times. The major distraction, however, was probably the mounting anxiety and anticipation I experienced knowing that Rob and I would be driving down to Chip's immediately after my meet. We would join Dan, Jack and Nellie who had traveled to Chip's home in Sonora the day after Doug's party.

As soon as I could get showered and changed after the meet Rob and I bought a six-pack, "travelers" as we called them, and headed off down the road, making good time in the Mustang. The following day we all went to a nearby ski area, rented a couple of toboggans and had a wild and crazy time speeding down the slopes, tumbling out of the toboggan, and engaging in some "free for all" wrestling matches. We arrived home soaked to the skin and with huge appetites, which Chip's Mother superbly accommodated.

Cindy was on my mind as Chip, Dan, Jack and I arrived back at the dorm the next day. During semester break I had had spare time on my hands so I had made a book of magazine cut outs similar to the book she made for me after Christmas. I took the book over to her that first night back and she really liked it.

She called me one night later in the week and asked me to come over so we could talk.

I got over to her dorm in a few minutes time, but wasn't very anxious to hear what I was about to be told.

"Let's go outside," I suggested. She agreed, so we walked up the sidewalk a short distance.

"Dave, this isn't going to be easy," she started. "I care about you a great deal, and we always have so much fun together." She paused a few seconds. I noticed she was visibly shaken by the ordeal she was putting us through, so I had to respect her honesty and forthrightness. "I'm so confused," she muttered. "I'm sorry, Dave, but I have to tell you that I still have feelings for a guy back home, and it's not fair to you to give you any hope of us having more of a relationship than we now have."

I took a big swallow before I spoke. "I understand, Cindy. And I know about your friend. Benny told me the other night, so it didn't come as any surprise to me tonight. Yeah, we did have some good times, didn't we? I was getting quite attached to you, you know." Boy, was that understatement.

"Yes, I know. And I feel so bad. But I had to tell you now, yes?"

"You're right. I'd better go, Cindy." This was still difficult for me even though I was expecting it. I was face to face with the sweet, friendly, attractive young lady that I was falling in love with. I could feel my throat tightening up again.

She gave me a peck on the cheek and said, "I hope we can remain friends."

"Sure."

"Goodnight, Dave," were the last words I heard her say as she made her way to the dorm entrance. I turned and walked back to the dorm, head bowed, hands in pockets, just shuffling along, thinking nothing in particular, and holding my heart in my hands like it was a ten pound weight. I did, however, ask internally why I did this to myself.

I didn't accept things very well, needless to say, as was evidenced by some poor judgment the following Thursday night. Dan and Jack came over to Chip's and my room to visit. It was early and we all felt "chippy". Chip had a good idea.

"Hey, you guys, do you have much school work?" We all answered in the negative. "Then let's go out and raise some hell. I'll call Bill Nathan and see if we can go over to his place. We'll grab some wine at Magnolia on the way." Chip left to go downstairs to the telephone booth in the main lobby.

A few minutes later Chip was back. "It's okay with Bill. He doesn't have much school work either. I told him we'd be over there in about 15 minutes."

"Party time. Let's do it, guys. Go grab Brent, and we'll be out of here." While Chip was on the phone Dan had given Brent a heads up. "Tank", a friend of Brent's from high school and a fellow footballer, also joined us. We all piled into Chip's truck and stopped at Magnolia to buy a few gallons of Red Mountain wine. We paired off for the wine to make it easy. Chip and I split the cost of a gallon, Dan and Jack did the same, and so on. It was a heller of a night, one that Brent and Tank wished later had never happened.

After a couple of hours of drinking and having a great time we left Bill's for Sierra to raise a little hell back there. Brent and Tank had different plans, though. They went to Ramsey Hall, where Eileen, Brent's girlfriend, lived, and caused some different problems.

The next time we saw them that night they were back at Sierra, huffing and puffing as they beat feet away from Ramsey ahead of the police.

The police pulled into the Sierra parking lot shortly after Nellie's return, but we took him for a long walk away from the dorm and kept him out of the way for a while until things settled down and he was more prepared to deal with the police.

I needed a weekend break from Happy Valley, and it needed a few people to get the hell out of Dodge as well, so Benny's request to join him going up to Herlong to spend the weekend with his family was swiftly accepted. It also gave me an opportunity to reflect on my occasional negative behavior. I really needed to do better at keeping things in check, but I was simply caught up with a bunch of fun-loving guys that found many ways, albeit sometimes unconscionable, to have a good time. I know I needed to show some restraint. On a Friday after classes we got a lift to the highway outside of town and stuck our thumbs out for a ride up the mountain. We lucked out. Some high-school friends of Benny's were on their way home from Sierra College, a junior college near Sacramento, and stopped for us. We took in a Herlong High School basketball game, and I marveled at how the town business carried on with all the snow berms piled high on every street. Benny's Mother was Louisiana bred and was the sweetest lady you ever wanted to meet. She fixed some fantastic meals, and it was interesting to see what small-town life in California was like in the Sierra foothills. Benny's parents were salt of the earth and certainly unselfish. Benny's father was full-blooded Hispanic and worked for the state, and his mother worked as a secretary downtown, so they were definitely financially stretched to feed four boys in the family. Their house was small, with only three small bedrooms, but it was warm with their great hospitality.

Cindy and I gradually got back on talking terms again and were congenial to one another after avoiding and ignoring one another for a few weeks. She accepted my requests to join me for occasional trips our group made to the snow country. At the height of winter, we listened for snow reports on the weekends. Happy Valley, on the valley floor, never received any snowfall, but about 45 minutes up into the foothills above Magalia at a place called Miners Gulch, a good layer of snow could be found a couple times a year. When that happened, all of us – Jack, Dan, Brent, Brad, Rob, Benny and me – would quickly arrange a date for the day and fill Chip's pick-up truck for the trip. We always had a great time, getting soaked to the skin in the process and having the inevitable snowball fights, but suffered immensely on the trip back down the Skyway as we huddled, freezing, under an insufficient quantity of blankets that thankfully someone remembered to bring along.

The excruciatingly difficult part of our snow trips was the realization that the great time Cindy and I were having was fleeting and temporary. We would laugh and talk, and fall into one another's arms in the snow. I don't know why we did that to ourselves, because the conclusion of the day's activities brought such emptiness for me. We were graciously holding onto something that could not be, but by our occasional dates were reflecting an unwillingness to fully sever the relationship. We were admitting our frailties and prolonged the pain of the break-up. Gradually, we saw less of each other and had new partners in our lives. In an unusual situation two years hence, however, I would realize too late there was something there between us, but it would be me that said no.

One Sunday night that winter Dan and I walked over to the dining hall for dinner.

Half way down the food line we heard our names called out. Turning, we saw it was Jim and Bob Jurgensen, two freshman

Raiders, unrelated, that played on the freshman basketball team. "Come on over and join us," they offered.

"Sure, we'll be right over. Save us a couple seats," Dan called back.

Toward the end of our meal, Dan and I managed to drop some napkins over the candle flame and sat horrified as the resulting flames shot up in the air higher than expected. Startled, we doused out the remaining small flame after a few seconds of watching the napkins burn on the table.

Lillian was over in a flash, visibly shaken. We had obviously picked a bad night for some napkins to catch on fire in the dining hall. We had, in Lillian's eyes, broken rank from the established decorum of her special Sunday night meals. And I'm sure she was gunning for us. "Did you boys start a fire over here?" she asked in a soft, but slightly agitated, trembling voice.

Dan and I were not overly concerned about the deed and certainly failed to see the seriousness of the matter. After all, it was only a few napkins ablaze. "Yes, Mrs. Thatcher, but it was all an accident," Dan said, trying to get her thinking along the same way. We didn't realize the possibility of her taking the matter higher.

"Hhrrummph," she mumbled, turning away to return to her tiny desk station.

We were truly shocked out of our jocks the following Tuesday when we received a summons to meet with the Vice President for Student Affairs at 11:00 A.M. the next day. They were calling out the big guns. I wondered if he and the Dean that met with us about our Raiders problems compared notes. Oh, hell, we thought, what's going to happen this time? We were very concerned about this turn of events, and in fact were more than scared, but the real stunner was still ahead.

CHAPTER TEN

We arrived for our meeting a few minutes early and had a seat in the Vice President's outer office. Silence. How serious was this? We had no idea of what to expect, and the uncertainty had us petrified. All we did was light a couple of napkins on fire. Surely this couldn't mean expulsion. Or could it? The Vice President called us in and we walked in displaying great deference to him and his authority, knowing he had us by the balls and could make life miserable for us. We were humble and hoped our solemnity might help to keep him from sticking it to us.

He and I looked at one another, and eyes locked on the other's set of eyes. We knew each other. We had met.

He looked directly at Dan and made a question sound more like a statement when he said, "Will you please excuse us? Please go back out and wait in the outer office. Your brother and I have something to discuss." Dan did an about face and left the office.

I wanted to smile, but that would not have been very cool. Plus, I was still a bit petrified on the possible consequences of this meeting. After all, as far as I was concerned, it was still his show and he had the upper hand, but then maybe he didn't.

"We've met," he stated matter of factly.

Damn right we have, cowboy. "Yes, Sir, we have," I answered deferentially. When I saw him enjoying the pot up at the swimming hole at Trout Hole I knew at the time he was a senior college administrator, but did not know his title or position.

"That was a most unfortunate occurrence."

Damn straight it was, I was thinking.

"Yes, Sir, but I really do not care about our chance meeting. That's your personal business. I didn't even say anything about it to anyone."

"Good."

And that was it. No more conversation needed on the topic. He got up from his chair, walked to the door and opened it, and asked Dan to come back in.

We literally fell out of our chairs with his opening remark, "You do know you could be charged with a felony, or at the least, a misdemeanor?" I figured he was doing the hard core scare approach, just to remind us this was serious, but that he would ratchet it down a bit.

My first thought was that this sort of offense could mean expulsion, not to mention time in the gray bar hotel! Dan did not know what had been discussed behind the closed door, so his jaw dropped and am certain he thought the worst. He told me later that his hands and brow suddenly were clammy with perspiration, that his stomach felt as if it had been hit with a sucker punch, and that his thoughts were that we've had it, it's all over but the shouting, and he's going to nail our little butts to the proverbial wall on this. Dan was very apologetic. "We're very sorry, sir. We didn't realize the seriousness or implications of this. It won't happen again, we promise," Dan said in a tone begging for forgiveness, fairness and leniency.

Dear God, get us out of this mess and we'll be good forever, I prayed, although I felt he was not going to bring the hammer down on us.

After a few minutes of watching us grovel and get wimpy, he came out with a statement that gave us some temporary relief. "I'm going to refer your case to your Dorm Judiciary for a hearing and will instruct them to mete out whatever punishment they feel is appropriate. I'm personally letting you guys off."

"Yes, Sir. Thank you, Sir. We're sorry this happened," Dan stated.

I merely said, "Thank you, Sir," and got up from my chair to leave.

I was relieved that the disposition of this mess would be handled by our peers, and appreciated his attempt to scare the holy crap out of us.

With that we left his office, still a bit concerned over the prospect of this unknown body, the Dorm Judiciary, hearing our case. Our worst fear was that the group would use us, as troublesome Raiders, to set an example for other Raiders living in the dorm.

A few days later Mouse, a fellow Raider, approached us outside the dorm as we returned from classes, advised us that he was on the Dorm Judiciary, and that he would see what he could do for us. Thank God for miracles! Mouse would give it his best shot to protect us.

He came through. He told us it was a tough debate, with others on the group wanting a stiffer punishment, but Mouse rallied one or two others to his side and made a strong enough case for leniency. Our punishment was to perform four hours of work around the dorm. Oh, thank you, Lord, I said to myself in relief. Dan and I thanked Mouse profusely for his efforts on our behalf. "Hey, we're fellow Raiders, what did you expect?" he replied.

"I can't believe the outcome of this," I said. "At one moment the Dean is talking felony charges, and now the upshot of it all is working around the dorm. Kind of crazy, but we'll take it, happily."

"I know what you mean," Mouse said, adding, "but we had to levy some type of penalty. Someone will inform you of your exact duties around the dorm."

Greatly relieved, we thanked him again and continued on into the dorm.

A few days later a senior Resident Assistant told Dan and I that he was responsible for administering our punishment, and that two of the hours would be met by each of us picking up the newspapers and other trash around the dorm lounge each morning for two weeks. A couple weeks after that phase of the penalty, just when we thought they had forgotten about the other two hours, we were told that the final two hours would be worked off by scrubbing down the metal shower walls in each of the eight bathrooms, and that we had to do it that coming Saturday. We made it fun by flooding some of the bathrooms and got our punishment behind us.

CHAPTER ELEVEN

Winter at Happy Valley was not near as severe as in most other parts of the country for the simple reason that we didn't get any snowfall. But with the valley temperature dipping often into the 30's and 40's, combined with all too frequent rainfall that seemingly lasted for days at a time, things could be sometimes justifiably classified as dreary. On the weekends when those gray, drizzly days conspired against us, we either stayed in the dorm killing time, went to the library to study, or went to the gym to find something to do. For the most part, that favorite and much anticipated activity at Happy Valley, the outdoors kegger party, was in hibernation from December to March. That wasn't always the case, however, for occasionally we would don heavy coats and any type of available headgear and brave the elements for an outdoors kegger at Larry Sanford's or Doug's apartment complex.

The onset of Spring brought a groundswell of party activity. Jack came across the hall to my room one night after dinner to announce our good fortune in that respect. "Dave, Mandy asked me to her sorority party they're having out on the Sacramento River this Saturday. The sorority is providing all the beer and food. She said that Phoebe Miller plans to ask you to go with her."

"Oh?" I replied with more than casual interest. "Sounds like a lot of fun. I hope she does ask me. I'd hate to miss something like that." All I cared about was the party. I'd had a few dates with Phoebe, and at one time we kind of had something for each other, but at present we were just friends. She was, well, different. To look at, she was quite attractive, with her long, straight blond hair, a pretty face, and decent looking legs. She was short, about 5' 1", which was fine, and her only physical drawback was the few extra pounds she carried that seemed to be concentrated around an ass that was about one axe-handle too wide. But still, no problem, for she also had a bit of that extra weight strategically located in her boobs. I mean, she had a set of knockers on her that definitely compensated for the big "toilet lid", as Buzzard aptly called that part of the female anatomy. Bubbly personality, too.

Her major detriment, however, was her flaky personality and romantic inclinations that were as cold as an Arctic iceberg. Her Momma taught her well. Even getting to "first base" with Phoebe was not in the lexicon. Phoebe even resisted a goodnight kiss longer than a fraction of a second. On the occasion of one of our dates, when I was lucky enough to experience some heavy kissing, I easily concluded that kissing Phoebe was like kissing a wall. Phoebe didn't even french kiss. But she sure looked good in a swimsuit, which I had the pleasure of experiencing on one of our dates when she asked me to join her for a day at Deer Hole. Still, she was a prude, and that's why my enthusiasm for the prospective party out on the banks of the river was really associated with the unlimited beer and food, and prospects of having a good time with others at the party.

Jack and Mandy, and Phoebe and I doubled, with me driving Phoebe's gunboat 1962 Buick, and Jack and Mandy in the back seat hugging it up. Jack finally turned the tables on me from our memorable "double-date" our freshman year in his roomie's VW. I just didn't feel right about this date. I was not excited about spending the day with Phoebe, and had no illusion of any good romancing when the sun went down.

From the dorm, we drove south on Magnolia Street, crossed W. First Street and continued to Sixth Street. We took a right turn at the small grocery store on the corner that during the next two years would become our primary source of beer and cigarettes, and drove out Sixth until it became Pentz Road. In a few minutes we were out of town and passing through the rural farmland that was flat as a pancake and dotted with occasional farmhouses, barns, and stands of trees. About seven miles out Pentz Road we veered to our right, staying on Pentz Road for another two miles until we saw a mass of cars parked along the road, hugging the edge precariously on a narrow shoulder atop the levee that dropped off about six feet. (I know you don't care about that levee, but you will later). After taking a few minutes to carefully park the gunboat we walked along a well-worn path toward the river and party site that was invisible until we came out of the heavy shrubs and bushes. The path opened up onto a large beach area protected from view of anyone on the road and that was all set up for the party by the sorority.

Jack and I deposited our blankets and things and wasted no time in locating the keg.

"Jack, I suggest we get a cold one and lay back to enjoy this beautiful, sunny day and the cold beer courtesy of the Delta Crappa's."

"I'm with you," he answered as we excused ourselves from the girls, who were busy talking to sorority sisters.

We spotted Bill Nathan on our way to the keg so sneaked up behind him and Jack put a bear hug on him for a moment before letting go. "Bill, how the hell are ya," I asked, adding, "who the heck invited your sleazy act out here?"

"Screw you," he answered good-heartedly. "Tricia McVey asked me out. I don't think you guys know her. I've been seeing her a bit lately. Good chick."

"Sounds great. It's good to see someone else we know here," Jack said.

"Especially a Raider," I added. The three of us hung around the keg, talking and drinking more than our share of brew. Once in a while we would separate and pay some attention to the girls.

When it got dark, Jack and I went to our respective staked out areas where we both laid and sat on the blankets with our dates and caught some hugs. Phoebe thought it would be cute to pull a blanket over us. While I momentarily got my hopes up for something good to come of the privacy, it really wasn't necessary, for all I could do after repeated attempts was kiss her, although she did surprise me by engaging in some serious frenching. But after a while, that got old, so I spent most of the time making small talk. Fun. Would have been a propitious time to experience something I had read that went like this ... guys play with love to get sex, and girls play with sex to get love. Might have worked on the banks of the Sacramento River that night! While her behavior was expected, my frustration mounted as I laid my eager eyes on those voluptuous lungs of hers and said to myself, "what if ...?" Damn.

I was patient to let Jack do his thing until he suggested it might be time for us to head back to town. Thank God, I told myself. Back at the dorm that night Jack told me that he had had a nice time with Mandy. And I had to be with phony Phoebe!

Most of us made it back to town after the party with no problems. Poor Bill. We learned the next day that the drunken bastard drove his car off the levee and into a ditch! No one was hurt, but Bill paid dearly the next day to have his car towed out of the ditch. Bill and Chip were both made from the same mold ... if anything could go wrong while they were drinking, fate found a way for it to happen, not without a bit of their help, of course.

A week later many of us were back out at the Sacramento River, but it wasn't party time. Incessant Spring rains had resulted in mountain run-off and a swollen Sacramento River to near flood stage. The Dean had put out a call to campus organizations to help the local communities by filling and placing sand bags along the river levees. Fraternities answered the call, and much to the satisfaction of the Dean, about fifty Raiders arrived on site to help where we could. It gave us a good feeling to help local residents and put our occasional self-centered activities aside for a weekend. It was a good positive release of energy as well.

With Cindy and Phoebe both history, my dating that semester became infrequent. No problem. I was having a pretty good time hitting different parties and running around town on the Suzuki. On some nights, Chip and I would head off one way to a party, and Dan and Jack would go in another direction.

Forget the firebombs. Forget the trashcans through windows, the lounge furniture askew, and so on. The most heinous act committed in the dorm occurred the following week, just when things seemed to be fairly well under control after the Dean's letter and $20 fine after Christmas. Someone had the ability and the "balls" (well, and some lack of intelligence) to enter Ma's apartment and literally tip it upside down. When word spread, a number of us went downstairs to take a look, and saw for ourselves that the damage was not exaggerated. A few of us were accused because we had been seen leaving the area, but that was after the fact and we were able to make a successful case that we were only down there to look at the room. No, we had not done it!, we emphatically told the R.A.s. That was one "RF" that remained a mystery after we all departed Happy Valley College. No one ever even suggested they had anything to do with it.

Spring, for some reason, brought on a rash of fire alarms being set off in the dorm. The administration pleaded unsuccessfully for restraint. Because their pleas fell on deaf ears of the unknown conspirators, the men of Sierra Hall were told that with the occurrence of the next fire alarm everyone would be forced to vacate the building until the alarm could be deactivated. None of us were very thrilled about the idea when we heard the news.

"Oh, this ought to be just great," complained Chip in his most sarcastic tone.

"I agree," I offered, adding, "What if it happens in the middle of the night? Can you imagine us all staggering outside to play grab-ass while they no doubt take their sweet-ass time turning off the alarm and letting us back in?"

We got our answer much too soon, and consistent with our worst fears, we were already in bed. I was in dreamland. The loud, ear-piercing scream of the fire alarm rammed its unwanted way into our ears and created instant consciousness out of a deep sleep.

"Oh, shit," I resignedly muttered. Chip was louder and more vociferous.

"Gaawwdd dammnnit!!" he yelled at the top of his lungs as he swung his feet to the floor. Precious sleep destroyed.

We all filed outside, complaining and threatening to kill the bastard that caused an early reveille.

"This crap has got to cease," someone was heard to say.

By the time we got our sleepy, bitching butts outside on that warm night we were all awake and joking around. Half the guys were in their skivvies. Lights came on across the way in Lissen Hall as the girls heard the commotion and curiosity was piqued. In no time at all the scene was party-like. Taunts were thrown at the girl's dorm, to the perceived entertainment of the girls peeking through window blinds partially open. Everyone, at one time or another during the forced exit from the dorm, dropped their drawers and hung a "BA" toward Lissen. Our stay outside was surprisingly short, and never again were we required to go outside when a fire alarm was pulled.

Things weren't going too well for Ma. She had just found out that she lost a battle to rid the dorm of electric beer signs. Many of us in the dorm, and other housing units for that matter, were consumed by a fad to obtain beer signs of any type. It was so important to us that we sometimes would cut a class to visit a beer wholesaler before anyone else received like information that a new shipment of advertising products was expected. We would take anything, such as cardboard signs or plastic signs that advertised any brand of beer product, but our primary delight and quest was in obtaining electrical signs, clocks, and so on.

Ma certainly saw her boys carrying in armloads of these signs. But she had no idea of the affect until she entered a couple of rooms as part of an ordinary room inspection and saw for the first time a room lit up with countless electrical gadgets – lights flashing off and on, colored lights running a circuit in a continuous light show. Her first and only concern was not for safety but the impact the signs must be having on the dorm's electric bill! Her direction to us to remove the electric signs fell on reluctant and deaf ears, so she took the matter to the Housing Office. While there was some concern and sympathy in that quarter, we residents had effectively lobbied for retention of the signs and Ma was told to let the matter rest.

Much to her satisfaction, the fad was short-lived, which I am certain was the logic of the Housing officials in advising her to let it run its course. After a while, we all got rather bored with the signs and used them for target practice with footballs and anything else that could be thrown.

Maybe not for Ma, but it had been a good year for the college. More and more prospective students were applying for admission as the popularity of the school and word of its excellent academic programs, good professor-student ratios, and natural beauty of the campus spread throughout the state. The Department of Agriculture, some of whose students were athletes and members of the Raiders, had won some statewide competition, the Business School also had won some regional competition in Business Marketing, and the Cross Country team went to the NAIA national meet and placed very well. It gave us a lot of pride in sleepy 'ol Happy Valley College.

CHAPTER TWELVE

Western Week loomed big on the horizon. As was the case the previous year, we did not get involved in the festivities as part of the dorm organization. After all, we were Raiders. But more important, we knew we would have a better time free-lancing our way through the week. We didn't want our social activities stifled or dictated by the regimentation of the dorm activities.

On the Saturday prior to Western Week, Jack, Dan, Paul Mastros, a tall, dark-skinned junior college transfer that was one of the more well known Raider hell raisers, myself, and a few others went out to Trout Hole for a day of sun, beer drinking and swimming. Jack's brother Gary had traveled to Happy Valley for the start of our Western Week activities. As part of the fun I was a victim of a beer shower by Jack and Paul.

"Boy, this is the life," we kept saying to each other as we sat or stood on the banks of the swimming hole on that warm day in early April, taking in the natural beauty of the granite rock formations and oak trees surrounding and secluding us. It was peaceful and quiet at Trout Hole but for the steady sound of the gurgling water rushing downstream. The water shimmered like diamonds from the rays of the high afternoon sun reaching down through the trees, warming us.

"I wonder how the poor folks are doing?" Paul rhetorically pondered.

"Ah, an assumption erroneously made if I ever heard one," I replied. "What makes you think we're not poor, Paul?" I added in a not so serious tone. "We're just poor students."

"Yes, Dave," Jack contributed, "we may be poor students, but we are rich in our Happy Valley friendships and experiences."

"Well said, my friend," I replied with a grin, mocking his reflective tone.

During the ensuing raucous laughter, I suspect we were all thinking the same thing. Savor it. Fill the soul with joy, laughter, and camaraderie, and be thankful for moments like this among true friends. We were living for the moment. There were no jealousies, no rancor, no criticism, or selfishness. And very few worries. We were all too poor and naïve, and too consumed with drinking happily from our Happy Valley cup of life to be subject to all the trappings and challenges that would surely affect us in later adult years, not to mention the Vietnam War. We gave freely and asked not for repayment. The only payment was friendship. The purity of it was not forgotten, nor did it go unappreciated.

Things were not quite so rosy for Gary. "I don't know if Jack has told you, but I'm not doing that well with my studies or grades, so I'm enlisting in the Marine Corps at the end of the semester. I've talked to a recruiter and will be going to boot camp in South Carolina at a place called Parris Island probably in July. He didn't pull any punches with me and told me I would end up somewhere in Nam," he said.

"You're sure that's what you want to do?" Dan asked.

"I don't have many options, do I? If I'm going to do this, I want to feel pride as a Marine. I don't want the Army. I don't want to be on a ship. And the Air Force doesn't do anything for me. Yes, being a Marine is what I want to do."

"Well," I said, "you know we'll be thinking of you, Gary, and we can only wish you the best."

"Hear, hear," was the chorus as we all tipped our beers to Gary.

Jack was rather silent throughout the exchange. He knew he had a decision to make down the road, and he had a girlfriend to think about. We all knew we had decisions to make, but not quite yet, thank goodness. I am certain some of Jack's reticence was due to the fact that Gary was destined for the rice paddies and whatever hell that may bring.

After an enjoyable afternoon at Trout Hole we headed back to campus. We were all in a happy, rowdy mood, but we went a step too far upon our return to the dorm by causing some minor damage. At the moment, we thought it was funny, but I couldn't help feel shortly thereafter that we were wrong and it took away our innocence. We had all been involved in RF's around the dorm, but most, if not all, was playful stuff and didn't hurt anyone or incur any costly repair bills. I think we all made an unconscious decision at that time to cease any RF's around the dorm.

Later that same afternoon we would all feel hurt for Benny. He had spent the afternoon drinking with the Orland boys from the first floor and with a couple of their friends from Orland that had driven up for Western Week.

Western Week should have only been for the students and faculty of the college. Certainly the administration could not legislate and enforce a policy restricting the festivities to those affiliated with the school, but it's too bad that outsiders were allowed in. Granted, there was a lot of partying during Western Week, but we all knew each other and nothing really got out of hand. If someone was getting a little too carried away in a threatening manner, friends would pull him aside and settle things down. But that wasn't the case with outsiders, who visited the campus and took part in certain activities with a careless, irresponsible attitude. The outsiders just frankly got a bit overzealous in all the revelry.

The group visiting from Orland was no exception, and we just stayed away from them. Most of the outsiders weren't even in college, anywhere. They brought with them their same sleazy habits from their hometown bars.

The Orland visitors did learn a lesson, though it was a nasty and expensive one for our friend Benny. They had traveled to Happy Valley in a big, beautiful, shiny black 1964 Chevrolet

Impala, with leather bucket seats and big, powerful mill under the hood. Their mistake was in permitting Benny to take a short spin in it with one of the girls he knew from Lissen Hall. We had nicknamed her "Sally Mander". She was a tall, blond girl that didn't always play with a full deck.

I was sitting with Dan and Jack in their room when we heard a loud crash outside that sounded like a car collision. A look out the window confirmed our first thought, but we took a hard swallow when we saw Benny getting out of the now somewhat mangled 1964 shiny, black Chevy Impala, with traces of smoke escaping from under the hood, and attempting with unsure steps to leave the scene of the accident as quickly as he could.

We ran downstairs and outside to apprehend Benny to prevent him from being charged with hit and run. Benny was staggering slowly down the sidewalk parallel to the dorm when we met him.

"Benny, you alright?" I asked.

"Yeah. I don't believe what I just did. Sonovabitch if those guys aren't going to kill me," he replied. He was in a bit of a daze, and was incoherent from the booze and the shock of the accident. It was obvious he had come around the corner of Maple Street too fast to make the right turn onto Oroville Avenue and had smashed into a parked car on the opposite side of the street. "Mary's in the car, I think. I don't know how she is," he continued.

Mary was apparently all right. By the time we arrived she was out of the car and leaning against it watching Benny. It didn't take long for the Orland visitors to learn of the crash and to hastily exit the first floor rooms belonging to their friends in Sierra. They didn't much give a damn about the physical condition of Benny or Mary, and wasted no time in reaming Benny out and letting him know he would pay for the damages.

We took Benny away from them and sat him down until we thought he was okay to walk around a bit. We all sobered up real quick and stayed with him while the police took their statements and wrote up the report. Needless to say, the incident put a damper on Benny's Western Week, not to mention the remainder of his school year since he was emotionally wrung out, and on our enthusiasm for the moment. We would have to wait a few days before we knew the final outcome with the Happy Valley Police.

The next day Dan, Jack, Chip, Nellie and I went over to Baker Hall to visit our football teammate Brad and his roommates and to enjoy the swimming pool shared by Baker and Ramsey Halls on what was an unusually hot day for early April. The afternoon was not without a humorous incident. The dorm mother of Ramsey Hall, Mrs. Spencer, was well known for her strict enforcement of the dorm rules, crabby personality and disposition, and restrictive policy toward the showing of any signs of affection by couples in public areas of her dorm, as we found out from previous visits. A short kiss or holding hands would be met with a steely stare from a face with wrinkled forehead and pronounced squinting eyes that seemed to stay locked in position. She let you know she didn't approve without saying a word. Other times she was quite vocal.

We were having a great time around the pool that day when old lady Spencer walked into the pool area to check on things. She stood near the pool surveying the people and activities to ensure all were properly behaving themselves. The pool and deck were crowded.

We were talking about old lady Spencer when suddenly someone in the crowd around her gave her a gentle hip and shoulder. She tumbled into the water, came up sputtering, and got to the side of the pool. We laughed and laughed as old lady Spencer pulled herself from the water with the help of a good Samaritan, up the ladder, looking like a drowned rat. That compensated somewhat for Benny's unfortunate and traumatic incident the day before, and Western Week tempo picked up from there.

On Monday, we did the same thing as the previous year, walking across the athletic field after a weightlifting workout to attend a kegger at Raider Henry's. The weather was gorgeous, great outdoor drinking weather, so we removed our Raider sweatshirts, grabbed a cup of beer, and commenced to participate in the Raider's version of Western Week '66.

The only real difference in our attire from the previous Western Week was that we hit on the idea of obtaining vests to wear with our cowboy hats and boots. We had visited a Goodwill Industries outlet downtown and were lucky enough to find vests for all of us that also helped us stay within our meager student budgets. We then used tape to display "Raider Soph" on the back of each vest to announce our affiliation. With great pride we walked around campus all week wearing those vests, and wore them to most of the social functions we attended. Plus, our upper class Raider brethren were quite impressed with our distinctive outfits, creativity and display of loyalty and camaraderie.

Tuesday we also drank at Henry's, although somewhere along the way Dan left to be with Janie, his longtime girlfriend, and Jack disappeared to be with Nancy. I had my Suzuki, which helped in taking a girl I might meet to a party or someone's apartment, and also gave me the freedom to go wherever and whenever I wanted.

From Henry's I motored back down Colley and First Avenue, on my way to the quad where the Western Week projects were being constructed by the various fraternities, sororities and dorm groups. I had a very slight accident on the way, however. As I was turning off First onto Magnolia I spotted Dan and Janie on the corner, and while trying to talk to them in the process of attempting a U-turn did not pay attention to some gravel on the road and laid the bike down. I wasn't traveling fast, so got only a few minor scratches. I stood up, got back on the bike and pulled over to the side of the street where Dan and Janie were standing.

"You okay, bro?" Dan asked, smiling.

"Sure, I'm fine."

"Are you sure?" Janie asked, concerned. She was a sweet girl. Salt of the earth type. "That was a nasty fall."

"Yeah, I'm okay. Hey, have you guys seen Annette?" I asked. Annette was my latest flame. I really had the hots for her. She lived at Ramsey with Janie, and had expressed an interest in me. Guys like me take those kinds of expressions and run with them. But it wasn't a serious interest. Annette was a cute girl and was definitely more interested in dating around. Okay. I could dig it. But I still wanted to spend some time with her.

"No, we haven't seen her," Janie replied, "but she may be at the quad helping put up our project."

"Thanks," I said, and made a successful U-turn as I sped off up the street the short distance to where I could park my bike on the perimeter of the quad. I wandered around looking for Annette, and finally gave up. I was pretty wiped out from the beer at Henry's, so I laid down on the grass behind a quad project to take it easy for a while. I remember hearing some voices as people walked by and speculated on my condition. I'm okay, folks. Just taking a breather. I was awakened by Annette after an unknown period of time.

"Hi, Dave," I heard her say.

I slowly opened my eyes, and saw her leaning over me, her long brunette hair falling down toward me as I looked up into her pretty smiling face. "Annette," I said in surprise, "how you doin?"

"I'm fine. But how about you?" she asked, obviously knowing the answer, that I had been doing some serious drinking somewhere.

"Oh, I'm feeling just fine. Good party over at Henry's," I added, knowing she would appreciate finding out about a good party going on. She had already received word about the party.

"That's what I heard. I'd like to go over there," she added.

"No problem," I replied, satisfied that my night seemed to be looking up.

As I got up I observed she was dressed in a t-shirt and pair of carpenter's overalls. Not "haute-couture", but it didn't detract from her lovely face. We walked around the quad for a few minutes, and then I gave her a ride over to Henry's. I'll be damned, though, if that girl didn't disappear on me. I found her later that night at Henry's, but she had her arm around the waist of an ugly frat rat with no hair that I didn't like too much, so I just said, "screw it", and rode back to the dorm to get some rack time.

Wednesday night Benny, Chip and I went to the big, open Alpha Pi party held out in the orchard behind their fraternity house. On our way out in Chip's truck I asked Benny, "How are you making out after the calamity last weekend?"

"Damn. That was a bitch, wasn't it? I'm okay physically, and so is Mary, thankfully. I filed a report with the insurance company but I've still got a large deductible I have to pay. Guess I'll be working some overtime this summer at the lumber mill back home. And I got ticketed and have to appear in court next week. I hope they don't throw the book at me. It really has bummed me out this week, but that's the price you pay when you do something bonehead like that."

"I know what you mean, good buddy. I'm sure your parents have also expressed their displeasure, if I know them as I do."

"Oh, yeah. I just need to work through it all."

"Hey," I said, "here's the Alpha Pi house," trying to change the subject, "let's see what's going on and try to have a good time."

"I hear ya," added Chip as we pulled onto the large property containing the frat house and a huge orchard where people could safely mingle.

The Alpha Pi house was a super location for that kind of function because it was a few miles out of town and was therefore less susceptible to city police scrutiny. Hundreds of people milled around the dirt covered area surrounding the house, talking to friends, planning further activities for the night, or making their way to and from the keg. The word the next day was that the fraternity went through fifty kegs at the party. Ah, Western Week, you wonderful Happy Valley College tradition.

Thursday night Dan and I went to Rob Crozan's apartment for a party. We had met Rob through Brad and some of his friends from Concord. Rob was tall, a bit on the thin side, and had that "Ichabod Crane" look, but he was a nice, friendly guy that liked beer and parties.

After a short but enjoyable stay there, Dan and I hopped on the Suzuki to ride over to the college auditorium where the annual Western Week play was underway. I drove the bike up to the front door, nearly running into the damn thing, and we sauntered into the building. Walking down the aisle, we spotted Janie and Annette, who had saved us a couple of seats.

After the play Dan and Janie went one way, and Annette again pulled her disappearing act, so I drove the cycle to the other side of town to join a Beta Pheta function underway at KC Hall.

I knew a lot of the Betas, so it was no problem getting in to their party. Jim Preston, the guy Dan and I met in the class registration line our freshman year, was now a Beta and gave me carte blanche access to their parties. One of the Orland guys was there. Gary played on the football team and was quieter than his friends from his hometown, so we had a couple beers together and left. He had asked me for a lift home. No sweat, I had told him, so off we went, pulling out of the KC Hall parking lot and heading east on Norwood. In a few minutes I would be back at the dorm, in bed, after dropping off Gary.

The trip home was a disaster. That damn cockiness and exuberance I felt from all the beer got me in big trouble with the Happy Valley Police. Seconds after running a stop sign – I had not even slowed down, for I saw the intersection was clear and decided to blast right through – I heard the police siren and then, as I slowed down, saw the spinning red lights reflecting on the street, trees, nearby houses, and the chrome of the motorcycle handlebars. Holy crap, I said to myself, what the hell have I done now? Damn it. What a fool I was. This is it, I thought. This is really it. The ballgame is over. This is going to be the final nail in the coffin that's going to undo me. It will all catch up to me with this final incident. I was imagining the worst, such as a ticket, a night in jail, a heavy fine, maybe a suspended drivers license. Would I be kicked out of school? Maybe the Dean, too, would bring the hammer down on me. I could see him now – "Well, Mr. Pedersen, you escaped the other jams you got yourself into. You skated out, but not this time. Oh, no. I'm sorry, but you're suspended from Happy Valley College. Adios. Sayonara. Ciao." And of course there was Mom and Dad. Wait until they get a hold of me.

"Can I please see your drivers license?" the policeman asked in a confident tone that also said, "Gotcha". His nametag said Webb. I could read it okay.

Shaken, scared, sobered somewhat, and with slightly trembling hands, I handed him my license. I didn't say anything. What could I say? He caught my ass sure as shit.

"You didn't even slow down for that sign," Officer Webb said calmly. I'm glad he was calm. My insides were erupting in fear and disgust. "Did you see it?" he asked.

"Yes, Sir." We were still sitting on the bike. Gary hadn't said a word. There was nothing he could say in my defense, after all.

"Please get off the bike. I'd like to administer some tests."

Oh, shit, I thought. Damn! My legs felt like rubber, and my inebriated condition made me feel like I was walking on air and my world was spinning out of control. My muscles and joints felt uncontrollable.

We were standing on the sidewalk when he said, "Please walk down that line separating the concrete blocks, heel to toe, one after the other."

I thought I did okay, but Officer Webb said I was walking off the line and wobbling to each side. Then he gave me a couple other tests, which I also failed miserably. I had no idea what to do in situations like this. Gary didn't either. Could I have pleaded with him? Could I have said I would walk home? Would that have worked? I didn't know, and I was moments from the proverbial ax coming down and obliterating my life.

And then the miracle of miracles. Jim Preston, my Beta Pheta buddy, must have left KC Hall moments after we did, and as luck would have it, was travelling the same route down Norwood as us on his drive to the fraternity house.

He spotted and recognized us, for he pulled his black Volkswagen off to the side of the road in front of us, got out of his car, and in a mature tone that indicated he had been there before, said, "Officer, I know these two men. If you'll let me take them home, I promise you the bike will be left here and picked up tomorrow. I'll make sure they go straight home."

What balls! What frigging savvy for this 19 year old! He may have been reasonably sober, which helped.

"Okay", Officer Webb replied, to my complete and utter shock and surprise. "You take them straight home, and the bike stays here until tomorrow." Looking at me, he added, "I'll let you go this time, but there had better not be a second time."

"No, Sir. Thank you, Sir," I stammered. And with that, Gary and I made a quick exit of the crime scene, got into Jim's car, and were driven away.

As we got underway I couldn't thank Jim enough. He had literally saved my life. I had gotten a second chance, and breathed a tremendous sigh of relief for it.

I found out from Chip when he returned to the dorm that he and Bill Nathan had not been quite so lucky that night. Their wanderings had taken them by the Sigma Rho function at a member's house off 3rd Street. Chip and Bill had evidently displayed some bad manners and poor sense to ridicule certain of the fraternity's members, in obvious disregard of the fact they were outnumbered, as they walked by the front of the house. However, it took only one person, in the form of John Conzaga, a big, muscular guy that the average sober person would not want to tangle with, to effectively and easily "clean their clocks". Chip and Bill got the fight they were looking for, but they caught the raw end of it. I'm sure that both Bill and Chip were accustomed to enjoying more success in fist fights back home in the small rural towns they came from in the mountains of the Mother Lode, but Happy Valley was a bigger place and their luck ran out. They were both cut up and bruised pretty bad. In fact, Bill took some ribbing over the shades he wore around campus for a few days to hide a "shiner". Chip just laid low back at the dorm.

The following day a bunch of us sat around our table at lunch in the dining hall and reflected on the week. It had unquestionably been a fun week, but we lost our innocence in a manner of speaking. And things could have been worse. Benny's auto accident, my near visit to the "gray bar hotel" from the driving while intoxicated incident, and Chip and Bill's disgraceful defeat at street fighting. Fortunately, Western Week was just about over, and it would be time to prepare for final exams. But before Western Week ended we had an opportunity to help the school. The Dean contacted our Raiders president and asked if we could help clean up the front lawn in front of the Administration Building after the post parade Western Week picnic for students, staff and families as a service to the campus and a way of helping event organizers. We gladly accepted.

Dan, Jack and I had one other matter we had to resolve aside from the obligatory focus on finals. We had our heart set on being the successors to the Sanchez's apartment on Iris Street, and had earlier on asked them to provide our names to Mrs. Holley, the owner and landlady of the house. The apartment was undoubtedly the best location off campus. It was at the busiest intersection of student pedestrian traffic, as most students living south of First Street had to use the intersection to head to their apartments or fraternity and sorority digs. Having been advised by the Sanchez's that all was secure, we went downtown one day after classes to where Mrs. Holley worked, filled out a couple rental forms, and gave her a deposit to hold the unit for us for the next school year.

This was an exciting and satisfying moment for us, as we had looked forward with great anticipation to getting out of the heavily regulated environment of Sierra Hall and having a place of our own. The college required freshmen and sophomores to stay in dormitories and other administration-approved student housing. Having met that requirement, and being prospective upper-classmen the following year, we were free to make our own housing arrangements.

With the conclusion of final exams in late May, and with the knowledge that our grades for the semester just concluded would permit our enrollment the following year, we said goodbye to friends around Sierra Hall with a cheery, "see you next year … have a good summer." Dan and I would again be pumping gas at the Standard Oil station on Main Street in Walnut Creek near home, Nellie would be working with his father's floor-laying business, and Jack had a job lined up at a hotel in Oakland as a bellman.

While I looked forward to seeing friends from high school who would be home from college for the summer, the stronger emotion was the emptiness I felt as the dorm and campus emptied out, with students taking off in every conceivable direction to travel home. As fate would have it I had a late final, so had to stay until that scheduled requirement was completed. Students with earlier final schedules left school early in the week, so that the overall affect of the gradual mass exodus by the time I was done was that of a ghost town. I knew I would see Jack during the Summer since he lived only a few miles from my home, so the departure that affected me the most was to see Cindy pack her belongings into her parent's car and drive off.

I don't know why that tore me up so much, for we had not dated that semester other than the few snow trips in January, but to watch her leave and think of her being with her boyfriend back home in Manteca just ripped me apart and made me feel very lonely. We had gotten back on speaking terms, and talked once in a while, but while there was nothing serious between us I couldn't help feeling jealous that other people would be with her to share that pretty smile, smell the Shalamar perfume that drove me nuts, and maybe even hold her soft hand. It was very sad. And it wasn't just Cindy, but all the other close friends that I spent so much time with day in and day out at Happy Valley like Chip, Brent, Benny, Rob, and others. Those people now occupied a big part of my life, so it was difficult to accept the finality of the school year, the exodus of people, the sudden abrupt transition to the summer routine, and departure from a place that really was now "home", at least for nine months of the year.

So many great memories from the past year. It was consoling to know that only three months later we would be back at Happy Valley, and particularly that Dan, Jack and I would have an apartment together.

I was grateful for Dad's arrival at school with the trailer that would be packed with our belongings and my Suzuki, and that we would soon be on our way home. I was in a melancholy mood as we pulled away from Sierra Hall and drove by a Lissen Hall from which Cindy was conspicuously absent. Lissen looked and felt so empty to me. Maybe part of the reason for that melancholy feeling was a realization that another chapter of my life had come to a close. Dorm life, such an important part of the college experience for its new friends, camaraderie, adventures and physical proximity to the campus center, not to mention a measure of independence, was now a part of the past. Various dorm experiences swept through my mind as we drove away … Jack and I saying goodnight to Mandy and Phoebe, the water fights, fire alarms, walking back to Sierra after the evening meal, and of course, visiting Cindy until lockout time. The melancholy aside, the tragic and horrific realities of the Vietnam War would finally invade and affect our carefree lives during the next school year.

CHAPTER THIRTEEN

The summer had been a good one for Dan and me. We had worked the entire summer at the Standard Oil gas station in downtown Walnut Creek, and had even been able to have some fun along the way while working for the manager, "Big Daddy" Gene Romain. "Big Daddy" was 6'3" and weighed about 240 pounds, and was a little on the lazy side. His biggest mistakes that summer were scheduling Dan and me on the same shift. This was our third summer working as gas jockeys, and while we could pump gas, give an oil change, fix a flat, and do a lube job, customers were in trouble if they needed anything more when Dan and I were alone.

"Big Daddy's" station was small, but strategically located at the corner of Main Street and Mt. Diablo Blvd. in Walnut Creek. Drivers heading out of town via Mt. Diablo Blvd. often stopped at our station to fill up before getting on the freeway to Oakland and San Francisco. Also, Main Street was very popular with the younger crowd on most every night of the week, but particularly on Friday's and Saturday's when they would "cruise the main" for hours to show off hot cars and try to meet other people. It was a visual diet of clean, souped up '57 Chevys, Impalas, GTO's, and

Mom and Dad's convertible Grand Prix or Buick Riviera. From sunset until midnight traffic would be bumper to bumper, with people hanging out car windows and standing up in convertibles yelling at the people in other cars in an effort to get names or coerce them into going around the block and stopping so they could meet and talk. Sometimes, cars would be parked along Main Street and guys and girls would stand around or sit atop the cars and do their thing from there. The latter also saved on gas, which was no small matter for some of the charged up gas guzzlers.

Pity the poor visitor to Walnut Creek that rolled off the freeway on a Friday night and had to drive through town on Main Street. The local folks knew better than to get near Main Street at night, and were smart enough to take parallel side streets to get through town. Editorials were written to the local paper complaining about the unconscionable mess created by the cruisers, and City Hall tried to curtail the activity, but police and other authorities were ineffective in reducing the number of cars on the street. The police pulled cars over and ticketed them for faulty brake lights or failing to signal for a turn, but were otherwise powerless to do anything else.

With "Big Daddy's" location, the cruising created some entertainment for Dan and me during slack times. We would sit on a fence separating the station parking lot from Arthur's liquor store next door, and watch the cars and people slowly move past the station. Slack times were occasionally created for us when we ran out of one particular kind of gas and would yell out to people from our perch on the fence, "Sorry, we're out of gas - - you may want to go a block up the street to the other Standard station." We would both chuckle as the cars pulled away and we could continue our relaxation and uninterrupted observation of the cruisers. What was really fun was to see some yokel run out of gas while cruising. Made him very popular. Traffic would grind to a halt while he and his riders got out of their car and pushed it into the station.

The only difficult part of work that summer was when "Big Daddy" scheduled me on the graveyard shift for the entire month of July. I reported to work at 11:00 p.m. and was relieved at 7:00 a.m. the next morning. Working that shift was not all that bad. Things were definitely slow, so I used the time to read or tidy things up in the garage, and the only real work was sweeping down the gas pump areas with some soda ash that we stored in a large can.

Because robberies occasionally occurred at local bars and gas stations, I lived in constant fear of being robbed and beaten up or shot, so was happy to see police on their patrols during the night, and was certainly happy to finish my graveyard stint at the end of July.

I wasn't very good at sleeping during the day during my graveyard shift, so spent most of the month in a near comatose condition, never being fully rested. That played havoc too on my workout program for football that Fall. Dan and I were weightlifting at a former Vic Tanny's joint at the northern end of Main Street that had been bought out by a likeable guy named Del. Del showed us the proper way to use the weights and prescribed an exercise routine, but after that we were on our own. Dan and I also ran, sticking mainly to wind sprints at our former high school. I managed to stay in reasonably good shape even while I had the graveyard shift, but what really screwed me over was the diagnosis of hemorrhoids by a doctor at our local hospital in early August. Mom and Dad were out of town on a vacation when I finally cried "uncle" and took myself to the hospital, where on the same day the doctor did some minor surgery and sent me home with strict orders not to run or lift weights for a month. This shocking and miserable turn of events came at a most inopportune time - - I had to be in shape for football, and especially the "fitness test" for which the coach forewarned us to prepare. He had told us before the end of the previous school year that on the first day of practice the next Fall we all would have to run thirty 50-yard wind sprints in thirty minutes - - one per minute, and that each sprint would be timed in an effort to determine who was in shape, who wasn't, and who was consistently the speediest. I took the doctor's advice for the fist two weeks, but after that started gradually working myself back into shape.

I was using my Suzuki to get to and from the gas station and to friends around Danville. Sometimes Dan would hop on the bike and join me to wherever I was going. Other times we would ask

Mom for the car. Dad was still doing his right-of-way work for the utility company serving the Bay Area, so he was only home on the weekends. With only one car in the family, that put a lot of pressure on Mom to get us where we needed to go. For that reason, she would sometimes let Dan take the car to work for his entire shift, rather than play chauffeur if she really didn't have to.

Because of the constraints caused by only having the one car, Mom and Dad did not object when Dan told them he wanted to buy a motorcycle. I can still remember Mom's reply: "You know I don't like motorcycles because they're not safe, but if you get one you're going to use it to get yourself to work." Sounded reasonable. So Dan bought a motorcycle, a Honda 250CC Scrambler. I mean, that was a cycle! It was a lion compared to my 50CC pussycat, and was big and fast enough to legally be put on the freeways.

It was all well and good that Dan bought the Scrambler, but that immediately made me dissatisfied with my Suzuki. Therefore, later in the summer I bought a 250CC Scrambler myself, and couldn't wait to get up to Happy Valley for the upcoming school year. Dan's cycle had the stock silver gas tank, and mine had been painted a bright yellow. Our friends always knew when we had arrived at their homes to visit, for two Scrambler's pulling into a driveway with baffles removed made a lot of noise, especially when we revved the engine before turning it off. I don't suppose their mothers, nor the neighbors for that matter, appreciated the noise, but oh, well.

To celebrate the end of summer Dan and I terminated our work at "Big Daddy's" a few days early in order to ride our bikes up to the lake at Twain Harte. We packed a few things inside our sleeping bags, put on our letterman's jackets and Mom took a photo of us on the bikes at the top of the driveway. We then headed out of town for the mountains.

The trip up did have what could have been a major hitch. Just outside of Oakdale as we made our way up into the rolling foothills covered in a typical summer California dry, brown grass, I suddenly realized Dan was no longer behind me. He was nowhere to be seen. Worried, I made a quick u-turn and headed back down the road, only to spot him stopped and sitting on the shoulder. I pulled up beside him.

"What happened?"

"I don't know. The damn thing just stopped running."

"Gas?"

"I'm okay on gas. It's something mechanical; but I'll be damned if I know what it is."

We were not mechanically inclined so we were in deep do-do.

"Great. What do we do?"

"Let's fiddle with the engine and try to get it re-started so we can find someone that can possibly help us."

Well, we checked the spark plug wires, the choke, fuel line, and so on, to no avail. We were stuck in the middle of nowhere, with no gas stations, stores, phone, nothing in sight. So much for our few days at beautiful Twain Harte. During all this, the engine had cooled down.

"Give it another kick at the starter, Dan."

It fired up! I'll be damned. At least we got the engine running. With that, we pulled back out onto the road, traveling slowly and took a turn off the road onto a dirt road that lead hopefully to a house since there was a mailbox that suggested that someone lived nearby. A short distance up the dirt road we came upon a house and what looked like a decent size barn. We had come onto someone's farm and a friendly man that came out of the house to greet us having heard the motorcycles.

"Hello," he said.

"Good morning, sir," Dan replied. "We're hoping maybe you can help us. A short way down the main road my cycle stopped running. By sheer luck we were able to get it re-started, but have no idea what the problem is. Can we use your phone to call someone?"

"Why, sure," he answered, "but let me take a look at it. Maybe I can help you."

"Oh, please," I said. "We would appreciate anything you can do." I mean, we were not mechanics, and I am certain he had figured that out.

"Follow me, and wheel the bike over here," he instructed as we headed toward the barn.

It was immediately evident that the barn was where he stored his tractors and other equipment, and he shortly figured out the problem, installed a new this and that, and sent us on our way with a big smile and, "Glad I could help."

We were ecstatic, and rode back to the main road with renewed vigor, excitement and anticipation.

Our arrival in the small, quaint mountain village of Twain Harte provided both relief and pleasure, and predominantly the latter emotion.

We weren't worried about lodging, having decided we would either sleep on a porch at the lakefront cabin owned by the parents of our Aunt Nancy, or at the cabin of Rhonda's parents. Rhonda was the girl from San Francisco I had met the previous summer when visiting Twain Harte with some guys from Danville. And that's exactly what we did, for while Rhonda was not at the cabin, her parents remembered me and let Dan and I use a couple of lounge chair cushions to sleep on under the stars. They even invited us for dinner one night.

All in all, it was a fun three days, with lots of time spent on "the Rock" sunbathing and cruising around town at night on our cycles. We ran into a few guys that graduated a year behind us at San Ramon, and we joined up to form an absolutely unbeatable team at "jungle rules" volleyball. With jungle rules, it was okay to grab the net and use it to go after and spike the ball. We took on all challengers and didn't come close to losing a match. And we saw a few people we knew from nights there during our high school years when we would all sit for hours on "the Rock", sunbathe, talk, and play new card games. As we did during our high school years, at night we would all meet at the Frostop for sodas, ice cream, and more socializing. Good times.

A couple of days after returning home we were on our way to Happy Valley for our junior year. I had no way of knowing that my junior year would be the most fun and fulfilling at Happy Valley. It would involve new friends and affiliations, and finally some satisfying experiences with the opposite sex. But at the same time, the Vietnam War and military service obligation clock kept ticking louder and louder and louder.

CHAPTER FOURTEEN

Dan and I were eager to get to Happy Valley as we rode our cycles north through Davis, Yuba City and other valley towns along route 89. It was a hot day, and we had carefully planned a route that would keep us off the freeways as much as possible. California did not have a helmet law in those days, and Mom was unsuccessful in her exhortations to us to buy and wear helmets, but at least we were careful enough to take the much safer rural roads for the trip north from the Bay Area.

When we arrived in Happy Valley after the 3-hour ride our butts were numb and our bodies shook and quivered for a couple of hours. Honda Scramblers were not Harley Davidsons, or "hogs," and were not made for comfortable long distance traveling.

We found our belongings where we had left them in the apartment a week earlier when Mom's car was used to bring our things up. The most important item in the apartment was the TV that Mom and Dad loaned us. It was an extra so they were gracious enough to let us use it. We would get a lot of enjoyment from it, particularly watching football on Saturdays and Sundays. During that earlier trip we had obtained the key to the apartment from Mrs. Holley. The place was ours, and that really excited us. The transition from the Sanchez twins to the Pedersen twins was now complete, and we were already talking about the prospects of the first party we would hold at 309 Iris Street, apartment C. Jack had decided not to play football in order to concentrate on wrestling, so he was not due in town for another week and a half.

The apartment was furnished, so all we needed was bedding, towels, eating utensils and pots and pans. Here again, Mom and Dad outfitted us pretty well. The other nice feature about the apartment, and the reason why Dan and I had the money to buy the motorcycles, was that it would cost considerably less than the dorm. The dorm cost us about $800 the previous year, which included meals. The apartment rent was $75 a month, so split three ways cost us each $25. The three of us planned to buy a meal pass for the dining hall, but even with that outlay our total prospective costs for the year would be $200 - $300 less each semester. As it turned out, each of us struck a deal with Ed, the campus food manager, to work for our meals.

Dan and I spent most of that first day putting things away, cleaning the apartment, and running to a local grocery store to get some food and a few personal items.

The building at 309 Iris had five apartment units. The two in front, A and B, were single, studio-type units, along with apartment D, which was in the left rear side of the building to the right up a short flight of stairs. Also up the same stairs and occupying the entire back portion of the building was apartment E, a 2-bedroom unit. The entrance to our basement apartment was on the left side of the building and down a few steps. The outside appearance of 309 Iris was that of a nondescript, 1 ½ story, wood siding house built in the 1930's. In the front, steps about 10 feet wide lead up to apartments A and B, and a small overhang jutted out from the left side over the unit C steps and entrance. The house faced Iris Street, and was a few hundred feet from the busy intersection of Iris and First Street. Across the street from us was a small produce packing plant and warehouse, and our proximity to the campus was such that a good toss of a stone could almost reach the college library. Down Iris Street five blocks away from campus was Carter's Market, a small grocery store that would become our source of beer and cigarettes (Dan didn't smoke, but Jack and I liked a "tote" after dinner and with our beers occasionally.) The only other item we needed, a coin-op Laundromat, was across the street from Carter's.

Apartment C had a living room, eat-in kitchen, one bathroom, and two bedrooms. Our predecessors, the Sanchez's, didn't have the problem we faced since they didn't have a third person living with them. Since there were three of us, and each of us wanted the individual bedroom, we came up with a fair way to see who got the good bedroom. At least the second bedroom was definitely large enough for two people. Dan broached the subject first as we were unpacking.

"We need to figure out who's going to get the back bedroom," he said.

"I know. Maybe we can draw straws or pick something from a hat when Jack arrives next week."

"Sounds good. I'm sure he wouldn't mind having the room."

"True. Actually, my heart's really not in it. It doesn't bother me one way or the other. You two are the ones with girlfriends, not me. I can see where it would be nice to have a room to yourself so that you can have some privacy."

"Can't wait," Dan replied with a smile.

"Why don't you go ahead and put your things in the back bedroom now. I'll set myself up in the other bedroom."

"Done."

Double-days football practices were a bitch. Up early in the morning to practice from 8:00 to 10:00 a.m., and back over to the gym for practice from 3:30 to 6:00 p.m. At 9:00 in the morning, it was already 90°, and it was still hovering around 100° at 3:30.

After our post-practice meal in the morning we would walk across campus, and cross First Street to literally fall into apartment C. None of the units had air conditioning. There was normally five or six of us that collapsed at the apartment and laid around the cool basement unit until it was time to make the trip for afternoon practice. Jack had brought up a mono record player, which we simply called "the mono," in an earlier trip with his belongings, so we acquired some LP records and listened to music while relaxing or studying our football play books.

The group normally consisted of Stan, a sophomore and the son of Coach Johnson, Rob, Brad, Brent, and Dan and I. We all made frequent trips to the kitchen for ice water or to drink sodas that had been placed in the fridge in anticipation of hanging out. We were seldom hungry. Just thirsty after practice, during that period when the temperature was consistently over 100 degrees.

Dan had bought the new album by "The Association" that had "Cherish" and "Along Comes Mary" on it. If it weren't for the end of double-days I don't know which would have gone first, the needle or the record. We played that record over and over, and enjoyed it just as much with each time it played. Another record we played the hell out of had South Pacific instrumentals of some soft music like "Ebb Tide" and "Poincianna." I can still hear those tunes in my head, because they were frequently played at the end of our parties when couples wanted some romantic music.

We also spent a lot of time at the 1-mile and 5-mile swimming holes trying to cool off in the river and rest up for the afternoons. Occasionally, we turned on the TV back at the apartment to catch a news program. Otherwise, the mid-day programming was nothing to get excited about.

Jack's arrival on Saturday before registration week was welcomed. Double-days were behind us, and we were anxious to see our roommate.

Expecting Jack at any time, Dan and I were lounging on the front steps of the building when he arrived. We got up and walked to the car to greet him as he got out.

"Welcome to Iris Street, roomie" Dan and I said almost simultaneously.

"Thanks," Jack replied. "It's good to be back in Happy Valley, and especially to move into our "new digs." His smile said it all. He was excited about being back in town where he could again see his girlfriend Nancy on a daily basis and, with the apartment, have some privacy with her.

Moments after getting his things in to the apartment we decided it was time to find out who would have the back bedroom. We decided to pull pieces of paper from a hat, which seemed the easiest and most fair (someone mentioned using the "rock, paper, knife" method, but that was rejected). Dan was the elated winner, and Jack was a visibly disappointed loser. I didn't give a shit.

Dan was a gracious victor, however, and came up with a nice consolation for Jack.

"I know you wanted the room, too, Jack, so I'll tell you what. At the end of the semester we'll switch and you can have the room."

Jack answered with a relieved, "Thanks. I really appreciate it buddy."

Later that weekend after talking to Dan and Jack I decided to quit football. I could see I wasn't going to get much if any playing time. Plus, I didn't feel like working out every day, and in particular running up and down those damn bleachers in 90° to 100° heat with legs that felt like spaghetti after practice, for nothing. I knew all the team members well and felt that not being on the team would not change the friendships any. And I felt like dedicating my energy and time to gymnastics, which I was better at anyway. I had received a varsity letter both my freshman and sophomore years, so that told me I should concentrate on that sport. Jack understood and rationalized with me.

"Dave," he started, "I know how you feel. I decided to concentrate on wrestling for the same reasons. I knew I wasn't going to be a starter in football, or even play that much, so why should I waste a couple hours a day of my time out on the football field? I lettered last year in wrestling, and should be number one in my weight class this season. And I like competing for Mac." "Mac" was the wrestling coach, and a damn successful one. He recruited some outstanding wrestlers to Happy Valley and had perennial conference championship teams. Most of the other students that took classes around the gym complex knew "Mac" as the extremely candid instructor of Health 101. He taught the course by TV because his class was so popular and enrollment so high.

"Well, I appreciate your thoughts, Jack," I said. "It wasn't an easy decision to make, especially after completing double-days, the toughest part of the season. What a waste. Damn." I was glad the decision was made, but was disappointed in myself. It was time, though, that I realized my limitations with football. I had a strong upper body, but I was not gifted with extraordinary speed or strong, large legs. That was my shortcoming. It made competing against the others extremely difficult, even though I liked the contact and getting in a good hit.

We all settled in to apartment life and enjoyed our freedom. We didn't have to buy much food because of our deal with Ed to work for our meals at the campus dining hall, which was a fairly short walk from the apartment. The only things we kept in the fridge were eggs, mayonnaise, mustard, bread and hotdogs. Didn't keep beer on hand. We bought that as we needed it - - after classes on a Friday, or for a Saturday afternoon or evening party.

Consistently, at about 9:00 p.m. one of us every night would say, "study break…time for a dogger," at which time we would meet in the kitchen, cook some wieners in boiling water, and throw them onto a piece of bread smothered with mustard. We found them to be incredibly delicious, and at times would unanimously decide to prepare another round of doggers.

We bought a newspaper on the weekends, but our main source of news was the TV. After returning to the apartment from dinner we would turn on the evening local and national news programs. We received a steady dose of news about the war in Vietnam. That, and what we learned from our friends back home that had been to Vietnam, made us thankful for our student deferments. We could thank the President for that. He allegedly deferred U.S college students from the draft to maintain the support of the American middle class. But, make no mistake, it also planted a seed of thought on what lay ahead of us upon graduation. There was plenty of bad news coming from Vietnam. Buddhist nuns set fire to themselves in protest toward the U.S. It was clear that by the beginning of 1966, the President had become obsessed with the war. He and his advisors wanted to increase troops to 600,000 by 1968, which only fueled student opposition against the higher draft quotas and increased public opinion against the war.

We watched the news in silence, Jack and I taking puffs on our after dinner "totes" and obviously not worrying about the harmful side effects on our bodies.

Walter Cronkite told us about the build-up in South Vietnam, that there were now 375,000 troops there, that the country was spending over $25 billion a year on the war, and that the bomb tonnage was higher than that dropped over Germany at the height of World War II. He implied that LBJ treated it like a personal war, even selecting bomb sites, while sneering at critics. The film footage showed us some of the ghastly details - - villages set afire by "zippo squads," children burned by napalm, prisoners tortured, and the effects of chemical warfare.

What really got our attention was talk of the draft, which was experiencing a ten-fold increase. That scared the hell out of us. But, we weren't anti-war activists, and we certainly didn't have any notion to demonstrate against the war during the very infrequent demonstrations on campus. Very possibly like Norman, Oklahoma, for example, Happy Valley was far removed from the world of hippies, drugs, riots, and Vietnam. Ours was a passive dislike for war's sake. We did not favor it, but we didn't have an agenda to tell people of our dislike. We learned from the news that the centers of anti-war activity were the Berkeley's and Harvard's of the academic world. However, very little of that rubbed off on the students at Happy Valley, where the priorities were studies, sports, parties, fraternity pledging, parties, advance preparations for Western Week, and more parties.

We felt the reach of Uncle Sam getting closer when we learned of the abolishment of many student deferments and higher criteria for retention of such deferments. At the time, though, that II-S looked great and kept us safe as long as we maintained the proper course load. There were many students that didn't keep the course load and vanished from campus. Gone, just like that. Elsewhere, draft resistance intensified, particularly at the University of Chicago where students seized and held the administration building for three days. It was in the music, too, like "Alice's Restaurant," and we saw pamphlets to prospective draftees, to "arrive high" at physicals and strongly suggesting that if one wanted to fake the addiction scene in a big way they should use a common pin on their arm for a few weeks in advance of the physical. Many simply left the country for Canada. Poof!

During the recent summer, Dan and I had driven the few miles to Pleasant Hill where we had lived until the family moved at the start of our high school years. There, we visited Fred, our best friend from grammar school through junior high school, and listened in awestruck silence as he told us about his duty in Vietnam with the Army. Fred had tried college after graduating from high school, but was not a good student and uncertain of the direction he wanted his life to take. How many 18-year olds really did? I didn't. I just knew I wanted to go to college, and was operating under the delusion that I knew the career field I desired. Bullshit. Fred joined the Army.

"So, Fred, now that you are back from serving over there, how do you feel? Do you let the protestors affect you? I had asked.

Fred thought about my questions for a moment, and then let it all hang out. "I feel dislocated, like I really do not have a place in our society", he said. "I almost feel embarrassed, and I do feel a sense of shame that I served our country in Vietnam. Maybe I am just feeling what many in the country feel, a sense of guilt over the war. I am having a difficult time adjusting to life here. In fact, I am seeing a military Psychologist. I'm feeling a bit stressed, and I am drinking more than I ever did before going over there."

This is not good, I thought to myself, feeling bad I was asking Fred to talk about this stuff.

"What was it like in Vietnam, Fred", asked Dan.

"It was hell. You had to be on your game all the time, for there just wasn't any safe, secure place. We all knew we could be killed any time, any place. Especially in the field, there were enemy mines and booby traps to worry about, along with snipers. The thing was, you never knew who the bad guys were. They all looked and dressed alike. The one good thing was that if you were wounded, you could be in good medical hands in quick order. It wasn't like we took some territory, secured it and moved on. The only way we knew we were doing good was by how many Cong we killed, the body count. And even when me and my fellow Soldiers were over there, we knew that the U.S. people didn't give a shit about us and the guys going back, or what they had gone through. That's bullshit, you know, Dave and Dan?"

What could I say, so far removed from the war and the military. "You're right, Fred. It is wrong, and still is. And now there are even more protests against the war."

"Yeah," Fred mumbled. "You know, we had only a one year tour in Nam, but our goal was survival. We all counted the days.

When I first went to Nam, it was as part of a unit. But the replacements came in individually, and they were just lost in the shuffle. I really thought I was doing the right thing by going over there. My Dad fought in World War Two, as did your Father. And I bought off on the notion that we were fighting to stop the spread of Communism. It was my turn to fight. But we all knew over there that the President was not letting us fight the way we could and should to win the damn war."

During our conversation he told us about two twin brothers that we all knew from junior-high and that had gone to high school with Fred. The Baker twins, Gary and Larry, were popular in school and had many friends. They had both joined the Army, Fred told us, and both, at their personal request, served in Nam. Gary didn't make it back. Larry did come back, only to be killed in an auto accident within a month of his return to the states. Fred also explained that an old neighborhood friend of ours, a nice guy but none the less someone our parents didn't like us hanging around, had received numerous decorations from combat duty in Nam. Little did Dan and I know that later that year we would see our old grade school friend Ron for the first time in years and under very strained conditions.

It had come time for Dan and me to say goodbye to an old friend. There was no question that Fred was different. The war. As we left his house, we wished him well. "Fred, take care of yourself, and please come up to Happy Valley to see us some time. I think you would like it. Peaceful place," I had told him.

Death and destruction were daily news items on TV and in the papers. Occasionally we would see a column in the local paper announcing the war death of a local boy. His life was gone, snuffed out, by a senseless war thousands of miles away that by its own criteria and the irrational decisions of politicians was still building toward its climax and an ignominious conclusion.

Things went on as normal at Happy Valley, but the war news and military draft got our attention. We often had conversations about it. They normally ended with an unspoken question mark after something like the following.

"So what is going to happen to us when we graduate?" someone would ask.

"Good question," would be the reply.

"I sure as hell don't want to go to the rice paddies! Somehow that really doesn't turn me on."

"Plus it's dangerous."

"Oh really? There's got to be a way to legally stay out of that mess. I've heard some guys mention something about the National Guard or reserves where you would go to basic training and then attend monthly drills for six years."

"Damn, that's a hell of a long time," was the reply.

We had no idea what the hell we were talking about. War games were low on our priority list of exciting things to do, let alone engage in meaningful discussion about. And no one around Happy Valley was available to discuss options regarding the military. It was like it didn't exist. In hindsight, it would have been nice to have some counseling available along those lines, but the only counseling was academic in nature. The only advice available on military options was in a number of offices downtown, also referred to as recruiting offices. No way, Jose. Too early to talk to those guys. Later, maybe, but not now. The recruiters had one common goal, to get guys to sign up for active service.

But really, everything was fine. Dan had the sole bedroom, which gave him ample opportunity to snuggle privately with Janie, his girlfriend, at parties and during breaks from classes, and Jack and I shared the other bedroom. Dan was playing football, and Jack and I met often in the weight room to lift weights in preparation of our upcoming wrestling and gymnastics seasons. The Raiders were still an active group, and our letterman society, block HV, had a house, just like the fraternities. That expanded our party options. We didn't see Brent, Stan, Chip and Rob quite as often as before simply because they had rented a house on the other side of the campus, on Hopewell Street near the memorable Magnolia Street grocery and Bill Nathan's place. Chip and I spent a lot of weekend nights together, however, because we were the only two without girlfriends. Dan had Janie, Jack had Nancy, Brent was going with Eileen, Rob was starting to see a lot of Lynn with the fantastic eyes, and Stan was going with Judy. That cut into the amount of time we all had together, so when we did have a stag day or night we made the most of it.

And then there was "Rudy", our neighbor upstairs in apartment A. Rudy was a Chicano from Lemoore in "the valley" and was a starting offensive guard on our football team. He had transferred to Happy Valley after two years at a junior college near his home. Rudy was a super guy and always in a good mood, but once in a while he would get a little carried away and play his stereo too loud while we were trying to study. On those occasions, we would grab a broom and bang the handle against our ceiling until he got the message. He and a fellow football team member, Jimmy Halton, often came downstairs to visit. Jimmy was a good guy and had come to Happy Valley from another junior college in the San Joaquin valley.

We had a good group at "Iris." Mike, a super wrestler and perennial league champion, was in apartment B. He was a nice guy but on the quiet side. Between that and the frequent visits by his girlfriend we didn't see too much of him. In the back of the unit, in apartment D, was "Rocko" as we called him. Rocko was a couple years older than our group and played football. Rocko was big, muscular and built like a brick shithouse. He was good looking, had short blond hair, and somehow always had a tan. If there was any one guy on campus that could get a date with any girl he desired, it was Rocko. Seriously. Any girl. The three of us would often watch out our basement window to see what girl Rocko would be bringing back to his place. Our jaws would drop and imaginations run wild as we would see someone like Mary Jo, a tall, gorgeous, leggy blond, walk by holding his arm.

"Oh, damn," one of us would say, "there goes Rocko with Mary Jo. I'll bet he's going to screw her eyeballs out all night."

"I'd drag my balls over 10 miles of broken glass just to smell the toilet seat she sat on," someone else would say.

"That lucky sonovabitch. He gets more ass than a toilet seat," would be heard, and we would all bust out in laughter, followed by a yell, not loud enough for Rocko to hear, of "go for it…go for the P, Rocko."

In apartment E was "Manfred", a high-school classmate of Benny's in Herlong and a transfer from Sierra College, a 2-year school near Sacramento. Manfred was pre-dental, but still found time to drink some beers with us once in a while. While he was a serious student, he somehow had put together enough "scratch" to have a nice set of wheels. He drove a '64 Malibu Super Sport with big tires, a jacked-up rear-end, tuck 'n roll upholstery, a mean 327 engine, and a classy 4 on the floor Hurst gear shift. Neat stuff.

It was a dreary, wet Saturday in early October when Jack received a letter from his brother, Gary. We were just sitting in the apartment watching a college football game. Jack opened the envelope and read the letter silently, then shared it with us. Dan turned down the TV volume. He read, "Dear Jack: Sorry I have taken so long to write to you. I know you'll understand, though. I'm using letter-writing time to keep up with Mom and Dad. I know I did the right thing by joining the Marines, but it sure hasn't been easy. We think Summer in Lafayette is a booger. Well, let me tell you, you haven't experienced uncomfortable heat until you've been in South Carolina in July. And throw in a little something they call humidity, and Parris Island was a physical challenge. But, I made it out okay, and that's all that really matters. I'm at Camp Lejeune in North Carolina now, and thankfully it's Fall as I'm told this place can also get uncomfortably hot. I'm in infantry training, and it's actually kind of fun. And I'm in the best shape of my life. I'll bet I can take you in a wrestling match. I miss you and the guys back home in Lafayette, and those crazy roommates and friends of yours at Happy Valley. I'll bet you guys are having a great time there in 'paradise', like my last visit there in the Spring of this year. It looks like I will be here for a while after training, and do not know yet where I will be going next. But eventually I will get orders for Nam. That's when things will get interesting. Don't know yet where I'll be going. All I know is Nam. And to fight. I'll be ready, but it's still pretty scary. Hope I make it back okay in one piece. Take care, Bro. Your brother, Gary."

"Well, it sounds like he has his head screwed on okay and is ready for whatever they throw at him, and wherever that is in Nam", I offered.

"That poor bastard," Benny exclaimed. "We'll be pulling for him that he will be alright, Jack. I know you'll be worried sick over him, but keep your chin up, good buddy."

"I know. Thanks, guys. Okay, get the volume back up. We've got a good game to watch."

CHAPTER FIFTEEN

While it was nice that Dan and Jack had girlfriends, the presence of the girls in the apartment, particularly on weekend nights, created some interesting circumstances. I could not act myself at those times. As soon as I stepped in the unit, I was too often told, "Cool it, Dave, Nancy and Janie are here." I was usually inebriated at the time, which compounded matters. Often times I would simply walk back outside, crank up the Scrambler, and ride off somewhere else to kill some time before returning. Chip had the same problem on Hopewell, which we discussed occasionally.

It was about this time, which was just prior to rush week for the fraternities and sororities, that Rancher approached me again. This time I was at gymnastics practice. Rancher was a Raider that had pledged Delta Phi Sigma fraternity, a local house on campus without any national headquarters, ties, or charter. It meant they could do things their way.

"Dave," he began, "I want you to think seriously about pledging Delta Phi."

"Rancher, you know how I feel about Raiders and about the fraternities."

"Delta Phi's different," he would argue.

"It's still a frat, and I'm a "God Damn Independent", and that's how I see things."

"But you need to get into an organization with substance and tradition, which Raiders can't offer you."

"Rancher, Raiders gives me all I want. We have a great bunch of guys, have plenty of parties, and it doesn't cost very much. I couldn't afford a frat."

"Delta Phi won't cost you that much. The dues are only $50 a semester, and the only other cost you would have would be our annual formal dinner dance and the cost of living in the house, which would probably cost about the same as your apartment."

"I don't know. It's just not me."

"What would you say if I told you Benny, Rat, Wilson, Amus, Jack Evans, and Keith Moore, all Raiders, were seriously thinking about pledging Delta Phi? They're friends of yours, and would be your fraternity brothers."

"I'd be surprised."

"Well, be surprised, because they are. They've all told me they would be at our first meeting for new pledges next Wednesday night at the house."

"Interesting," was all I could say.

"Well, think about it Dave. We'd like to have you in."

"Okay," I said reluctantly, "I'll think about it, but I just don't see myself being interested." I probably didn't see myself wanting to pay the price. I had heard some of the horror stories about pledging a fraternity at Happy Valley, particularly Delta Phi, and wasn't exactly anxious to personally experience it. There were no rules on hazing, particularly with the local fraternities that were not governed by a national charter.

"Thanks," Rancher said as he turned and walked out of the gym.

I thought and thought about it. I mentioned it to Dan and Jack, receiving a cool reception from them on the idea. I also talked to Benny, who expressed much enthusiasm for the idea. That following weekend was another in which it was suggested I modify my behavior at the apartment. That, and other similar weekends, played a very large part in my decision to pledge Delta

Phi. I was looking for something different in my life at Happy Valley, and felt the fraternity experience would be rewarding. I attended the meeting and signed up to pledge.

Delta Phi was known for its severe hazing techniques. Experiencing it and hearing about it from my pledge brothers made me a believer. There were stories about one ex-pledge being thrown through a window. Some of the older, current members still had their Delta Phi brands on their stomachs. Later in the pledge semester a few of us considered doing the same when we became members.

A few weeks into the semester Rat quit the pledge class. Because he was the vice-president, a new election had to be held. By a near unanimous vote I won, which was a proud feeling knowing that my pledge brothers had faith in me.

Shortly thereafter the Wilsons also quit. My Raider friends were slowly abandoning the frat idea. They, along with other dropouts, said they were fed up with hazing and harassment. There was talk of forming a new fraternity, which was bold talk from people that just couldn't handle the regimented and required bullshit the members put us through. Most of the hazing was standard stuff and was tolerable. The severe hazing was administered to pledges that, in various forms, showed a lukewarm interest in the fraternity. They had either missed the important, though grueling, Monday night meetings, didn't show up on their assigned nights to singularly do dishes at the house and be subjected to a steady ration of shit from the members, or didn't learn the fraternity history. The latter was most evident when members threw questions at you while alone doing dishes. They at least gave you a metal World War I military helmet to wear so your head was protected from flying objects.

Benny took some early heat for one reason or another and was visibly disturbed as we talked at his apartment one night. He had called and wanted to talk. Fortunately, the call was received in the early evening, unlike many of the calls that came to me from members at 1 or 2 in the morning suggesting I drive out to such and such a place to pick up a pledge brother that had been taken out and stranded. Those late night calls prompted me to move my sleeping quarters to the couch in the living room near the phone to keep it from ringing too many times and waking Dan and Jack. Neat.

"Hi Benny, what's up?" I asked as I walked into his apartment living room. He really looked upset and that worried me.

"Dave, I just don't think I can continue pledging. I don't know why, but the members are really giving me a hard time, just like they did to Rat, Jack and the Wilsons."

I couldn't believe what I was hearing. "Of course they are, Benny. They're treating all the Raiders the same way. I'm not exempt. They're testing our commitment, don't you see? They want to know quickly just how serious we are about becoming members."

"Well, I guess you're right, but that's still no excuse for the way they've treated me. And Donna is really concerned too. Just the other night when she was here they came by, got me outside, and reamed out my ass. In front of her, of all things! That's bullshit, and I won't stand for it! I've had it."

"I can understand how you feel, buddy, and I don't condone what they did in the presence of Donna, but just try to work through it. Forget it if some of them want to act like assholes. Some day you'll be a member and you can tell them to screw off."

"No, I've made up my mind. I'll tell Rancher tomorrow that I'm through." Rancher was Benny's big brother, who served as a sponsor, protector, and counselor. He wasn't going to be too thrilled with seeing another Raider bite the dust. Rancher knew some Raiders could fit in with the Delta Phi's and was personally hurt with every Raider dropout. "I'm sorry, Dave," Benny continued, "I thought I really wanted this, but I guess I'm just not willing to pay the price. The hazing is too much. What are you going to do?"

"About what, Benny?" I was in another world, overwhelmed by the disappointment that now all of my Raider friends had dropped out.

"About pledging. Are you going to stay in?"

I sat quietly for a moment, staring at the wall across from me, not seeing what was on it, but trying to think everything through, particularly the dialogue that had just occurred. I turned to look at Benny, a new revitalized sense of commitment giving me strength of purpose, and said slowly and with conviction, "Benny, this pledge class started one month ago with 21 guys that said they wanted to be Delta Phis. With your exit, we now have 14. All my Raider buddies have dropped out. One of my reasons for joining was to go through this pledge semester with people I knew well and liked. That's all gone now. Am I going to drop out? No way, Benny. This is a challenge, nothing more, and I plan to see my way through. I don't know how I'll feel after I get in, and right now I don't much give a shit. All I know is, I'm going to do it. And I say that knowing the hazing will get even more physical and demanding."

"That's good. I wish I felt the same way, but I don't."

"I understand, Benny, I really do, and this is not going to affect our friendship."

"Good," he replied.

"Well, I gotta go. I've got some studying to do yet tonight, and you never know what's going to happen in the middle of the night." I smiled, and he replied in kind with a sheepish smile and chuckle.

"That's true."

"See you tomorrow around campus, buddy. Take care of yourself."

"Thanks, Dave."

The wind blew hard in my face racing the Scrambler back up Magnolia Street to Iris. I kept reminding myself over and over that I was going to hang in there, come hell or high water. It was just something I had to do. They weren't going to force me out.

I worked hard as the vice president, and because my pledge class president, Mick, came up with lame excuses too frequently on why he couldn't make the mandatory Monday night meetings or join us for some RF'ing of our own against the active members I guided the pledge class and was the whipping boy for problems perceived by the active members. We all finally had enough of Mick's malingering, so one night went to his apartment unannounced and "talked him" into resigning. I became the "dung shitty president", which was in concert with the feelings of my pledge brothers as well as the actives. If I was going to take the shit, let me at least be the president and exercise some control.

The harassment wasn't always one way. We occasionally showed some balls and pulled some pranks that we knew were going to cause some real hell at the following Monday night meeting. Like the time we let off a smoke bomb in the frat house at 1 AM and watched safely from around the corner as the house filled with smoke and actives came stumbling and coughing out of the house using every expletive known to man. The real problem with that, however, turned out to be the hole burned in the foyer rug that was a constant reminder to the actives whenever we pledges had the displeasure of being in the house.

On another occasion we stole the dining room benches from the house at 3 a.m. in the morning, which made mealtime the following day for house residents a real disaster. We ran into some difficulty when told to have the "sonovabitchin' tables" back by noon and didn't. That night our "group activity" was to retrieve the tables. We got all of them, but for one. We were sure a girl at the Yum-Yum Apartments, where they had been placed on the roof the previous night, had taken one. She gave us a hard time, but eventually changed her mind after a bit of gentle "persuasion".

Without question it was an interesting semester. I didn't spend too much time with Dan, Jack and other Raiders, but the late Fall semester was rather quiet socially anyway due to the weather and it's effect on holding outdoor social functions.

Our pledge Hell Week started with 13 guys. We finished with 9. I couldn't believe that some of the guys would endure all the hazing for an entire semester yet quit in the final week. The hazing had taken on more extreme measures and obviously tested what turned out to be 9 of us to the max. It was an incredible week of mind games, physical hazing, and total abandonment of any thought to schoolwork. Hell Week demanded our full-time attention 24 hours a day, and it was during this time that the 9 of us became even tighter as friends and pledge brothers. Teamwork and commiserating were the structure of the week. We marveled at how insanely creative the actives could be and were scared shitless of them.

We were given instructions for the next two days by Rich, my big brother and the pledge master at 12:30 in the afternoon on Friday of Hell Week. Among other things, we were told to wear our grubbiest clothes and to bring an extra set of grubbies. This was it. At least, we hoped like hell that this was to be the culmination of Hell Week!

Just prior to reporting to the house for a 6:00 PM muster Friday night we all sat at my apartment. What a deal. Everyone else in Happy Valley was out partying on that night and here we were huddled in my place shaking and fearful of the unknown that was just ahead once we set foot in the yard of the house. Just before leaving my apartment we all took a tranquilizing pill! What a lot of good that turned out to be! It was useless, to say the least.

After an unexplainably wild, physically and emotionally draining and frenetic weekend it was over. Pledge semester and Hell Week were behind us, and the nine of us that made it through from the initial group of 21 were members. After initiation, we went down to a bowling alley in town where a member, Gus, bartended. After a few beers there we went to the Silver Room, where I used Gus' ID to drink. I was 20 at the time, and Gus was 27.

Dan and Jack were demonstrably happy that pledge activity was over too. It really didn't mean anything to them that I was now a Delta Phi, but they were relieved knowing there would be no more phone calls in the middle of the night. Benny came by the apartment later that day.

"Congratulations," he said, adding, "I'll bet you're really glad it's over and you made it through."

"Thanks, Benny. Yes, it's over. Whew! I can't and obviously couldn't explain to you what actually took place because of the oath we took. The experience we pledges went through is one I shall never forget and can only talk about in detail with other fraternity brothers. I told myself I would finish and I did. I think all of us that just pledged have some mixed feelings about certain of the members, but that's something we will learn to put behind us and deal with."

"Yeah, I'm sure you feel that way. Let me see your pin and sweatshirt."

"Sure, it's in my room." I showed the articles to him and could see and feel his personal disappointment that he didn't stick with it. But neither of us said anything, and nothing was ever said in the future. We just both understood, and left it that way.

After all, Benny, for so many reasons, would always be a "brother" to me anyway.

The remainder of the semester was catch-up time with studies. I had some serious "booking" to do to make up for lost study time while pledging, and staring down the gun barrel of final exams.

There was a new person in my life at the conclusion of the semester. The girlfriend of Rancher had a roommate named Cynthia. While I didn't date her that semester, I visited with her and occasionally studied with her at her apartment.

The end of the semester brought plans to live at the fraternity house for the Spring semester. Benny would move in to take my place at Iris Street.

CHAPTER SIXTEEN

My first order of business upon returning to Happy Valley after Semester break was to move my limited amount of worldly belongings from Iris Street to the fraternity house. I had an armload of clothes as I walked through the gate of the fraternity house yard and caught Lucky coming out the front door.

"Hi roomie," he bellowed with a smile as he saw me.

"Hey, Lucky, how you doing?" I replied.

"Doin ' just great. On my way over to see Anne and maybe take in a show. Need any help?"

"No, thanks," I answered. "What I do have I can handle in a couple more trips."

Even with a jacket on it was evident that Lucky had a great build and chiseled physique. Small waist, broad shoulders, and muscular arms. It was common knowledge that he had once entered a Mr. America contest, and he still worked out regularly at a gym downtown. He was friendly and out-going, and I was pleased to have him as a roommate that semester. Prior to the end of the previous semester he had approached me and told me that his roommate, Rich, my big brother, was moving out. He then asked if I wanted to room with him. I had answered yes unhesitatingly, knowing we had much in common. One of those commonalities was that we both owned a motorcycle, but then that was not unusual, for about half of the Delta Phi's owned bikes, and it was a common sight to see about 12 or 15 motorcycles lined up and parked along the street curb in front of the house. Another nice thing about my new roomie was that he owned a Triumph sports car, which he occasionally loaned me when I was desperate for a set of wheels for a date or some other purpose.

"Okay, Duke," he replied. "See you in the morning." Duke was the nickname my pledge brothers had given me and it hung on around the fraternity.

I had not known Lucky prior to pledging, but had occasionally seen him at Delta Phi parties with his current girlfriend, Anne, who was from a high school near my hometown and was a pretty blond that was a song leader at Happy Valley that year.

With a great feeling of anticipation for the upcoming semester I got myself settled in at the house. The room Lucky and I shared was small and on the first floor, near the community head on that floor at the back of the house. But that didn't bother me, for there was adequate closet space, a study desk, and I had the bottom bunk. Plus, Lucky often spent the night at his girlfriend's apartment, so I had the place to myself often. That worked out particularly well when I brought a girl back to the house.

The previous semester had been very disjointed. I seldom did anything socially with Dan and Jack and the guys at Hopewell. Of course, with the exception of Chip they all had girlfriends anyway, so it was a moot point. My studies had also suffered during the pledge semester. There were too many occasions in which I put off studying in deference to pledge activities, and too many mornings when I slept in and missed a morning class because for one reason or another I had been up late the previous night "putting out pledge fires."

During the upcoming semester I was determined to have control over my social life, get my grades up, and to participate in Delta Phi or Raider functions as I chose. My Raider friends respected me for pledging and joining the fraternity, and not a soul held my fraternity association against me. It was probably because they also knew that I was a "God damn independent" at heart, and that I would be around at their parties. I had proven something to myself, that I finished what I started, regardless of the price, and I think that self-assuredness manifested itself in a certain attitude that caused me to be even more independent.

I was not enamored with my election to the fraternity office of Sergeant-at-Arms, for that forced a level of commitment and involvement I had not planned on. However, I dutifully performed my elected duties and attended most of the fraternity business meetings. I attended most of the fraternity socials, but otherwise spent very little time around the house. It was a common sight for me to be seen leaving the house after dinner each night, taking my books either to Dan, Jack and Benny's place at Iris or to the campus library. Many of the members noticed my marginal relationship with the fraternity, but to their credit and to the credit of Delta Phi, the unspoken understanding was, "once a Delta Phi, always a Delta Phi," regardless of one's level of commitment and involvement with the house activities.

Another reason for studying elsewhere was that I was carrying a heavy load of classes that semester and found it necessary to get away from the constant activity and distractions around the house. The library and Iris provided quiet places to concentrate on my demanding Statistics and Macro Economics studies.

Because Cynthia lived with Laurie, Rancher's girlfriend, Rancher and I hung out together a bit during the early part of the spring semester. Rancher also had a motorcycle, and was in Block HV, having earned his varsity letter in football. We had a number of other Block HV members in our house - - my big brother, Rich, had lettered in water polo, as had Rob Van Siclen, another brother. Rancher and Mike Keller had lettered in football, and Jeff Pleau got his in wrestling. In fact, in the pledge class for the current spring semester were a couple more varsity wrestlers. We prided ourselves in being known as the "jock fraternity."

I was in my room at the house studying one night when Rancher poked his head in through my doorway and asked a question that was posed frequently during my first month in the house.

"Hey, Duke, want to go over to Laurie and Cynthia's?" Sometimes it was more of a statement, implying that I had little

157

choice because both girls wanted to see us that particular night. Something like, "Duke, let's go over to the girls' apartment," or "Laurie and Cynthia would like us to come over. Let's go."

I would stop my work, look up at Rancher and smile as I leaned back in my chair. It was a good thing I booked hard during the day and early in the evening, giving me the confidence to comfortably answer in the affirmative.

"Sure, Rancher, let me clean up a bit and I'll be right with you." I really didn't clean up in the sense of a shower and all. I just took a "Right Guard shower" and put on some Brut and away we went on our motorcycles.

Rancher and I rode our bikes down Iris Street, did a "Hollywood stop" at First Street, and sped down Magnolia Street past the gym towards 2nd Avenue. We pulled up in front of the girl's apartment, and revved the engines before shutting them off. The girls opened the door before we had a chance to knock.

"Hi girls," Rancher beamed, "What's cookin'?"

"Hi," Laurie answered. "We were just sitting here waiting for you guys to arrive. Got tired of studying." Neither girl was very serious about school, but was having a good time faking it.

Rancher gave Laurie a hug, but I didn't do the same with Cynthia. I really didn't know her that well yet, and plus the fact I was not intent on getting serious with her or anyone else; that would have ruined my semester. Cynthia was not someone I would fall for anyway. She was tall, about my height, and was cute but didn't have a face that caught looks. But she was a nice person, and fun to be with, which was all I cared about. She was someone to visit and a much needed female companion. She was not the first girl I had spent any time with since Cindy. Cindy had dumped me the previous year, and later that same year Annette was illusive and a moving target. Pledge activity during the recently completed semester had conveniently occupied all my time. So Cynthia was a pleasant change.

"We don't have anything special to do," Cynthia advised us, "so you guys don't mind just sitting around and watching TV, do you?" She smiled and I noticed something else about her. She had some sexy eyes, and I got a feeling she wasn't a "goody two-shoes" that I kept having the misfortune of meeting. She just looked a little nasty, like she wanted to get down and get with the program.

"Sounds fine to me," I said. "I wouldn't mind just laying back and relaxing and enjoying this great company." Boy, that's enough to gag over.

"That's very sweet of you," Laurie responded.

The girls lived in a modern 2-bedroom apartment. The kitchen and living room were downstairs, and both bedrooms were upstairs.

After a couple of hours visiting, watching TV and catching an occasional hug with our friends, Rancher and I excused ourselves and promised the girls we would look for them on campus the next day. Rancher and I went to the girls' apartment about one or two nights a week, and I even took Cynthia out on a date one night. She and Laurie thought I was hooked, that I was becoming the steady boyfriend of Cynthia. But I wasn't. In fact, after about a month I started seeing less and less of her. She just wasn't my type, and there was no sense trying to convince myself otherwise, or leading her on if that were the case.

The last time I visited Cynthia was a momentous time in my life, for it marked a transition into manhood. Considering I was 20 years old, it was about time! I got laid for the first time in my friggin' life.

As was normal for a Saturday night, I had been out drinking and carousing on the motorcycle. I had started with a few beers at the Oasis, a Raider hangout at 3rd Street and Cherry. The "O", as we affectionately referred to it, had a long L-shaped bar, a soiled and worn wooden floor, cheap beers, and the best damn hotdogs and potato salad in Northern California. The "O" was frequently a last stop before going home late at night. There, one could curb a severe case of the munchies. The doggers were foot long, loaded with tomato, relish and onions and the buns were steamed. Whenever Buzzard was there and an order for a hotdog was called out for pick-up, the walls would reverberate with his yell, "Dogger!" Everyone expected the yell and laughed like hell. The biggest problem I encountered on leaving the "O" was remembering on which side of the building I parked my motorcycle. Fortunately, I had a small area to reconnoiter. I wasn't always so lucky when I rode my bike to football games and had to park out in the parking lot. It sometimes took me a little while to find my bike because I had been shit-faced when I parked it and after 2 hours in the stadium stands sobering up I completely lost track of its whereabouts. The real problem was when I thought I had parked it on Magnolia Street in front of the gym! All the walking sobered me up even more, however.

Sam and his wife, Daisy, were the owners of the Oasis. They didn't let the fact they were in their 60's diminish their enjoyment and rapport with the regulars. We were all on a first name basis with Sam and Daisy and loved them. They ran a tight ship, but were tolerant when things got a little carried away, like the time one of the Wilson twins brought in a large box of fresh vegetables and we ended up splattering the floors and walls with them. What a damn mess that was! Sam just told us to clean it up before we left.

But back to Cynthia. From the "O" I had gone by Brad's apartment and drank a few beers with he and Bo, one of his roommates, before going back to the fraternity house. I wasn't ready to call it a night, so I called Cynthia from the pay phone in the front lobby.

"Hello," she answered as she picked up the receiver. She sounded rather distant.

"Hi, Cynthia, this is Dave. How you doing tonight?"

"Oh, hi," she replied in a monotone voice. "I'm doing OK, I guess. Just sitting around and watching TV. Laurie's out with Rancher."

"Oh?" I queried. "I'm at the house. I've been to the "O" and stopped by to have a few beers with a friend. I really don't feel like calling it a night. Okay if I come over?" Her reply surprised me, for I didn't expect her to be that friendly toward me since I hadn't been seeing her much at all lately.

"Yeah. That sounds good. Why don't you come over? I'd like to see you."

"I'm on my way," I answered.

"Hot damn," I said to myself as I hanged up the phone, went to my room to splash on some Brut, walked back down the hall, out the front door, and bounded down the steps to where I had parked my bike a few minutes prior. The engine was still warm, so I kicked the bike into 1st gear immediately after cranking it over and sped away from the curb toward Cynthia's and some company.

We exchanged some pleasantries as I made my way into the apartment, and I could immediately sense her loneliness that night. She was acting quiet and wasn't her usual animated, talkative self.

"Can I get you a beer?" she asked.

"Please. As if I haven't already had enough of those tonight. The "O" was wild earlier this evening."

"I haven't been there," she replied as she walked back into the living room with my "Oly", as we termed Olympia beer, and one for herself. "I think I'll ask Laurie if she wants to go there some night."

"I don't know if you want to go there, Cynthia. The place is a Raider hangout and things can get a little out of hand sometimes."

"Well maybe not, then." She smiled, indicating she was getting back to her usual self. The TV was on, and I plopped myself onto the comfortable mini-sofa.

"Mind if I sit with you?" she asked.

"Please do. I'd like that. Thanks for the beer, by the way."

"Oh, you're welcome. I'm glad you called. I was feeling quite lonely tonight." She snuggled in next to me and put her arm around my shoulder.

"This may be a good night," I thought to myself.

After watching TV for a while and finishing our beers she put the empty Oly cans down on a nearby table. Between her expressed loneliness and my mild inebriation, the natural thing occurred. I gently pulled her closer to me and we kissed, long and hard. We held each other tight. A few minutes later she asked, "Do you want to go upstairs?"

I didn't want to be too hasty in my reply. No sense in implying it was the first time I had been made an offer like that. "Yes," I replied, feeling mellow from all the beer consumed that night.

She got up, grabbed my hand and walked me to the stairs that would lead us to her room. "I wonder how often she's done this before?" I asked myself as we walked up the stairs. Don't get me wrong now. It was just a rhetorical question, for at this point I could really give a darn. I would care later, however, as the reader will soon find out.

We entered her room and sat down on the side of the bed, not saying anything to each other. I put my arms around her and we kissed while I carefully and slowly guided us to a prostrate position on the bed. We kissed and let our hands wander over one another's body, searching, and being deliberate even though we wanted so badly to get past the foreplay and make love. It wasn't much later that we each began to work on the other's clothing. A belt here, a zipper, a sweater, pants, and so on. We were naked and in each other's arms. She pulled me on top of her and things took the natural course. Maybe she did perceive it was my first time! We lay together afterwards and kissed some more and she held me tight, like she didn't want me to leave. We spoke soft words to one another.

After a while we got dressed and went back downstairs. We both knew it would not happen again. By chance, I had called her at a time when she was feeling lonely. Everything had come together that night by fate and was now history.

"Goodnight, Cynthia," I said as I began to open the front door to let myself out. I gave her a little hug and a peck on the cheek.

"Bye, Dave." She was turning away as I exited the apartment.

I felt numbed as I rode the bike to the house. I felt some measure of euphoria but I also could not ignore the emptiness that sat in my gut. Had I just taken advantage of a lonely girl? Only Cynthia knew the answer to that question.

On the following Monday we crossed paths on campus.

"That should not have happened Saturday night. I feel bad about it," she said in a very sincere and somber tone.

I didn't know if she was trying to tell me she was not that kind of girl, or that she hadn't meant to do it with me. There was a difference.

"Yeah, I know what you mean." What the hell else was I supposed to say? After all, everything considered, it was still the first time I had gotten laid. It sure beat thinking about it!

"Well, I've got to get to a class. See ya," she said as she turned and headed for the other end of campus.

Before the whole business was over, I found it necessary to talk to her one more time. And it was the toughest phone call I had ever made in my life, for a personal problem of severe proportions ensued from our time in bed that night.

CHAPTER SEVENTEEN

On Wednesday, two days after I had seen Cynthia on campus, I was sitting in my 7:30 AM business class when I started feeling little shots of pain in the head of my penis. "What's this?" I asked myself as I tried to pay attention to the professor and take notes. One-half hour into the fifty minute class the occasional shots of pain had developed into a throbbing pain, and then into a steady pain that made my penis feel like someone was putting that proverbial glass rod up it that Dad told Dan and me about at 15 years old when he explained the World War II horrors of syphilis for our "birds and the bees" thing. His was quite a "speech". It was more like a bombing run than a strafing run and scared the holy crap out of us as the reader can deduce from what I have just explained. I was in agony and had broken out into a cold sweat. What made matters worse was that I was in the front row, and I know the professor wanted to ask me if I was feeling okay. "I'm okay, Sir," I would have haltingly blurted out. "Sure. It's only my penis. It feels like it's on fire. Otherwise, I'm all right. Don't mind me, but I feel like I could use major surgery right about now, or at least an emergency room."

I literally hung on, not knowing how I did so. I should have gotten up and excused myself, but I didn't and couldn't. "What the hell was going on?" I screamed to myself as beads of sweat formed on my forehead. Mercifully, the bell finally rang and I quickly dashed out the door, down the steps and out of the building. I was still in pain, but it helped to be walking, and it was great for my morale to know I was making a beeline for the student health center. What I would say to the nurse upon my arrival to the center was far from my mind. My steps were short and choppy, and I was slightly hunched over as I crossed the quad and walked past the CAC building. The center was now in view across 1st Street and I couldn't get there fast enough. My pain and slow progress made it feel like I was in slow motion. I couldn't recognize anyone I saw, for all the faces blended together in a giant blurred collage.

It was my first time to the medical building so it took a few moments to get my bearings and find the registration desk. I walked up to the counter and realized this was a time for candor.

"May I help you?" the nurse asked.

Oh, hell, this was it. How do I tell this lady my penis is in excruciating pain and I feel like I'm going to die? "My penis is very sore. It's quite painful." I tried to talk on and get the word penis behind as quickly as possible. The word penis was only a P sound, but it may as well have been a neon sign advertising my retched condition.

She appeared to understand and to have witnessed or handled this very same sort of crisis before. "Please fill out this card and I need to see your student activities card." Damn. Fill out a card? I asked myself. I'm ready to collapse on the floor right here and die and she wants me to fill out a damn card? I did as she asked, and was then told to have a seat in the waiting room. Her casual means of handling the situation caused me to think that I might live after all and that my problem was not that serious. Either that or she was a real veteran and cool under fire, or wanted to see this heathen suffer for a while.

I disguised my agony while waiting in the lounge by engrossing myself in a Life magazine. No Playboys here, damnit. But even if they had, I don't think that would have been the most propitious time to look at photos of naked women. I kept thinking to myself that this was a hell of a price to pay for the right of passage into manhood. After what seemed like hours, but was only a short 15 minutes, my name was called out and I was lead into an examining room. I explained my problem to the doctor and gave them a urine sample. His diagnosis was a mild form of gonorrhea, and he gave me a prescription of antibiotics to fill at the health center pharmacy. After being assured that my malady wasn't that serious and that some penicillin should cure me in a few days, I left the examining room, picked up my medicine, and got back to the house as quickly as I could to take the medicine and lay down.

Was I ever shocked to see that the color of my first pee after taking the medicine was orange! It stayed that way for the week I took the medicine. The guys at Iris got a big kick out of it, and I thought it was comical myself once the pain disappeared and I knew I was going to live.

"Hey, look at this stuff, you guys," Benny yelled out from the bathroom to Dan and Jack after I emptied my bladder in their toilet.

Dan and Jack rushed in and we all got a good laugh looking at the bowl of orange pee. "Well, look what Cynthia gave Peapecker," Jack laughingly stated.

"I don't know if it would have been worth it," Dan added.

"Hell, how was I supposed to know? It's over with anyhow," I replied. "Except for one thing. The people at the health center told me I should call the girl involved and inform her of my problem."

"Oh, my," Jack exclaimed. "Are you going to call her?"

"Yeah. I have to, really. I don't think there's much choice in the matter. Someone needs to tell her she's spreading something. I'm sure not looking forward to it, though."

A couple days later I called Cynthia and explained what had happened to me. When she expressed her disbelief and tried to rebut me, I simply told her she was the only girl I had been with lately. I didn't feel like explaining she was the only girl in my entire life with which I had intercourse. It was a short conversation. I had done what was right, and now I just had to cure my ailment. I never talked to Cynthia again after that phone call.

Cynthia and I occasionally crossed paths on campus, but we didn't acknowledge each other. In fact, as time progressed and some of the trappings of the counter-culture, hippie movement and anti-Vietnam war activity found their way to Happy Valley, I noted that Cynthia was dressing in the unkempt fashion popular among hippies and had let her facial appearance and hair go the same way. Even Brenda, our dorm homecoming queen candidate the previous year and one of the girls from our ice cream fight one night at the dorms, and a very pretty girl, had let herself go too. She was seen around campus dressed slovenly and wearing rimless glasses that made her look like John Lennon.

I'm sure both Brenda and Cynthia were disciples of Timothy Leary, an advocate of drugs. Wasn't it he that had said, "Expand your consciousness and find ecstasy and revelation within?" Of course, the use of marijuana, hashish and LSD was an expression of their new religion of love and freedom, of which drugs were the sacrament. The music of the times spoke to the counter-culture. The Doors, Jefferson Airplane, Mamas and Papas, Richie Havens, and so on. While our group went more for the Motown sound of Smokey Robinson, the Supremes, and Little Anthony and the Imperials, not to mention some of the great party music by the Righteous Brothers and Glen Yarbrough, there were times when we liked the music of the counter-culture. I particularly liked "The Doors", and on any given Friday afternoon after classes I could be seen sitting on the front steps of Dan's apartment at Iris Street with a cold beer from a sixer I had just brought back on my motorcycle from Carter's Market at 6th and Iris, and with the sound of "The Doors" hit "Light My Fire" blaring from the stereo in Dan and Jack's apartment. I would sit in smug enjoyment and satisfaction, saying hello to friends and strangers walking by on the busy student thoroughfare of Iris Street on their way to dorms or apartments. If I wasn't sitting on the apartment building steps I was sitting or reclining on my motorcycle. Either way, I was in hog heaven in Happy Valley. Each time I went down into Dan's apartment to grab another beer out of the fridge I would give Raquel Welch a wink. She displayed her curvaceous body on a poster hung on the wall above the TV. Ah, our sex symbol of the 60's.

As was common fare on the evening TV news, the media spoke of the increasing tempo of war activity in South Vietnam, of increasing casualties, and of heightened war protest coming from all quarters such as Harvard professors, Martin Luther King, and the extremely vocal crowd at Berkeley.

After dinner one night I walked into Dan's apartment in time to hear Jack talking about some information of great import to all of us, and caught the tail end of a conversation about one of our former freshman football teammates.

"Talk about crazy stuff happening," Benny said, adding, "remember Rich, the second string tackle behind Brad? I heard he bailed out of school and headed north to Canada."

"Why," I asked, stunned.

"His grades were hurting and he had to drop some classes. When he unexpectedly received his draft notice in the mail he apparently told his family he wanted no part of the military, did not believe in the war, and was heading out of the country until things settled down," Benny explained.

Jack said, "That's sad, really sad. I cannot imagine someone being that desperate so as to leave the country and their family. Swenson told me about a National Guard program that is taking people right now. It's an officer's program and those that are accepted go to a special officer candidate school for six weeks this summer. I'm thinking seriously about trying to sign up," Jack explained. Swenson was a good friend of Buzzard's and a year ahead of us academically, so he was looking for a Guard or reserve unit in anticipation of being classified 1-A when he graduated in June.

"That sounds pretty good, Jack," I replied. It was good information, but I did not share Jack's enthusiasm for the simple reason that I had not yet given all that much thought to post-graduation in terms of what my options were. It was something in the back of my mind, but I wasn't planning that far ahead. Jack obviously was, particularly since he and Nancy were very serious. I'm sure he didn't want to be forced to say "bye-bye" when he got his degree in his right hand and a change in draft status in his left. I didn't know at the time if the "A" in I-A meant "available" or "got your ass."

"Sounds like you're going to do it Jack," Benny added. Benny was pretty much a follower, but he was cautious. He was like me and in no hurry to commit. Plus, going to play Army for a good part of the summer wasn't our idea of fun.

"Yes, Benny, I really am. I want to get this business over with and find a Guard or reserve unit as soon as I can. I know it means training this summer, which will mess me up financially for my senior year here, and drilling on weekends once a month for the remainder of this semester, but I'm willing to accept that. I just hope they're not going to ask for some money under the table. My father told me recently about a National Guard recruiter in L.A. that was taking kickbacks from guys eager to get in his unit. He would put them at the top of the waiting list. Swenson and I are going to Sacramento in a couple of days to talk to the recruiter there and see about signing up. If he says anything about money I'm gone. Bullshit on that. I haven't got the money, anyway, and I'm not going to take the risk of putting my ass in a sling."

Dan and I both told Jack we would think about it and let him know our decisions the next day. I felt that joining would be the right thing to do, but the timing was lousy. I was doing well with a full course load and was having a good semester socially, so I didn't feel like getting myself involved with premature Army duty. I passed on it, as did Dan and Benny. The truth be known, I was simply having my best semester at Happy Valley and wasn't ready to make a major decision like that.

Later that week Jack returned from Sacramento with good news. "I'm in," he exclaimed as he walked into the apartment. "And so is Swenson. We go to our first drill in Sacramento three weeks from now. Wow, what a relief. I'm glad that's behind me."

"That's great, Jack," I told him. "Did the recruiter ask for some money?"

"No. Swenson and I had talked about that on our way down there. If he had said anything about paying him we were going to walk. We were also going to turn him in."

"Heavy. I would say good thing he didn't try anything," Dan interjected.

"So what time are your drills, 'ol buddy?" I asked.

"We have to be at the drill hall at 7:30 in the morning, so we'll probably leave here about 6:00. I'll let Swenson drive. With his lead foot in that loaded El Camino of his we'll make it in time."

"Oww. Lovely. That's mighty early, Jack. You going to be up in time?" Dan asked, giving him a smile acknowledging that Jack was not known to be a morning person. Later, Jack would tell us how he learned to sleep while standing in formation!

"I don't have any choice, do I? I have to be up and ready when Swenson gets here."

The effects of the Vietnam War, which aside from Jack's brother Gary and a few friends had been entering our peaceful lives on pussycat feet, now came in like a screaming Navy A-6 Intruder on a bombing run over a Vietnam jungle. There was nothing subtle about it. No blood. No time spent in the rice paddies. Just a commitment by one of us in this case to spend part of the next six years in a uniform, not to mention the likelihood of Jack's Marine brother serving in Vietnam. A commitment and decision we could not have foreseen when we reported to Happy Valley College in 1964 as freshmen. But then, who knows beforehand what the affects of war will be? With both World Wars I and II, the war touched most men the same. They enlisted, went to boot camp, and they fought because our great country, or our allies who believed in the freedoms enjoyed in our country, had been attacked. It was the right thing to do. This war, however, was different. A lot of people that did not believe in the war and did not support it were being drafted into service. I had read that earlier in the year the opinions and positions of senior administration staff for the President and a growing number of congressmen started to swing against the war. And there was a sense of the government's growing isolation from the public, with expressions such as, "the establishment is out of its mind." While it may sound trite, our particular group at Happy Valley had neither an emotional nor attitudinal orientation – we didn't vocally support it, and yet we were not opposed to it. We just had other things to do and felt that putting on a uniform at that particular point in our lives was not exactly in the best interest of our health. But so much for reason. The war in Vietnam was now marginally affecting us.

CHAPTER EIGHTEEN

The semester was my best at Happy Valley, due to a social life that was harmonious and full in every respect. I was finally enjoying a degree of success with the opposite sex. I studied hard, which paid off in excellent grades, and I played hard. There were only a few times that I drank too much, at many a keg affair, and did a lot of running around weekend nights on the motorcycle.

I dated a girl named Shelley for a while, who at 5'1" had the biggest set of knockers my eager hands had ever felt in my still formative years of sex education. I had some good times with her, but there was no serious relationship.

In fact, one night during the period I dated Shelley I picked up her best friend and dorm roommate, Pat. Fred, my best friend from grade school in Pleasant Hill, whom I had grown up with and who was attending Diablo Valley College after returning from Vietnam, had told me some interesting and provocative stories about Pat from when she was attending DVC. On the particular night I picked up Pat, I had been to a few places drinking and was cruising around looking for some pick-up potential. During my many cruising activities I sometimes ran into Shelley, and other times I went calling on girls I knew and even those I knew marginally. I would simply knock on doors where I knew certain girls lived, hoping one would invite me in to visit.

I had taken Pat for a ride on the motorcycle, which she thoroughly enjoyed, and then stopped at the fraternity house. Unfortunately for us, Shelley had seen us riding around, which was probably the reason for a very strange occurrence that night. Pat and I had had an abated sexual liaison that evening in my room. After I took a quick shower we were getting ready to leave the room when I heard a slight rustling noise, looked around, and sighted a shoebox on the windowsill. At that time of the year I kept the window open. When it was put there I did not know and what may have been observed and by whom was also a mystery. Upon examining the contents, I found a mouse in the shoebox! I believe that it had been placed there by none other than Shelly, and I suppose the implication or message was that the little furry animal was a "rat."

Myrna was another girl in my life, but thank goodness the association was brief, occasional and short-lived. The association began one mid-week night while sitting around the fraternity house trophy room with a few of the brothers on old sagging, overstuffed couches that were in dire need of being replaced. The furniture was absolutely horrid and had probably conveyed with the 1930's era structure when the fraternity bought it.

"Hey, let's go to Myrna's," someone suggested. The mix of boredom and horniness was evident.

"Who's Myrna?" I asked.

"You haven't met Myrna, Duke?" another brother queried with a hint of incredulity.

"No. Never heard of her or met her," I replied.

"That settles it. Duke's going. Let's go to Myrna's," he said emphatically.

We hopped into a car and sped off toward the other side of town, driving up the Boulevard and making a left onto 7th Street where we pulled up in front of a two-story apartment building that appeared to be in the low rent district. We walked up a couple flights of stairs in a dimly lit stairwell and one of the guys rapped on the door. The guys were in pretty good spirits. I still had not figured out what this was all about. Myrna was expecting us so she was quick to answer the door.

"Hi boys," she said. Myrna wasn't very pretty. And she wasn't big, either. She was downright tiny and petite, with stringy black hair, and was wearing a robe. She must have been ready for sleep when the call came from the house.

"Hi, Myrna," the guys said almost in unison. I didn't know her, so I just said, "Hi." "We brought a new brother with us. Myrna, this is Dave," Phil said.

The light finally turned on for me. Myrna pulled trains for the brothers of Delta Phi. That also explained why she was in a robe. She was ready for action.

"Hi, Dave, how are you?" she said, but with very little of a smile. She was probably thinking that the small number of Delta Phi's that initially received her favors were now taking advantage of her good nature. Still, she must have had a healthy appetite for sex.

We sat around in her small living room for a few minutes making small talk before one of the guys grabbed her by the hand and without a word led her to her bedroom. While Myrna was preoccupied we joked around a bit and checked out her refrigerator.

My turn finally came. I walked into her darkened bedroom and sat on the edge of the bed.

"Go ahead and take your clothes off," she said.

"Sure," I answered, and began stripping down to my skivvies.

"Are you Dave?" she asked.

"Yep, that's me." I should have known there was going to be a problem, for I wasn't feeling overwhelmingly excited about this experience. I got into her bed and under her covers, and put my arm around her frail body. And this was supposed to be good sex? I asked myself. I may as well have been putting my arms around a picket rail fence.

It didn't work. I couldn't bring myself to kiss her, and there was no stimulation in my loins. No heat, nothing. Not even the high level of testosterone in this normally horny 20-year old made any difference. After about 15 minutes of realizing it wasn't going to get up, I mumbled to her, "Well, I guess it's just not going to happen tonight."

"That's okay," she said. "But you can come back some other time."

"Okay," I said. I wasn't ready to tell her I would be using the "rain check" any time soon. I got out of bed, got dressed and walked out to the other room, where fortunately no one asked me how it all went. No "kiss and tell" action after Myrna. If there was a next time, I thought to myself, I'll have to be drunk.

Myrna also was gullible and vulnerable. The next time I saw her was a week later in the house, and I had just hit the sack. I had no sooner closed my weary eyes from studying when I heard a hell of a commotion coming from the foyer.

"Come on, Myrna, you can do it! Go! Go! Hurry! You're doing great, keep it up!" A chorus of cheers and encouragement was coming from half a dozen guys at the foot of the stairs and an equal number at the top of the stairs. What the hell was going on? I asked myself as I quickly got out of bed and walked up the hall toward the foyer.

I arrived in time to see Myrna nearing the bottom of the steps, taking the steps as quickly as she could. A rapid thump, thump, thump, could be heard over the screams of encouragement. What was even more outrageously funny was that Myrna was naked as a jaybird and her little tits were bouncing smartly with each step she took. A robe was then flung down the steps so that she could re-dress.

"Myrna, that was good, but you're still a little shy of the record," she was told by an enthusiastic brother.

"I think you need to try it a couple more times, Myrna," someone else offered with equal passion. "I think you can break the record tonight."

Myrna had been told that it was a Delta Phi tradition for girls to start dressed in a robe at the bottom of the steps, race to the top, undress, and race down the steps to see how fast they could perform against a stopwatch. Myrna was obviously the only one stupid enough to engage in the activity.

I stood in the foyer, amazed, and laughing with a few of the other brothers standing around. What a trip, I thought to myself. Wait until Dan and the others hear about this.

"Okay, Myrna, get ready. On your mark, get set, go!" the brother screamed. I watched her little body tear up the steps as fast as her legs would take her. The guys yelled encouragement and told her she was on a record-setting pace. Before I could see her I heard her feet lightly pounding on the steps as she made her way down.

She hit the foyer floor, her little chest heaving, and with a serious look on her face. Competitive spirit. "You did it, Myrna, you set a new record! Congratulations!" A couple of guys put their arm around her and congratulated her. She was smiling from ear to ear and was obviously pleased with her achievement. She was oblivious to the fact that she was standing around naked until someone handed her the robe and she slowly put it on.

I walked back to my room, chuckling to myself, and wondering what other strange and unusual experiences lay ahead.

The next weekend I made a point to take Brenda out. Brenda and I had a date the previous weekend when she invited me to the annual Sadie Hawkins Dance at the college gym, where the girls asked out the guys. We had a nice time, but I pulled a few stunts with some Raiders buddies, Benny and Buzzard, that did not enamor me to Brenda by the end of the night. And that's what I reminded myself when I arrived at the house that Friday eve of my date while the brothers were having a function with the Gamma Delta's. At the house I had a nice talk with Cindy, with whom I had not spoken for quite some time, and I did not help myself to the keg.

One quite memorable kegger was held at Tim Ballantine's apartment on an overcast and drizzly Saturday. The kegger had been planned since early in the week, so we had our fingers crossed that it would not rain. No such luck. Even though it rained some, the kegger's spirit was not dampened. Jack and I went over on my cycle, dressed for inclement weather. Dan and Benny were on Dan's cycle, and dressed likewise. The keg itself was in the back of a truck belonging to Tim's roommate, Pete, and a large bag of peanuts had been provided.

It was a typical kegger. It didn't take us long to get a buzz on, and then it was looney-tune time. A construction crew's tractor got started up, a road sign was demolished, and a sad-looking bicycle was destroyed. Jack and I wandered upstairs to Terri Millikan's apartment where we drank and listened to records. Terri had gone to high school with Dan and me. Dan and Benny were elsewhere, we later learned, playing "games" with a willing girl named Mimi. The story was good for a chortle. To top things off, a few of the guys, after leaving Tim's, found a dead cow and deposited it that night on the front doorstep of a girl's dorm. The incident made front page in the next day's Happy Valley Gazette.

We also had a lot of keggers at the house Joe Knapp, Brent's old roomie at Sierra, rented out on West near Paige Avenue. Rob, a fraternity brother of mine, and I went out to Bob's one particular Friday afternoon for a kegger. We got a good heat on, and then went back to the fraternity house for a social with the Tri-Delt's. The folks at the social didn't much appreciate our "enthusiasm" when we stormed in to the house and began raising hell in front of our dear guests from the sorority.

That wasn't the only time the brothers let me know my rambunctious behavior was not condoned. On a few occasions, Harvey, a pledge brother, and I would attend socials blitzed and do some crazy things, such as a "dead gopher." Doing a "dead gopher" meant falling to the floor on your back, sticking your arms and legs up in a semi-rigid position and then slightly jerking arms and legs with your eyes closed. It created an unusual and unforgettable effect when people were caught off-guard and the element of surprise was successful. The fraternity had an unwritten rule against a member in the position of being on his back on the ground at a social function, even accidentally from a fall. Bad decorum, I guess. So that made Harvey and me doubly popular, and was why we inherited the nicknames, the "social renegades."

CHAPTER NINETEEN

On a sunny, warm Saturday Dan, Jack, Benny and I were at Hopewell having a few beers with our good friends living there. "Tank", Brad and a few other guys also stopped by so we decided to all chip in for a keg. "Stork," a Raider and basketball player, was also there with some of his fellow sophomore Raiders.

About three beers into the afternoon the subject of spring break came up. It was only a few weeks away.

"Hey guys," Jack began, "What do you say we go somewhere for spring break? I've always wanted to visit Palm Springs and see what that place is like during the break." Palm Springs was the place many west coast college students headed to during the annual spring break ritual. East coasters trekked in droves to Ft. Lauderdale to party and let it all hang out, while Palm Springs was the chosen destination for west coast students. Palm Springs didn't get the numbers that Ft. Lauderdale did, but that was because of the many other spots around L.A. that students gravitated toward – Manhattan, Hermosa and Redondo Beaches, Laguna Beach, Malibu Beach, and the many surfing spots – and the fact there were more colleges on the east coast. A lot of students crossed the border to Mexican destinations like Ensenada and Mazatlan.

"Wow, that's a great idea," plugged Chip.

"I think it's a super idea, too" said Rob, "but do we really want to fight the crowds in Palm Springs?"

"Why don't we go to San Diego?" Brad asked. "My sister and her husband, who is in the Navy, live near there and I'm sure they would let us stay a night or two."

"Are you sure, Brad?" I asked. "Ten guys sleeping on their living room floor? Sounds nice, but I doubt they would bite on that idea."

"No, I'm sure there wouldn't be a problem. They're a neat couple and would love to have us," Brad replied with honest conviction. "I'll give them a call though."

"Yes. Do check Brad," I suggested.

"Ok, so we head south. How do we get there?" asked Chip. "My truck won't hold us or get us there and Rob's Mustang won't cut it. That leaves one possibility, unless we rent something."

"No, we're not going to rent a camper," I stated firmly. I remembered all too well the disaster after my senior year of high school. This was a whole different group and I envisioned us bringing back a camper in pieces at best.

All eyes turned to Stan, the coach's son.

"Hey, are you guys serious?" he asked, raising his voice to punctuate his alarm. Stan had a car, and although it wasn't big, it could be made sufficient. His car was a '54 Chevy sedan that was in good working order.

"Sure, we'll just remove the rear seat and create a larger seating area in the back," Rob suggested. We all walked out to the car, beers in hand and expectations running high.

Peering inside the car, we all had some doubts about capacity, but by this time we weren't going to let anything stop us.

"No sweat," Jack offered. "We really have no choice, anyway, do we guys?"

"No. This is it," I said. We had no idea how taxing the long drive would be on our collective patience, however.

About two beers later, with excitement and anticipation high, our itinerary had been planned and commitments had been made. We would rendezvous at Dan's and my house in Danville, drive to San Bernadino to pick up Stork, go to the L.A. beaches, then to

San Diego, and also visit Tijuana across the border. We had heard juicy stories about TJ and wanted to experience it for ourselves. Some of it, anyway.

Before departing Hopewell that day we had also nicknamed the '54 Chevy "The Gozinya." Three weeks later, on the Friday on which spring break started Dan and I traveled to Danville. The following day Stan, Rob, Chip and Brent arrived about 4:00 in the afternoon in the Gozinya. Jack came from his home in nearby Lafayette and Brad drove over from Concord. Mom and Dad had been asked well before about using our house as the rendezvous spot and had cheerfully agreed. They were wonderful about that type of thing. Any of our friends, regardless of number, were always welcome and would get a feast set out before them and a place to sleep if needed. They enjoyed seeing our friends from Happy Valley. Plus, this gave Mom a chance to show off her stuff in the kitchen. Both she and Dad contributed, for Dan and I had requested our favorite meal—BBQ rotisserie chicken, spaghetti, tossed salad and garlic bread.

We all ate till we were uncomfortably full, and then everyone passed out an endless amount of compliments for the excellent dinner. We all crashed early, anxious for our morning getaway.

After a large breakfast that included Dad's famous Swedish pancakes, and ensured we wouldn't have to worry about eating until late in the day, a photo of the group standing against and on top of the Gozinya was taken.

We got underway after picking straws to see who got to sit three-abreast in the desirable front seat. That meant there was five of us in the back of the car either leaning against the side panels, against the back, with head sometimes smacking against the rear window when the car hit a bump, or with back to the front seat. Any way you cut it, it was tight quarters in the back. Stan drove starting off, and Brent and Dan sat in front, leaving Jack, Chip, Rob, Brad and me in the back.

We were all in pretty good spirits heading down the coastal route. Once we got past the Monterey area we made some stops in San Luis Obispo and Santa Barbara. The surfing spots like Malibu, Huntington Beach, Newport Beach and Laguna Beach that we had heard so much about in Beach Boys songs and wanted to visit would come later when we arrived in the Los Angeles area.

We were ecstatic when we hit the L.A. area, confident that we weren't too far from Stork's home. Wrong! We all learned simultaneously that L.A. was a big place. Because we thought we were close to Stork's we elected not to make any more stops to stretch the cramped legs of the unlucky bastards sitting in the back. It therefore seemed like an eternity as we made our way through Ventura and Oxnard, Thousand Oaks, then dropped out of the mountains into Santa Monica where we headed east through greater L.A. city, Pomona and Ontario before finally arriving, sore, yet cheerful and thankful, at Stork's home in "San Berdu." Like my parents had done, Stork's Mom was ready for us with a great dinner, and afterwards we all sat in front of the TV to watch the NCAA championship semi-final round basketball game between UCLA and Houston, featuring Lew Alcindor and Elvin Hayes. A great game.

The next morning we were up early and on our way to the famous L.A. beaches. Of great import was that Stork was able to take one of the family cars, thus giving us relative traveling comfort for the next few days. We headed straight for the Newport Beach area, and after driving around that area for a while and experiencing heavy crowds we headed south a few miles to Laguna Beach. We spent the day sunbathing and body surfing in some poor surf, but Stork gave us some encouragement for the next day.

"Tomorrow we'll go to the "Wedge" where we're sure to have some better surf. And it's within walking distance of my uncle's place." Stork had mentioned the fact that we could probably stay at his uncle's. He just didn't happen to mention it to his parents. His uncle was out of the area, so Stork figured we could sleep in his yard.

The "Wedge" was famous for bodysurfing. We had seen photos in surfing mags of massive waves bodysurfed by experts. While we looked forward to visiting the "Wedge," not all of us were that anxious to subject our bodies to its waves.

We grabbed a case of beer and some wine before arriving at Stork's uncle's place. We relaxed in the yard, drinking and soaking some rays under the late afternoon sun. The place was a typical small beach house with a wooden fence surrounding a small front yard. The patio in the front yard, where we were lounging, was brick. One of those grassless, easy to maintain yards. As we all prepared to go to bed we wished we had grass, for the brick was a bitch to sleep on under our sleeping bags. Jack was "conveniently" feeling a bit under the weather with a cold and slight temperature so he slept in the Gozinya.

We awoke with aching bodies added to hangovers.

"Stork. Great idea to stay here and save a few bucks, but my body's hurtin' from those damn bricks," Rob declared.

"Yeah, me, too," Stan chimed in. Before things got out of hand and Stork was made to feel like shit over what had happened, a couple of us took the offensive.

"Hey. It was fine, and we all had a good time last night, so what the hell? I say we think about getting some breakfast and then having some of the dog that bit us before we go to the beach," I said. "Someone go get sleeping beauty up in the Gozinya so we can get some "grease". I'm so hungry I could eat the south end of a north bound horse."

After breakfast we stood around the patio having a couple beers before walking to the beach. The beers would also help allay some of our fear about challenging the "Wedge." Arriving at the beach, feeling our usual obnoxious selves after a few drinks, we found the surf perfect. Directly in front of where we placed our towels we had some good surf to play in. To our left, a short walk down the beach, was the unmistakable area referred to as "The Wedge." The surf that day was thankfully smaller than normal, which meant there was a chance we could try to body surf "The Wedge." The euphoria of the beer also made us a bit foolish, for we all stupidly got the crazy idea to run charging into the water and do well-timed full-body slams into breaking waves. The waves were not large enough to hurt us, but large enough to let us know who would come out on top. Laughing, we did this over and over until we got up the courage to hit "The Wedge."

Catching waves at "The Wedge" was exhilarating and satisfying, and we did that for the better part of an hour before deciding it was time for lunch and our departure for San Diego.

We timed our arrival for the dinner that Brad's sister, Ruth, and her Naval officer husband, Bill, planned for us in their government quarters at Imperial Beach. She was smart and had laid out taco fixings for the nine hungry individuals that descended on their small house. That night we laid sleeping bags on the carpet floor and commented on the welcome change from the previous night's bricks.

The following day we spent the afternoon at San Diego area beaches and talked about our plans for the night.

"Well, guys, this is it. TJ tonight," I reminded them. Snickers abounded as the guys thought of the stories we had heard.

"Do you think there really is a place called the "Blue Goose" and that the stuff goes on there like we've been told?" Chip asked.

"Yep. I think so, Chip," Stan replied.

"We'll soon find out," I said.

"It's the real thing," Brad added.

"I suggest we all stay together going around TJ tonight. I've heard that you're safer in groups and that the crazies and police are less likely to bother you if you're in groups," said my brother.

"Sounds like a weiner," Jack said. "There's no sense taking our chances. I'd hate to have someone throw away the key on us."

"We'll be alright," Brad assured us. "Just don't do anything stupid like buying a bar hostess a drink or touching any of the women."

"We'll just watch the show," I stated. "This is going to be great. I can't wait."

TJ was just like we had been told. We had driven to the nearby border where we parked the cars and walked across to the Mexico side. We were all wearing our block HV letter jackets, feeling that might also discourage anyone from bothering us. As soon as we got across the border we were accosted by small kids trying to sell us any number of things. Before we covered the few hundred yards between the border station and the outskirts of the city we heard a phrase from a small boy we had often been told about, "My mother, she is a virgin." We all looked at each other and laughed. "Yep, we're in TJ, fellas," someone exclaimed.

We hit a few bars, having a beer at each one before moving on. We finally got to the "Blue Goose", anticipating a show. We weren't disappointed. We sat a couple rows back from a small stage surrounded by a single metal bar. On stage, a girl was dancing to the blaring music. She was wearing only a G-string as she went through the motions trying to keep to the rhythm of the tinny sounding music. She moved around the small floor, and when she got next to the rail, that is when the real action started with the front-row spectators eager to make contact in numerous ways.

"Damn, I can't believe that," said Happy Valley's answer to Mr. Clean, Brent.

"Neither can I," I replied, "but it sure is a great show."

After watching the show for a while we walked back outside, all of us talking excitedly and simultaneously about what we had just seen. The next bar was a little different experience. As soon as we walked in the door to the darkened foyer each of us was met by a young lady that was topless. Wow, this is fantastic, I thought to myself. Fortunately, we were all ready for what came next, for we had been advised to put wallets in a front pocket and keep our hands on them as much as possible. As soon as the hostess met me she pushed her body next to mine, put one hand on my crotch, rubbing vigorously, and used her free hand to search with equal vigor and obvious intent for my wallet. Her left hand went from pocket to pocket, until she found the one with my hand in it. She tried to gently pull my hand free, but being unsuccessful, decided to escort me to a table. The other guys were experiencing the same. I sat at the table drinking a beer I ordered from her, listening to her rough English.

"Will you buy a beer for me?" she asked.

"No," I replied.

"Why not?"

"I just don't feel like it." This went on for a little while. I knew she would give up soon and leave, but until she did I just kept taking in the sight of her bare breasts. She finally tried another tact.

"There is a room upstairs. I do it all," she offered.

"How much?" I asked out of curiosity.

"Ten dollars."

"Naw. Not tonight."

"You don't think I am attractive?" she asked. New tact.

"You look fine. I just don't want to go upstairs with you." All this time she was sitting next to me still "massaging" me. And she knew she was getting somewhere. Occasionally she would let her hand slip over to where she knew my wallet was, but she also found my hand still in that same pocket. It wasn't the most relaxing way to have a beer, but I was casually enjoying her entreaties to me and I was starting to feel a few sheets to the wind. It was definitely a unique experience. I was trying to make the most of this encounter and still keep myself safe and out of trouble as I sure had no idea of what might await me upstairs.

"I do it under the table. It is dark here," she pleaded. "You are ready," she observed. Damn right I was ready, but this wasn't the time and place to let things go any farther. I did want to see Happy Valley, family and other friends again, and certainly did not want to spend any time in the "TJ gray bar hotel." I looked around. All the guys still had hostesses snuggled up next to them. We looked at one another in delight. We would be talking about this place for a long time.

"No, not under the table either," I finally responded. I could tell her patience was growing slim. With a loud sigh she said, "bastard," and left the table to try her luck with the next unsuspecting guy that came through the door. The other guys experienced the same thing, so we all moved to share the same table where we finished our beers and moved on elsewhere in the dirty, unkempt city that obviously had no bounds on indecency, a fact we obviously knew first-hand. Before leaving TJ we all bought small black-handled switchblade knives that we hid in the liners of our jackets. Dan and I also bought one of the stock TJ pieces of art. It was a bullfighter and bull painted in bright, gaudy colors on a felt-type material with a cheap wood frame. It was bought as a gift for Mom and Dad. We were certain they would appreciate it.

We were a bit nervous approaching the U.S. side of the border station, afraid of being caught with the knives. It turned out that there was no reason to be fearful. The border guards gave a big smile as the nine of us in letter jackets went through the station. We showed them the painting and other small artifacts and souvenirs purchased. They could see we had not bought any liquor to bring across, and asked if we had purchased anything else.

"No, Sir," we all answered, with Brad adding, "maybe too much beer," to which the guards laughed and told us to have a safe drive back. We talked about TJ and our experiences on the way back to Imperial Beach, but gave no gory details at the house.

The next day we said farewell and thanks, and drove to L.A. But before leaving beautiful San Diego and its lovely beaches we stopped at the Marine Corps Training Depot and said hello to an older cousin of Dan's and mine that was stationed there and was a Captain in the Marine Corps. We did not get into any conversation about the war as that would have been inappropriate. We drove to Eileen's house in Anaheim where we were served a great dinner by her Mom. That night, Brent and Eileen, Chip and Brad went to Disneyland. The rest of us opted to stay at the house and lay back.

The following morning we had a group photo taken in front of Eileen's house and then drove to Huntington Beach where we did some bodysurfing, clowned around for camera shots, and watched the surfers shooting the pier. We again used Stork's uncle's place to crash, and the next morning Stork headed back home and we all piled into the Gozinya for the long drive north. By this time we were a bit worn-out and ready for the end of spring break.

After an agonizingly long, uncomfortable ride, during which tempers actually flared a bit, we arrived in Danville. Jack headed home to Lafayette and Stan, Rob, Chip, and Brent continued on to Happy Valley.

When we all got back together in Happy Valley we shared stories of our trip among ourselves and with others eager to hear of TJ.

CHAPTER TWENTY

Midway through the semester the talk around the gym was about the upcoming NFL football draft. Would Jerry Sanchez get drafted for his punting skills? He had been contacted by a few teams so expectations were understandably and justifiably high.

We were all excited and happy for Jerry when it was learned that he had been drafted by the Baltimore Colts. What a thrill, particularly for a player from a small, non-scholarship, Division III school to be taken in the draft. Jerry planned a party at his apartment and close Raider and Block HV members were invited. Our whole group was extended an invitation. I took Sue Belmont, a roommate of Nancy and Janie, Jack's and Dan's girlfriends, and Chip was taking Karen, a girl living in Ramsey Hall that he had been dating for the past few months.

It was a great party, and everyone was having a super time. Jerry's girlfriend, Mary Jane, had decorated the apartment in Colts Blue and White, and there were cutouts of horseshoes adorning walls and doors. I mean this was big time stuff! And, Jerry even wore a large horseshoe cutout pinned to the back of his shirt.

There was an occurrence that damn near destroyed the party and almost caused Chip to get his lunch, even though he wasn't directly responsible. Chip's date drank like a fish, and couldn't hold her booze. She had definitely had too many after the party was a couple hours old.

People were standing around in small groups and large groups, talking, drinking, laughing, and just having a nice time. Jerry was constantly being congratulated, and was extolling his chances at making the team. A loud cacophony of sound permeated the entire apartment, but not so loud that anyone missed the loud tongue-lashing given Chip's date, Karen. For she, in her greatly inebriated state that short changed her ability to reason and fully grasp the significance of the event we were celebrating, had unbeknownst to anyone walked up behind Jerry and crisply and cleanly ripped the horseshoe off his back!

"God damn you, you damn bitch," Jerry roared.

Mary Jane was equally demonstrative, and also let Karen know what she thought of it all. And all partiers stood frozen, watching the unraveling scene and wondering what Chip would do. Chip was pissed at Karen, too, but was also trying to cool off Jerry to no avail. When things started getting a bit heated between he and Jerry, Chip chose the right course of action by grabbing Karen and making an early, unplanned exit from the party.

The party wasn't the same afterwards. The horseshoe was destroyed and would not be placed back on the shirt. Jerry and Mary Jane kept mumbling to everyone how pissed they were, and so the rest of us just continued partying and slowly made our exits, albeit prematurely.

A couple nights later Dan and I received a call that would cause us great pain and fear. Put another way, it scared the hell out of us. I was at Dan's when the phone rang.

"Hello," Dan said after picking up the receiver. It was evident it was our mother calling.

"Hi, Mom. How's everything?" he asked. Mom didn't call that often, so I'm sure Dan was thinking there was a problem. He told her we were fine and that all was well in Happy Valley, and that I was there because we were all studying together that night.

I didn't know what Mom was saying, but it was easy to read my brother's reaction. His face froze and his grip on the receiver tightened. There was great concern in his voice when he spoke. "How's Ron doing?" He listened intently.

A few moments later, he asked Mom, "Has Fred been over to see him?"

Dan's words became slow and pained. "Whereabouts is he in the hospital?"

Dan almost dropped the phone. His next words stumbled out. "Oh, my God. I wonder how bad it is?"

She was evidently explaining something to him.

"I'll tell Dave, and we'll try to get down there as soon as we can. Good talking to you, Mom. Love you, and give our love to Dad. And I'll say Hi to Dave from both of you. Bye."

Dan hung up the phone slowly, and told Jack, Benny and me what Mom had just told him. "Mom said that Fred's mother called her today to say that our old friend Ron Kowalchick was just flown back from Vietnam where he got shot up pretty bad. He had surgery on his leg yesterday and he's now convalescing at Oak Knoll Naval Hospital in Oakland. She thought we would want to see him."

"Oh, man, how bad is he, Dan?"

"He lost a few inches from one of his legs. He's going to be there for a few weeks before being moved elsewhere." Dan halted for a few seconds, then added, "He's in the amputee ward. Mom gave me the address of his ward. I don't believe this."

We were all stunned and speechless, and there was a good measure of fear. The war kept getting closer. First, there was news of school acquaintances getting shot and killed in Vietnam. Next, Jack's brother enlisting in the Marine Corps and Jack making the decision, obviously a wise one at this point, to join the National Guard. And that was followed by news of a good friend from our grade school days arriving back in the states minus some of his leg. Sonovabitch. We didn't need this kind of drama in our lives! Was it any wonder why we were always so alert for news of the draft? Or why we sometimes got a little carried away in our partying? Any week could have been our last at Happy Valley depending on which way the draft winds might blow.

But just because we were not volunteering and anxious to join and serve did not mean we had a disregard for the men fighting in the rice paddies of Nam. I'm not sure what we felt toward them. Respect? Admiration? Gratitude? That almost sounds patronizing, doesn't it? We felt compassion, particularly for the families of the many who did not return alive. At least Ron had come back alive. And so had Fred. There were so many, however, that weren't so lucky. And in Happy Valley we lived day to day under the illusion that it was the other guy that got drafted and was sent to Nam. Not us. We've got our student deferments. Hopefully, they would leave us alone and at least let us finish school. We certainly didn't know, and could not know, the real trauma our military were bearing up under, except for cases like Ron's.

A few sobering days later Dan and I drove to Oakland in a borrowed car. We would see Ron that afternoon, spend the night at home, and return to school the next morning. It was a quiet drive. Talk about having your gut in your throat. We didn't know what to expect, especially having to visit an amputee ward. Oh, shit, help us through this one, God. And help Ron, dear God. We were numb. Scared. This was way out of our Happy Valley milieu.

After parking the car in a central parking lot of Oak Knoll Naval Hospital in the southern rolling hills area of Oakland we stopped the first person we found to ask directions around the hospital grounds. The grounds were filled with countless long, one-story, white wood-frame structures with green roofs from World War II days. We found Building H-9 and asked again for directions to the east wing. With dubious bad luck we entered at the opposite end of the wing from Ron. We walked slowly and carefully down the middle of the wing. Beds lined each side of the building. Some of the men were in traction of one type or another, some sat on the sides of their beds, a leg or an arm visibly missing. Some were up and about on crutches, again without a leg. One guy had no legs at all, his body supported on a small platform as he made his way down the floor. I had never felt so speechless, empty, and angry in my entire life. What right did I have to be here, healthy looking, among these men who had obviously put their lives on the line and had come out less than whole? I felt like crying. The whole mess was tragic and unnecessary. What sort of a future did some of these guys have? My peripheral vision was on over-drive on that day in Oak Knoll Naval Hospital in March of 1967 and in a manner of speaking went far beyond the whitewashed walls of the amputee ward to an unknown future filled with dread and foreboding.

We spotted Ron's bed about three-quarters down on the right side. He was sitting up and smiled as he saw us approaching. At least someone could smile. What courage!

"Hey, Dan and Dave. It's great to see you," he said. "This is a real surprise."

"Hi, Ron. How you doing, 'ol buddy?" Dan answered.

"Hi, Ron," I said. We shook hands.

"I'm doing pretty good, really. At least I came back alive," he said cheerfully. "How have you two been, anyway? I haven't seen you in years."

It was great the way he turned the conversation around to us. He knew we felt uncomfortable, and was trying to get us more relaxed. "We've been just fine, Ron," I started. "You know we're up at Happy Valley. Great place. I've lettered in gymnastics, and Dan got his letter in football."

"That's great," he said. "You guys knew that Tim died a couple years back, didn't you?" Welcome to reality. Tim killed in Nam. Ron an amputee. We're just twenty years old and this shouldn't be happening.

"Yes. We did. It's really sad," Dan replied. Tim was one of the neighborhood guys our age when we were growing up in Pleasant Hill. Dan, Fred and I hung around together and were best friends. Ron and Tim lived a block over, and a guy named John was two blocks away. Our parents didn't like us playing with the three of them. I suppose some rumors had gotten around about them, and our parents felt that Ron, Tim and John were all a bad influence on us. Oh, we still sneaked over to their houses once in a while, and sometimes we got caught and paid for our mistakes. I remember Ron in particular. Ron was in my class in the fifth grade, and one Monday had brought in a program from the Cal-Michigan State football game that had been played that weekend in Berkeley in the Fall of 1956. He proudly showed us a picture in the program of his cousin who played for

Michigan State. Ron's program was no match, however, for the San Francisco 49ers programs brought in on Mondays during the football season by Diane Travis. Her father had season tickets to the 49ers home games played in beautiful, cozy Kezar Stadium in Golden Gate Park in San Francisco. Since she liked me I was always the first to see each program. In fact, Diane had asked me to a birthday party for her brother, Billy, that year. Reluctantly, my parents had let me go, even though they couldn't figure why a girl was asking a boy to a party!

Ron went on to tell us how he was injured and about his operation. I could tell he didn't want to speak too much of the horror stories from over there. The war was the shits. I needed no reminder. He did, however, tell us of a couple of incidents and skirmishes he was directly involved in. And he showed us his Purple Heart. He was so proud. Dan and I sat there listening, spellbound, becoming more frightened of the possibilities for us, but feeling pride for Ron and caring for his welfare, while we were still behind and safe in the states at Happy Valley College.

After about a half hour of visiting and catching up on old times in the neighborhood he was starting to feel some pain and discomfort so suggested that we should probably leave. With lumps in our throats we tried to put on cheery faces as we shook his hand, wished him well, and said our goodbyes.

As Dan and I drove toward home we each kept seeing over and over a picture in our minds of the amputee ward we had just visited at Oak Knoll Naval Hospital. That screaming Navy A-6 Intruder on a bombing run over a Vietnam jungle again, reminding us of a war getting increasingly closer to our personal lives. By early 1967, over 6,000 American troops had been killed in Vietnam, and the plan was to deploy about 470,000 troops by the end of 1967 against a backdrop of declining public support. From that point on, we became more motivated to explore all other military service possibilities in an effort to stay out of the Army and out of the rice paddies. Time would tell, however.

Admittedly, my only motivation for staying out of Vietnam was a fear of physical harm in an increasingly and seemingly senseless war, and a war not being fought by the United States like a war should be fought, to win conclusively. None of us were convinced about the "domino affect" the president was espousing. The politicians were fighting the war, and many Americans felt the government was pulling a bit of "flim flam". We just were not getting the truth, and the Vietnam War was being misrepresented to the people. Unlike Jack, I was not trying to elude danger because of an emotional relationship with a young woman. Jack obviously did not want that relationship compromised by the war. There was no one in my life at that time that fit into that category. A short while from then, however, that would change and I would be driven by the love and promise of a future with someone.

Dan and I headed back to Happy Valley the day after visiting Ron at the hospital. It was a quiet ride, as one might expect. We were deep in our own thoughts about the war, casualties, and how we would meet our obligation.

Immediately upon returning we organized a Raiders blood donation event at the local hospital for shipment to Oak Knoll Naval Hospital. It was the least we could to support the troops.

The next weekend I felt like getting away from it all so I visited a high school friend named Paul who was attending the University of California at Davis. I bummed a ride from a friend going to Sacramento, and arrived at Paul's apartment complex just north of the campus at about 3:00 in the afternoon. Paul, his roommates and their girlfriends already had a party going, and were big into the Mamas and the Papas. "California Dreamin'" and "Monday, Monday" still ring in my ears when I think back on that day. We drank some beers together, and a few of the people I noticed were hitting on some "grass", and Paul and I moved on elsewhere for some other parties.

They were good parties, but just didn't have the wild abandonment and excitement that our Raider parties had at Happy Valley. I suppose it could be speculated that the more intellectual set at Davis partied in a more subdued fashion than the Cal rejects at Happy Valley.

My ride picked me up Saturday night and with a still fuzzy head I slept most of the way back home an hour and a half away.

I was over at Iris Street the next day in time to catch the guys before they went for their weekly grocery shopping. The four of us, Dan, Jack, Benny, and I came out of the apartment to find "Sam" loitering about. "Sam", a Bassett hound, was our friend, and was obviously in the area looking for leftovers and steak bones that the guys customarily put out for him. He didn't need the extra food. His owner was a senior administrator at the college, Dr. Jenkins, who I am sure fed him well. We used to clown around with "Sam" and marvel at how much he resembled his owner, or visa versa. "Sam" even made the front page of the paper one year bedecked with New Year's confetti and a hot-water bottle sitting atop his head, ears hanging straight and low to the ground.

The Jenkins lived on the next street over, and we occasionally could hear "Sam" let out his trademark howl, a low-sounding, elongated "baarruuuww." Once in a while we heard "Sam's" howl at close range when he got a little cocky demanding food at the door to Apt. C.

"Hey, Sam," Benny called out.

The dog waddled over, tail wagging, and we all gave him a short pet before turning toward "the Volv", as we affectionately called Nancy's car. She often left the cream colored, '65 Volvo with Jack so he would have the wheels to come visit her. We also used it for laundry runs and grocery shopping trips.

Grocery runs were a riot. From the moment we piled into "the Volv" we were half in stitches, anticipating the crazy things we would do at the store. Grocery shopping for us was a release. It got us away from the books, off of Iris Street, and far from any worries on our collective minds.

There were a number of food stores closer to Iris but we were in the mood for a little ride and wanted to go to a larger store, so we headed through town, picked up Valencia, then turned left on Myrtle, traveling the short distance to a shopping center that had a Be-Lo supermarket.

We piled out of "the Volv" and into the store we went, single file. Jack grabbed a shopping cart and everyone started talking at once entreating on what should be purchased first. However, since Jack had the cart, he led the way. I didn't need anything, so I just followed. I was along for the fun, anyway, trying not to think of the Economics paper I should have been working on.

Our mark was left in each area of the store we visited.

We were all so wasted from the shopping experience that we sat relatively quiet in "the Volv" all the way back to Iris. Another fun, tumultuous grocery shopping trip to let off some steam. Back at Iris, however, it was time to get serious again about some studying.

In fact, we all got serious about studies during the following few weeks, which wasn't an easy task considering our building anticipation level for the upcoming Western Week. While it was always the same basic format and programs, we would undoubtedly find a way to make it different and better than previous Western weeks.

CHAPTER TWENTY-ONE

Western Week for me had an ignominious start. My Statistics professor did the unthinkable—he scheduled an exam during the week. Fortunately, the test was to be on Tuesday, which meant that I would only be out of action Monday night. No professor scheduled an exam for the latter part of the week, for students could barely stand up by that time, let alone have their faculties together to take an exam! I did not attend Presents Monday night, which was no great loss, and studied over at Dan's. I knew when Presents was over, for I could hear all the commotion outside from people walking to their dorms, apartments, and frat parties, and at that time I ventured back over to the fraternity house to allow myself a little bit of fun at the traditional post-Presents kegger there.

I spotted a girl that I had been noticing on campus and was anxious to meet. She was a freshman and lived in Lissen Hall, and did not appear to be with someone. I was standing on the front porch, which was about six feet above the ground, so I had a commanding view of the swarms of people that now milled around the yard. I saw her approaching the steps to the porch and hoped she would come up on the porch. She did, and I took the opportunity to meet her.

"Hi," I said.

"Hi," she replied, smiling. "You're not drinking," she observed.

"Not tonight. I've got an exam tomorrow. I'll let loose afterwards."

"A test? I thought professors didn't give tests during Western Week," she stated.

"Myth. Some do. Most don't. My name's Dave."

"Hi, Dave. I'm Debbie. What's your test on?"

"Statistics," I told her. I even said it without stuttering. The word could be a tough one to say sometimes.

She wrinkled her nose and gave an "ugh" sound.

"Where do you live, Debbie?" I already knew but asked anyway.

"Lissen Hall."

"Oh, I spent my first two years living in Sierra Hall. Had a great time."

"Yes. I like it, and I have a good roommate. There she is over there. Hi, Nancy!" she yelled across the yard, waving at her roommate. "Where do you live now?"

"Here. I'm in the fraternity."

"Where's your room?" Somehow I gathered she was asking only out of general curiosity.

"Right down the hall there." I saw her beer cup was near empty, so I offered to escort her to the small barn in the back of the house for a refill. On the way, I unlocked the door to my room so she could peek into it, and also showed her the trophy room on the way. We got to where the kegs were stationed, along with the long lines. One of the servers noticed me.

"Hey, Duke, need a beer?" It was one of the pledges, bless his soul.

"Sure do. Thanks." I stuck the cup into the waiting hand, ahead of those in line. Just in case people didn't appreciate what I did, the pledge set them straight.

"He's a Delta Phi, and gets head of line privileges." There were a few grumbles, but nothing more. After all, the beer was free to all.

"Thanks," Debbie said. "This is all I'm going to have. I really don't want to drink too much tonight."

Spoken like a true freshman, I thought to myself.

Debbie was a pretty girl, was about 5'2" tall, and had a fascinating walk. She stood erect and straight, which complimented the very nice figure she had. She had short, dark hair, and olive skin, and I noticed that night for the first time that she had magnificent eyes. I would later buy a poster that was a print of a Keene figure with its characteristically large, wondrous, and penetrating eyes.

We chatted for a while, and then Debbie let me know she needed to return to her dorm. I offered to give her a lift on the motorcycle, which she quickly and eagerly accepted, and led her to the front curb where the cycles were parked.

I took Debbie home, telling her it was a pleasure to have met her, and returned to the fraternity house where I promptly hit the rack. It was later than I had planned on staying up, but not too late to have a few lingering thoughts of Debbie before falling off to sleep.

I did well on the exam the following day, and upon getting out of the classroom headed for Iris Street where the residents of 309 Iris had planned a kegger. The kegger was a huge success, and we went through four kegs. We placed the keg off the sidewalk toward the back of the house where there was plenty of room for people to mingle. Many of the Raiders were there, and a lot of close friends. There was a lot of socializing and some serious beer drinking. The only RFing was by Buzzard when he started yelling "Cameel...camel-jockey's" in reference to the foreign students from the Middle East in the house next to 309 Iris. They wisely did not show their faces. Later that night Buzzard ripped off the bamboo curtains that hung on the outside of the windows facing 309 Iris. It was unanimous that the Tuesday kegger at Iris during Western Week become a tradition.

From the kegger we all went to the quad where a steak dinner was being served and projects were being erected by the various organizations. Most everyone walked the very short distance across the lot next to ours, then crossed W. First Street, walking by the library to where the projects were going up. However, Chip and I went to and through the quad on our motorcycles. Professor Mervin, the college treasurer quickly ordered us off before any trouble started. Before leaving the quad, however, I gave a delighted young boy a ride on my motorcycle, and caused a few missed heartbeats by gunning my motor before charging off in the opposite direction, away from Professor Mervin.

Chip and I took the bikes back to Iris and returned to the quad on foot, but we grabbed another cup of beer to take with us. We wandered around the projects, talking to folks we knew while they worked hard putting up the projects, and also attended a dance in the quad.

I had made the mistake of taking my fraternity beer mug to the quad, for sometime during the night I misplaced it. "Where the hell is my mug?" I kept asking others at the dance. Dan was asking everyone also. In fact, Debbie, who I had conveniently run into at the dance, told me the following day that Dan and I spared no one in our queries about the mug.

At the conclusion of the dance I walked Debbie home. I was really distraught over the presumed loss of my fraternity mug with the nickname Duke emblazoned, but was in great spirits the following morning when the mug was found sitting on Dan's windowsill outside the apartment. I did not know how it got there!

I was becoming somewhat infatuated over Debbie, but Western Week partying took precedence. On both Wednesday and Thursday afternoon our group attended keggers at another traditional Raider site, Paul Mastro's apartment on Rio Petaluma. It was a pretty setting, with a narrow street separating the older homes, now rented out as apartments, from the creek and tall trees lining its banks on both sides. There was very little traffic, so it was a peaceful, safe place to congregate and drink beer. From the kegger Wednesday night we went to Ghost Town, where I laughed my ass off at the poor souls going through the Block HV egg toss initiation rites.

I consumed my share of beers both nights, so wandered from party to party, event to event on the motorcycle with whoever wanted to join me.

Friday afternoon I attended a kegger at Ballentine's on Ranchero. It was a great party, and early on promised to be as good as the previous Ballentine kegger during which we started the tractor and dumped the cow on the women's dorm front porch. A couple former "flames" of mine were present, too.

"Hi, Phoebe," I said as congenially as I could. I was hoping she wouldn't have any flashback to the aborted apology attempt by Dan, Jack and me for our bad treatment of her while I lived at Sierra Hall the previous year. Apparently, it was history.

"Hi, Dave," she beamed, giving her head a little shake that sent her long, blond hair dancing from side to side. She had really beautiful hair. "How have you been? Gee, I never see you anymore."

"Oh, I've been fine, Phoebe. I guess we just don't go to the same places. But I've been around." As a sorority girl she wouldn't be seen in the Oasis, at any Raider parties, or at even the Block HV house. She might not even attend any functions with my fraternity, those wild guys with all the "choppers". "Where you headed?" I asked.

"I'm on my way to Terri's apartment. Do you want to come along?"

"Sure," I answered. Terri was a sorority sister of Phoebe's, and a friend of mine from high school. We walked across the courtyard from where the keg sat and walked upstairs to Terri's. Phoebe had a bottle of sloe gin with her, so I imbibed on some sloe gin fizzes between cups of beer.

The three of us sat in Terri's apartment, talking about Marshall and Little Daisy candidates, and how the Greeks were "burned out" with all the organized festivities they were expected to participate in during the past week. "In fact," Terri said, "I'm not even going to the rodeo tonight. I really don't care who wins Marshall and Little Daisy." I made a mental note that I wanted to get to the rodeo at a decent time.

So much for plans. I was having a good time visiting with Terri and Phoebe, and on one particular trip across the yard to the keg spotted an old flame named Annette, yelling a few unkind words at her.

"Dave," Ballentine told me, "you're rude, crude and socially unacceptable, but you're a good man, anyway," he shouted.

"That's right," I answered.

"Having a good time?" he asked.

"Sure am, Tim. In fact, I'd better get my ass out of here if I want to see any of the rodeo."

"I would say so, but it looks like you're running a tad late. I would say the rodeo is almost over."

"You might be right, Tim, but I'm on my way anyway. See ya." With that, I hopped on my cycle, started it up, and sped toward the fairgrounds at the other end of town. I arrived at the gate in time to see the last event. Disappointed that I hadn't arrived earlier, I compounded things by going to the dance at the auditorium on the fairgrounds. I was pretty wasted, so let a couple fraternity bothers take me home. A third brother drove my cycle back to the house.

As hung over as I was Saturday morning, I decided to join the other fraternity brothers who were riding their motorcycles in the parade that day. I managed to get on my jeans, cowboy boots and a vest. Mom and Dad, who had come up for the parade and lunch on the front lawn of the college Admin Building, were quite shocked when they noticed me in the parade, to say the least. After lunch with Mom and Dad, Brad, Dan, Jack, Chip, me, and a few others went to the "slide" out Alamo Road to swim and relax for the afternoon.

It was after that weekend that I started seeing a lot of Debbie and calling her in the evenings. The sad thing was that there was only a month and a half of school remaining, which meant a summer of separation ahead. I didn't want to think about that at the time, however. I took her to movies, a few keggers, on motorcycle rides out in Birdwell Park on its winding roads bordered by lush vegetation and the creek, and visited her dorm. In Birdwell Park we often stopped at secluded spots to be alone and share some intimacies.

The first weekend after Western Week, though, I took Toni Abramowiz to the Block HV letterman dinner-dance. It was a big affair, and Toni was a good friend, a Physical Education major, and a cute girl with a great personality, so I felt more comfortable taking her vice Debbie, who I was just getting to know. Toni and I often crossed paths in the gym where I spent a lot of time weightlifting. What a night!

"Toni, you look great," I exclaimed when she walked into the dorm lobby area from her upstairs room. She was with Donna, Cindy's roommate in the dorm. Toni and I were double dating with Benny and Donna, so I had picked up Benny earlier at Iris.

"Thank you, Dave," she replied. "You and Benny sure look nice tonight." It wasn't very often the girls saw us in coat and tie, which was just as well, for we much preferred our jeans, t-shirts, Block HV jackets, and low cut "black con" tennis shoes.

"Thanks, Toni. Well, let's go. I'm sure the party has started." I had traded wheels for the night with Dave Smith, my fraternity brother and fellow pledge class member—he had my cycle, and I had his Volkswagen. The four of us went to a cocktail hour at the apartment of a Block HV member. It was crowded, but fun, and Toni and I started drinking screwdrivers.

Toni may have felt she had to stay up with my drinking pace, which was agreeably slow, but shortly after arriving at the party she stated, "I'm going to keep up with you, drink for drink."

"Why would you want to do that?" I asked.

"I'm sure everyone thinks of me as a tee-totaling female jock," she answered, adding, "plus, I'm in a good mood tonight and really enjoying the evening. It's going to be a great night." I should have seen the potential disaster in her commitment, but I didn't. We went back to the liquor table a few times, and I ensured we had "good" drinks. The party was loud and festive, and everyone was having a good time "warming up" for the dinner dance afterwards.

Toni never saw the dinner dance.

Just prior to the time people were leaving to get to the Kiwanis Hall downtown for the dinner dance, the four of us departed, stopping en route at Lissen Hall so the girls could freshen up. Benny and I waited downstairs in the lobby for what seemed like hours. In our inebriated condition, we were acting our normal, boisterous, rowdy selves talking to others and cracking jokes.

Finally, Donna ventured downstairs and broke the stunning news.

"Dave," she lamented, "Toni drank too much at the party and is sick. She can't go anywhere right now. She feels terrible that she let this happen."

I wasn't in a sympathetic mood, and let some anger show. "Oh, hell. Great. That's just great." I stopped myself. I wasn't going to let it ruin the good mood I was in from the party and the vodka. "Are you ready to go, Donna?" I asked.

"Yes, but let me run back upstairs and see how Toni is doing one more time," she replied.

"Okay," I said.

"I don't believe this," Benny said to me a short while after Donna walked back upstairs.

"It's alright, Benny. I'll take you guys to the hall and then go get my cycle back from Dave. Do you think you can get a ride home from someone at the dinner dance?"

"No sweat."

"Good. Here's Donna," I replied as I saw her come through the door separating the lobby from the stairwell and the forbidden, off-limits-to-men zone above.

Dropping Benny and Donna off at the Kiwanis Hall, I drove to Dave's apartment on Ranchero, surprising him with my premature return. I was happy to find Dave there, for I was in a "testy" mood now and wanted my motorcycle back to roam. Dave understood and was happy to get his car back. Jean probably didn't like motorcycles anyway.

I raced off toward the Oasis, where I had a few beers.

By the time I left the "O" I was feeling pretty mellow. I kicked the stand up on the cycle and cranked it over. I now had Debbie on my mind, so I drove over to Lissen Hall and called for her from the lobby phone. Thank God, she was in.

"Debbie?" I asked in an expectant tone when I heard her voice on the other end.

"Yes?" she asked. "Dave, is that you? What's happened? I thought you and Toni were out. Nancy said she saw you two and Benny and Donna come into the dorm earlier tonight, and that you had told her you were going to a dinner-dance. She also said you and Benny looked like you were having a good time." She giggled a bit as she made that observation.

"Yes, that's right," I answered. "Well, to make a long story short, Toni got sick, so I took Benny and Donna to the dinner and then went to the Oasis. Are you busy doing anything right now?" I really wanted to see her.

"No. I'm just studying." Oh, my goodness, I thought to myself. Studying on a Saturday night at Happy Valley.

"Could you come downstairs for a while so I can see you?"

"Sure. I'll be right down."

Hot damn, I thought to myself. Debbie was downstairs about 10 minutes later, looking lovely in just a pair of jeans and a sweatshirt. After a nice visit I climbed on the bike and drove off. I found my way to the Beta Pheta house, noticing some activity there, parked the bike and walked in to look for a few of my Beta Pheta friends. I found Jim Preston, who after giving me a cup of beer asked if I wanted to join him in crashing some parties.

By the time we got back to the Delta Phi house I had had enough activity for the night. I passed out shortly after my head hit the pillow of my bed. Mercifully, my head did not spin, although all the indicators of a hangover welcomed me to the following day.

After getting my strength, I called both Toni and Debbie, and ended up taking both of them on motorcycle rides. I wanted to show Toni there were no bad feelings about the unfortunate occurrence the previous night. She felt miserable about the episode, but I convinced her everything was okay.

I took Debbie to a show that evening. I knew that Lucky, my roommate, was staying at his girlfriend's apartment that night, so made the suggestion that Debbie and I go back to the fraternity house. It was the first time I took her there, and we just layed on top of my bed listening to some records of Lucky's. I could feel her willingness for intimacy, so held her in my arms and we kissed passionately. She excited me as no other girl had ever done before. There was a sensuousness and mystery to her that stirred my emotions, not to mention her body pressed against my chest and her physical attractiveness. I knew better than to try anything more than passionate kissing and hugging, feeling that if she and

I were to spend more time together the romance would come naturally. I took her home after a wonderful evening together.

A friend of Benny's from his hometown was looking for a roommate for the following year, and because I didn't want to continue living at the fraternity house and wanted to get back to Iris, Jim and I made an agreement to share the two-bedroom apartment E at the back of 309 Iris. Jim was a serious student, but joined us for a few beers occasionally. He and I would get around Happy Valley in style in his 1964 Malibu Super Sport.

I saw Debbie most every night, and we were quickly becoming a pair on campus. I felt so good when with her, and so empty when away from her. I longed every day for the evening, when I would take the short trip to the dorm on the bike to visit with her either in the lounge or on walks to the nearby creek and it's secluded areas. I was head over heels and developing some very strong feelings toward her.

I now knew what Dan and Jack had previously experienced when I was wondering why they spent so much time with their girlfriends and had so little time for the guys. During that timeframe, I either was in class, studying at the library, or at the dorm with Debbie. We had talked about the upcoming summer, and while we didn't exactly live that close, I was encouraged realizing that her home in San Rafael, across the bay from Danville, was only about an hour away. The trick, however, would be to find a way to get to San Rafael. I was optimistic that I would manage to see her somehow or another. The unpleasant thought of having to go a week without seeing her during the summer was bothersome, however.

As the spring semester drew to a close campus activities dissipated to a trickle. Students were earnestly preparing for final exams, with many trying to make up for an entire semester of poor study habits. Because I worked hard all semester with my classes, final exams did not cause any undo trauma. That also meant I was able to justify continued evening trips to Lissen Hall to visit Debbie.

Final exams came and were over, and I was never so happy as to get out of my last exam, my Business Law final. My plans, as discussed with Debbie beforehand, included a bee-line to the "O" for a few beers with the other guys, then a visit with Debbie later that night. She was also to have her last final that day.

The "O" was hopping with celebrations over the conclusion of final exams, and the place was packed. Dan and Jack were already there, as well as Buzzard, a number of the Orland gang, and a host of other Raiders. I parked my cycle outside and walked in to a tumultuous welcome.

"Hey Pecker," a number of people yelled.

"Grab a beer, it's party time," was heard.

"Hey, everyone, it's over!" I yelled. I knew it wouldn't take long to make up for the head start some of the other guys had.

As we bellied up to the bar or stood around near the food service window conversation turned to reflections on various final exams, but mostly to what lay ahead for the summer.

"Buzzard," I asked, "what are you doing this summer?"

"Back to Fillmore to pick oranges again. Another hot, shitty summer lies ahead," he replied.

"How about you?" he asked.

"Well, at the moment it looks like I'll be pumping gas again for Standard Oil."

"Don't feel bad, Dave," Jack interjected, "at least you'll be able to make some money for school next year. I've got eight weeks of National Guard Officer training in the desert at Fort Irwin which means I'll get in about two to three weeks of work at the end of the summer if I'm lucky. I don't know what I'm going to do for money next year for school, but my folks have said they'll try to help out when they can. Maybe I can work a couple jobs during the school year. And working during Christmas break will be crucial." Poor Jack, I thought. What a hell of a way to spend a summer. But the consolation was that he wouldn't be classified 1-A for the Army draft when he graduated.

"How about you, Dan?" Buzzard asked.

"I'll be working in an electronics manufacturing plant in Richmond owned by Janie's uncle. It'll sure beat pumping gas," he observed.

We all chuckled and harassed Dan a bit over his good fortune in getting summer employment help from his girlfriend.

"Hey, screw you guys," he said good-naturedly. "I'll take it. I don't give a damn who helps me."

The owners of the "O" were in good spirits, and particularly enjoyed seeing a full house with happy, drinking customers. A few days from then the "O" would be almost deserted, and business would be dead until the start of the fall semester in September.

In between beers I made a couple quick trips to Lissen Hall to see Debbie. I had called, but she was not answering the subsequent pages by the front desk operator. I was becoming increasingly anxious to see her as the night went on. Not until my third trip to the dorm did I notice a note taped to the front door addressed to me. I was not expecting such an occurrence and feared for the worse as I took the note off the door.

I opened the envelope to find the following:

"Dear Dave:

I'm sorry I couldn't see you tonight. My ride unexpectedly decided to leave tonight instead of tomorrow. I hope you have fun tonight and did well on your exams. Please call me."

Short and sweet, I thought. I was really devastated, for my expectation level on seeing her had really built up. All kinds of thoughts and emotions ran through my head. Why hadn't she at least tried to call me? She knew I would be at the "O". And yet, in a small, though incongruous way, I felt a little bit relieved that I would be spared the discomfort and agony of saying goodbye to Debbie not knowing when, or even if, I would see her next. I folded the note, placed it in a pocket, and went back to the "O", now more than ever ready to let off some steam. All the guys were still there, so I bought another beer and got back into the celebration.

One of the guys suggested I call Myrna and that we make a little trip to her place, but I was not ready for her and had no inclination to crawl into her sack. No, thanks.

The next day Dan and I were packed and ready to go when Dad arrived with a trailer in which we put the motorcycles and our belongings. I had already moved out of the fraternity house and left a number of things in the apartment at the Iris apartment that Jim and I would share the following semester.

One could tell the Vietnam War was catching up to us that Summer. Jack was going off to Fort Irwin in the California desert for National Guard training, and Rob had told us the week prior that he was going to San Diego for the first segment of his Naval Officer Training.

One of the first things I did upon arriving at home was to call Debbie. Mom and Dad agreed to let me have the car for the upcoming Saturday so I could drive over to Marin County to visit her. It was great seeing her, plus I had the good fortune to get a summer job through her neighbor. He worked for a large, national trucking firm headquartered in Oakland, where he was a senior manager. I would be working in the Finance department doing some statistical analysis work. It worked out beautifully, for it turned out that a neighbor in Danville also worked there and was able to give me a ride to and from work.

Debbie and I were able to see each other every weekend. Sometimes I was able to have the use of the family car for Saturday and Sunday. The drive to Marin County took me over the Benicia Bridge, through Vallejo, and over Black Point Cut-Off. Each time I made that trip, I thought of seeing Debbie and the corresponding excitement level skyrocketed as I drove over the last large hill on Black Point Cut-Off and saw the hills of Marin County ahead. A few more miles and I exited the highway, making my way toward her house.

Dad fortunately had a company car, so my taking the family car did not leave them without transportation. Of course, Dan needed the car at times too, although Janie lived only a few miles from Danville and was usually able to get the use of her mother's car for their weekend dates.

On the rare occasions when I was unable to get the family car, Dad drove me as far as Vallejo and I hitch hiked to Marin County. Hitchhiking was safe and a normal occurrence in the 60's, so it was never a problem getting a ride. On a couple weekends I got a ride to San Rafael from Debbie's neighbor, Mr. Richards, after work on Friday, spent the entire weekend at Debbie's, and went back to work Monday morning with Mr. Richards. That was the "cat's meow", for I would have three nights with Debbie instead of the normal one.

During my weekend visits we normally went to Stinson Beach, a favorite place of hers and spent all day laying on the beach and playing in the ocean surf. We packed huge "dagwood" sandwiches for lunch. Her choice of swimsuits accentuated her fine body and I would literally go nuts looking at her as she lay close to me on her beach towel. I wanted to hold her and caress her more than the public setting permitted. I could not get enough of her, and took advantage of every possible opportunity to hold her and touch her fantastic body.

When the weather wasn't nice, or we wanted to do something different, we drove to San Francisco to take in its' many beautiful sights. A day in Golden Gate Park meant strolls among the many trails, sitting arm in arm on a bench next to one of the lakes, or visiting the Aquarium. We went to Fleishacker Zoo, to the boardwalk on the ocean where we would also walk on the beach and watch angry waves pound the shore, and to Union Square to watch the multitudes of people and to window shop at the large department stores. Ghiradelli Square was always a fascination, and we often had a deli sandwich at a favorite restaurant there.

And other times we stayed in Marin County and visited Sausalito with it's many specialty shops, the Kettle restaurant for a deli lunch, and the Broadway building with it's "Little Lombard Street" leading to countless shops up and down four levels. Sausalito was a romantic place for us, particularly because we often looked through the window of Eaton's and marveled over its exquisite jewelry. Sitting on the benches along the waterside we watched the sailboats twisting through San Francisco Bay waters and observed and listened to the squawking seagulls searching and clambering over scraps of food in the water. I even splurged one night and took her to dinner at the Ondine. Saturday night at the "No Name" bar in Sausilito was always fun.

Evenings on those precious weekend visits normally meant a drive-in movie, of course. We were rarely interested in what movie was playing and hoped it wasn't too obvious! Even when we had been to the drive-in I looked forward to our return to Debbie's home, for we would sit on the couch in the living room and normally played the album, "A Man And A Woman" which was fantastic mood music.

One weekend Dan joined me for a trip over to Marin County. He was going to stay at Brent's Saturday night while I was visiting Debbie. Brent had called and asked us to visit. He had said he wanted to discuss something with us. Dan and I pulled into his driveway and got out of the car, still discussing and speculating over what Brent wanted to talk to us about. He met us at the door, and led us into the living room where we were surprised to see Eileen. San Rafael was a long way from Los Angeles, and she wasn't just in town for a weekend visit. Her parents, we knew, could not afford to fly her up for something so frivolous. Eileen was not her usual ebullient, bubbling self, and had a reticent look on her face. Dan and I still hadn't figured it out when Brent broke the news to us.

With a very solemn face, and with a hand in one of Eileen's hands, he looked at us and said, "Eileen and I think highly of you two and therefore wanted you to be the first to know. Eileen is pregnant and we'll be getting married this Summer." Eileen looked down momentarily at the floor, too embarrassed to look at us.

Holy shit. Dan and I looked at each other, then back at Brent and Eileen. This kind of news was beyond our imagination, and because we were sensitized after many reminders from Mom and Dad that we would be on our own if we ever knocked someone up, we were stunned and felt frightened and concerned for Brent and Eileen.

"Wow," was all I could say. That didn't do wonders for Brent and Eileen, I'm sure, for they were looking for our support.

Dan was more helpful. "How do you guys feel?" he asked. "What do your parents say?"

Brent replied, "We're a bit frightened, but we'll be okay. We made this mess for ourselves, so we need to accept it and work things out. Our parents are hurt and disappointed, but they've told us they will help where they can." Brent was an honest, conscientious, hard working, stand-up guy, and he was treating this new episode in his life like a man and as I thought he would. This was in character. It was obvious Brent and Eileen had discussed this. I saw the same spirit and effort that we saw in him on the football field, where he overcame lack of size with a heart as big as a melon.

"Good," I said. "You guys will be okay, and you don't have to worry about any negative thoughts from us. I know I speak for Dan when I say we understand and feel your disappointment. We also appreciate the challenges you have lying ahead. We'll help you in any way we can. And I am certain others in Happy Valley will feel the same way. We're friends."

"Thanks," Eileen said, speaking for the first time. A smile on her face told us our attitude lifted a big weight off her shoulders. She was obviously very worried about what their close friends would think about their predicament. "It means a lot to us to have told you and to get your support. We sure made a mess of things," she added, looking at Brent. Her eyes said she needed all the help he could muster.

"What about school next year?" I asked.

"We'll be in Happy Valley," Brent answered with conviction. "We're not going to let this stop our educations. We'll find a way to make it."

"Great," Dan replied. "I'm sure you can find a nice apartment that's affordable."

"Yes," Brent said. "We'll both take courses this Fall, and Eileen will be out of school in the spring. She'll finish her education later, I'm sure of that." He squeezed her hand, and gave an optimistic look that told her he meant what he said. She smiled back at him, understanding and acknowledging what was to be. "Eileen's going to fly back to L.A. Monday to continue working down there, and will come back up here in August when we'll get married and go up to Happy Valley to find an apartment."

"And Brent's going to play football this year," Eileen added enthusiastically. "He should not be denied that, regardless of the circumstances." It was plainly obvious that they were in fact to receive some help from their parents. Brent wasn't on a scholarship, since Happy Valley was in a non-scholarship conference, but would have had to work more than the normal two hours a day that all of us worked in the school food services operations.

"Everything's going to be all right, you two," I stated with sincere optimism.

"Thanks. We hope so," Brent answered. Brent, of all people, would find a way to make things work.

With that, I politely excused myself. I was anxious to get to Debbie's a few miles up the freeway. "I'll see you about 4:00 o'clock tomorrow, Dan, okay?"

"Sounds fine. See you then and say Hi to Debbie."

"Say hello to Debbie for us, Dave," Eileen added in a cheerful tone.

"I shall, and thanks. See ya." I quickly strode to the car. I couldn't wait to see Debbie and to hold her in my arms. As I drove the short distance to her house I reflected on what had just taken place at Brent's. Even though Debbie and I had not made love, what happened to Brent and Eileen still scared me enough to be super cautious when and if the moment came when Debbie and I would show our feelings for each other with intimate love-making.

The Summer passed all too quickly, particularly so after Debbie informed me that she had decided to enroll in a special 2-year nursing degree program at a local junior college. She was extremely serious about her studies, and had decided she wanted to be in an accelerated degree program rather than the long, drawn out four-year program at Happy Valley. I was pleased for her professionally, but completely devastated by the dual thought that we would now be three hours drive apart and that the likelihood of seeing each other every weekend was extremely remote. I knew I could trust her, and she assured me so, but I still had concerns. She also sought my devotion. I told her I didn't want to date anyone else, which was so easy to say when she was in my arms and I looked into her eyes. Little did I know that I would be the one to compromise that trust, on more than one occasion during the ensuing school year.

On a mid-week day, a day before class registration for me, I rode my cycle to Debbie's to say goodbye before continuing on to Happy Valley. Dan was already at school for football practices, and had told me that Jack, Benny and my new roommate, Jim, were also in town, along with most of the other guys, again particularly due to football. It was almost like deja-vu with my Freshman year. I wasn't playing football my senior year, so many of my close friends were in Happy Valley ahead of me.

With a lump in my throat as big as a grapefruit, and shoes that felt like lead weights, I said goodbye to Debbie.

"You take care of yourself," I told her. "I'll be thinking of you always, and I'll write often. Be good, okay?" I still needed her reassurances!

"I will. Don't worry. I'm really going to be busy with my studies. I won't have time for anything or anyone else. Have fun, okay? But you be good, too."

"Don't worry. I love you, Debbie." I was starting to get choked up, and had to get the hell out of there.

"I love you, too, Dave." I could sense she was also choked up. I held her one last time, gave her a big squeeze, and kissed her affectionately. Taking my arms away, I cranked over the bike's motor, kicked it into first gear, and raced off. I couldn't look back. Plus, the prospect of a three- hour ride to Happy Valley on the motorcycle was not pleasant. I had the emptiest feeling in my stomach I had ever experienced. Even saying goodbye to Mom and Dad my freshman year didn't cause such an emotion, for I was anxious for school and prepared for the goodbye. This was different. Debbie and I had really developed a close and a bonding relationship. It really tore the hell out of me and created a profound loneliness I had never before felt.

It was a long, sad three hours to Happy Valley, and nothing could change that. Even seeing all the guys again could not compensate for the emptiness I felt from leaving my love Debbie behind and three hours away. Something told me this would be a very different kind of school year for me. I was in extremely familiar surroundings, but felt an imbalance. The person I cared about the most was far away. We were all changing as we entered into our fourth year of college and approached 21 years of age. And the distant drumbeats of war from across the Pacific Ocean were getting louder and closer all the time.

CHAPTER TWENTY-TWO

I was in love with Debbie, and missed her terribly. This had a pronounced affect on my behavior at Happy Valley as I started my senior year. I inadvertently cut myself off from a lot of the social ties that were my mainstay in previous years. Oh, sure, I still got around, but not with the frequency that had made me look like a social moving target the year before.

During the week, my studies came first. I was taking a heavy load so I could graduate in June and get back down to the Bay Area and closer to Debbie. Accelerating my course work was my focus as I consciously made plans for the future based on Debbie. As well thought-out as those plans were, however, there was one matter that I had very little control over—the draft. Uncle Sam was taking 36,000 young men a month, and I knew for a fact that I would get a diploma in one hand the following June and a 1-A draft classification in the other. Great. Just great. I had to do something to keep the 1-A from materializing, which meant I would explore all legal options—medical, National Guard, anything. Why did I have to go and fall in love and create this monster dilemma? The stress, anxiety, and most of all the uncertainty plagued at me constantly. I "banged my head" against a wall trying to study all week fighting the temptation to dwell on Debbie. On Fridays when she was not coming up, I usually bought some beer, drank in front of Iris, and then cruised around on my motorcycle searching for a kegger to put my loneliness at greater distance.

I wrote to Debbie about two or three times a week, and then even rode the cycle downtown to drop the letter in the Post Office for early mailing the next day. When I could take it no longer, I called her, even though I could not afford the phone bills. The nice thing was that she was always home when I called, and it was fantastic hearing her voice, albeit so distant.

My roommate, Jim, and I got along fine, and took turns cooking dinner. Whenever we fixed steaks it was a sure bet that somewhere in the process we would have flames in the broiler pan. Nothing like a little melodrama before dinner.

Oftentimes during the week, and on weekend nights, I visited Toni. Toni and I became close friends after the dinner-dance fiasco. At her apartment, which was a short walk up Iris and over half a block on 4th Street, we often sat around talking and playing cards. She had some neat roommates, which made the visits even more fun, and one of her roommates pressed my shirts for me for a quarter apiece. I paid Toni to type some of my school papers. She knew I missed Debbie a lot, and consoled me, trying to make things easier on me. I appreciated her friendship and her understanding.

Things had changed so much from my earlier years at Happy Valley. Because Dan and Jack had steady girlfriends that they spent a great deal of time with, I rarely saw them on the weekends. Brent and Eileen had an apartment on the east side of town living in the same complex as one of the Sanchez twins and his wife, Mary Jane. Rob Maguire had a girlfriend, Lynn, as did Stan, one of the roommates at Hopewell. Chip dated off and on. The parties went on, just like before, but it seemed like the pace was different. It was probably because we didn't get as crazy and obnoxious as we did in our first three years of Happy Valley. We weren't breaking things or bullying our way around a dance floor, that's for certain.

Maybe the sobering and thought provoking reality of world events was a factor. Certainly the marriages were. All of us except Jack were staring down the gun barrel of the draft. And like a dummy, I was accelerating my studies to graduate on time! Most of the guys had figured on extending their studies, what they referred to as "the five-year plan." Put off Uncle Sam another year. Why not? Most everyone didn't want to leave Happy Valley anyway. Why leave "paradise" to return to smoggy L.A. or the crowded San Francisco Bay Area? What was the hurry to go out and earn a living or face the draft? Life at Happy Valley was self-perpetuating, whether it was Block HV activities, the Greeks (I had a fraternity brother who in his mid-30's could not cut the proverbial umbilical cord), or Western Week. And one could always find something to do. The sororities always needed some guys around expert in carpentry to help them with homecoming floats and Western Week quad projects. That also created opportunities to find someone to date. Hey, open a hamburger stand in town and stick around for a while! Just don't let the Summer heat and blahs get you down. Plus, housing was cheap.

Our Raiders buddy and my fraternity brother, Rancher, was denied the opportunity to hang out in Happy Valley for he was taken from us early. He had been up at beautiful Lake Tahoe during the previous Summer scuba diving with a businessman friend from town. King Neptune got him. He never surfaced from a dive in the mile-deep, cold, clear, blue waters of Lake Tahoe. Rumors spread that the catastrophic accident was faked, that he was heavily burdened with debt and up to his butt in financial problems, and that he was probably in 'ol "Mehico" drinking cold beers on the lovely sandy Mazatlan beaches.

And "Taco", our neighbor and football teammate at Iris, was different that year. He had always been Mr. Happy Go Lucky. Nothing bothered the lovable, fun-loving Chicano. His '45 Dodge was missing that year, too. We found out why shortly after returning to school. All of us were torn up when we heard the news about the car accident. Taco and a popular guy on the football team, Jimmy Halton, had stayed in Happy Valley for the summer. One night, after they had been drinking heavily, they were carousing in Taco's car. Taco had lost control, didn't make a turn in the road out by the river, and the car slammed into a tree. Taco came out all right, but Jimmy died from his injuries. The guys on the football squad were devastated and dedicated the season to Rancher and Jimmy. Taco kept to himself much of the time and really quieted down, so we didn't see much of him. It was amazing how so many different incidents were impacting our previously carefree lives. Benny with his car accident, Jack joining the National Guard, Rob going to Naval Officer training, a Sanchez married, Brent and Eileen married, Rancher taken from us, Taco in an accident that killed one of our football buddies, our grade school friend Ron back from Nam missing part of his leg, and another friend, Tim, dead from the war. And two of our freshman football buddies were casualties of the war. Paul and Tim had both let their class loads fall. Eventually, Paul took off for Canada, and Tim left school with a severe case of depression. No one was immune…the war, the draft, relationships, but there was still motorcycle riding and party hopping for me that served as a temporary equalizer.

There were times when I decided that if I couldn't be near Debbie I didn't want to be around anyone. I had favorite roads on which I took the motorcycle to escape or beat the boredom, mostly to fight the loneliness of Happy Valley without Debbie. Where Pizon's Pizza stood on Colley Avenue, just over the creek, a left turn put me on Birdwell Avenue, a winding, twisting, tree-lined road. I often took the bike out that road as fast as I could, leaning into turns with exhilaration. The twisting part of the road ended at Glenwood, which I took to Colley Avenue, making a left turn to head out toward the river and it's isolation.

I also took rides through town, picking up Hibiscus Way, speeding or cruising through beautiful Sutter Park, thick with foliage. I saw couples somewhat hidden in secluded spots along the creek and envied them. I wanted to be with Debbie in one of those hidden-away places. At Sutter Oak, or at the swimming hole at Five-Mile, I turned around and went back the same way I had come. But I was never in a hurry to return to Iris, for that meant acute loneliness or studying, the latter difficult to do at times.

The loneliness got the best of me a couple of times. On one of those occasions the evening started at the Beta Pheta house around the corner from my fraternity house. I had reverted to being somewhat of a Raider independent, although I of course maintained my Delta Phi membership, so I roamed from place to place to drink beer with friends.

On a warm Fall Friday night I pulled up in front of the Beta Pheta house and parked the motorcycle. My old friend Jim Preston had told me on campus that day to come by the house as the fraternity was planning to have a kegger. I spotted Jim up on the large front porch.

"Jim!" I yelled. "How's it going?"

"Just great, Dave. Come on up." When I got up on the porch Jim put a cup of beer in my hand and I recognized a few other guys I knew well. I knew many of the Beta Phetas and they never had an objection to my occasional appearances to drink with them. And they never charged me.

"Thanks. How's everyone doing?" I asked.

"It's Friday night, and the beer's cold. What else matters?" someone replied.

"You got it," I said. The conversation was animated. I decided to bring up a memory from the past. "Jim, remember that night a couple years ago when you happened along at just the right time to help me out of a bad jam with the police?"

"I sure do," he said.

"No repeats, right?" I said in jest.

"Right. I'm just glad I was able to help you. And then you turn right around and smash up my car! What a way to repay my kindness!" He was laughing, as were a few of the others standing around the keg.

"Oh, thanks for bringing that up, Jim, old buddy."

I couldn't help chuckling myself, even though I remember being deeply distressed when the incident occurred the previous year. I had borrowed Jim's VW bug to drive up to Herlong to see a girlfriend. Coming back down the mountain the next day I failed to negotiate a turn after hitting some unseen ice on the road and spun out. The car headed into the embankment on the other side of the road and left the car with a crunched in right fender. I was pissed. What would Jim say when he got his car back in such a condition after loaning it out? Actually Jim had been pretty good about it and even referred me to a car body mechanic who did the work for a decent price. The expense wiped out my living allowance for a couple weeks, however.

"You're welcome, my good friend," he said, laughing.

I stayed at the Beta house for about an hour or so, then said goodbye and thanked them for the brew. I got on my bike, and headed for my fraternity house, where a large party was in full swing. I wound the bike out those two blocks, and upon taking the turn on Hemlock Street from 4th lost control of the bike. I laid that sonovabitch down. I don't know which hurdled the farthest on the asphalt, me or the bike. The bike and I were about 5 feet apart from each other when we came to a rest. Needless to say, the noise got the attention of a lot of people at the party, many of whom saw me promptly get to my feet virtually uninjured but for a scrape on my knee and a mean strawberry on my left elbow and forearm.

Someone from the fraternity house yard yelled out, "Duke, you okay?"

"Yeah, I'm fine," I answered. I couldn't feel a thing, almost. I walked over to the bike, got it to an upright position, straightened a foot peg out, started it up, and drove to the front of the house to a hail of cheers and hoorahs. After examining my injuries, I decided I needed some medical attention, but not an emergency room. And I knew they didn't have a first aid kit in the fraternity house. I had the bright idea to drive to Cindy's apartment to get some medical attention and do some more socializing. Cindy and I were on good speaking terms, and I was good friends with her other roommates, Donna, Sue and Carol. They lived out W. 2nd Street, near Brad Steven's apartment, so off I went.

I banged on the door, hopeful that Cindy would be home to give me some first aid. In my inebriated state I was looking for some sympathy and attention, and it would be great to get it from Cindy. Sue answered the door, surprised to see me unannounced.

"Hi, Dave. It's a surprise seeing you. How are you?" she said in her sweet voice.

"Oh fine, Sue. Except for a little matter of some injuries I sustained a few minutes ago falling off the bike."

"How bad is it?" she asked. "Let me see."

I showed her the knee, with the torn jeans, and the strawberry on my elbow and forearm. I hadn't had a chance to wash them out, so there was a lot of dirt and small gravel pieces evident. It was also beginning to hurt.

"Oohh. You took a nasty fall. Well, let's see if nurse Sue can help you out. Come on in."

"Thanks, Sue," I said, gratefully. I didn't need to ask where Cindy and her other roommates were. As we walked into the living room Sue said, "Cindy, Donna and Carol are at the TKE, Gamma Delta function at the TKE house." Sue was in a different sorority, Tri-Delt's.

"Oh," I replied. I was in good hands with Sue, and could not have had more attractive help. She was tall, with long brunette hair, and had a very pretty face. In fact, she had been a homecoming queen candidate during the past football season and had come in a close second in the voting.

She washed my strawberries out and found some gauze and tape, and actually did a pretty fair job of getting my wounds properly cleaned and dressed. When she finished I complimented her on the first aid and thanked her profusely.

"You're very welcome, Dave. Just be a little more careful on that bike, okay?"

"Okay, Sue. I know what you mean. I'll see ya. Take care." And I was gone, back to the Beta Pheta house to look up Jim.

Jim and I drove over to the TKE house, where we took a little razing from some of their members for showing our faces. But we knew a number of other TKE's and were "safe" from any serious confrontation. I talked to Cindy for a while, and Jim found a girlfriend of his to talk to while I was preoccupied. Cindy was anxious to leave the party, so we discussed the idea of going somewhere together. I said goodbye to Jim, and Cindy gave me a ride back to my bike. From there, I followed her to her apartment. Sue had gone somewhere, so we had the place to ourselves.

We shared a couple hours together on the couch, and it brought back fond memories of an earlier time hugging to music by Johnny Mathis, Glen Yarborough and the Righteous Brothers. It wasn't homerun time, but we definitely picked up where we left off before the break up about two years ago. Before I left that night she asked if I wanted to attend a barbecue the next night with her at a sorority sister's apartment. I said, "Yes, that would be very nice."

"Good," she answered. We agreed that we would meet at her apartment, and that we would go over in her car. I can't imagine why she didn't want to go on my motorcycle.

The next day, I thought about the previous night. While Cindy and I really didn't do anything except for some heavy kissing, I was disappointed in myself. Would it bother me if Debbie had done something similar? Damn right it would.

The barbecue was a lot of fun, and fortunately Debbie's old dorm roommate, now a sorority sister of Cindy's, was not at the party. At the party, Cindy expressed a wish, albeit a half-hearted one I feel, that we could go back together again. "Cindy," I replied, " I really enjoyed last night. It felt nice being close to you again, but I care a lot about Debbie. I'm extremely happy with her, even though we don't see much of each other." That was the end of any conversation on the topic. Still, I felt like a real jerk about what I had done to Debbie.

One night the following week as I was sitting around with Dan, Jack and Benny in their apartment, the conversation turned to Vietnam.

"What do you plan on doing about the draft when you graduate?" Jack asked. The guys knew I was accelerating my studies so I could graduate the following June.

"I don't know, Jack. I honestly haven't the slightest idea what course to take," I replied. Like everyone else, I was on my own. I would have to resolve the matter myself.

"For whatever it's worth," Benny started, then hesitated a moment, "don't even try to get into any of the local reserve or Guard units. They already have waiting lists. Unless you have some great connections you're wasting your time."

"Yeah, that's what I heard," I dejectedly stated. "I've been told about some units around Sacramento. Maybe I'll try down there. It's worth the effort." My relationship with Debbie changed the complexion of things tremendously. I too often ran a horrifying scenario through my mind that went like this: Debbie and I would be going steady or be engaged to get married when my "number would come up" and I would be standing on her doorstep saying goodbye, asking her to wait only two or three years for me while I was sloshing around in the rice paddies. For some reason, the thought of her waiting for me didn't seem realistic, and the notion of losing her was not a pleasant thought.

"I've heard some cases where guys have been exempted, you know, 4-F, due to some strange medical condition," Jack stated. He was trying to be helpful and encouraging, but hell, I was a perfect physical specimen and in excellent health. Fit for duty.

"Well, there is one thing," I replied. "Ever since I had that gymnastics injury my freshman year my left shoulder isn't as flexible as it should be. I can't rotate it or lift it like my right shoulder." I lifted my right arm, extended, in a circular motion upward, then did the same with my left arm until it "locked" in a position about 10 o'clock.

"Wow, that's really something," Dan indicated with surprise.

I decided to see a doctor about it. The next day I called and made an appointment with an orthopedist. A couple visits to the doctor resulted in a diagnosis of limited motion in the arm and the offer of treatment by cortisone shots. I took the written diagnosis information for future use, and declined the shots. Still fit for duty.

Two strikes against me—no local reserve unit and no significant medical problem that would make me 4-F. I was healthy enough to go off to war. So much for that.

Grab a few beers, sit on the front steps of Iris, put on "The Doors", "The Good, The Bad, and The Ugly", or a James Bond movie soundtrack, and lay back. What the hell? Let the chips fall where they may. Right! No, I would keep trying.

Debbie drove up to Happy Valley every second or third weekend. It was fantastic when she visited. She generally arrived about mid-afternoon, with me anxiously waiting outside for her. We would go up into the apartment, and I would usually give her time to at least remove her coat before I slapped a big, affectionate hug on her. We talked for a little while before laying down on the bed for the special moments of closeness. I was eager to touch her and feel her searching, caressing hands. Ecstasy.

When finished with our much-anticipated tenderness, we would lay on the bed, close together and remind one another how much the other was missed. Eventually, we went out for some dinner, then find a party.

The weekend of October 28th was special. I had decided to give her my fraternity pin as a symbol of my devotion to her. I had suggested in one of my letters that I had something I wanted to give her, so that when she arrived that Friday she was keyed up and excited to learn more about what was in store. The apartment was empty as we entered it. That was something great about Jim. When he knew Debbie was coming up he spent very little time at the apartment. Gave us lots of privacy. The only problem was that the only bathroom was off my bedroom, so he just sneaked through in the mornings.

I put on some mood music—my favorites, like Johnny Mathis, Glenn Yarborough, Johnny Rivers, and an instrumental that had string renditions of some music with a South Pacific Islands flavor, and Debbie and I engaged in intimacies so eagerly awaited from the previous time we were together. Afterwards, before we went out to a party I had been invited to, I felt it was time to offer her the pin. There was some uncertainty in my mind as to whether or not she would accept it.

"Debbie," I said with some hesitation, "I would feel very honored if you would wear my fraternity pin."

Her reaction and its' obvious sincerity was beyond my expectations. "Oh, Dave, I'd love to. I was hoping so much this would happen. I'll wear it all the time." We hugged tight enough to stop our breathing and added a long kiss to punctuate our expressions of love for one another. I was very taken by her sincerity, and she was equally moved with my asking her to wear the pin. I helped her put it on the green sweater she was wearing, and we went off to the party. She sat on my lap during much of the party and occasionally would turn to kiss me, saying, "I'm so happy, Dave." I felt like a million bucks. More so than ever before I now needed to get hot on finding a reserve unit so this sweet little thing wouldn't get away from me.

That Sunday night she called me from home to tell me how happy she was, how happy her parents were, and to tell me that it was all because of her excitement about the pin that she got stopped for speeding by a highway patrolman and received a ticket. Nothing to worry about though, she told me, and we laughed it off.

I was really acting strange from the longing I felt for Debbie and the pressure of the draft. Benny, Dan and Jack got a little irritated with me at times. Occasionally, while studying with them in their apartment, I would suddenly become restless and disenchanted with studying. I would pack up and go to the "O" for a couple beers. There was normally quite a crowd on those Wednesday and Thursday nights, made up of those who either had late morning classes the next day or took school lightly. I was either one or the other, depending on the circumstances.

Along with Toni, one of my other female friends was a high-school friend of Cindy's named Kathy. She and her twin sister, both of which had beautiful blond hair and pretty features, had gone to American River Junior College their first two years and had transferred up to Happy Valley that year as Juniors. Kathy was very friendly and probably a little lonely, for she would occasionally drop by Apt. E to talk. We would sit on the steps outside and chat about a multitude of things. We often ran into each other at the laundromat up Iris Street at the corner of W. Sixth Street. If I had not been pinned, I'm sure I would have been interested in more of a relationship with Kathy or to resurrect a relationship with Cindy, for that matter. Or Toni.

As a good friend, I came to her aid one Saturday night. We were at the same party and she was obviously quite drunk. Afraid she might be taken advantage of I offered to take her home. She accepted. I stayed around for a little while to make sure she was all right, and then returned to my place to retire early.

Life just didn't seem quite fair about then. My love was three hours away, and life wasn't very uncomplicated anymore. Gone were the simple days of early years at Happy Valley when all we really cared about was engaging in small time sports programs, be they football, gymnastics, wrestling, or soccer and keeping our grades up so we could stay in school. I doubt very many of us really had much of a cogent idea of how we were "preparing ourselves for the future" but we generally studied hard and took our class work seriously. We were in college because college was the thing to do and we certainly wanted to be there. And we wanted to improve our odds at landing decent jobs and careers after college. Fortunately, Happy Valley was inexpensive, so that made going to college affordable. Besides sports and classes, we lived from Friday to Friday, on the lookout for the best parties to attend. We had such great times together drinking beer, going to swimming holes, listening to music, and "R.F.ing." The only thing we took more seriously was stretching our meager finances and getting a keg back for the deposit. We didn't even take our partying seriously—it just happened. Other times, we made things happen.

Our lives were becoming complicated by the complexities of an unknown future revolving around girlfriends, jobs after graduation, and the draft. Plus, I guess we were growing up, maturing, and preparing to face life after college. Even the partying I did on weekends Debbie wasn't visiting lacked vitality. I hit Ranchero apartments with old friends, but had an empty feeling. It just wasn't the same. My love interest had a definite impact on my final year of school.

My most relaxing times were sitting in the sun straddling the motorcycle listening to good music coming from Dan's apartment on a Friday afternoon. I remember well one drizzly Saturday afternoon during football season. In an effort to get out of the rainy weather I went to the "O", where I ran into friends, had a couple beers, and watched a fabulous performance by USC and O.J. Simpson against Notre Dame. I got back to our football stadium in time to see the conclusion of the Happy Valley game and to follow some of the players into the locker room.

The following weekend Happy Valley was playing at U.C.-Davis, so by pre-arrangement, Debbie talked her parents into driving up for the game. That way, she and I could see one another, and our parents could sit together and visit during the game. I got down to Davis early that Saturday and looked up my good friend from high school, Jerry, that was in our group that spent a week at lake Twain Harte before my sophomore year and that was in a fraternity there. He lived in the house, which fortuitously was a stone's throw from the football stadium.

I met Debbie and her parents and led them into the stands to where my parents were sitting. Greetings were exchanged and we settled into watching a football game that turned into one of the longest in conference history due to not one, but two heart attack incidents on the field. One involved a player, the other an official. Shortly into the second quarter I made a move.

"Mom and Dad, Debbie and I are going to take a walk," I said doing all I could to act natural and not look like I had ulterior motives. I have a feeling her parents knew exactly what I had in mind. My parents may not have made a connection then, but it's a sure bet they wondered what we had been up to when we returned an hour later!

"Sure thing, son, hurry back," Dad replied. He was intent on the game and watching Dan play.

Down the bleacher steps we walked. "Where are we going?" Debbie asked.

"You'll see. We're going to my friend's fraternity house." Debbie may have missed the physical contact between us as much as I did, but she was a bit skeptical of traipsing off in a strange place to see just another fraternity house. Yes, I was resourceful when it came to finding a way to have some privacy with Debbie for a little intimacy.

"Are you sure you want to do this? Our parents may wonder where we've been?" she asked. She was obviously a little worried about this little caper.

"We'll be alright, and we won't be very long. It's right over here," I said as the house came into view after exiting a nearby stadium gate. I led her into the empty house, then upstairs to Jerry's loft room. There, I didn't hesitate for one second to take her into my arms and kiss her passionately. All those feelings of longing and loneliness at Happy Valley, mixed with a growing fear of the unknown, found release as we laid down on the bed and began to search each other's anxious bodies with a pent up passion.

The worry I was feeling about the draft was temporarily allayed. The fear of losing Debbie was always more pronounced

229

after intimacy, and continued to eat at me because of growing uncertainty about the future. The time close together was so satisfying, but I could never get enough of her. Thirty minutes after intimacy I wanted to touch her gorgeous body again. For that reason, it was so difficult saying goodbye to her after the game when she left with her parents. I told her I loved her, and that I was glad she came up to Davis for the night. I also assured her I would write real soon and call her later in the week.

CHAPTER TWENTY-THREE

Like much of the rest of the country, the residents of 309 Iris watched Walter Cronkite and listened to him describe the events unraveling in South Vietnam and in our nation's big cities. During the summer we had watched film clips of the massive rioting in Detroit and were told of the $44 million in damages and 42 dead. Cronkite told the country that 50% of U.S. aid to South Vietnam went into the black market, and about the increasing number of draft dodgers and conscientious objectors. Canada remained an alternative for many. We sat in silence, each with our own private thoughts, listening to the quickening tempo of ugly news. More and more Americans were being drafted and a painfully increasing number were coming back in pine boxes. Support for the war slackened. In October, 35,000 war critics marched on the nation's capital. The U.S. policies were increasingly questioned by the public. Divisiveness became more pronounced. One was either for or against the war in Vietnam. I sat on the fence, philosophically, but wanted it to be over. I could look myself in the mirror and know I was not being a coward. I just had no interest at this point in my life in fighting a war in Southeast Asia that I felt would not impact me or the country, although I suspect that may have portrayed a lack of understanding in international affairs. I had other plans, other priorities. The protests were manifested in many forms—musical shows, marches, sit-ins, pacifist folk songs by musical artists like Joan Baez. One particular poster is remembered—it asked, "What if they called a war and nobody came?" But its' timing seemed poor, for a war was already underway, with no end in sight.

The war was taking its toll on Vietnamese civilians as well. Women and children caught in the crossfire or assumed to be helping the North Vietnamese communists. Their homelands were bombed and strafed by both sides, the result being burned, scarred, rapidly aging bystanders.

Much of the protest activity, we were told, was taking place on college campuses. Sit-ins and strikes were prevalent. During the Fall semester of 1967 demonstrations on campuses totaled over 200, and almost one-half of Americans surveyed said the war was a mistake. Draft cards were burned. News reporters taped groups of people chanting, "Hey, Hey, LBJ, how many kids have you killed today?" and "Hell, no, we won't go," for TV news broadcasts. Harvard seniors exclaimed they would rather go to jail or into exile rather than go in the Army. We just sat in Apt. C and shook our heads. Occasionally, someone would utter, "Those assholes" in reference to the protestors and hippies. While we wished the war would end, we were not vocal to the point of radicalism or butting heads with U.S. policy. To us, the protestors were "kooks" and took their objections too far. In retrospect, our feelings probably derived from our being in a "comfort zone" in terms of quality of life and our reluctance, maybe unconsciously, to question things. After all, this was Happy Valley College, and life there was idyllic and quite agreeable. Being miles from Berkeley and San Francisco, and especially from Washington D.C. and other hotbeds like Boston and Chicago, was a factor. The news we received was obviously one-sided, and our perceptions were supported by our lifestyles. While my own future with respect to Uncle Sam's military forces was uncertain at best, I did not lash out at the source of that uncertainty. Things would somehow fall into place in due time, hopefully for the best. I knew that one way or the other I would wear a uniform. It was just a question of what service and under what conditions.

At Happy Valley, protest was low-key and infrequent. Occasional demonstrations took place in the quad, replete with greater numbers of students heckling the smaller number of demonstrators. "Otto bomb," a singular courageous presence in 1966, had now found more people who felt as he did, and he was always in the front of the protest groups. The demonstrations were over-dramatized by the town press corps, who greeted us in one of their newspaper editions with the expression, "Happy Valley College is a hotbed of liberalism in a valley of conservatism." Nice try. Sounded good, though, and the locals really got stirred up.

Editorials were sent in to the paper and printed, and the town council discussed the matter in their chambers, voicing their "concern."

In fact, my "friend" from Trout Hole and the dining hall "fire" episode disciplinary meeting, the Vice President, contacted me and asked if I could arrange as many Raiders as I could muster, wearing our blue sweatshirts, to be present at an upcoming anti-war demonstration in the quad. He told us to make our presence known but not to engage in any policing activity. We were sixty-strong, and the demonstration was peaceful.

If the town's leaders had toured the campus area on any given weekend night, or even some Wednesday or Thursday nights for that matter, they would have undoubtedly come away with the strong impression that normal college life was alive and well at Happy Valley. Ranchero Avenue apartments had their usual Friday keggers thanks to the Orland crew and other neighbors, the "O" was generally packed with revelers, the Raiders had their parties, and the fraternities usually had a party going.

In fact, if they had come by 309 Iris one particular night that Fall they would have observed a hellacious orange throwing fight perpetrated by Chip, Rob and Stan from Hopewell. They had picked up a couple boxes of decaying oranges, pulled up across the street in front of the agriculture warehouse, and started blasting 309 Iris with a steady barrage of the rotten oranges. After running out of ammo, they entered Apt. C to "make peace", only to fling a shaving cream pie in the faces of Dan and me before sprinting to their car and beating feet back to Hopewell. We weren't going to take it lying down, so we hopped on the motorcycles, sped over to Hopewell where we started gathering some oranges, and threw a few at their front door before being invited inside the apartment. There, Dan and I were greeted with a "Happy Birthday." Surprise! What an ingenious way to be led to a surprise party with many of our friends in attendance! It was a great feeling to know we had friends such as those who gathered at Hopewell that evening.

Sports were still a big part of the lives of many of us. On TV we watched Lombardi's Packers on Sundays during football season, college football on Saturdays, and the amazing Lew Alcinder of UCLA during basketball season. Spring meant baseball, and we watched stars like Sandy Koufax, Ted Williams, and Tom Seavers. Palmer and Nicklaus dominated golf, and Bobby Hull stole the hockey show. That Fall the NFL had expanded to 16 teams and started the eventual demise of the AFL in name.

The town naysayers also missed our mud football game one rainy Saturday in November in which about 16 of us—the Hopewell group, plus Brent, Iris Street guys, along with Brad, his roomies, and a few others—met at Rosecrans Elementary School to create a sloppy, chewed up grass field during 2 hours of tackle football in the mud. Cindy and Sue happened by, so I raced home on the cycle to get my camera so they could take some photos of the motley crew. After the game we cleaned up and met back at Brad's for a kegger.

No, things were not going to hell in a hand basket at Happy Valley, but our contribution to "normalcy" was not printable news.

I was one of the few people at Happy Valley to have seen San Francisco's Haight-Ashbury first hand. But it was no big deal. On a particular visit to Debbie's in early November she and I one day went via Haight-Ashbury to visit her sister who was attending a nursing school in San Francisco.

We observed first hand the notable environment of the love children and the flower children. I parked the car and we walked a couple blocks. It was a sunny day so the residents and groupies were out milling around. Some were panhandling tourists for loose change, and others sat around listening to a guitarist.

The scent of marijuana hung in the air. People were dressed in colorful, patterned shirts, and many wore headbands around long hair. Loud music could be heard coming from a number of the old frame houses. An open front door to a house revealed an openness created by a lack of furniture. Other than the panhandlers, everyone was minding their own business, oblivious to strangers strolling the streets curious to view the hippie lifestyle. Beads hung from around the necks of most of the love children, and most were either barefoot or wore some type of sandals. Looking at singular persons or couples sitting on steps seemingly immersed in thought reminded me of the Bob Dylan song, "How does it feel…how does it feel…like a complete unknown, like a rolling stone." Many of these people came from middle class homes and were either escaping from or searching for something, or both. I often wondered how serious their beliefs really were. How strongly did they feel? Was there a feeling of commitment, or was this just an excuse to isolate oneself from the mainstream of society? Something made many of them turn their backs on friends and families and strike out in another direction. Were they escaping parents that didn't care? Were they looking for some attention or some notoriety? How many of them were honestly and uncompromisingly disgusted with the U.S. presence in Vietnam? How many really felt that their opinions and actions mattered? How many really cared…about anything?

These and other thoughts ran the gamut as Debbie and I quietly strolled this unique domain. I admitted to myself there was a measure of romanticism in their existence, but I could not see myself living their lifestyle. After all, I didn't have any strong feelings one way or the other on the issues many of them thrived on. I was part of a loving, caring family, and I was in the process of preparing myself to soon become a member of the business community somewhere.

It wasn't until I was among them that I realized how different my attire was from theirs. My Levi cords, low-cut black converse and madras print shirt contrasted obliquely with their flowered shirts, denim pants, long hair, beads and headbands. Two very different worlds separated only by belief systems. We partied differently, too—I drank beer and "spooly-ooly", and they smoked pot. But I'll bet we both occasionally drank cheap wine.

Back at Happy Valley later that month of November, I decided it was time to try another National Guard unit, this time making the long trek to Sacramento to do so. Dan, Jack and Benny wished me good luck as I prepared to drive down on that Tuesday of Thanksgiving week. My former fraternity house roomie, Lucky, had been nice enough to loan me his Triumph, so with a mix of hope and pessimism I headed down Highway 89.

Jim Preston told me about a Guard unit. He had heard about it from a friend. In discussing the matter with Dan and Jack over the previous weekend it was their opinion that I personally visit the unit. I wanted to simply call the Sergeant I had been told to contact, but we all eventually agreed it was best to make a face-to-face appeal to join vice doing so by phone. It was too easy to be told "no" over the phone. A personal visit would show greater interest.

I was as nervous as a whore in church when I pulled into the parking lot of the large stucco building called the "drill hall" and couldn't keep from feeling pessimistic. On the front of the building in large blue letters were the words, "California National Guard." I had not had much trouble finding the location in West Sacramento.

Once in the office spaces I asked for the person whose name I had been given.

"Excuse me," I said, "I'd like to see First Sergeant McKee."

"Is he expecting you?" a guy in an Army uniform asked.

"No, but I was given his name as the person to talk to about getting into the unit."

"Oh," the disinterested soldier replied. "We're at our max, ya' know. We're not taking anyone," he added without interest as he took another puff of his cigarette and looked at his Popular Mechanics magazine.

"Well, I still want to see him. I've come a long way."

"Sure. Just a minute." The soldier returned a short time later. "Go on down the hall. He's in the last office on the right."

"Thanks," I said, walking down the hall holding my heart in my hands. This is bullshit, I thought to myself. I tapped on the doorframe since the office door was open.

"Come in," the portly, but friendly, First Sergeant said.

"Hello, sir, I'm Dave Pedersen and I was told you might be able to help me."

"Oh?" he replied, probably more out of curiosity as to who had steered me his way, for he knew damn well why I was there.

"Yes, sir. I'm interested in signing up for your unit."

"So are a lot of other guys," he said. "Where are you from?"

"Happy Valley. I'm a Senior there and will be graduating next June."

"You made a long drive. You should have called me and saved yourself a lot of time and expense."

"Well, I felt it would be better to come and see you in person. I'd sure like to get in, sir." Without getting on my hands and knees, I was begging. Give me a damn break.

"Yes, I see. Well, Dave, I just can't help you. I've got a waiting list with over 500 names on it. Have you tried a unit up in Happy Valley?" he asked in an effort to bring me down softly.

"Yes, I have. Same story. Waiting list."

"All I can tell you is keep checking around. And call back to check on the status of my list. I'll put your name on it, but don't be encouraged. I've only taken in a few guys during the past three months. It's tough."

"Yes, sir," I replied. I was in a bit of a daze at this point. Hopelessness smothered me like a blanket. My world seemed to be caving in around me. "Thanks, and goodbye." I walked slowly back up the hallway and past the front desk where the unconcerned soldier sat looking at his magazine.

The drive back to Happy Valley was slow and painful. I kept asking myself what I was going to do. Things were looking grim. I wanted so much to have Debbie in my life after graduation, but at the rate things were going I was going to have an M-16 in my hands first. Why did this have to be happening? Why now? Why did I have to be deeply in love? What shitty timing!

Along the way I stopped at a gas station in Yuba City to call Debbie. I had told her I would call after the meeting in Sacramento.

I had been too distraught to look for a phone immediately after my session with First Sergeant McKee, and just wanted to "play like a sheepherder and get the flock out of Dodge."

"Hello," Debbie answered after picking up the receiver.

"Hi, Debbie. It's just me."

"Dave! How are you and how did it go?"

"Nothing promising at all, Debbie. I feel miserable."

"Oh, no, Dave. Oh, I wish I could be with you right now," she said in a loving way.

"And I wish I could be with you, babe."

"Where are you calling from?" she asked.

"I'm at a gas station in Yuba City," I answered. "This has been the longest drive of my life. It just doesn't look good for finding a unit. They're all full and have waiting lists."

"You'll find one, Dave. Just keep trying. Are you coming down Thursday for Thanksgiving?"

"Yes, I can't wait to see you. I've got to go. This call is getting expensive. I love you, Debbie."

"I love you, too, Dave. See you in a few days. Bye."

I hung up the phone and dragged my miserable ass back to the car. The one good thing was that I got Lucky's car back in one piece and in good working order. No accidents or car problems, thank God.

I told Dan and the others about my bad news as soon as I arrived at Iris. They tried to be encouraging, but I could see the handwriting plainly on the wall. Reserve and Guard units were full and I was healthy. Guess who was going to get a 1-A classification notice in June? The idea of foregoing graduation did not cross my mind. I was taking 19 ½ units that semester and was on target to graduate in June. Plus, I wanted Debbie in my life more than I had ever wanted anything in my life. When together, she gave me so much happiness and satisfaction. When apart, I lived on hope. I was committed to her and to leaving Happy Valley in June. All the fantastic memories of the three previous years there were now secondary. I now worried about what Debbie might do if I could not get into a Guard unit. What would she do if I had to report to the Army and give them the next two years of my life? Two years sounded like an eternity.

And the way things were going I'd probably find myself in a rice paddy. Naw, they wouldn't send a college graduate to the rice paddies, I thought to myself. Bullshit, was my reply. They have no conscience. A draftee is a draftee. You'll go where they want to send you, to where Fred and Ron went. I had absolutely no idea what to expect. None. I still hadn't visited the friendly Army recruiter to talk about enlisting or find out what other jobs might be available. I wasn't that desperate yet.

We had a great relationship, but I'm sorry, Debbie wouldn't accept my being drafted. I could see it clearly. She was young, pretty, and would be available, and I did not have the nerve to speculate with her about our future if I got called up. No way. I wasn't going to put us through that emotional knothole. And that was assuming I came back alive. There were certainly no guarantees that I would be fortunate enough to do so. A lot of guys didn't make it back, and I could be one of them. I didn't think Debbie would want to take that chance. She would break things off rather than live with hope day to day that I would come back.

All these thoughts ran through my mind as I went to bed that night. I kept seeing First Sergeant McKee, hearing his rejection, and seeing the complacent desk jockey soldier. I saw no hope. I felt despair. I was destined to be a ground-pounder in Nam, and I would lose Debbie. Screw the world. Sleep came with difficulty that night.

The following night, I went to the "O" for a couple beers after the Block HV meeting. Tom Santos gave me a ride back to Iris, and although my plans were to head south the following day I decided to thumb a ride to Debbie's that evening. I was chomping at the bit to see her and be in her arms, particularly after the fiasco with the Guard unit in Sacramento earlier in the week.

I walked into our apartment and saw Jim sitting in the living room reading. "Jim, are you doing anything real important right now?"

He gave me a puzzled look. "No, he said. "Why?"

"I wonder if you could do me a real big favor. I'm anxious to get the hell out of here for the Thanksgiving break, and I would really appreciate it if you could give me a lift to the edge of town so I could thumb a ride to the Bay Area."

"Sure," he answered without hesitating. He gave me that shit-eating grin of his, and was probably thinking, "you really are horny."

"Great. Thanks, Jim. Give me a few minutes to pack some things." About 15 minutes later we were driving through town, out Broadway toward Highway 89. We turned left on E. Park Avenue and swung onto the entrance to the highway. Jim was good enough to run me a couple miles down the road.

"Thanks, Jim. I really appreciate this. Have a good Thanksgiving," I said as I hopped out of his car with my athletic bag.

"Sure. I still can't believe you are doing this. Give me a call if you strike out and need a ride back to the apartment." I looked around. No phone booth. Oh, well.

"Okay. Thanks." Jim made a U-turn and was gone. About ten minutes later, at 10:30, I got my first ride. It was a good one, getting me all the way to Yuba City. My ride was with a couple of old winos, and I shared some of their wine on our way down the road. In Yuba City, I had a little more difficulty obtaining my next ride. Finally, after what felt like an eternity, a local farmer picked me up. The old guy was going to Sacramento, which was a bit out of my way, but I took it anyway. His pickup smelled like he had carried all varieties of farm animals in it, but I just kept reminding myself how much I had enjoyed being around farms when I was a kid. I got accustomed to the strong odor after a while.

The old farmer with the stubble beard asked, "Where you headed to?"

"San Rafael."

"San Rafael? You've got a long way to go!"

"You're right. I've got a girlfriend down there I'm going to see."

"Oh. Well, you shouldn't have too much trouble getting down there. Lots of traffic headed that way from Sacramento."

"I hope I don't have much trouble. I was almost giving up hope back there in Yuba City until you stopped. I had my thumb out for a good thirty minutes."

"Is that so? I usually don't pick up hitchhikers. But you looked like a clean-cut kid with your school jacket on and all."

"I really appreciate your stopping," I said. He went on to tell me about his small farm and what stock he raised. Along the way he pulled out a pint bottle of whisky and asked if I wanted some. I politely turned the offer down. I was already feeling the negative affects of the wine I had drank earlier, as well as the beers I consumed at the "O".

He dropped me off in Sacramento near a freeway interchange. There, I really lucked out, for a guy came along soon after and gave me a lift to Davis. A couple Air Force guys picked me up there and got me as far as Fairfield, the site of Travis Air Force Base. My last ride was from an Air Force Sergeant who was going to Hamilton Air Force Base, which was located only a few miles from San Rafael. This put me in great spirits, for I would be within walking distance of Debbie's house from where I intended to get let off. The Sergeant was a nice guy, and we talked about a number of things, including the Vietnam War, which made the trip go that much faster. As we approached the turnoff for San Rafael I told him where I could be let out.

"I'll take you all the way, if it's that close," he offered.

I was leery of allowing a stranger to pull up in front of the house, so I politely told him no. "It's Okay. I appreciate it, but you can drop me off just up ahead. I can walk the rest of the way."

"Okay. I'm in no hurry, so just thought I would offer to take you all the way to your girlfriend's house." He didn't push it, fortunately.

I walked the short distance up the road to Debbie's neighborhood, and then I let myself in through the gate to the backyard. I found the "hide-a-key", and unlocked the side door to the garage. Once in the garage, I turned on a light and found the spare key to the kitchen door. I was trying to be as quiet as I could. It had never crossed my mind to call Debbie to tell her I was coming. I had wanted to surprise her.

And I did just that, including surprising the hell out of her parents when they got up the next morning and saw me sleeping on the couch. I had helped myself to a pillow and blanket out of the hall linen closet and fallen asleep on the sofa in the living room.

Her parents took the shock well and didn't express any anger. They just kept remarking how quiet I had been for everyone to sleep through my entry. I always have been a soft walker.

I spent the next few days of the school break at Debbie's and really hated having to head back up the road. I had called Brent during the weekend and arranged a ride back to school with he and Eileen.

During the school year I tried to keep myself as busy as possible to keep from thinking or worrying about Debbie. Besides my heavy course load, I also served on the Student Judiciary Board of the college. The Student Body President, Ed Groller, had selected me to serve, the same guy that had a somewhat questionable past with the school administration. I took a little good-natured razing on my appointment. Maybe Ed did too. I also got very involved in Block HV Society, attending all their meetings at the Block HV House out at 9th and Chester Streets, after which we normally went to the "O" for a few beers.

On the weekends Debbie didn't visit I worked with the concession stands that Block HV operated at the football and basketball games. It kept me occupied, plus I acquired more than a sufficient number of points to allow me to attend the Block HV dinner-dance free.

I spent a lot of time at the "O", oftentimes shoulder to shoulder with other partiers. Actually, Wednesday and Thursdays were more crowded than most weekend nights, with students getting a head start on the upcoming weekend. Beer got spilled on pool tables, but Juanita didn't object too much. The place was a gold mine and I'm sure she could afford to clean or re-cover the tables when necessary. One of my main reasons to visit the "O" was to eat those fantastically delicious hot dogs and superb potato salad. Wow, what a treat that was. I just about lived on that stuff.

The "O" was great fun, for people got rowdy and the excitement meter stayed high. Juanita loved it so long as things didn't get too much out of hand. As you recall, she didn't even get that upset about the vegetables thrown around inside the bar a year earlier. On those rare occasions when girlfriends were left behind and our old group got together, either at the "O" or out Humboldt Road to have a keg at "the slide" or inner tube down Little Butte Creek, all hell broke loose and it was like old times in our more carefree freshman and sophomore years.

CHAPTER TWENTY-FOUR

Later that month things got rather tense as I watched the evening news in Apartment C with Dan, Jack and Benny. Walter Cronkite was telling us about the Tet offensive in Vietnam, and about how the Viet Cong were unleashing their greatest offensive thrust of the war with over 70,000 troops. Within a 72-hour time frame the Cong had captured the large city of Hue and fought their way to the U. S. Embassy in Saigon. It was only a short time earlier that we had sat in front of the TV and heard stories that the communist forces were thought to be exhausted and were losing their punch, but America had been mistaken in the enemy's capacity to withstand pain. Like any other sovereignty the North Vietnamese resisted any foreign intervention. At that time the U. S. forces in South Vietnam numbered 500,000 troops. I would say that was plenty of U. S. forces.

"Bomb the fuckers!" Benny exclaimed.

"Really. Why the hell won't we go in there and fight a war like war should be fought? We're the U. S. This thing's dragged on long enough. Why can't we get it over once and for all?" I stated.

"I agree," said Jack. "We've lost thousands of lives in a crazy war over what? Either end the damn thing or let them fight it out for themselves. Who gives a rasty you know what about who controls who over there?"

"They're playing games," Dan interjected. "We've all been fed a bunch of misinformation." He was alluding to General Westmoreland's reports that we had the war in hand, that the Cong were letting up. Cronkite called the war a "military stalemate", and rightly so. Of course, this bit of opinionating didn't much help me and many other prospective draftees. We were under the illusion that the U. S. was winning, which went far to allay our fears about being drafted. I kept hoping that the war would either end soon or phase down to the point where draftees were no longer needed. There were plenty of guys that wanted to enlist. Maybe their numbers would be sufficient to carry on a slackened war effort. But no such luck.

In February of that year we learned that Hue had been recaptured and that the communist forces, which we always seemed to see wearing black, had been driven out of Saigon. Westmoreland told his bosses and the country that 42,000 Cong had been killed and that Cong plans had gone awry. But he wasn't too convincing, for by this point in the war the U. S. had lost 16,000 men, with over 100,000 wounded. The war fires kept burning. In his 1964 campaign for the presidency LBJ had told the American public that our young men should not be fighting a war 10,000 miles away. Let their young men fight the war, he exclaimed. Right on, LBJ. The Tet Offensive shattered the illusion we all had that circumstances over in Nam were different. And then Westmoreland asked for 200,000 more men, which thankfully was not supported by Johnson. There were claims we were wasting our resources and the lives of our young men in the rice paddies.

One of the more lasting impressions of the war was seen live by millions of TV viewers as the Saigon Police Chief summarily executed a Viet Cong with a pistol shot to the head on live camera.

"Oh, my God", Jack mumbled as we sat in horror and watched the dead Cong crumple and fall to the ground.

"I don't believe what we just saw," I said. "That was live!'

What else was new? Nothing surprised us anymore with the war. Young people were becoming more vocal and vehement in their protest of the war. They were more and more alienated from their elders. "Don't trust anyone over 30" was a popular slogan among the counter culture. Their elders were making the decisions to continue a fruitless war that would take young people thousands of miles from their homes and all too often return in a pine box.

It was February and I was getting closer to the moment of truth. If I did nothing, I would be drafted by the end of June. As soon as my draft board received official notice of my graduation I would receive a re-classification to I-A in the mail. What the hell? Why fight it? I was beginning to think. But instead of giving in I started to think about enlisting in the Air Force. Take my chances there with a three or four year tour of enlistment. Debbie and I could still get married and she could join me wherever I was stationed, assuming it was not Vietnam. It would beat the rice paddies. I had thought about taking the test to be an officer, but to me being an officer implied a longer commitment. Whatever I ended up doing, I wanted to get in and get out. Get it over with so I could carry on with my life. But the question lingered of who to trust for straight information.

The one good thing that came along early that year was "Laugh-In" with Rowan and Martin. We at Iris were regular viewers and loved the wit and humor and the way the actors created comedy from the serious issues of the time.

The agony of the USS PUEBLO capture and the plight of CDR Butcher and his crew also hit the news about that time frame. The hate, anguish and disillusionment transitioned from 1967 and made 1968 a year to remember, or forget. The Tet Offensive, while costly in lives to the communists, succeeded in turning American opinion against the war. Most Americans were beginning to think that we had made a mistake by our incontrovertible involvement, that we should have used those vast consumed and squandered war resources to improve our economic position against the likes of Japan and Germany and to take care of our own poor.

As if our struggle overseas wasn't enough, new troubles on the home front erupted with the assassination of Martin Luther King on April 4th and the riots and violence in 125 cities across the country precipitated by that heinous, senseless act. Thank God we were in sleepy Happy Valley, miles from the riots and even further from the violence in Vietnam.

The clock kept ticking on me.

On any given night we would be watching the evening news after dinner and one of us on an alternating basis it seems would throw out useless exclamations and epithets toward the sources or causes of our frustration or anger. "Damn hippies," or, "that damn LBJ", or "those asshole commies". That really didn't help much, but we vented some of our pent-up emotions. One night we talked a bit more about the hippies.

"Those hippies may have the right idea", Benny observed.

"What do you mean?" Jack asked.

"Well, many of them have found a way to stay out of Vietnam, and I suppose the only thing they really worry about is where they get their next meal, their next hit on some grass, and a piece of ass", he replied. A little laughter and guffaws ensued.

"That may be the case," Jack said after things quieted down, "but you won't find me taking up their cause."

"I don't think that's Benny's point, Jack," I stated. "I think he's merely reflecting on the basic difference in lifestyles and emotional trappings between us and them."

"I think they're screwed up," Dan interjected. "Look at Brenda Howe. One year she's homecoming queen and song girl, and everyone's sweetheart, and now she's a hippie. She looks like shit. Doesn't take care of herself, wears shabby clothes and is generally rarely seen. I'm sure she hangs around a similar group of people."

"I agree. She looks like hell and has let herself go as she has become more enamored with the so-called hippie lifestyle. I haven't talked to her, nor have any of you I suppose, so we don't know what she believes in. But is it really important? There are so few hippies around here that they are rarely seen other than when all twenty of them gather in the quad to demonstrate."

"As far as I'm concerned, they can live the hippie life," Jack broke in. "But I don't like their demonstrations."

"Spoken like a true Guardsman," I replied jokingly. "Some day you may be breaking up one of their demonstrations here or in Berkeley."

"Maybe," Jack answered. But I could tell he didn't relish the thought.

"But to get back on Benny's comment," I interjected, "the hippies do have an intriguing lifestyle. We're always hearing about the flower children and the free sex. I wonder if Brenda's in to that?" I mused.

"Some lucky bastard may be getting some of that," Benny offered. The conversation stopped for a moment as we reflected on that possibility, for Brenda had a nice body, but was known in earlier years at Happy Valley to be on the prudish, chilly side.

"You know," I continued, "you may freak out a bit when I tell you this, but I remember some of my thoughts from that day that Debbie and I walked around Haight-Ashbury a few months ago. I told Debbie as we walked among the hippies and their environs that I was slightly envious of them. She was taken aback with such an observation, and asked me to explain myself. She was almost in disbelief. After all, this was a conservative, beer-drinking jock telling her he thought the hippies were okay and onto something.

"I reminded her that most of the hippies were for some reason or another exempt from the draft, and told her about my friend Ron who had come back from Vietnam missing part of his leg. I told her about the visit to the hospital by Dan and me to see Ron and how shook up we were. I didn't know where I stood on the war. It was a U. S. effort, yes, and we should support it, but it seemed we were doing something the South Vietnamese should be handling themselves. Our guys shouldn't be getting shot up. The war effort was a joke, and we in America didn't really know what was going on.

"But my friends and I were brought up not to question what was happening in Nam. Most Americans were that way about the war. The President says we should fight, so we fight. She had replied that that was how her Father, a retired Marine Corps officer, felt about the war. I then relayed to her my frustration and why there was some envy. Graduation was drawing near, I told her, and I had no idea what to do about military service. I loved her, and I didn't want to go away for a long time and take the chance of losing her. She told me not to worry, and that she would wait for me, but that didn't help matters much. The hippies are 'free spirits'. Sure, that's mainly because of the drugs they're on, but they don't have the emotional upheaval, the uncertainties, and the unanswerable questions that I have. They go from day to day. No big deal. Smoke a little pot. Float through the day. Just think about their next demonstration, if they're really into what they say they believe."

"Yes, but do you really want to live like that, Dave?" Jack asked.

"No, and I'm not saying I want to be part of that lifestyle with its drugs and ten people sleeping in a room in Haight-Ashbury. I'm just saying this whole mess about the war, the draft, and my plans for a future with Debbie is driving me up a wall. I don't know what the hell to do. I wish I didn't have these damn worries. You're fortunate, Jack. You committed early on. You're in a Guard unit so you know where you'll be a year from now. I don't have that luxury," I exclaimed.

"You had your chance, Dave," Jack quietly reminded me.

"I know. But back then I was not mentally ready to commit myself to what you're in. I wasn't prepared to commit myself to the military, an unknown quantity."

"Well, Dave," Benny said with all sincerity, "if it makes you feel any better, Dan and I are in the same boat, with one exception. We're not finishing school until at least another semester after you. We have more time to work something out."

"Yeah, bro," Dan said, "just hang in there. Maybe you'll manage to luck out and get in a reserve or Guard unit."

"I should be so lucky. This is February and June is just around the corner. I've tried to find a unit here and in Sacramento. The problem is, I don't have any contacts, clout, or whatever, to help me get in. The guys that know someone, or slip some money under the table, are the ones getting accepted. I refuse to pay anyone for preferential treatment, so color me not taken."

"Well, you did make your point," Jack commented. "I'm sure things aren't easy for you. Debbie's one good-looking young lady, and I know how you feel about her. Things will work out."

"I hope so, Jack." With that we got up to collect our books and do some studying. I couldn't study, however. I had Debbie on my mind, so I faked studying for a while before closing the books.

On a much different note, the month ended with Eileen and Brent having their baby. They decided to name it after Jimmy Halton, our former football teammate that lost his life the previous Summer in the auto accident with "Taco". We all knew the baby would create even more financial and emotional challenges for Brent and Eileen, but we also were confident they would find a way to make it okay. We obviously had no idea what they were experiencing with their new responsibilities in taking care of a baby. Brent was already working evenings and weekends now that football season had ended, so we did not see much of them but for rare occasions. So much for their carefree years at Happy Valley College.

CHAPTER TWENTY-FIVE

I was working in the Student Union again that semester, which was no different from all the previous semesters at Happy Valley. The prior semester I had worked only one hour each day, Monday through Friday. During the Spring semester, however, I worked one hour three days a week, and two hours on the other two weekdays. The job gave me a little spending money, and helped fill the days since I was no longer involved in sports.

On those many valley sunny days that drew and kept many students outdoors, I spent a lot of free time sitting in the quad yakking it up with fellow Raiders and fraternity brothers. A good friendship developed with Tim Raley, a junior soccer player that was from the Lafayette area. After mentioning the Raley name to my folks some time earlier my Mom had dragged out an old photo of Dan and I and Tim's older sister, Bonnie, sitting naked together in a wading pool at the age of three, when we had been next door neighbors. Our family had moved out of the area a year later. We all had a good chuckle when I showed the photo to Bonnie and Tim.

Sitting in the quad was also super for bagging rays and looking at all the girls wearing their Spring fashions.

In March Tim bought my motorcycle. Anticipating the need to buy a car soon after I graduated and needing the money to do so, I put the bike up for sale. I really wanted to hold off selling it until after Western Week in April, but Tim was an interested buyer and had just the opposite idea – he wanted the cycle in time to use it during Western Week. Selling the "bumble bee" was akin to parting with a good friend. While I had owned the bike a little less than two years, there were so many great memories and it had been such reliable transportation for me. The latter created the biggest impact, for I felt "stripped", naked, stranded the moment I watched Tim ride off with the bike. I had become so accustomed to always having my own transportation for the past three years, not being dependent on anyone. I could come and go anytime and anywhere I pleased. Not having a car in a place with a moderate climate like Happy Valley rarely presented a problem, for in the past my dates and girlfriends preferred going somewhere on the back of a Honda 250 Scrambler.

It really hurt seeing the motorcycle driven away by a new owner.

Well, the bike was gone. It was nice while it lasted. I had other things to focus on, so I did the best I could to put the matter out of my mind. It hurt a little, however, whenever I saw Tim cruising around on the "bumble bee". It reminded me of the freedom and pleasure I enjoyed at one time with the motorcycle.

With Easter Break approaching I was looking forward to going home to Danville and spending some time with Debbie, whose break coincided with mine. It was for that reason I was more than a bit confused after a phone call from her. It was the Wednesday night prior to Easter Break.

"Hi, love, how you doing?" I asked, eager to discuss plans for the upcoming week together.

"Oh, I'm doing fine. I miss you," she said in that soft, romantic voice of hers.

"I miss you, too, love, but in a few days I'll be down there and we can spend some time together."

"Dave," she started, and then after a short pause continued, "I know you want to come over here so we can be together, but I'm not going to be in the area."

"What?" I asked in some shock. I was totally unprepared for this little surprise. I was looking forward to spending a lot of time with her, of going to our favorite beach at Stinson Beach, of going to Sausilito and San Francisco (where I always had the opportunity, and the need, to do the city on less than $5 a day). "I don't understand. Where are you going?"

"I know you can't believe this, Dave, but a girlfriend from high-school that now lives in Montana has asked me to visit her. I'd really like to see her. I'll only be gone a week, and then we can be together again."

"Okay, love, but you know I'm disappointed and will miss you," I replied dejectedly. My initial reaction was disbelief and certainly great disappointment. After all, we were physically separated during the school year, and now had an opportunity to be together most of the week during the break. But I wasn't going to push it. If she wanted and needed to spend a week with an old girlfriend in the Big Sky Country of Montana, so be it.

"Thanks, Dave.   I knew you would understand. I'm really going to miss you, but you know that. I'll call you from Montana a couple times, okay?"

"Sure. I'll miss you, too, love." I was extremely deflated.

"What are you going to do during the break?" she asked. "I think you ought to go on a trip. You've been studying so hard this year taking that heavy load. You need a break, and to do something different."

"I don't know what I'll do. Maybe I'll just stay at home." We hung up with each of us saying "I love you". When I hung up the phone I told the other guys about it since it was their apartment my phone calls came to and they were right there sitting in the living room studying. They were in some disbelief as well, but left it alone.

The next day I was sitting in the quad with Tim Raley and told him about the phone conversation with Debbie the previous night.

"Say, why don't you join me for the few days I plan to spend at the beach in Santa Cruz during the break?" Tim asked.

"That sounds good, Tim, but I don't know." The thought of spending a few days at any beach excited me, but in my subconscious mind I didn't want to leave the Bay Area because my sixth sense was telling me Debbie wasn't going to Montana but was in fact planning to be at or near her home.

"Come on. Debbie's going to Montana, and you go to Santa Cruz. I think it will do you some good to get away for a few days."

About that time, I remembered an expression my Uncle Harry used that went like this – "Don't complain, don't explain". "Well, alright," I resignedly said. He was right. I may as well go somewhere and have a little fun. Maybe I could somehow see her on the weekend before returning to school.

On Monday morning of Spring Break Tim drove over from his house in Lafayette to pick me up. We drove to Santa Cruz, experiencing the normal weather conditions that caused second thoughts about making the drive to the beach. It was sunny and warm when we left Danville, and the same all the way down Highway 17 through Fremont, San Jose, and Los Gatos. Once into the mountains between San Jose and the Pacific Ocean, however, we hit the usual fog bank that hung among the trees and hills and blanketed the area. Sometimes the fog lies in the mountains and has already burned off in the lower altitude of the oceanfront. All too often, though, the fog still shrouds the town of Santa Cruz and all one can do is hope for an early burn-off. At times, the fog never burns off, which means a wasted trip. That day, however, we were in luck, for the sun shone bright as we dropped out of the mountains and entered the city limits of Santa Cruz. Hot damn!

The area held many memories of days spent in and out of the water in hopes of natural bleached hair for that surfer look, of catching a good day of waves for body-surfing, and of hours spent walking along the boardwalk with its' arcades, food stands, and carnival-type rides, not to mention all the lovely girls at the beach. And I still had fond memories of that trip home from Santa Cruz with Dan and our high school friend, Rick, in Rick's Mother's flashy white '66 Valiant convertible with the 8-track tape deck, when we met some girls after asking them to pull off to the side of the road where we talked for a while and got to know one another.

Tim and I spent the day on the beach, and even ran into his sister and her boyfriend who had come down just for the day. Leaving the beach we went to a motel to get a place to stay for the night. I checked us in, and told the desk clerk I was by myself. A few minutes later, Tim sneaked into the room. We checked out the next morning having paid only for a single.

We had decided to drive further south to Carmel, in hopes of securing a free place to stay with friends living in the area, namely Jack's parents. Mr. and Mrs. Layton had a nice home within a couple hundred yards of the beach and at the foot of the main street running through town. After strolling among the many specialty shops in town until the morning fog burned off, we spent the day on the beach. Carmel has a picturesque beach, but the surf is lousy for body surfing. Probably just as well for the quaint area, for the lack of good surf keeps a lot of the riff-raff away.

About 4 o'clock we walked over to the Layton's and knocked on the door. The always friendly, out-going Mrs. Layton opened the door, surprised to see one of her son's roommates from Happy Valley standing there with a stranger. We hadn't even shown the courtesy of calling her to give her a warning.

"Well, hello, Dave," she said, greeting us with an ever-present big smile. "This is a pleasant surprise." Mrs. Layton was really good people, and liked Dan and I very much. She was always pleased to see us visit, whether at their former house in Lafayette or now at the beach house.

"Hi, Mrs. Layton. This is a good friend from Happy Valley, Tim. We were in the area so thought we would pay a visit."

"Hello, Mrs. Layton. It's my pleasure," Tim said.

"Hi Tim. I'm pleased to meet you. Why don't you both come in? It looks like you've been at the beach."

"Yes, ma'am, we have. We were at Santa Cruz yesterday and decided to visit Carmel," I replied.

"Oh, that's smart. This is a much nicer area than Santa Cruz," she offered, a little biased I'm sure. The socio-economics of Santa Cruz ranked far below that of the greater Monterey-Carmel area with its million dollar oceanfront homes and 17-mile drive in nearby Pacific Grove. "Can I offer you a drink? I'm sure you're thirsty." Just what the doctor ordered, I thought to myself.

"Please." I looked at Tim. "A beer will be great."

"Sounds good," Tim added.

"Sure you don't want a mixed drink?" she asked.

"Thanks, but a beer is just fine," I replied. We sat in a sitting room that had a large picture window providing a view of small pine trees and sand dunes across the street from the house. The trees hid the ocean that was at the foot of the gently sloping hill. A short walk down through the trees and along a well-worn sandy trail exposed the advancing, retreating foamy surf of the Pacific Ocean. With the window of the sitting room open we could hear the constant crash of the waves. The sun's late afternoon rays through the window warmed the room as the three of us carried on a conversation about Happy Valley, current affairs, and numerous other topics.

It was a very relaxing visit, particularly after a few beers. Mr. Layton was on a business trip, and Jack's sister Mandy was visiting friends in the Bay Area. Carl, the youngest of their four children, was out with friends and due back any time. Along the way, Mrs. Layton asked the hoped for question.

"Why don't you boys just plan on staying here? There's plenty of room, and I'd rather like some company."

"Oh, thanks, Mrs. Layton, but we couldn't do that," I feigned.

"Don't be foolish," she chided. "Of course you can stay here." With two sons our age, she knew damn well what we were up to.

"Twist our arms," I said, knowing that we could relax around beautiful Carmel the next couple of days. "Thanks, Mrs. Layton," I said.

"Just don't expect any fancy dinners," she added.

"We'll eat whatever you want to put on the table. In fact, we could go into town to eat. We don't want to be a burden on you," I replied.

"Don't be serious. I look forward to cooking for a couple of extra people."

After that, we helped ourselves to another beer. As I sat in the sitting room with the rays of a setting sun streaking in, listening to the crashing surf, feeling the euphoria from a few beers and being in the company of good friends, I wondered to myself does it really get much better than this? This was heaven, and I wanted it to go on forever. But, yes, I did miss Debbie, and wished she could be there to enjoy the experience.

Mrs. Layton broke the tranquility with a question that unfortunately brought me back to reality. "Dave, what are you going to do about military service?" she asked.

Disguising some minor annoyance at hearing the subject, I gave a brief answer. "The whole business is still up in the air. I'm trying to get into a reserve or Guard unit, but failing that I'm giving serious thought to enlisting in the Air Force. It's better than getting drafted.

"I agree," she said. "We're so happy Jack got into that Guard unit, especially as an officer." She was very proud of him. "And Jack's brother is doing okay in the Marine Corps. He just received orders for Vietnam," she added. She didn't say anything else. She did not have to, for I could tell by her voice and the look on her face she was worried about him.

"Yes," I replied. "That's nice, but I had no desire to follow Jack's path at that time. I'll take my chances elsewhere," adding, "I'll say a prayer for Gary." I just wanted to get the mess over with any way I could and do it in a way with the safety odds in my favor. Pushing a desk in the Air Force would be safer than carrying an M-16 in the Army.

After dinner Tim suggested he and I go downtown and see if any women were wandering around. "Dave, let's walk into town and see what's happening."

"Sounds like a good idea, Tim. Mrs. Layton, if you'll please excuse us. And thanks so much for that delicious dinner."

"Why, you're very welcome, Dave. I've enjoyed our conversation. I'll give you a spare key so you can let yourselves back in tonight. It's a lovely evening for a walk into town."

Tim and I walked to the end of the short road the Layton's lived on and turned left up the path that paralleled the main street of Carmel. We wandered into some of the shops and "window shopped", admiring the fashions in the men's clothing stores in particular. We stopped at a deli and bought a can of beer to carry with us, and spotted a couple girls that seemed to be wandering aimlessly like us. We struck up a conversation.

It turned out that the two girls, Lisa and Sharon, were visiting Carmel for the week and were from Marin County in the San Francisco Bay Area. We found a bench along the street and sat down to enjoy our beers and talk. We did some people watching, too, which is always intriguing in a place like Carmel with its mix of well-to-do residents and a whole spectrum of tourists or visitors. The visitors ranged from hippies to those with some bucks that were staying at the more exclusive bungalow-type motels nestled in discreetly among the shops and hidden behind clusters of stubby pine trees.

We polished off our beers, walked back inside the deli to buy another round, then by mutual agreement walked down to the beach. It was a fogless, moon lit, star-bright night as we followed the path down to the parking area at the bottom of the hill. Passing through the parking area our feet touched the sand of the beach that sloped gently down to the water's edge.

"It's a beautiful night," I said to Lisa, the girl I was with. "Let's walk down a ways and find a place to sit and listen to the waves crashing onto the beach."

Lisa wasn't what you would call pretty, but she wasn't dogmeat, either. She was wearing a pair of dark slacks, and a blouse and sweater, prepared for typical, cool oceanfront weather. She had a tiny nose, and a small mouth, and her dark hair swooped up in a distinct curl at her shoulders, kind of like the Mary Tyler Moore look. It was apparent that she took good care of herself and spent a lot of money at her favorite hairdresser. She was thin, and had a nice figure.

"That sounds fine to me," she replied.

As I sat down she maneuvered her body to sit close to mine. I was silent for a while, drinking in the solitude of the place, its beauty, and the sound of the surf. Because of the clear skies it was possible to see the whitecaps from the breaking waves as they rushed to shore before being spent on the sand or rolling back out to sea. Lisa was nestled close. We had something in common.

We were both lonely and were mesmerized by the setting. But that's as far as things went. Debbie was on my mind and was back home … or in Montana. Or wherever.

The next day Tim and I met the girls on the beach. We played in the surf a bit, bagged some rays, and all walked up into town to have a deli sandwich lunch. About 3:00 o'clock the girls left to drive back home to Marin County, but not until we all exchanged phone numbers.

On Thursday Tim and I drove back to the Bay Area. I called Debbie that night, taking a chance she might be home from Montana, if she had ever gone there. She wasn't home, so I talked to her mother. Her mother could no longer contribute to the masquerade Debbie had created with her story of going to Montana.

"Dave, she's not in Montana. She's in the area here."

"What?" I asked in astonishment. "I don't understand. What's going on?"

"She's at Letterman Hospital at the Presidio. She has wanted for a long time to have some surgery done on her nose. This week seemed like the best time to do it, and she didn't want you to know about it or see her. That's why she tried to convince you, unsuccessfully she felt, that she was going to Montana. I hope you understand and aren't too upset with her."

"Oh, my God," I mumbled softly. "Yes. Yes, I understand. Is she okay? Has she had the operation?"

"Yes, she had the operation Tuesday. She's still in the hospital and will be released Saturday. She has a lot of bandages on her face at this time."

"Do you have her phone number? Do you think she'll let me see her?"

"Yes, here it is." She gave me the phone number, which I wrote down on the first piece of paper I could find. It was at that time that I realized my hands were trembling. Debbie in a hospital. Damn. I hated hospitals. And she was in one right now, recovering from an operation. I knew it must have taken her a great deal of courage to have the surgery performed, and I now realized how concerned she was with the shape of her nose. A nose job. Damn again. She didn't have to do it! Why did she?

261

She was beautiful just the way she was. Obviously, she was more self-conscious about it than I realized. But she had never talked to me about it or let on like it was a concern or worry of hers. She had her reasons.

I thanked her mother for the number, hung up the phone, and quickly dialed the hospital.

"Hi Debbie," I said after being patched through to her room. "It's Dave. How are you feeling?"

"Hi Dave. You know," she observed, disappointment obvious in her tone of voice.

"Yes. Your mother told me. She couldn't hide it any longer."

"That's okay. Are you mad at me?"

What a silly question. "Mad at you? For what? I understand why you tried to convince me you were going to Montana, but I do wish you could have been honest with me."

"I know, but I just didn't want you to know what I was doing or to see me right after the operation."

"Can I come in and see you?"

"I look terrible, Dave."

"I don't care, and I'm sure you look fine. I love you, Debbie, and want to be with you."

"And I love you, too. Yes, I'd like to see you."

My heart was pounding. I wanted to be with her so damn bad I could scream. Damn, I missed her. "I'll come over tomorrow afternoon, okay?"

"Good. I'd prefer it be the afternoon anyway. Plus, some of the bandages are being removed tomorrow morning."

"Great. I'll see you then. About 4:00 o'clock."

"Okay. I'll see you tomorrow. Bye. I love you."

"Bye. And I love you." I couldn't wait for the next day.

At 4:00 o'clock Friday I walked into Letterman Hospital and asked for directions to Debbie's room. Between Oak Knoll Naval and Letterman I was beginning to see too much of military hospitals. I walked into her room and found her sitting in a chair. She was in a nightgown and robe, and had a large bandage covering her nose and much of her cheeks. Her eyes and mouth were exposed. Those beautiful, penetrating, mysterious eyes that so intrigued and excited me. She gave a half smile when she saw me, and it was evident the bandages restrained her from more pronounced facial expression. I walked quickly to her chair and she stood up, reaching out her hand to mine. I leaned toward her to kiss her on the forehead. With her free hand she waved me off and simultaneously jerked her head back slightly. "No", she said softly, pointing at her nose. She then said, "we shouldn't. I don't want to take a chance of you accidentally bumping my nose."

"Oh, yes, you're right. That would be terrible. Can I slowly just put my lips to your forehead, though?"

"Okay, but move very carefully." She leaned her head slightly forward, putting her free hand near and over her nose. I likewise moved with great caution as I touched my lips to her forehead.

She gave me a little smile. "I look terrible, don't I?"

"Of course not, Debbie. Please don't say that. You are the beautiful girl I love. I'm just glad to see you're okay."

"Alright. How was your week? Did you go anywhere and take my advice?"

"Yes. Tim Raley and I went to Santa Cruz, where we ran into his sister and boyfriend, and to Carmel, staying at Jack's parents." That sounded good, like I stayed out of trouble.

"That's nice. Did you have a good time?"

"It was okay. Just spent a lot of time on the beaches and laying in the sun."

"Yes, you have a nice tan. I look terrible, and have lost the little tan I had."

"Don't be silly. You look great. And you'll get your tan back soon."

"It will be a while. I'm not even supposed to lay in the sun after the bandages come off."

We talked for a while, holding hands the entire time. It was getting close to dinner time and the end of afternoon visiting hours, so it was time for me to leave. "I'll try to get over to see you Saturday night after you return home, okay? I've missed you, Debbie."

"I know. And I missed you. I hope you can come over Saturday. Dave, we can't do anything for a while, you know. I can't take any chances of my nose being touched accidentally.

"That's all right," I told her, giving her a little extra squeeze of the hand. "Bye. I'll see you tomorrow. Remember I love you."

"I know, and I love you, Dave. Drive safely."

"I will. Bye. Say Hi to your parents for me." I walked out the door with my heart in the pit of my stomach. I didn't want to leave her all alone in the hospital. I felt a little better, though, knowing that her parents and sisters were coming to visit her that night.

I was able to drive to Debbie's the next day, arriving about one o'clock. I had to get the car back that night, so it was going to be a short visit. But at least I was able to see her again before returning to Happy Valley. Before I left her home we talked about our future. It wasn't easy for me, for I was the one staring at a tour of duty in Army greens in some hellhole around South Vietnam. I felt extremely defensive and vulnerable when the subject came up. There were so few options, with only one of them good. I knew I had a legal responsibility to serve my country. I wasn't going to buck that. Moral responsibility was pushing it. It was a matter of how I would serve. And where. And when. There were so many unknowns.

We were sitting out in Debbie's backyard at a picnic table, facing each other across the table. That was certainly not my favorite positioning. When around Debbie I wanted to be as physically close as I could be. She did that to me. I wanted to be touching some way or another. Was it the sexual libido, or a sense of insecurity? Who knows? Who cares? It was just a simple fact of life.

"Dave," she said, "you're graduating in June. My father says you'll be classified 1-A for the Army draft. What are you going to do?" She was genuinely concerned and sure went right to the nub of the matter.

The problem was I didn't have any great answers, at least nothing that would show her that our relationship and seeing one another could go on virtually unimpeded. I could feel what she was thinking. She was a desirable, beautiful young lady that wanted to know if I was going to be in her future, and wanted to know what I was doing about it. She needed reassurances, but realized there were no guarantees. What could I tell her? Zip!

I wasn't going to flim-flam my way through an answer to her question. And I needed to be sensitive to her female perspective. I would just be honest and up front about the whole thing.

"Debbie," I replied, pausing to put my thoughts in a logical order, "most of all, I love you very much. But in answer to your question, it's all such a mystery right now. I've been trying like hell to find a reserve or Guard unit. You know that. It's the ideal solution. That way I spend a few months in training somewhere and can return to the Bay Area. And then all I have are weekend drills."

"What if you get called up?"

"That's a very big if, and I would say I hope it doesn't happen. They're taking enough draftees now that the reserves don't need to be called up. Plus, in the grand scheme of things, I would certainly much prefer to take my chances with getting called up in the reserves than getting drafted and definitely heading to Nam."

She then asked the killer question, the one that sent shockwaves through my body and soul, tightened my gut and scared the holy crap out of me. "What happens if you don't get into a reserve unit, which does look slim at this point?"

"It's either the draft or I enlist. If I let myself get drafted, it's a two-year hitch. To enlist means a four-year duty. You know what going in the draft means. I'd probably end up in Vietnam. If I enlist, I could be stationed anywhere, maybe be lucky enough to get near here, although it's a remote possibility at best."

"I think you ought to take your chances with the draft. It's only two years, Dave, and it would go by fast. I'll wait for you. I really will. I still have another year of school anyway, and I'll be very busy. Four years is a long time if you enlist. But then I have to say that if you enter the draft and get sent to Vietnam I will worry myself sick over you. What would happen if something terrible occurred? I could not deal with that, Dave. Oh, sweetie, I am so torn over this. I want you to enter the draft, serve your two years, get out, and we can move on with our lives, but then I think about you getting hurt. Or worse." Her body shuddered involuntarily and her eyes suddenly moistened.

And as far as the four-year hitch in the Air Force I wanted to pursue, she didn't have to say anything. It was apparent she wouldn't want to leave home prematurely and drop out of the special nursing program she was now enrolled in so that she could join me wherever the Air Force might elect to station me.

I let it sink in, and allowed the thoughts to bang around in my confused mind. I could see the handwriting on the wall. Somehow or another I was going to lose Debbie. I did not want to think that way and therefore tried to hold the proverbial yet probably unrealistic hope that some way or another our relationship would survive the uncertain times ahead. The more I thought about it my options were not good. Setting myself up for the draft sucked. And signing up for four years in one of the other branches of the military also sucked. Not good.

"I know what you mean, Debbie, but I'm not anxious to serve in Vietnam. I don't have to remind you of my visit to Oak Knoll Naval Hospital and of friends of mine that got killed over there. That scares the hell out of me. I don't want to take that chance, Debbie. Is that cowardly of me? Does it make me any less a man? Or an American, or a patriot? Has apathy so colored my feelings and direction that I shun what should be a responsibility to serve in Vietnam? This is hard, Debbie. I do not know where objectivity starts and leaves off. I only know that I love you."

"No, it's not. But maybe you'll be all right. And it's only two years."

"And it only takes one bullet, Debbie, and there are a lot of them flying around over there, not to mention all the deadly booby traps the Viet Cong have dreamed up. That's a risk I prefer not to take. If I have a four-year tour, maybe you could join me when you finish your program."

"Yes, that's possible. But it's something I'd rather not think about now. I don't know if I want to leave this area, Dave. And if I don't, will our relationship continue? Will we still have the same feelings for each other?" In other words, will a long distance relationship survive?

This was starting to hurt. I got a knot in my throat. This is what it was coming down to. How strongly did she feel about me? She felt strong enough to say she'd wait for two years, assuming I didn't come out of Nam in a body bag, but four years was an iffy proposition at best. I sat silent, unable to speak. I looked past her at the trees in the yard. The yard. Other houses. Permanency. Something I could not enjoy at present or in the near future. What future was there for me? What was my future?

"Everything's going to be all right," she said, sensing my depression and melancholy mood, and the uncertainty with which she presented me. "I'll be here for you. Don't worry."

"Okay," I mumbled, barely audible. "I just wish I knew what was going to happen, that I had a crystal ball. I can't stand it."

"Neither can I," she replied.

We held hands, and I stared into her eyes, trying to read something there. Anything.

I did see worry and concern. She was sincere, I could tell. A short while later it was time to leave. Holding back a choked up voice, testimony to the emotion building up in me from the love I felt for her, and the fear of losing her, I said my goodbyes and got in the car for a lonely drive back across the flat, uninspiring desolation of Black Point Cut-off.

CHAPTER TWENTY-SIX

A couple of weeks later at Happy Valley everyone was getting the Western Week itch. The event was starting the next week and people were anticipating the great parties and all the associated festivities. I had decided to make it a Western Week to remember, even though I was without the motorcycle. Maybe it was just as well, for I "tied one on" every day starting with Monday. Opening day for me meant a six-pack of beer at Iris with some friends, followed by attending "Presents". Our general rowdiness in the front row almost got us kicked out. I'm sure people were cussing those damn Raiders! From Presents we went to my fraternity house for their annual Monday post-Presents kegger.

On Tuesday, Jack, Dan, Benny and I, with some help from "Rocko", organized the second annual Iris Street Raider kegger, and as was the case the previous year, we had a large crowd and went through four kegs. Lots of drunk cowboys, yes! We made numerous trips between the kegger and the quad to observe the quad projects being erected by the various Greek and other organizations. We were totally obnoxious, and friends smartly declined our offers to help. The annual free steak dinner in the quad slowed us down a little that night, however.

Wednesday morning we dragged ourselves out of bed and half stumbled across the street toward the quad to enjoy the free pancake breakfast. That afternoon I helped conduct the bike races around the front lawn of the school. After the bike races, I joined a large group of people watching the traditional jumping frog contest participated in by the girls. My old friend Annette was a contestant and was wearing what looked like the same carpenters overalls she was wearing at Western Week two years prior. Screams of encouragement filled the afternoon air in front of the Administration Building.

Annette was in the next group. She and the three other girls in her "heat" took their places and put frogs into position at the line. Annette didn't make out too well, either. In the excitement of things, with everyone yelling, and Annette and her fellow contestants screaming and jumping to motivate their respective frogs, Annette inadvertently got off balance with an overzealous jump, and came down smack on top of her poor frog! Time-out was called to clean up the mess and take away the remains, and poor Annette got sick, ditched her shoes and wasn't the same for a little while that day. It was a nasty mess all the way around. Word of the incident spread fast and Annette was an instant celebrity on campus.

Late afternoon that day meant the traditional Wednesday Raider kegger at Mastro's on Rio Plumas, followed by a trip up Magnolia Street to the stadium parking lot for "Ghost Town" and its' carnival atmosphere. I laughed heartily at the new Block HV inductees being splattered with eggs, and even threw a few eggs myself. I also tried the "Bucking Horse" ride, a 55-gallon drum rigged up to a bunch of ropes that were pulled in every possible direction by members of the sponsoring agi fraternity. They couldn't get me off, but I suffered raw, sore hands in the process. I was sitting rather forlornly in front of Iris later that night, wishing Debbie could be there with me, when Dan and his new girlfriend, Sue, returned. We talked a while and Sue tried to lift my spirits.

I had a make-up test Thursday in Geography that I hadn't even studied for, so as a means of rebelling against a professor who would be insensitive enough to schedule an exam during Western

Week I simply walked in, signed my name, and promptly walked out, to the surprise and astonishment of the professor and fellow classmates. No one was going to ruin my last Western Week, test or no. I was doing well in the class anyway, but would have to work my fanny off the rest of the semester to get a decent grade. Then it was back over to Rio Plumas for another kegger at Mastro's.

I expected Debbie up on Friday, in the late afternoon, so until her arrival I passed the time away sipping on some hard cider. Got that mellow feeling real quick. She was running a little late, so when she finally arrived we were due to head to the fairgrounds for the Western Week rodeo. I went nuts seeing her pull up, for I had not seen her since Spring Break a few weeks before. She looked great, and was bubbling with excitement over being back at Happy Valley at Western Week time. She let me know it was okay to kiss her, as long as we were careful about her still healing nose. I kissed her right there in the front yard and held her so tight I almost hurt her. When we stopped kissing she caught her breath and jokingly said, "Boy, you really did miss me!"

"More than you'll ever know, babe," I replied. "How about a quick drink inside, and then we need to be on our way to the rodeo. I'm competing this year, you know. First time ever, and I'm really excited about it. Me and two other fraternity brothers are in the calf-saddling contest. That should be a real screamer, especially since we'll all be ripped and will be lucky just to see the calf, let alone put a saddle on it."

She laughed, knowing I wasn't kidding about our Delta Phi prospects. She had been to one rodeo event, but neither of us had been a contestant nor among the contestants on the far side of the grounds opposite the grandstands. The event I was in required my fraternity brothers and me to first put a saddle on the terrified animal and then for one of us to ride it over the finish line.

We drank some hard cider in the apartment, and hopped in Debbie's car. I had my contestant number so I showed it at the south gate of the fairgrounds and we were waved through. We drove through the open field to the back of the rodeo grounds where we saw all the other contestants, their cars, and the many livestock trailers and trucks that had transported the animals to the fairgrounds.

I spotted Dan, Jack and Benny, who were in an event representing Raiders. This was the first year Raiders had been recognized officially to gain entry in the rodeo events. It helped that the student body president was a Raider, the same one who had appointed me to the Judicial Appellate position. Debbie and I joined the others and worked some more on the hard cider I had brought with me.

I was feeling "relaxed" when our event came up, but I was a little nervous about the idea of getting a saddle on the calf. Sure, it was all meant to be fun, but it would be embarrassing to fail altogether. The fun part was the anticipation and standing with friends in the contestant area getting loose for the event. Well, the time finally came and Jay, Jerry and I ran around the inside of the arena trying to lasso our calf to the cheers and yells of spectators. The calf was predictably uncooperative, so I thought I'd rough it up a little. Wrong! When I tried to "tackle" it, I ended up the worse for wear with my body being thrown to the ground and trampled over. I received a nice little battle wound, also called a "strawberry", on my left shoulder. We finally got the saddle on the calf, but were too late in getting it over the line. Someone else beat us to it. But we had fun, and didn't fail miserably.

After the rodeo Debbie and I returned to Iris Street to meet up with Dan, Jack, and my parents. We talked for a while and when mom and dad left to return to their motel I lead Debbie to my apartment where we spent the night.

On Saturday we all went to the parade and then watched Dan play in an exhibition rugby match. Rugby had just arrived at Happy Valley that year and the new team was playing a "B" side from an established club in the San Francisco Bay Area.

Sunday Debbie departed in the early afternoon for her three-hour drive back to Marin County. We hadn't talked much about my military service status, and by not doing so she could undoubtedly deduce that I was still in limbo.

In recent weeks I had been talking to Chip about his post graduation plans. He had already signed the papers to enlist in the Air Force. "I didn't really see any other choice," he said. "I'll be damned if I'm going to let myself get drafted, and I know it's impossible to get into a reserve unit. I tried to sign up for one down close to home, in Sonora, thinking I had some connections, but it fizzled out on me." There was that Navy A-6 roaring in again. This time it was Chip.

"Yeah. I know what you mean. What are you going to do in the Air Force?"

"Not sure yet. I took the test and they just said I'd be doing something along administrative lines."

The word "administrative" sounded like music to my ears, compared to bullets and hidden bamboo rods. "Chip, who did you talk to?"

"It was a Tech Sergeant Holmes in the recruiting office downtown. Why don't you go see him?"

"You know, I think I will. I'm in the same predicament as you. Time is closing in on me, and I'd rather enlist than take my chances with the draft. The idea of enlisting doesn't exactly light Debbie's fire, but I also need to keep in mind how I feel about all this."

"That's right. You've got to do what's right for you, what you really want to do. I'm sure you have heard the expression that if things are meant to work out for you and Debbie, then they will."

"I think I'll go over to that office tomorrow."

"Good luck," Chip answered.

The next day I walked downtown and introduced myself to Tech Sergeant Holmes, the local Air Force recruiter. We had a good talk, and he was very positive about the opportunities in the Air Force. He likened that branch of the service to a business, which I suspect the Air Force felt would resonate with prospective college graduates, and explained in general terms why he felt that way. He said he was sure I would be placed in the administrative job series somewhere, and told me I would need to take a test. I left his office assuring him I would return a couple days later to take the test that would determine where my strengths lay. As an afterthought, I suspected that business was good for Sergeant Holmes and that he was meeting his quotas for recruits. While enlisting in the Air Force was not my number one option, I felt good about my meeting and my decision to look into it as I walked back to the apartment on that pretty, warm Spring day.

A couple of weeks after taking the test Sergeant Holmes called me to advise of the results. "Strong administrative test results," he indicated. "If you enlist we'll send you to basic training for eight weeks, and then you'll go to a special school to learn Air Force administrative skills."

"Sounds good to me," I told him. "When would I go?"

"When do you graduate?"

"June first," I said.

"Well, you could go home for 30 days and then return here to sign up, at which time you would be given a physical and await orders to training."

"Okay. I'll be in touch with you. Am I assured a slot?"

"Yes, so long as you sign up by 30 June."

"Where would I be stationed?" I asked.

"I couldn't tell you that. The only thing I can guarantee is your specialty field."

"I see. Well, like I said I'll be in touch with you before June 30th," I said, adding, "I guess the ball is in my court, as they say." I felt good that I had something lined up, that things weren't being left to chance anymore and that I finally had some sort of plan. And I had a good feeling about being in the Air Force. It seemed to be a good organization and I felt I would fit in well. I knew I wasn't going to let myself be drafted, but I also told myself I would keep knocking on doors of reserve units. And I needed to talk to Debbie.

I called her that night to tell her the news.

"That sounds nice, Dave, but four years, and you don't know where you'll be stationed.

"I realize that, Debbie, but I have no other choice. I have to do something," I emphasized. I could feel the tension and her displeasure with the Air Force idea. "At least now I know what I'll be doing to meet my military service obligation. Maybe I'll end up at Hamilton Air Force Base or Travis. Even Beale in Yuba City isn't that far away." Then again, I could be stationed anywhere in the bloody world. I think they had Air Force bases in Greenland.

Wouldn't that be a sweetheart assignment. Granted, I had no earthly idea where I would be sent.

"But what if you get sent somewhere else?" I sensed the tension building.

"I don't know. For goodness sakes, Debbie, I'm doing the best I can in a very tough situation. I've said it before and I will say it again. I really do not want to get shot at. I guess we'll just have to let time take its course and see what happens. I love you and don't want to lose you. At least this way I'm reasonably assured of living through the Vietnam War. Did you know that this is the worst year of the war, and that the U.S. is suffering an average of one-thousand casualties a week, Debbie, and the highest amount of deaths from the fighting over there? I really do not want any part of it."

"That's true, and I think you're right, especially the more I hear my father talk about the war and all its casualties. Things will work out okay, Dave. I just know it. I love you. I really do," she said in the sweetest way.

I hung up the phone and returned to my studies. I really felt relieved after talking to Debbie, particularly in her acknowledgement that maybe I was making the best decision. Maybe things would turn out all right. I just wanted to get it over, although a four-year enlistment was undeniably the long way to do it. Finals were approaching and I didn't want to botch anything up at this late stage in the game. I wanted that diploma June first, and even though Happy Valley had so many great memories that could never be duplicated, I wanted to graduate and move on.

I had a number of interviews for jobs with different business firms, mostly located in the San Francisco Bay Area, and had received an offer letter from a large department store chain to enter their Executive Development Program. I decided I wanted to go into retailing, so had focused my interviews there. I wasn't interested in banking, and didn't have the skills for accounting work. The interviewing companies understood the ramifications of the draft, and all indicated they would hire and work around military service. I accepted the offer from the department store firm and was later told by return letter to report to their downtown

San Francisco store for training on July 15th. The thought of getting a paycheck either from my prospective employer or the Air Force excited me, for I was anxious to buy my first car, so excited in fact that I almost got talked into buying a nifty little 1966 Austin Healey convertible from an Iris Street neighbor. I finally told myself not to rush things, and that I didn't have the money yet anyway.

While still a little muddy, my future plans were taking some shape. I would either be working in San Francisco for a while, which would put me close to Debbie, or I would be going into the Air Force. It was that simple. But the final fallout of the Air Force proposition left many question marks. Oh, well, what the hell! Progress!

Finals came and went, and I went on rounds to the professor's offices to check on scores and grades. I passed everything, and knew I would graduate. Hot damn. I made it. It was both a happy and a sad moment. Nothing it seemed could replicate those four memorable years at Happy Valley College, particularly my first three years. It was like living in a dream world. Referring to Happy Valley as "paradise" or "Shangri La" was not a stretch. There were such great friends, experiences, camaraderie and fun, and certainly enough dilemmas to give me a somewhat steep growing up curve. Those early carefree years were a wonderful memory. But a future away from Happy Valley lay ahead, and with Debbie in the middle of it. I hoped.

CHAPTER TWENTY-SEVEN

Three things occurred within a couple of weeks after graduation and returning home to Danville. One of them I had no choice in doing. Another I both needed and wanted to do. And the other I wanted to do come hell or high water, ignoring an uncertain future.

In the first week of June, on the first working day following my arrival in Danville, I borrowed my parent's car to drive to nearby Martinez where I was required to inform my local Selective Service office of my recent graduation from college. Goodbye student deferment. My college deferment was officially history and I was now a healthy prime target for the draft. Put more simply and bluntly, my butt now belonged to Uncle Sam. He was now going to call the shots.

On my way home I stopped at the local British Motors car dealership in Walnut Creek. I needed to do something crazy to dilute the Selective Service experience. I immediately fell in love with a few of the used MGs on the lot, particularly a baby-blue 1961 MG Coupe. I knew it was foolish to be thinking of buying a car, but I needed a set of wheels and I convinced myself I would worry about any consequences later. Plus, my subconscious yearned to support my father's opinion that I was impetuous and impulsive when it came to buying something. If I wanted something, I wanted it now. I was not into delayed gratification. Not next week, not next month. Dad was just the opposite. I remember the time he wanted a simple transistor radio. How did he obtain it? He contacted his Norwegian cousin, who captained one of the world's largest oil tanker ships, to bring him back a transistor radio after his next trip to Japan!

Well, I bought the car for $1300, convincing the dealer of my good credit and future upcoming employment with the department store in San Francisco. I obviously didn't tell them I was choice bait for the draft, and I neglected to explain the scenario regarding the Air Force. The dealership simply saw me as a recent college grad that had a job offer. That's all it took.

A few days later, after getting the hang of driving my nifty MG around, I drove into San Francisco to visit a discount jeweler with whom Dad had dealt. He was also a good friend of the owner. I would have much preferred to get the engagement ring I was planning on buying for Debbie at one of the fancy jewelry stores in Sausilito we had so often visited, like Eatons, but that was way above my price range. And Dad opined that, "why go to a jeweler downtown when you can get the same thing at a discount store in the city?" He showed me the catalog. The pictures looked okay, so what the hell, right? I'll bite.

The store wasn't paying front footage on Market Street in San Francisco. It wasn't even paying second floor footage. It didn't even have a bloody shingle hanging on the wall at street level. It did have an elevator access, however, which I took to the third floor, pushed a bell, and was let in. I guess this was how the jewelry business was conducted in cities. I introduced myself and asked for Fred. Moments later Fred appeared, smiling, asking how my Dad was, and ready to do business. I had a small budget for the engagement ring, and Fred understood, so he showed me the best diamond ring he had for the money and I bought it. I was to come back to pick up the ring a couple of days later.

Damn, I was just moving right along. I sure didn't convey any appearance that I was terribly worried about the future. And I really wasn't. You could say I had blinders on, or maybe that I was in denial of something evil lurking out there, but I was just focusing on Debbie. To hell with all the rest. I had a job starting July 15th in the city, I had a set of wheels, and I had plan B, which was enlisting in the Air Force. At that point I was in fact deceiving myself to think that the Air Force was plan B, for it was quite in fact plan A. I conveniently didn't think often about plan B. Maybe if I ignored some of the more distasteful options they might go away. Everything was up for grabs if I needed plan B. I was making plans and living as though there was no Vietnam War, no Air Force enlistment, and no draft board hungry for my warm body. I was living under a big delusion that somehow everything was going to work out, as if a reserve or Guard unit would in fact call me and ask me to join. And no, I wasn't smoking dope.

I picked up the ring on Thursday and continued on through the city, past the big Buddha in the window of a private residence on Bay Street, over the Golden Gate Bridge and up highway 101 to San Rafael to Debbie's to surprise her that night with the ring.

Arriving at her house I acted as normal as I could, even though my insides were in a near frenzy with excitement and anticipation over getting her away from the house to put the ring on her finger. I had no doubt in my mind that she would say, "Yes," for we were deeply in love, and we had talked a great deal in recent weeks about a future together and her willingness to wait things out for me.

On a gorgeous California night we drove out of town a short distance on the road to Stinson Beach. I turned off on a side road and parked the car with a view of the hills that the evening coastal fog was slowly creeping over on its course further inland. Her sixth sense may have been telling her something was up, for she didn't even ask why I had pulled off onto a road we had never been on before. Earlier, at the house, I had merely suggested we take a little drive. Of course, doing that sort of thing also gave us the opportunity to be alone and share intimacies in private. She was always responsive when I suggested a drive somewhere to be alone.

After sitting in the car a short while and talking about the day each of us had had, I decided it was time to pop the question. I suddenly found myself short on words, so just said the first thing that came to mind. "Debbie, you know I love you very much. I hope that some day I will be your husband."

Before I had a chance to go on, she looked at me with those beautiful eyes and said, ever so softly, "yes, I know, and I want to be your wife. It will happen, Dave, I just know it."

"Debbie, I bought something for you, and you would make me the happiest guy in the world if you would accept it and wear it." I pulled the box from my jacket pocket, opened it, and took the ring in my thumb and forefinger to carefully extract it from the box. I admit that the method I used in giving her the ring was not very creative, such as having it served up in a drink or dessert at a fancy restaurant or in a scoop of Baskin Robbins ice-cream, but by Debbie's reaction I could tell I had done the right thing. Amidst a beaming thousand-dollar smile and true surprise, she was overjoyed as I placed the ring onto her finger.

"Oh, Dave. Oh, Dave. I can't believe it. I love you so much," she said as she clasped her thin brown arms around my neck and kissed me repeatedly.

"I love you so much, babe," I told her in return as we held tightly to one another and lost all consciousness of our surroundings, and most of all an uncertain future. There were no guarantees of anything. I could end up in Vietnam and come home in a pine box. I could enter the Air Force and be stationed for a few years in Greenland or Europe. I could get hit by a Mack truck the next day for that matter, but you know what I mean. The only guarantee was that I was going to serve in the military. We stayed in the parked car for a bit longer to hug and kiss and enjoy the satisfying closeness.

"Let's hurry back," Debbie suggested. "I'm so excited, and I do want to tell my family the wonderful news as soon as possible. Oh, Dave, I'm so happy."

"I can't wait till we're together always, Debbie," I affectionately told her. It was an expression both of us used when we were together and sharing sweet thoughts.

"I know, and I can't either, Dave. I hope it's soon," she added. She looked at the ring repeatedly as we drove back through town to her parent's house.

Her parents shared our excitement and were genuinely happy for us.

I explained everything to my parents when I returned home that night, and the next day Mom informed me that she was going to have a combination graduation-engagement announcement party in our honor the following weekend. I wasn't overly thrilled about having such a formal event, but Mom was obviously determined to have the function so I was not going to try to discourage her.

Two major events occurred the following week. On Tuesday I received a new draft card in the mail. As expected, it had the dreaded classification 1-A. Although I was expecting such a re-classification, the combination of the speed with which the new card was issued coupled with the unmistakable 1-A that I read on the card caused my heart to sink and my nervousness over the entire situation to escalate. I had admittedly been rather impervious to my vulnerability in recent weeks, ignoring possible negative consequences, but the mail that day brought me swiftly back to reality. It wasn't now a matter of what I was going to do; it was simply a question of when I would make the call to the Air Force recruiter in Happy Valley to tell him I was ready to sign up. I still had almost two weeks before the June 30 deadline, so I would call around the 28th. Why hurry? I rationalized that the Air Force would have me for the next four years.

That night I called Debbie to break the bad news to her. She was devastated, but trying to look ahead to the light at the end of the tunnel. She was encouraging, saying, "Don't worry, Dave, everything is going to work out alright for us. I love you, and don't forget it."

In my anguished state, it was easy to say to myself, "I'm glad you feel like that. But this is a real disaster. Your life isn't being turned upside down. I'm the one that is being pulled away to Lord knows where, to give the next four years of my life to the Air Force. What will I be doing, where will I be, and will you still be there for me?" The cynical insecure part of me had doubts on the latter, but that was a demon I had to deal with.

The next night, Wednesday, I was in downtown Walnut Creek on Broadway in a men's clothing store, Grodins. I had to get out of the house and Broadway, a short street with interesting specialty shops great for window shopping, was a good destination and distraction. In Grodins I was looking at some sport shirts (Gant shirts like my good friend Jack encouraged me to buy … if I could afford them!), when a salesman approached.

"Can I help you?" he asked nicely.

"No, thanks, I'm just looking," I replied.

"The Gant's are very nice shirts," he offered, obviously trying to perk some purchasing interest on my part. That wasn't going to work for me, however, for I didn't have any money to spend. He didn't know that, though.

"Yes, I know. A friend of mine from college wears nothing but Gants."

"Where do you go to school?" he asked. He appeared to be interested in the conversation, and not solely to sell me a shirt.

"Used to. I just graduated from Happy Valley College a couple of weeks ago."

"Ah. Happy Valley. I know some people that went there. I even went to one of your Western days celebrations. Had a great time."

"Western Week."

"Yes, that's it."

"I had four great Western Weeks and four great years at Happy Valley. I really hated to leave, but life does go on."

"Doing what?" What are your plans?"

"Well, I've got an offer from the Emporium to start as an Executive Trainee next month. But I've got a little problem."

"Oh, what's that? Let me guess. The draft."

Perceptive guy. "Yep. Just got my 1-A card in the mail yesterday. They didn't waste any time re-classifying me."

"Don't feel bad. Many friends of mine are experiencing the same thing right now. Have you thought of another branch of the service?"

"As a matter of fact I have. My plan right now is to sign up with the Air Force. It's four years, but at least I should get more out of it. I'm sure not looking forward to leaving my girlfriend in Marin County, though."

"That's smart on your part," he replied. "But maybe your girlfriend can join you after your basic training."

I couldn't believe I was having this conversation with a total stranger in a clothes store in Walnut Creek. It seemed oddly out of place, but he was a nice guy and it did me some good to talk out some of my concerns. "Well, I hope she can join me. We got engaged last weekend, but I just hope she'll wait for me. Tricky business nowadays, you know?"

"Yes. I agree. I'm glad I don't have that problem with my girlfriend. I'm not going anywhere."

"Oh? How are you so fortunate, if I may ask a rather personal question?" I asked, with obvious envy.

"I'm in a reserve unit. In fact, I've been in the unit about two years now. I was lucky to get in. Hey, you might want to try my unit. They probably have a waiting list, but what the hell? Give it a try."

"I'm sure they're filled up and with a waiting list, just like all the other damn units I've tried from Happy Valley to Sacramento. Sure. I'll go for it. Where's the unit located?"

"Over in Sausilito. Here's the phone number of a Major McIntyre that you need to call." He wrote down the information and handed me the piece of paper, which I carefully placed in a pocket. He had also written his name on the paper.

I liked it already. Sausilito was such a beautiful place, and it was hard for me to envision an Army base in or near that wonderfully idyllic setting. "Thanks," I told him. "I'll call him tomorrow."

"Sure thing. Hey, you want to buy a shirt?"

"Not tonight, but I may be back," I told him as I walked out, smiling. I think he understood.

"Good luck," he said, also smiling. He knew I had more important things on my mind than trying to pick out a shirt. Plus, a Gant shirt wouldn't fit in over in Nam. I was excited about having a contact for a reserve unit, knowing whom I could ask for and also having a name to drop, but I was not optimistic about my chances of getting in. I had experienced too many doors closed in my face already, and I was now in the bottom of the ninth inning, with two outs.

The next day I got up early. If I had something to do I liked to get up and get an early start. None of this lounging around all morning and losing half a day. I drove to a pay phone booth in Sausilito from where I called Major McIntyre.

After a couple rings the phone was picked up. My heart was in my stomach and my mouth dry. This was a biggee. "Eighty-first division, second brigade. Major McIntyre speaking."

Great. I got directly to the man I had to talk to, not having to go through a "gate guard" that would try to fend me off. "Major McIntyre, my name is Dave Pedersen. We have not met, but I was talking to a Gary Finelli last night in Walnut Creek and he gave me your name and number. I would very much like to talk to you about any possible openings in your unit." What a dumb thing to say … so did one million other guys!

"Yes, Mr. Pedersen. I wish I could help you, but I'm sure you can understand I have a long waiting list of men that also want to get in this unit." He sounded like a very nice gentleman over the phone. He had an even, controlled voice, and I could detect a trace of empathy in it. But that did me no good. I was feeling devastated again. Same old shit. But something told me to try harder.

"I see. Well, Sir, I'm in Sausilito right now calling from a pay phone. I would like to come in and see you nonetheless."

"Yes, that would be okay. But I can't promise you anything," he said. It was an opening that gave me a possible, yet remote, ray of hope. He gave me directions, telling me I had to go through a long tunnel under the mountain and to just observe the lights at the tunnel entrance.

"Thank you, Major. I'll be right there."

I found the one-way tunnel okay, and went berserk waiting for the light to turn green to let me in. Coming out of the long tunnel I was in a desolate valley, with the brown, dry hills above and to the west of Sausilito to my right, and the hills separating me from the entrance to San Francisco Bay and the Pacific Ocean to my left. There were no buildings to be seen anywhere, which seemed so peculiar considering the proximity of San Francisco and the Sausilito-Tiburon area. It was definitely a government land reserve. I was driving west on a winding two-lane road that eventually took me to Fort Attlebury with its two reserve center sites consisting mainly of light tan colored two-story buildings from World War II vintage. The buildings looked like old barracks.

I parked my car among the buildings and from where I stood could see the Pacific Ocean about 500 yards in front of me. The water looked gray due to the fog that still hung low over this southernmost tip of Marin County. I could also hear the low, long sound of a foghorn sending out its rhythmic warning signal to boaters and ships to beware of the dangerous rocky shoreline. I hoped the dense, eerie fog was not an ominous symbol of bad news ahead. I've always loved the sound of a foghorn. I walked down some steps from the road to the landing of the Major's office building. I then walked in a single doorway, up a flight of stairs that opened up onto a long hallway. The place was very quiet, and for good reason. The Major, I concluded, was the only person working in the building that particular day.

I went about halfway down the hall, my steps echoing off the narrow passageway walls. The floor was a green linoleum tile that had recently been waxed and buffed, and the walls were gypsum board painted a pale green. This was a very simple, unimpressive military office building. I found the Major's name on the wall near a door and knocked.

"Come in," a welcoming voice said.

I opened the door to a nondescript, spartanly furnished office that consisted of a large gray metal desk, which the Major stood behind, a gray metal filing cabinet with glass coverlets, and a couple of standard gray metal chairs that had a thin cushion of green vinyl. Probably all government-issue, I thought. A nameplate on the front of the desk had a bronze oak leaf that represented the rank of the owner, the letters "MAJ McIntyre" centered, and some other emblem on the right side that probably signified his Army career field.

I said, "Good morning, Major, I'm Dave Pedersen. I just spoke to you a short time ago on the phone. Thank you so much for seeing me this morning. I wanted to come in and talk to you about the unit."

"Yes. Yes. Come in and have a seat. The Major looked friendly. He wore glasses with thick lens, and had military length black wavy hair. He had a slight twitch with his eyes, and his overall demeanor helped me relax and gave me some hope that he might be reasonable. "Tell me something about yourself," he said.

I quickly surmised this was an "interview". I emphasized activities I had been involved in while in high school and college, and told him about my career plans in business now that I was armed with my bachelor's degree. I also told him about Debbie, our recent engagement, and happened to mention that her father was a retired Marine Corps colonel. This really got his attention, particularly when I described further what line of work Debbie's father was presently engaged in as a civil servant at the nearby Presidio in San Francisco and that his last duty assignment prior to retiring was with the Joint U.S. Military Assistance Group in Saigon, or JUSMAG as it was called. I could tell he made a mental note of it. I indicated that I was looking into the Air Force, and had only a short time before a commitment was expected from me.

"Very interesting. Tell me, Dave, would you be interested in the officer corps?"

This was not time to make distinctions between being enlisted and officer in a reserve unit. "Oh, yes, Sir, I would." At least that sounded good. I was prepared to do or say anything at this point.

"Well, that may be one possible way we could get you in," he suggested.

"I see. Well, I'm interested, Sir."

"I think you could fit in nicely here," he confided.

Holy cow. What was this guy suggesting? Was I going to make it in? "I hope so, Sir. When would I know, Sir?" Boy, I was laying on the "Sirs" big time, and like it was the nicest word in the English language. Of course, at that juncture, the word "Sir" certainly seemed the most appropriate word to use. And after all, I was in the presence of a military officer.

"I'll check my records, Dave, and will try to get back to you as soon as possible. I realize the deadline you have. I can't promise anything. I'll have to see which of our specialties may have an opening. What I want you to do is go to the Presidio to take an aptitude test so we can see which specialty field you can enter. I'll call ahead to say you are coming over. You're in luck. Today is a scheduled test day."

"Yes, Sir. Thank you, Major. I've enjoyed talking to you and having the pleasure of meeting you."

"Yes. Likewise. You appear to be a fine young man." He gave me directions to the building at the Presidio and I stood up to leave.

"Thank you, Sir. I'll wait to hear from you."

My spirits were flying sky high as I walked down the hall, down the steps and out of the building into a dreary, overcast day at Fort Attlebury. Screw the weather. The weather didn't bother me, for I had accomplished my objective. I asserted myself with the Major by saying I wanted to see him and was successful in doing so. Going in to see him face to face made a significant difference in the outcome of the day. Now I was on my way to take an exam. Hopefully, he would receive the results back from it soon and could make a decision. Wowwee!! Damn, there was hope after all. Maybe his interest in me stemmed from the status of Debbie's father in the Marine Corps. Who knows? Hey, what the hell. Whatever works.

I flew across the Golden Gate Bridge, found my building at the Presidio, and reported in for the exam. I concentrated on every question and did the best I possibly could, for it had the potential of being my ticket to an only slightly disrupted future, but nonetheless one on which I could make plans with Debbie.

Before leaving the Presidio I called Debbie's father to tell him the good news. He asked me to whom I spoke at Fort Attlebury, so I supplied him with both a name and phone number and all the pertinent details. He didn't suggest he would call the Major, and I didn't ask.

As I drove home to Danville a plethora of thoughts and reflections cascaded like Bridal Vail Falls in Yosemite. As we commonly told one another at Happy Valley, "I was chippy." Said another way, which is why I kept telling myself, "This is it, Dave. This is it. Right down to the friggin' final hour." I couldn't believe it. I tried to prevent myself from being too optimistic, for there was certainly no guarantee and no sign for such, but I couldn't help it. Debbie was more than ever like the Sirens in Greek mythology. I was captivated by her and pulled to her in so many ways. She was the center of my life. I loved her very much and wanted a future together for us. I gripped the steering wheel with fervor as I drove up Bay Street in San Francisco, this time ignoring the beautiful homes lining the marina, and especially the house with the big bay window and a huge Buddha sitting in it looking out onto the bay from its second floor perch. I continued up the Embarcadero before making my way onto the expressway leading to the Bay Bridge and the Oakland side of the bay.

It had turned into a beautiful, sunny day. The fog had burned off, awaiting late afternoon when it would again creep in over the hills of the city. San Francisco was a fantastically beautiful place. Driving along the Embarcadero reminded me of seeing off my grandparents many years ago on an ocean cruise to Grandpa's home in Honolulu. He was born in Honolulu of Spanish parents in 1896, and always had wonderful stories of his youth in that city. In fact, my Mother told me that Grandpa's Father was married to Hawaiian royal blood but that the marriage had ended in divorce. Seeing the merchant ships tied up also conjured up a statement made by the Norwegian uncle on my Dad's side when my brother and I were in high school. My Dad had been born in Norway and "Uncle Peder" was a cousin of his. Uncle Peder had told us one night while we dined in his Captain's quarters, "Maybe some day if the timing is right I can take you boys on one of my voyages to Japan and the Persian Gulf." I had never forgotten that offer. And he could make it happen, for he was the Captain of one of the world's largest super tankers. I still held the dream, for my Norwegian blood gave me the yearning to travel and a sense of ease and comfort the few times I had been on small and large vessels in open water. I wanted to see the world. I didn't want to stay in Happy Valley like so many of my friends. My world went much farther, across the oceans, to the Orient and to Europe. I wanted to see those places and walk among their cities and people at some point in my life. Given half the opportunity to travel, color me gone, but not with Debbie in my life. Not now. Debbie trumped my desire to travel.

Right now, however, I was racked with high anxiety over the prospect of getting into a reserve unit, and of being able to tell Debbie, "I'm just going to be away for four months, then we'll be together forever." Getting into a reserve unit would solve my most immediate concern. The one weekend a month drills would be a piece of cake and gladly attended in view of the alternative. Debbie was everything at that point in my life, and everything else took a back seat, including travel. Sure, my new job was also foremost in my mind, but nothing would happen if the draft or Air Force got me. I couldn't believe it. I had only about ten days in which to contact the Air Force and lock myself into a commitment there. Ten days! My hands got sweaty on the steering wheel as I realized how critical the timing had become. "Oh, Lord," I prayed, "Please make this happen. Please allow me to get into that reserve unit so I have a better idea of what my future will be." I really did not know if praying would work, or that He would listen to me, for after all, I had told him four years previous that I wanted to enter the ministry and I backed out. I lowered my head for a fleeting instant, eyes closed, as a symbol of my hope and despair, while speeding across the San Francisco-Oakland Bay Bridge, thankfully ahead of rush hour traffic.

Upon arriving home I explained the events of the day to my parents. They were cautiously optimistic themselves, and were of course hoping for the best. They knew how much I was agonizing over the situation.

I called Debbie, who kept repeating, "Oh, Dave, I hope it works out for you this time. If it does, you won't be gone that long," she observed. She was feeling some wear and tear emotionally from this business also, up and down like a yo-yo with the engagement and the knowledge that nothing in the short run was guaranteed. We literally were on the fence and had no idea of which way we would fall.

The weekend at Debbie's was different. We were both filled with hope that I would get the desired phone call soon, and yet we were simultaneously frightened by the consequences of bad news. The disruption would be traumatic. It was almost a somber weekend. Little was said about the prospects of being accepted into a reserve unit. We didn't have to say much, knowing what was on one another's mind. Occasionally throughout the weekend one or the other would offer a statement of hope and optimism, and that things would work out all right. We'll make it, we reminded ourselves. We took in a drive-in movie, so we could snuggle, and spent the day Saturday at the Cliff House overlooking the Pacific Ocean with its angry waves pounding against the rocks below. We walked hand in hand at nearby Rockaway Beach and drew hearts in the sand. I alternately gazed into Debbie's mysterious eyes and at the ocean's horizon, intrigued by what I knew lay beyond, for I knew the world's geography.

It was tougher than normal saying goodbye to Debbie on Sunday, knowing time was getting short for a resolution to our dilemma.

Two days later, on Tuesday, I got the phone call of a lifetime.

I was in the backyard at home bagging some rays when the phone rang. Dashing into the house, for every phone call could be THE call, I picked up the receiver and heard the new but distinctly familiar voice of Major McIntyre.

"Hello," I said into the receiver.

"Could I speak to Dave Pedersen, please," the person at the other end stated.

"This is Dave Pedersen speaking."

"Hello, Dave, this is Major McIntyre. How are you today?"

"Just fine, Sir, and you?" I said that knowing my gut was in knots and that I was praying like crazy for some good news. This phone conversation was BIG. It could impact the next four years of my life, if not more.

"I am doing well, thank you. I have some good news for you." In the instant that he paused I thought I would lose all self-control. I couldn't believe my ears. "There is a slot for you in the unit and it is yours if you wish to take it."

If I wish to take it, he asks? I couldn't get the words out fast enough, and was tripping over them with a near stuttering reply. "Oh, thank you, Sir," I gushed with unabashed delight. "Yes, Sir, I'll take it. I sure will. That's wonderful news."

"Well, I was very impressed with you, and your test results came out good. You'll be receiving orders in the mail to advise you of a reporting date for basic training, and after basic training you'll be going to Supply School."

"Sounds wonderful," I replied. "What do I need to do at this point?"

"I've scheduled you for a physical at the Oakland processing center for next Wednesday. Otherwise, all you can do is await your orders."

"Yes, Sir. Do you have any idea of where I will be going to basic training?" I couldn't believe I asked such a question, for it made no difference to me where I went for that eight-week period, but I was excited and making conversation.

"No, I don't. You may be fortunate to get Fort Ord, but there's no guarantee. It's all a matter of the Army filling its' quotas."

"When will I be ordered to report?"

"Probably in the November time frame. That would be about normal. There's normally about a two to three month delay in processing. But I'm sure that will fit into your plans okay?"

"Oh, yes, Sir. It certainly will."

"Well, that's all I have to tell you at this time. How's your uncle?" he asked.

I knew immediately to whom he was referring, and it clicked that I had better not attempt to correct him. If he was under the illusion that Debbie's father was my uncle, fine, so be it. Don't blow it at this point by trying to correct him and possibly confuse the poor guy. "Oh, he's fine, Sir. Doing very well, as a matter of fact."

"Very good," he answered. "Please give him my regards."

"Oh, I will, Sir." Geez, the way he was talking in such deferential terms one would think my "Uncle" was a General! Great, I thought. I could use all the help I could get.

"Goodbye, David. I'll see you when you report after your training."

"Goodbye, Sir, and thank you so much for all you've done. I'm very grateful to you and will make a good Soldier."

"You're welcome, David, and I am confidant that you will be a good Soldier." He was sincere, but the tone of his voice told me he had heard such gratification many times before from happy reserve enlistees. "Goodbye," he added.

"Goodbye again, Sir", I said, and hanged up the phone.

I immediately let out a prolonged scream of excitement and joy. "I did it. I did it," I yelled repeatedly, and explained the good news to two bewildered parents who had come rushing into the kitchen upon hearing my screams of joy.

It was truly a miracle. The process started so many months before in Happy Valley to locate and get accepted into a reserve unit was finally over. I flashed back to the many miles put on cars borrowed from friends, of sorrowful calls to Debbie to describe my feelings of despair and frustration after repeated failures to find a unit, and of alternate plans made in the event they were needed. So close. So damn close. If it hadn't been for the good fortune of talking to a stranger in a clothes store in nearby Walnut Creek and making the extra effort to see the head of the reserve unit personally, I would not have felt the tremendous sense of relief and happiness that the phone call from the Major had brought, and I know that I would have been on my way into the Air Force. Entering the Air Force, I speculated, would probably have spelled the end of my relationship with Debbie, for as strong a relationship I felt we had, and as much as we meant to one another, something told me she would not have followed me to my permanent duty station, wherever that might be. The distance apart would have killed the relationship.

I called Debbie that night to tell her the wonderful news. We talked long, not really saying anything much, and just filling the phone lines with "I love you" and "I can't wait to be with you always". That kind of stuff. We were both feeling such relief, and with it the hope of being together always. The last thing I said to Debbie before hanging up the phone, choked up with emotion and relief, was "Everything is going to be alright, Debbie. I will only be gone four months."

Later that night I thought of most of the guys at Happy Valley. They still had their student deferments, and were still removed from the trauma and anxiety of what I had just been through. Although it was a part of growing up and meeting responsibilities and obligations, I still was not overly thrilled about playing Army off and on with monthly drills for the next six years of my life, but I would meet my duty and be a good Soldier.

What a transition during the past four years, from a carefree existence predominated by a very active college athletics and social life that saw limited parameters on behavior, to the realization that the next week I would be standing naked in a long line of Army inductees in a highly regimented environment to get a physical prior to military service. I reflected back on those hysterically funny and outrageously crazy days under the sun at Happy Valley College. I knew mine was a special experience, with both good and bad, fortunately mostly good, and for which I was very grateful and blessed.

CHAPTER TWENTY-EIGHT

I lucked out and was ordered to basic training and advanced individual training at Fort Ord near Monterey, California, only about two hours drive from Danville. I was nervous as hell as my parents dropped me off the day after Thanksgiving at the reception center on post and said goodbye. The good folks in the reception center checked my gear and asked a few questions about the things I had packed. I knew better than to pack a coat and tie, but Playboy magazines had to go, as well as any "civilian attire", which my parents took back home with them. I was then escorted to another nearby building where I would first meet my fellow basic trainees. We were on the second deck of an old, wooden, open bay barracks structure for a few days during processing. Our hair was shaved off, we were issued our uniform items, and we got our first exposure to pulling KP, or kitchen patrol, on an Army post. Our uniforms included a small white tag sewn above the right pocket on our fatigues shirts. They were called "maggot tags", but were intended to alert others on post that we were trainees. There had been a number of meningitis cases recently among trainees so the post officials wanted to keep us separated from the rest of the base population.

Shortly after arriving at our temporary quarters I made friends with a couple guys that were also from the Bay Area. Mike was from Castro Valley and a recent graduate of the California College of Arts and Crafts, and "Wally" was a Harvard Law School graduate now practicing in his hometown of Palo Alto. As it turned out, many of the guys were, surprise!, college graduates and were from places all over the country. One had graduated from East Carolina, a couple from Valparaiso University in Indiana, another from Washington State, and a large group from Hawaii. All in all, it was a good group.

On day four we were ordered to pack up our duffel bags and to board a "cattle truck." The truck took us across the post to the basic training barracks, where we had our first undesirable experience with a yelling, screaming, barking drill sergeant who obviously wanted to let us know who was in charge and where we fit in the whole scheme of things.

"Get your fuckin' asses off that truck you lowly maggots!" a very strack drill sergeant screamed repeatedly. "Park your butts in front of the building and stand at attention!" he continued. I could tell this guy meant business. Standing in formation I noted his nametag said Becker. Drill Sergeant Becker was a stocky, well-built man with a blonde regulation moustache about the shape of Hitler's. His DI , or Drill Instructor, cap was low over his forehead, so all we could see of the top of his head was some short, regulation-cut blond hair in the back. In fact, it wasn't until the last weekend of basic that we ever saw the top of his head. He always had his "Smokey Bear" cap on. His olive drab uniform, with the three sergeant stripes, was clean, starched, pressed, and appeared to be tailor cut for him. The bottoms of his trousers were perfectly round where they were tucked sharply into black combat boots that were spit-shined. We would find out later he put cardboard at the bottom of his trousers to make them look perfectly smooth and round. He was the perfect looking Army drill sergeant and commanded fear and respect from the first moment we set eyes on him and heard his thundering voice.

From the first roll call we also found out Drill Sergeant Becker had a good sense of humor. One of the guys in our platoon was named Bruszesllacz. He was simply called "alphabet" by the DI.

The Hawaiians were referred to collectively and individually as "pineapples".

I was in Wally's squad, along with a couple of the pineapples and one of them, Marc, was also a Harvard Law School grad and a recent Presidential Executive Fellow. Marc was a short, cheery sort with an uncharacteristically deep voice, and he wore black horn-rimmed glasses. He looked very much the intellectual he was. Mike, my friend from Castro Valley, was in another squad, but since our platoon occupied the same half floor of the open bay barracks we were able to spend some time together after supper. My bunkmate was Phil, who hailed from Salinas, just outside the back gate of Fort Ord, and who had to start each morning with a cigarette as soon as his feet hit the floor. Phil was younger than most of us, having just graduated from high school. He wasn't inclined toward college, being a musician in a band, and was taking no chances with the draft. A tight group was formed between the college graduates, and we would most every night congregate in the room shared by Wally and another squad leader, Bill, who had just finished school at the University of Missouri.

Eight weeks of basic training is certainly no picnic, but there were some enjoyable and memorable times. My older cousin, now Major Pedersen, was assigned to a Marine Corps tenant command on the post. When visiting me on Sunday visiting day he always left a six-pack of beer behind. At an appropriate time Wally would put out the word quietly for a "staff meeting", at which time each of us in the group would enjoy a beer in the privacy of Wally's room. During that time at basic, one beer would give most of us a good "buzz".

Drill Sergeant Becker was usually good for some crazy stuff, like the time he punished us for poor results on an inspection of our living spaces by bellowing out at post-lunch formation, "Second platoon fall out on the double and fall back in with foot lockers on your right shoulder!!" We couldn't believe our ears, but obviously did as directed. Each of us ran into the building, back down the steps and out the front entrance to form up with a footlocker where our M-14 rifles usually were on our shoulders.

The other DI's were howling with laughter as they observed the commotion.

During our roll call formation early in training Drill Sergeant Becker one day ordered that whenever we came out of the building for a formation we had to yell, "second platoon, second to none!" When the yelling was unsatisfactory, we had to run back upstairs, form up, and do it again. But the DI was also moderately compassionate. During week six after marching as a unit to the nearest Post Exchange facility for haircuts, he permitted us to stay in the area long enough to have a limit of two beers. The beer tasted great and the action by our drill sergeant was great for morale, plus it gave us a little spring in our steps as we happily marched back to the barracks.

I saw Debbie once on a Sunday during the entire eight weeks. Like I did with my parents when they visited, Debbie and I sat out back of the barracks at one of the picnic tables and enjoyed some home cooked food she had brought along. I wrote to her frequently, but her letters to me were not as frequent and became less so with the passing of the short time apart ("We're going to be okay, hon, it's only four months of separation and then we can plan our lives without having to worry about me going off to the rice paddies of Vietnam and getting shot at"). And I tried to look at it as just the two months since I was lead to believe we would be allowed to go off base on weekends during our specialty training after basic. I called her when I could get to a phone, but that wasn't permitted until after the midway point of basic training. This was difficult for me considering I was the one that was isolated on an Army base and out of the mainstream of things with no options.

Drill Sergeant Becker became a little more relaxed and conversed with us in casual settings during the last two weekends of training. In fact, on one day during the last weekend of basic we spied him washing his motorcycle behind the building, so a bunch of us went over to talk to him.

"Good morning, drill sergeant," I said, adding, "That's a good looking motorcycle you have there."

"Thanks. Yes, she is a beauty, and I get a lot of pleasure from riding it around."

"How much longer do you have, here, Sir?" Phil asked.

"About four months left on my current orders here, then I go to Nam. I have asked to be sent there for my next tour. I want to be a part of what we are doing over there and make my contribution."

"Yes, Sir. It sounds as though you have given it a lot of thought and it is the right thing for you to do," I said. Considering who he was and all, there really was not much else to say.

"I have, and it is what I want to do. I believe in what we are doing."

He was actually normal. He told us he was from Illinois, and had been in the Army three years. In civilian clothes, and with no DI cap covering his head, he came across as being an average guy. He was our age, and was making a career out of the Army. He was a confident man, a professional Soldier, and had always commanded our respect. He was also in excellent physical condition, despite the few beers he told us he had at the end of each day. He had a friendly smile, and was actually quite likeable.

I don't know if it was because of the typical love-hate relationship that developed between us and Drill Sergeant Becker because we were recruits, but I found myself slowly developing a greater respect and admiration for my superiors in uniform. Obviously, Drill Sergeant Becker, and even the Company Commander, a bozo of an Army Captain, was in an extreme position of authority. When the drill sergeants said, "Jump!" we asked, "How high?" But Drill Sergeant Becker also taught us to have pride in our platoon, in our unit, and to work together. But after all, that was the essence of basic training – teaching teamwork and pride.

I remember the time I helped a fellow platoon member with PT, physical training. We were on a big sandy field, and the DI that was leading the PT had purposely put Miller, a very poor physical specimen, over a pool of water. Seeing him struggle with pushups, I stayed upright on one arm and tried to help him with my other arm. I felt bad for him and wanted to help. I was being a good team member, but I felt bitterness toward the DI. At one point I could tell that Drill Sergeant Becker said something to the other DI. I decided then and there I would follow Drill Sergeant

Becker "up any hill", an expression I learned from returning Vietnam vets.

There was one unusual and most unexpected occurrence toward the end of basic training. Our Sergeant Major called me into his office after morning formation and said I was to report to building NH140 and that transportation was being sent for me. I was more that a bit surprised to see my cousin.

Stunned, I still rendered the required military respect by standing at attention and saluting him.

"Private Pedersen reporting as directed, Sir."

He saluted. "Hello, Dave," he said. "You can call me Bill."

"Yes, Sir. Bill." This would not be easy after seven weeks of calling everyone Sir that was ranked higher than a Private.

The meeting was short. He told me he was assigned to a Counter Intelligence unit and asked me to keep my ears close to the ground in the event I might hear any discussion or see behavior that was subversive in nature within my training company. With that, we chatted for a few minutes and he dismissed me, knowing I had to return to my training unit. I had to chuckle later while thinking about the matter, wondering what my Sergeant Major and the company chain of command was thinking.

The best day of basic, graduation, finally arrived, and it was tough saying goodbye to Drill Sergeant Becker. There were a lot of reasons for this, including the camaraderie, the respect, the admiration for what he stood for, and certainly the courage he displayed in wanting to go to Nam. We all put on our Class A dress uniforms that Saturday morning, having sewed on our little gold, single private stripes shaped like butterfly wings in the down position, and pinned on a red and yellow ribbon we had been provided, and marched around the parade field for the ceremony. I felt immense pride wearing the uniform.

That night our small group was invited to my cousin's quarters on post for a party. His wife put out a lavish spread of spaghetti, rotisserie chicken, tossed salad and garlic bread, along with some fantastic carrot cake and we all drank our fill of beer. Getting real food was such a delight. Basic was behind us, history.

On Sunday morning we were taken in small groups to the main part of the post where most of us would be in various AIT schools. I felt a quiet, unemotional sense of pleasure in looking around at the basic training area as we departed. It would be the last time I had to set foot in it. Gone was the exercising while standing in line for chow, the forced marches carrying our heavy M14 rifles with the heavy wood stocks, and the malicious treatment of basic trainees by permanent party personnel assigned to our barracks galley who took sinister pleasure in needlessly overworking trainees assigned to KP duty.

Most of us in the Supply School were granted leave after our first week. We first had to "police" the area around our barracks, then pass a personal appearance inspection Saturday morning before being permitted to depart the post. I got a ride from a friend going to Oakland, where my parents would meet me. Soon after arriving home I drove over to Debbie's for the night.

To put it mildly, I could not wait to see Debbie and to again hold her in my arms. Never mind how horny I was. I was wearing my Class A uniform. I figured I was still on orders, so what the hell. But the main reason for wearing the uniform was pride, and I wanted Debbie and her father to see me at least once in uniform. In retrospect, with him being a former officer, and me showing up with an E-2 stripe, he probably deep down could give diddly squat about my uniform. Plus, I looked good in it. Luckily, it fit me tight and accentuated my large, muscular upper body. Anyway, I changed into civilian clothes shortly after arriving at Debbie's.

I was totally unprepared for what happened that day. Any way you cut it, it came across as a shock and was painful. Debbie was acting a bit strange, and late that afternoon when I was trying to find some privacy somewhere to snuggle she came up with the very surprising announcement. "Dave, I know this is going to hurt you, but I have decided to give you back the ring." I could see it was upsetting her, too, but I tried to find out why she had made the decision that ran totally contrary to all the things we said to one another about a future together and the magic of my getting into a reserve unit to meet my military obligation.

"Why, Debbie?" I asked plaintively. "I don't understand. I love you, Debbie. I've only been gone eight weeks," I pleaded. "You told me repeatedly you would be there for me even if I went in the draft for a two year tour of duty. And now this after only two months apart?" I was getting choked up, but didn't want to permit any tears. I certainly was not ready for this. She was my Siren, my life, and I had based so many plans on a life together with her. This surely could not be happening. It was too surreal, and it sucked the air and life out of me like a big, surprise punch to the gut.

"I don't know why, Dave, but I just can't go through with it. There is a part of me that still loves you, but I guess I just don't want to get married yet. Please understand. I don't care about dating anyone else. That's not it. In fact, I haven't been seeing anyone else. I feel terrible about this. I really do."

Her statement that she did not want to date anyone else did not help me in dealing with her exit from my life. It was apparent to me that the thought of marriage scared the hell out of her. She was still so young, and was a pretty girl. She didn't want to tie herself down yet. I could understand that, and had to respect her decision, but the thought of someone else being with her, in her arms and touching her tore me up like I could not believe.

"I understand, but I can't stand the thought of losing you," I told her.

"I know. Dave, I'm not going to date anyone," she again stated. "But I just can't continue wearing your ring. I'm sorry." She walked out hurriedly and closed her bedroom door behind her.

Stunned, and too shocked to realize she was probably doing both of us a favor by putting off any talk of marriage, I walked into the kitchen. Her father happened to be standing there, so I leaned against the counter, both hands gripping it, and looking out the small kitchen window, told him, "Debbie just broke off our engagement. I can't believe it. She's called things off," was all I could say.

He turned to me, shocked himself, and said, "What?" in an incredulous tone. "Damn her," he mumbled, asking, "Where is she?"

"In her bedroom," I answered.

He called out her name as he left the kitchen to go talk to her. "Debbie!"

I stood in the kitchen, my hands still bracing myself up against the counter. I looked at the ring I held in my fingers, then out the window to the front yard and the neighbor's house across the street. I kept shaking my head. Damn, I thought to myself, I've lost her. Had I lost her? Could we continue dating as if nothing had happened? Or could I give her a long time alone to work through everything? I don't know. I took the message that there was enough finality in her voice, notwithstanding her plaintiff that she was not going to date anyone, to suggest that I needed to retreat and let her live her life and sort things out. Plus, I was going bye-bye for the next two months back down to Fort Ord, so I would not be nearby to try and maintain some sort of a relationship.

Debbie's father returned a couple of minutes later. "I don't understand her," he said in disgust.

I saw no reason to stick around. Talking to her at that time was not going to change anything. I walked to her bedroom door and knocked on it. When she opened the door, teary-eyed, I told her I was leaving. She walked me to the front door, where I let myself out. I looked back at her, myself fighting back tears, and simply said, "Goodbye." There was really nothing else to say or do. All I knew was I felt a burning in my throat and emptiness in my heart I had never ever felt before.

"Goodbye, Dave," she replied, and before I turned to walk down the pathway to my car I could see through the glass storm door that she had turned and walked briskly back toward her room.

I felt immense hurt and pain and I was somewhat eager to talk to someone about the break-up, other than my parents who I simply told of the break-up and said very little more. I looked forward to seeing Mike, who by pre-arrangement would be giving me a ride back to Fort Ord Sunday night. Maybe I was simply looking for some sympathy.

That weekend held more surprises. Mike and I had just pulled onto Highway 17 toward San Jose for our drive back to Fort Ord when I told him of the break-up between Debbie and me. He turned his head slowly, eyes wide and mouth slightly gaping open, and then said, "Dave, would you believe that Sandy also broke things off with me this past weekend?"

"Nooo," I said in disbelief.

"Yes," he replied. "I don't believe it."

"What an incredible coincidence, Mike."

"Yes, I agree. She just said she wasn't in any hurry to settle down. She also said we could still date, although I don't know if I want to under those circumstances. We'll see."

"Almost the same situation as with me, Mike, although Debbie said she wasn't interested in dating anyone else."

"Right," he answered sarcastically. "Don't believe that, good friend."

"I know. As if it really makes any difference. So what. We're not together, so she doesn't owe me squat. So, how about that? We both got the 'ol brown helmet on the same day. Put'er there, Mike." He chuckled. I stuck out my hand and we shook, in a bonding sort of way.

On Monday night I walked to the post library after dinner. I was anxious to write a letter to my Uncle Peder in Rotterdam, The Netherlends, where he and his wife lived. I asked him if the offer still stood for the job and voyage to the Orient and Persian Gulf. I put Debbie out of mind as best I could. She was out of my life, and I decided to formulate other plans. Somehow, some way, those plans would involve travel. Maybe I would finally have the opportunity to see what lay beyond the horizon I had often looked at longingly and dreamily from Stinson Beach and Rockaway Beach.

Mike and I shared rides to the Bay Area every weekend during the eight-week AIT school, and we often walked together after supper on base to meet other friends from basic training at the Post bowling center. There, we would drink a few beers and share stories of basic and AIT and talk of plans after the completion of our training.

Things were pretty relaxed during AIT. The only time we had to form up in formation was when we marched the short distance back and forth to the Supply School a few blocks from the barracks. We could walk casually to the mess hall for meals, and there was no longer a requirement to do various PT exercises while waiting in the chow line as we had been required to do in basic. We generally were released for the weekend by 11:00 o'clock Saturday morning, and there was no KP duty, thank God.

Wally and I kicked butt in Supply School, achieving final grades of 99.8 and 99.6, respectively. In fact, the officer in charge of the school scheduled us for a brief the last week of school to obtain a verbal critique from us.

The last weekend of AIT I had driven my little MGA down from Danville and left it parked at the Layton's in Carmel for the week. Mandy Layton had obligingly given me a lift back to the post on that particular Sunday night.

On the last day of AIT Wally and I went to the paymaster's office to get paid and walked through the other necessary offices to get processed out of school and active duty. When finished, I said goodbye to him and told him I would look him up back at Fort Attlebury, where he was assigned to a Supply School Instructor unit. Saying goodbye to my other new friends from AIT, and promising to look them up if I were ever in their neighborhoods, I lifted my full duffel bag to my shoulder and walked to the post exchange to catch the bus to Carmel. The exchange was located just up the street from the bowling center, and a few blocks down from the library, where I had spent many a weeknight evening writing letters and reading magazines.

The bus to Carmel was on time. With an indescribable anxiety and mounting sense of relief I hopped on the bus and paid my fare. I was filled with exuberance and felt light-headed as I took my seat and awaited our departure. I reflected on the past sixteen weeks of my life there at Fort Ord, and all that had happened, both good and bad. I was eager to leave, to put it all behind me, and yet there was a somber side because of having to say goodbye to new friends that shared common challenges in Army training and to now familiar surroundings. And there was Drill Sergeant Becker, who wanted to serve in Vietnam, who I respected so very deeply.

My life could take form again. I was hoping I would be lucky enough to get an affirmative from Uncle Peder, and was optimistic I could arrange to make up the missed drills. I could simply put in some extra drill time during the week at Fort Attlebury before my voyage to compensate for the few months I would very likely be away.

Finally, for minutes seemed like hours sitting on the bus awaiting departure, the bus pulled away from the bus stop. I took one last look at the pale green, wooden frame buildings that had represented my temporary home, looking to the left into the AIT, 4th Training Brigade area as we passed by it. I then looked to the right, at the bowling center that had provided many fun hours of camaraderie and beer drinking. I was now alone. My friends from basic and AIT were scattered in every possible direction. Would I see them again? I would see Mike and Wally, but the others? I knew one thing for sure, unless there was a real emergency, none of us would serve duty in Vietnam. In retrospect, it was amazing how things had changed from when I was sweating a load over my military obligation and trying to make plans with Debbie, who obviously was no longer in my life. The latter thought produced a sad, melancholy feeling, emptiness, and some pain. My thoughts then moved ahead, to that blue 1961 MGA sitting in Carmel a few miles away that would help transform me back to civilian Dave as it took me north to the Bay Area and my social playgrounds of San Francisco, Sausilito and Tiburon.

The bus headed south from Fort Ord and onto the four-lane highway separating the main post from the Pacific Ocean. We passed by the rifle ranges visible along the highway to my right between the road and the beaches. I remembered laying on wet sand at those ranges firing at targets with my M14 in the rain. What fun. We traveled through Seaside and Monterey, making the requisite stops. When the bus pulled up to and stopped at the main street of lovely Carmel I got off and lugged my duffel bag down the street toward the ocean beaches to where the Layton's lived and where my getaway car was parked. I felt great and light on my feet, even though the duffel bag, filled with five thousand standard government-issue items, weighed a ton. Thankfully, my walk, which was longer than I had anticipated, but which could not faze me at this point, was downhill all the way. The day was sunny and clear, which made it all the more sensational for me. I had orders in my pocket that certified I had completed sixteen weeks of Army active duty training. The realization of it all gave me a sense of euphoria, and caused me to smile at everyone I passed by and to offer greetings. If you know Carmel, however, a Soldier in uniform humping a duffel bag is not a common sight. The tourists hump large wallets, figuratively. This was indeed a special day.

Arriving at the Layton's, I knocked on the front door, which was then opened to reveal the always smiling, happy face of Mrs. Layton.

"Hi, Dave! Come in," she cheerfully exclaimed.

"Hi Mrs. Layton. Thanks, and how are you?" I happily stated.

"Oh, I'm just fine," she answered. "And I'll bet you're feeling pretty good yourself, aren't you?"

"Oh, yes. I feel great. I'm so happy that's behind me.

"Can I offer you a beer, Dave?"

"Thanks. I appreciate it, and any other time I would eagerly say yes, but I'm kind of anxious to get up the road." I could not believe I was turning down a beer, especially one that could be enjoyed with Jack's wonderful mother sitting in front of that picture window looking out to the Pacific Ocean. But I couldn't wait to get away from this particular part of California and put some real distance between Fort Ord and me so I could start the next chapter of my life. "If I could just use a room to change out of my uniform I would really appreciate it."

"Certainly. You can use Carl's room right there," as she pointed to a bedroom down a short hallway from where we stood in the foyer.

"Thanks," I told her and proceeded to the room. A few minutes later I emerged in civilian clothes, with duffel bag in tow, ready to make my getaway.

"Mrs. Layton," I called out, for she was not in sight.

"Yes, Dave," she answered as she walked in from the living room.

"Well, I guess I'll be on my way. Thanks so much for everything. I really appreciated it, particularly your letting me leave the car here for the week. And please say hello to Jack, Gary and Mandy, as well as Mr. Layton."

"Oh, no problem, Dave. In fact, Carl and Mandy's friends have been asking all sorts of questions about the car. They all like it. Mandy's been telling them the car belongs to a cute, funny guy that went to school at Happy Valley with her brother." Mandy, I remembered, had seen me in action a number of times at Happy Valley.

"I see," I said, smiling. "Well, time to go. Thanks again."

"You're very welcome, Dave. Have a safe drive."

"Thanks. Bye," I said. I gave her a hug before walking out the front door and heading for my car. I squeezed the duffel bag into the back of the car, a tight fit, and drove away. I took one last reflective look at the base, this time on my right as I traveled north. I remembered all the times I had looked out from the post onto the busy highway, or had looked at the cars zooming by as I stood on the rifle range behind barbed wire fences. I had wished so much I was in one of those cars because they represented freedom. And I thought about Drill Sergeant Becker with another group of basic trainees.

Now I was feeling the freedom. I was on the road, zooming north, and the barbed wire fences were on my left and right, and not restraining me. And all those guys at the range were looking at me traveling by on the highway, free as a bird. Twiddlee-dee.

So there I was, cruising along, making good progress toward home, when the not so unexpected happened. My engine died. I swore loudly, knowing exactly what had occurred, having lived through the experience a number of times before when the engine just up and quit for no reason. At least no reason I would be privy to. I had just passed Morgan Hill and was approaching San Jose, so there was very little commercial or residential activity near me. So there I was, my emotional, feeling good, bubble bursting as I sat on the side of the road. In the past, if I waited long enough for the engine to cool down I could get it re-started. I sat there, eyes closed for what seemed long enough. I said a little prayer and turned the key. No luck. I waited longer. Finally, the engine kicked over. I threw it into gear and sped off, hoping of course I would get to Danville without any more problems.

I got home to Danville about 8:00 PM without any further mishaps, unpacked and put my feet up to relax. But I couldn't relax. I was wound up tighter than a drum, and I wanted to do something, celebrate. I couldn't just sit around home that night. So I grabbed a snack and informed Mom that I was going to Happy Valley. She understood.

"Just drive safely," she said as I backed out of the driveway.

I went straight to Dan's apartment that he shared with Brad, Rob and Bill Gouvea, arriving about midnight. Unfortunately, they were all in bed asleep. I left their place and drove to a couple of apartments where some former female friends had lived, but no one answered my knocks on the doors, so I went over to Iris Street, where I found some old friends sitting outside their apartment enjoying the nice Spring evening. I told them about my past four months and they sat in awe as it sank in that I had been fortunate enough to get into a reserve unit. More significantly, I think they were reminded of the reality of the Vietnam War and decisions they too would soon have to make. I cheerfully accepted the cold beer they offered me, and after downing it I excused myself to go elsewhere. I drove around town for a while and couldn't find anything else to do. The doors I knocked on at night in the past were no longer available. I went back to Dan's and crashed on his sofa.

The next morning over some breakfast I told Dan and the others some of the highlights of my duty at Fort Ord. All of them but Rob were still in limbo regarding military service and had not yet made any decisions on how they would perform their duty. They told me they were all going to Palm Springs for Spring Break that coming Sunday and invited me along. I told them I would be happy to join them.

Later that day, which was Friday, I drove back to Danville in my little MG. On Saturday the guys met at our house, ready to head off to Palm Springs the following day. I wasn't to be with them, however.

I went to bed that night with all intentions of going to Palm Springs, but I sensed a stronger desire to do something else, out of that mold of the same thing. I awoke Sunday morning with a strong, unexplainable urge to go to Hawaii. I don't know how the idea germinated. Maybe it was because I just needed a different adventure at that point in my life. And maybe because it represented that "unknown" out there over the horizon that I had daydreamed about so often from the California shores. It wasn't Tahiti, but it was still paradise, and I wanted part of it. Nothing was going to stop me. I didn't have to report back to my job in the city until I had advised them I had completed my training and was ready to return, so that was no problem. And I didn't have my first drill until the next month. I walked into the kitchen to join others for breakfast.

"Good morning," I said to everyone.

"Good morning," was the reply.

"Well, I've decided to go to Hawaii," I stated abruptly. Silence followed.

The guys couldn't believe it. I'm sure they all wished they were also going to Hawaii, but then, they were still poor students. Not that the Army paid very much, but I had been collecting some pay. "What?" Dad asked in some shock and surprise.

"I'm going to Hawaii. I'm going to drive to the airport, buy a ticket, fly to Honolulu, and then find a motel to stay in for a week or two." I was very sure of myself. It was going to happen. I wanted a real break from the past four months and the ordeal with Debbie. I wanted to spread my wings, too, and travel. This was a start.

"Are you sure you're not doing this because of Debbie?" Dad asked.

"Sure, I know what I'm doing. That may be part of the reason, but that's not all that bad. I need to do this, Dad. I need to get away for a little while."

"Oh, Carl, stop it," Mom said in a scolding tone to Dad. "I think it's a great idea. I wouldn't mind going to Hawaii myself." Boy, that last comment really quieted him down, although he gave me a puzzled look and a little frown. Remember, my Dad is the guy that waited six months for a new transistor radio from Japan brought over on a ship by his cousin Peder!

With that, I sat down at the table to enjoy Dad's Swedish pancakes before packing some things and driving myself to San Francisco International Airport. After breakfast I had called United Airlines to book a seat on a flight.

Within two hours time from when I left home I was on a flight to Honolulu. It was a great vacation, and I ran into some Happy Valley girls that invited me to stay at their Waikiki apartment. I also called my Army "pineapple" friends and visited relatives on my mother's and my grandfather's side of the family. My great-grandfather had come from Spain as a whaler and had settled in Hawaii, where he had jobs on the old Damon Ranch and operated a saddle shop in downtown Honolulu. Maybe it was no wonder that with my Scandanavian blood and my Hawaiian Islands ancestry I had the desire to travel and to see the world. Some day, I fervently hoped, I would have a permanent job that required and permitted me to travel extensively. The bug in me to travel was strong and unrelenting, and undeniable.

I also told myself, while walking on the sands of Waikiki, and sitting under the lush greenery of the outdoor bar at the stately Royal Hawaiian Hotel sipping a cold beer, that it would be a long time before I let myself be in another serious relationship with a woman. I wanted my freedom and no romantic entanglements. I had plenty of time for that, if it was to be. There were other things I wanted to do. Plus, losing Debbie after returning from Army basic training still hurt a lot. I even had the thought of moving to Norway to live when my Army Reserve obligation concluded. Maybe I could learn Norwegian and find a job there.

My stay on Oahu completed, I flew back to San Francisco, retrieved my car from the long-term parking lot and returned home. There was some mail waiting for me. I casually glanced at the few pieces, my attention drawn to the piece on the bottom, which was unmistakably from overseas. It had a Dutch stamp. I stared at it, hopeful of good news. I was not disappointed. With fine penmanship, but with a very slight Dutch slant to his surprisingly good command of English, Uncle Peder had written the magical sought after words:

Dear David:
I vil be in Richmond, California, on the 21ˢᵗ day of June. You are velcome to join me if you vish for our upcoming voyage to the Persian Gulf and Japan...

EPILOGUE

It is December, 1969, over a year after reporting to Army Basic Training. I met Uncle Peder's ship in Richmond, California, in June earlier that year and we immediately set sail for Saudi Arabia to load a shipment of crude oil. From there we steamed to Yokohama, Japan, to drop off part of our load of crude. Yokohama offered a few firsts for me. It was the first time I ate sushi and raw squid, which smelled horrible, and used an outdoors open urinal that was common at many bars. I went for jogs on the immense Yokohama waterfront plaza near the piers and some nice hotels and wearing a San Francisco 49ers tee-shirt got a lot of looks from the local folks. Leaving Yokohama, we went to Long Beach, California, to drop off more crude oil at a refinery there, then sailed up the coast of California to Richmond to offload the remaining oil at a Standard Oil refinery. My voyage with Uncle Peder on his ship, the "Martita", was an experience I shall never forget. I was able to start seeing the immense world around me, starting with the Persian Gulf and Japan, and it more than heightened my desire to travel the world.

I am working with an insurance company in their regional headquarters in Menlo Park, California, and am attending monthly Army Reserve drills at Fort Attlebury. I am living in Mountain View with Al, who grew up with one of my Happy Valley College buddies. He is attending grad school at Stanford, played football at San Jose State, and was a member of Theti Chi fraternity. His frat brothers like my Happy Valley style at their parties and have made me an honorary member of their house. I had made up the drills I missed during the three-month voyage on the Martita. The drills aren't so bad. We often go off base at lunch to buy some wine and sandwich materials which we bring back on the base and take to the top of one of the hills that command a fantastically breathtaking view of beautiful San Francisco, the Golden Gate Bridge, and the Pacific Ocean. In fact, I recognize the view in many television programs and movies made in San Francisco. After lunch, we force ourselves back to our barracks-type office building where we prepare ourselves for our annual two-week annual active duty training. Things could be worse. The Vietnam War is still raging on, and still taking thousands of young men's lives. They will never be able to sit on top of that hill near Sausilito and take in the panoramic view of this gorgeous little corner of an immense world, nor will they be able to live fulfilling lives with friends and families, get married, raise a family, enjoy the many wonders of this beautiful Earth, and on and on.

It's not fair. None of it is fair. The country is still divided. Nixon promised to close the door on Vietnam by announcing in June of 1969 that he was withdrawing 25,000 troops. But that's too few and too late.

I have remained in touch with friends. Jack is working for the same insurance company as me. His National Guard unit was called up for two weeks in August to quell riots in Los Angeles, in an area called Watts. Rob was selected for Navy Flight School and is in Pensacola, Florida, learning to fly jet aircraft. There is little question that he is destined for bombing runs over Vietnam and I hope to God he comes through the war okay. Jack's brother, Gary, the Marine, was medivac'd out of Vietnam with shrapnel wounds one month before he was scheduled to complete his tour of duty, but has recovered and is finishing out his Marine Corps tour at Camp Pendleton, California, with full use of all his limbs. My former dorm roomie, Chip, who had of course hoped to get orders to Beale Air Force Base in Yuba City, California, a few hours drive north of his home in Sonora, instead was sent to Danang, the big, sprawling base in South Vietnam, and recently wrote me he has orders for Minot Air Force Base in North Dakota. Other than the occasional attacks by the Viet Cong, he is still safer on the base than out in the country. Benny and my brother Dan lucked out and were able to get appointments in my same reserve unit at Fort Attlebury, thanks to the good graces of Major McIntyre. They are both presently in basic training at Fort Gordon, Georgia. I heard from Benny that Cindy was engaged to be married to our former dorm buddy, Tim Ballantine, the guy that returned to school our sophomore year with the new Corvette. Our freshman football buddy, Paul, was allegedly still in Canada. Oh, I almost forgot to mention Rancher. A Delta Phi pledge brother of mine that has stayed in contact with me and is still in Happy Valley called to say a strange piece of mail had recently arrived at the fraternity house. In it was a single piece of somewhat rumpled paper that had the simple words, "Hedde be, brothers. I am doing okay in Mexico." At the bottom was the name, "Rancher." Nothing else. No address, nothing. Was it for real? Did someone else send it? The envelope had a postmark of Mexico City, so there really was no way of telling where Rancher was hanging out, assuming he had sent the letter.

That leaves Debbie. I had some time to kill between my release from active duty training and meeting the Martita for the voyage, so in April I called and visited with her. It was not the same. She was distant. I called Debbie's home a month after the completion of the voyage and was told by her Mother that she was engaged to be married to an Air Force officer stationed at nearby Hamilton Air Force Base. I guess I should have been an officer! But I have no regrets. My life is mine and is on a path I enjoy.

A drill weekend turned my life upside down in a way I had not anticipated. I was standing on the second deck of the building my unit drilled in when Wally told me news I did not want to hear. "Someone told me that Drill Sergeant Becker was killed in Vietnam last month."

I froze in my place, looking into Wally's face, not believing what he had just told me, not wanting to believe it. No, it couldn't be. I had thought the Drill Sergeant to be invincible. He was the loyal, "strack", professional Soldier that I admired. This just couldn't be, I kept telling myself. Drill Sergeant Becker dead? DEAD?

I turned from Wally and walked down the stairs, slowly opening the door. I turned left out of the building and started walking down the narrow road separating similar barracks-type buildings used by other functional units. About a hundred yards away the road stopped, emptying into a large sloping area mixed with grass and small red gravel rocks. We used the area for our marching formation training and infrequent physical training. When I entered that area I started running, as fast as I could, through the training area and onto another road below that ended at the large sand beach a few hundred yards ahead. I ran and I ran, onto the beach, feeling my combat boots sink heavily into the giving sand. My progress was slowed, but my effort was sustained. I wasn't going to stop until I was totally winded and could go no further.

I was mad. Mad at the Communists that killed Drill Sergeant Becker. Mad at the dumb, senseless war, a war that saw no victor, saw no end, and saw so many lives, military and civilian, snuffed out. "For what?" I repeatedly asked myself. I couldn't figure it out.

I ran hundreds of yards on that desolate beach on the western side of Marin County that very few people ever saw, my lungs finally telling me they would soon run out of oxygen for legs that wanted to keep pounding the sand in fury, despair and anger. The world seemed messed up, and now because of it a person I hardly knew, who alone commanded so much respect, was gone from this Earth. This man, who was only my age when he whipped us into a cohesive unit at Fort Ord, would never again experience the many beautiful things life offered.

I staggered to a stop, falling to the sand, arms spread out, gasping for air. "No. No." I kept repeating.

All was still and silent. Even the seagulls and the foghorns. No one was near. I lay spent on a lonely beach, trying to sort things out. And then I remembered Drill Sergeant Becker's statement that one weekend day behind the barracks about wanting to serve in Vietnam. Being there was what he had wanted. Being a professional Soldier, he knew the consequences, the risks. While I could not accept it then, he had. He believed in the struggle and was prepared for whatever the cost might be. Serving in Vietnam was an end in itself, so much like the early Greek athletes and their "Agon". Sports were not a means to an end, but an end in and of itself. That probably was how Drill Sergeant Becker saw his role in the war – not a means to anything, but doing what he felt was right, as part of his duty in uniform and the oath he had taken. His duty, his mission in life was to serve his superiors and his country. We should all be so lucky to not get caught up in means to any end. Enjoy life for what it offers you. Be thankful. Don't get caught up on the details. There really didn't have to be a reason for everything. He died knowing the effort was the right thing to do. It was about having the courage to make the commitment to something in which he believed.

I actually felt cleansed. More importantly, I considered myself fortunate to have known an unselfish man like Drill Sergeant Becker, knowing too that my life would be different for it.

And it was. The next day I called Major McIntyre and drove over to Fort Attlebury to see him. Entering his office, I got right to the point. I explained the news I had received the previous day from Wally and told him how much I admired Drill Sergeant Becker.

"Sir, I've given the matter a lot of thought," I said. "I want to go active duty. I want to do this for Drill Sergeant Becker. But more important, I want to make up for my indifference toward the war and our Soldiers when I was in college. I want to emulate the professionalism and ideals of Drill Sergeant Becker, and I know no better way to do so and to honor him and all he stood for than to take the oath and go on active duty, wherever the Army needs to send me. This is a matter of honor and redemption, Sir, and I would also like to apply for Officers Candidate School."

He was somewhat stunned by my revelation and my decision, for seldom had he heard that type of request. Normally, as he had heard from me over a year previous, it was just the opposite. Guys wanted to go reserve duty.

"I can help you with that," he replied, and I could sense his pride in making that statement.

One week later I was back at Fort Attlebury. I had requested that Major McIntrye swear me in, and that he administer the oath of allegiance that would officially place me on active duty with the United States Army. At my request, Debbie's father was also present.

"I, Dave Pedersen, do solemnly swear that I will support and defend the Constitution of the United States against all enemies foreign and domestic, that I will bear true faith and allegiance to the same, and that I will obey the orders of the President of the United States, and the orders of the officers appointed over me, according to regulation and the Uniform Code of Military Justice, so help me God."

Printed in the United States
85023LV00003B/55-57/A